"I thought [we might] talk a little business," said Lucifer Jones.

"I don't believe we shall," said Doctor Ho.

"Why the hell not?" Lucifer demanded.

"Reverend Jones," Ho said, "you are perhaps the only man of my acquaintance with even less regard for the laws and morals of society than I myself possess. While I do not necessarily consider that a failing, it does make it difficult for me to trust you."

"Well, as I see it, Doctor Ho, you got two choices. You can take me on as a partner, or have me as an enemy. Now, if we become partners and you really do take over the world, you could give me a little chunk of it, like say Australia. If on the other hand you'd rather have me as an enemy, you're not taking on me but the Lord as well."

"There is a third alternative, you know," said Doctor Ho.

"Yeah? What is that?"

Ho pulled out a pearl-handled revolver. "I can kill you right here and now . . ."

"Resnick is thought-provoking, imaginative, mordantly funny—and above all galactically grand."

—*Los Angeles Times*

Turn the page for more raves for Mike Resnick . . .

Praise For
The Genius of
Mike Resnick

"Resnick occupies a peak all his own in the mountains of science fiction."
—*Analog*

✠✠✠✠

"Resnick has a beautiful style."
—*Science Fiction & Fantasy Book Review*

✠✠✠✠

"Resnick's tales are ironic, inventive and very readable."
—*Publishers Weekly*

✠✠✠✠

"Mike Resnick not only writes fast-paced, entertaining science fiction, but adds some intelligence and thought as well."
—*Amazing*

✠✠✠✠

"One of the most daring and prolific writers in all science fiction . . . he always delivers."
—**David Brin**

✠✠✠✠

"He's addictive . . . one of the best storytellers to hit science fiction in years."
—Frank M. Robinson

✠✠✠✠

"Mike Resnick has written some excellent space adventures."
—*Locus*

✠✠✠✠

"Resnick is a reader's writer, one who can be counted upon to deliver a dependably entertaining read."
—Michael Kube-McDowell

✠✠✠✠

"You may come away from Mike Resnick's books with considerably more than a rousing good tale."
—Jo Clayton

✠✠✠✠

"The most versatile and entertaining madman writing science fiction today."
—Jack L. Chalker

✠✠✠✠

ALSO BY MIKE RESNICK

WALPURGIS III
THE SOUL EATER

Published by
Warner Books

ATTENTION: SCHOOLS AND CORPORATIONS

WARNER books are available at quantity discounts with bulk purchase for educational, business, or sales promotional use. For information, please write to: SPECIAL SALES DEPARTMENT, WARNER BOOKS,1271 AVENUE OF THE AMERICAS, NEW YORK, N.Y. 10020.

**ARE THERE WARNER BOOKS
YOU WANT BUT CANNOT FIND IN YOUR LOCAL STORES?**

You can get any WARNER BOOKS title in print. Simply send title and retail price, plus 50¢ per order and 50¢ per copy to cover mailing and handling costs for each book desired. New York State and California residents add applicable sales tax. Enclose check or money order only, no cash please, to: WARNER BOOKS, P.O. BOX 690, NEW YORK, N.Y. 10019.

MIKE RESNICK

LUCIFER JONES

WARNER BOOKS

A Time Warner Company

This book about my
favorite fictional character
is dedicated to
Carol,
my favorite nonfictional character

If you purchase this book without a cover you should be aware
that this book may have been stolen property and reported as
"unsold and destroyed" to the publisher. In such case neither the
author nor the publisher has received any payment for this
"stripped book."

WARNER BOOKS EDITION

Copyright © 1992 by Mike Resnick
All rights reserved.

Questar is a registered trademark of Warner Books, Inc.

Cover design by Don Puckey
Cover illustration by Darrell Sweet
Cover lettering by Carl Dellacroce

Warner Books, Inc.
1271 Avenue of the Americas
New York, NY 10020

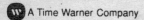 A Time Warner Company

Printed in the United States of America

First Printing: November, 1992

10 9 8 7 6 5 4 3 2 1

CONTENTS

CAST OF CHARACTERS

Inspector Willie Wong, who has run out of names for his sons, and possesses a platitude for every occasion.

General Chang, a warlord's warlord.

Doctor Aristotle Ho, an Insidious Oriental Dentist who dreams of world domination.

Sir Mortimer Edgerton-Smythe, who will stop at nothing to bring Doctor Aristotle Ho to justice.

Rupert Cornwall, an Australian scoundrel with a passion for rubies, wealthy women, and real estate.

The Scorpion Lady, a beautiful but deadly smuggler with a truly outstanding pair of lungs.

Baron Steinmetz, who creates a homemade man out of spare parts in his basement.

Harvey Edwards, former halfback, now the fastest rickshaw puller in Macau.

Mr. Mako, diminutive Japanese detective who specializes in judo, disguise, archaeology, and jealousy.

Cuddles, an authentic Chinese dragon.

Sam Hightower, full-time Abominable Snowman and part-time ghost.

Capturing Clyde Calhoun, world-famous hunter who brings 'em back alive. Not intact, but alive.

Lisara, a 111-year-old virgin who has taken up the High Priestess trade.

King Philbert of Sylvania, who bears a remarkable resemblance to our narrator.

Gustave the Book, half-man, half-thing, and all gambler.

Erich Von Horst, a prince among con men.

Princess Griselda, who knows what, if not who, she likes.

Mr. Tall and *Mr. Short*, who share a taste for lost continents, easy money, and indiscriminate bloodshed.

Akbar, a learning-disabled elephant.

Count Basil de Chenza Lupo, an aristocratic werewolf.

Lady Edith Quilton, the richest widow in Rajasthan Province.

Quesadilla, the notorious Clubfoot of Notre Dame.

Sherringford House, the world's greatest consulting detective, who is always brilliant if not always correct.

El Diablo, a bull with an attitude.

And our narrator, the *Right Reverend Honorable Doctor Lucifer Jones*, a handsome, noble, and resourceful Christian gentleman who has certain unresolved differences with eighteen separate Asian and European governments over the finer points of the law.

PART I

EXPLOITS

(1926–1931)

1
The Master Detective

They say that there are a lot of differences between Hong Kong and some of the African cities I had recently left behind. Different people, different cultures, different buildings, even different food.

Of course, there are a lot of similarities, too. Same lack of consideration for those who are bold enough to tinker with the laws of statistical probability. Same steel bars in the local jail. Same concrete walls and floors. Same uncomfortable cots. Same awful food.

Truth to tell, I'd had a lot more time to consider the similarities than the differences. I'd gotten right off the boat from Portuguese East Africa, checked into the Luk Kwok Hotel (which thought-fully rented its rooms by the hour, the night, or the week), spent the next hour in a local restaurant trying to down a bowl of soup with a pair of chopsticks, and then, realizing that my funds needed replenishing, I got involved in a friendly little game of chance involving two cubes of ivory with spots painted on them. It was when the third cube slipped out of my sleeve that I was invited to inspect the premises of the local jail.

That had been five days ago, and I had spent the intervening time alternately trying not to mind the smell of dead fish, which is what all of Hong Kong smelled like back in 1926, and gaining some comfort by reading my well-worn copy of the Good Book, which I ain't never without.

The girl that brought my grub to me was a charming little

thing named Mei Sung. She was right impressed to be serving a man of the cloth, which I was back in those days, and I converted the bejabbers out of her three or four times a day, which made my incarceration in durance vile a mite easier to take.

As time crawled by I got to know my fellow inmates. There was a Turkish dentist who had gassed a British officer to death in what he assured me was an accident and would certainly have been construed as such by the courts if he hadn't appropriated the officer's wallet and wristwatch before reporting the poor fellow's untimely demise. There was a young Brazilian student who sweated up a storm and kept screaming things about anarchy and tyrants and such and keeping everyone awake. There were two Chinamen dressed all in black, who kept glaring at me every time I finished converting Mei Sung. There was a Frenchman who kept saying he was glad he killed the chef, and that anyone who ruined *sole almondine* that badly deserved to die.

And there was me, the Right Reverend Honorable Doctor Lucifer Jones, out of Moline, Illinois, by way of the Dark Continent, where I'd done my best to illuminate the dark, dreary lives of the godless black heathen despite certain minor disagreements with the constabularies of fourteen countries which culminated in my being asked to establish the Tabernacle of Saint Luke on some other land mass. But I already wrote that story, and I ain't going to go into it again, since anyone who's read it knows that I'm a righteous and God-fearing man who was just misunderstood.

On the fifth day of the thirty that I was to serve, they gave me a roommate, a well-dressed Australian with expensive-looking rings on all his fingers. His name was Rupert Cornwall, and he explained that he had come to Hong Kong because Australia was a pretty empty country and he liked crowds.

"And what do you do for a living, Brother Rupert?" I asked him, by way of being polite.

"I'm an entrepreneur," he said. "I put opportunists together with opportunities, and take a little percentage for my trouble."

"I didn't know being an entrepreneur was a criminal offense in Hong Kong," I said.

"I was arrested by mistake," he answered.

"You, too?"

"Absolutely," he said. "I expect to be out of here within the hour. And what about yourself? You look like a man of God with that turned-around collar of yours."

"You hit the nail right on the head, Brother Rupert. That's what I am: a man of God, here to bring comfort and spiritual uplifting to the heathen."

"What religion do you belong to?" he asked.

"One me and the Lord worked out betwixt ourselves one Sunday afternoon back in Illinois," I said. "Hell, the way I see it, as long as we're upright and holy and got a poorbox, what's the difference?"

He broke out into a great big smile. "I *like* you, Doctor Jones," he said. "Where's your church located?"

"Well, I ain't quite got around to building my tabernacle yet, Brother Rupert . . . but I'm taking donations for it, if the spirit's come upon you and you're so inclined."

"I don't have any money with me," he answered. "But look me up after we're both out of here, and I might have some work for you."

"Work wasn't exactly what I had in mind," I said distastefully.

"When you hear what I have to offer, you might change your mind," he said.

"Yeah?"

He nodded. "I could use a man of the cloth in my operation. I think we could enter into a mutually profitable relationship."

"You don't say?" I replied. "Well, I suppose I could always take a brief fling at the entrepreneur business before I erect my tabernacle, God being the patient and understanding critter that He is."

He reached into his vest pocket and handed me his card. "That's my business address. Remember to call on me."

Well, I could tell we were hitting it off right fine, and I was going to ask him more about our pending partnership, but just then a guard came by and unlocked the door.

"They made your bail again, Rupert," he said in a bored voice.

"Was there ever any doubt?" asked Rupert smugly.

"You get arrested by mistake a lot?" I asked as he was leaving.

"Almost daily," he said. "Personally, I think they're just jealous of my success."

Then he was gone, and I was left with my thoughts until Mei Sung came by for another conversion, which left me so exhausted that I thought I might grab a quick forty winks. I had snored my way through about twenty of 'em when the door opened again, and the guard gestured me to follow him.

"Did somebody make my bail, too?" I asked, thinking of Rupert Cornwall. He just chuckled and kept leading me down one corridor after another until we finally came to a little cubbyhole, which was filled with a desk, two chairs, and a pudgy Chinaman with a natty little mustache and goatee. He was dressed in a white linen suit, and hadn't bothered to take his Panama hat off even though we were inside.

"Sit, please," he said, smiling at me.

I sat myself down in the empty chair while he nodded at the guard, who left the room.

"You are Mr. Jones?" said the Chinaman.

"Doctor Lucifer Jones at your service," I said.

"That what we must talk about," he said in pidgen English.

"About whether I'm Lucifer Jones?" I asked, puzzled.

"About whether you are at my service," he said. "Because if not, then you go back to cell for twenty-five more days."

"Are you the guy who made my bail?" I asked.

"No one make your bail," he said. "Please sit back and relax, Doctor Jones. I am Inspector Willie Wong of Hong Kong Police Force. Perhaps you have heard of me?"

"Can't say that I have, Brother Wong," I answered. He looked right disappointed at that. "Why are you wasting your time with me, anyway?" I continued. "You ought to be trying to find the ungodly sinner that stuck that extra die up my sleeve."

"That no concern of mine," he said, holding up a hand. "But am prepared to make deal, Doctor Jones. You help me, I help you."

"Yeah?"

He nodded. "Man in your cell named Rupert Cornwall."

"What about him?"

"Rupert Cornwall biggest gangster in Hong Kong."

"Then why did you let him go?"

"Beauty is in eye of beholder," said Wong.

"I beg your pardon?"

"Old Chinese proverb. Perhaps it not translate very well." He paused. "Let Rupert Cornwall go for lack of evidence."

"What has all this got to do with me?" I asked.

"Patience, Doctor Jones," said Wong. "Penny saved is penny earned."

"Another proverb?"

He nodded. "Very wise of you to notice. You are man we need."

"Need for what, Brother Wong?" I asked.

"Need go-between. Rupert Cornwall trust you. You will meet with him, learn about operation, report back to me. Then, when time is right, we strike."

"How long you figure this'll take?"

He shrugged. "Maybe week, maybe month, who know? Too many chefs spoil the soup."

"I don't know, Brother Wong," I said. "After all, I only got twenty-five days left to serve."

He broke out into a great big grin. "You not acquainted with Chinese calendar, I take it?"

"How long is twenty-five days on a Chinese calendar?" I asked.

He shrugged again. "Maybe week, maybe month, who know?" He looked across the desk at me. "We have deal?"

I sighed. "We have a deal."

"Good. Knew I could count on man of cloth."

"How do I report to you?" I asked.

"He know what I look like, so you will report to me through sons."

"I don't know how to break this unhappy tiding to you, Brother Wong," I said, "but I ain't got no sons."

"I have twenty-eight," he replied distastefully. "All currently unemployed and available to work for honorable father."

"Twenty-eight?" I repeated. "I don't envy your missus none."

"Have seventeen missuses," he answered. "Fifteen currently suing for back alimony. That's why move here from Honolulu."

"My heart bleeds for you, Brother Wong," I said with as much sincerity as I could muster on the spur of the moment.

"Whenever I become depressed over situation, I just remember old Chinese proverb: Watched pot never boil." He got to his feet and walked around the desk to stand in front of me. "I think for this case we use Number Nine and Number Twenty-Six sons."

"What are their names?"

"Just told you: Nine and Twenty-Six. Ran out of names after Number Five son was born."

"What do you call your daughters—A through Z?"

Wong threw back his head and laughed. "You fine fellow, Doctor Jones. Wonderful sense of humor. Sincerely hope Rupert Cornwall not cut your tongue out before case is over."

"Uh . . . let's just pause a second for serious reflection, Brother Wong," I said. "Old Rupert wouldn't really cut my tongue out, would he?"

"No, not really," said Wong.

"That's better."

"Would have one of his hired killers do it for him."

"You know," I said, "upon further consideration, I think the Lord would want me to serve out my full sentence. After all, I was caught fair and square, and somehow this seems unfair to the just and honorable man who sentenced me."

"Whatever you say, Doctor Jones," said Wong. He went back around the desk, opened the drawer, and pulled out a sheet of paper that was subdivided into hundreds of little squares. "This help you pass the time."

"What is it?" I asked.

He smiled. "Calendar of Chinese week." He tossed me a pencil. "You can mark off each day with this. Will bring new one when you run out of lead."

Which is how I became an operative in the employ of the Hong Kong Police.

* * *

You'd think that the biggest gangster in Hong Kong would operate out of one of them beautiful old palaces that overlook the ocean, or failing that he'd set up headquarters in a penthouse suite in some luxury hotel. So you can imagine my surprise when I wandered down a couple of back alleyways and found Rupert Cornwall's place of business to be a run-down little storefront right between a fish peddler and a shirtmaker.

The whole area smelled of incense and dead fish, and there were lots of tall men dressed in black and wearing lean and hungry looks, but I just ignored 'em all like the God-fearing Christian that I am and walked up to Cornwall's door and pounded on it a couple of times. A muscular guy who looked like a cross between an Olympic weightlifter and a small mountain let me in and ushered me through a maze of unopened cardboard boxes to a back room, where Rupert Cornwall sat in an easy chair, smoking a Havana cigar and going through the Hong Kong version of the *Daily Racing Form*.

"Doctor Jones!" he said. "My dear fellow, I hadn't expected to see you again for almost a month!" He paused and looked around. "We just moved in here a few days ago. I used to operate out of one of the hotels, but my overhead was killing me."

"Yeah, I know how expensive them luxury suites can be," I agreed.

"Luxury suites nothing," he corrected me. "It was making bail two and three times a day. Ah, well, you're here, and that's all that matters." Suddenly his eyes narrowed. "Just how, exactly, did you get here so soon?"

"I'm a fast walker, Brother Rupert," I answered.

"I thought you were incarcerated for thirty days."

I shrugged. "Time flies when you're having fun. I guess I'd been there longer than I thought."

"Yes, I saw little Mei Sung," he said with a grin. "Well, are you prepared to discuss the details of our first business venture?"

"That's what I'm here for, Brother Rupert," I said.

"Fine," he said. "I want you to know up front that I am an honest businessman who would never dream of harming another soul, Doctor Jones."

"I could tell that right off," I said.

"I seek no commendation for my work," he continued. "I'm in the import/export business, hardly a noteworthy or romantic occupation. I pay my bills on time, I treat my help well, I have virtually no social life, I avoid the spotlight at all costs. In point of fact, I am a *laissez-faire* capitalist of the highest order. And yet, there is a local official who has harassed me, threatened me, tried to drive me out of business, and caused me a considerable loss of revenue."

"No!" I said, shocked.

"Yes, Doctor Jones," he replied. "I have borne his enmity silently up to now, but he has become an intolerable nuisance, and it is my intention to so embarrass him that he is forced to resign from his position, if not leave Hong Kong altogether."

"What does this have to do with *me*, Brother Rupert?" I asked.

"I cannot proceed with my plan alone. For your complicity in ridding me of this vile and obdurate man, I am willing to pay you the sum of one thousand British pounds sterling. What do you say to that?"

"That's a right tidy sum," I allowed. "Just who is this here villain that we plan to put out of commission?"

"A man named Wong."

"Would that be Inspector Willie Wong of the Hong Kong Police?" I suggested.

"The very same. How is it that you come to know his name, Doctor Jones?"

"Oh, they bandy it around a lot down at the jail," I said.

"Have you any compunctions in helping me rid decent society of this man?"

"Not a one," I said. "Why, did you know that every single man he arrested swore that he was innocent? We certainly can't have a man like that riding roughshod over the people of this fair city."

He broke out into a great big smile. "I believe we understand each other perfectly, Doctor Jones. I *knew* I had selected the right man!"

"How do we plan to deal with this menace to social stability and free enterprise?" I asked.

"Willie Wong's reputation rests on the fact that he has never made a mistake, never arrested an innocent man, never let a guilty one get away," said Cornwall, puffing on his cigar. "If we can publicly embarrass and humiliate him, I believe his honor will demand that he retire from public service."

"And just how do we aim to do that?"

"I have it on good authority that the Empire Emerald, the largest gemstone in all of China, will be stolen from the Fung Ping Shan Museum tomorrow night," he said, leaning forward in his chair. "I will arrange that every clue points toward you, and knowing Wong, he will almost certainly bring you into custody within hours of the robbery. It will then be revealed that he has wrongly arrested a man of God, and that, furthermore, the emerald was stolen by one of his own sons." He leaned back with a satisfied smile. "What do you think of that?"

"I think I want five hundred pounds up front and the name of a good bondsman, just in case something goes wrong," I said.

"Certainly, my dear Doctor Jones." He pulled out a wallet thick enough to choke a small elephant and peeled off five one-hundred-pound notes, which he then handed over to me. "I distrust a man who doesn't look out for his own interest."

"Okay," I said, stuffing the money into my pocket. "What else do I have to know or do?"

"Very little," he said. "Spend an hour browsing at the museum late tomorrow afternoon, perhaps get into a slight altercation with one of the tourists so people will remember seeing you there, keep off the streets between midnight and two o'clock in the morning, and put *this* in a safe place."

With that, he handed me a small cloth bag that was closed with a drawstring.

"What's in it?" I asked.

"Take a look."

I opened it up and found a lump of coal about the size of a golf ball.

"*That*, Doctor Jones, will prove to be the undoing of Willie

Wong. Hide it well, but not so well that a thorough search cannot turn it up. While you are spending the night in jail and his men are ransacking your room, my own operatives will plant the real emerald on one of his brats.''

"An emerald this big is an awful high price to pay to get rid of one bothersome policeman," I said.

"He costs me more than that every week," said Cornwall. "It will be money well spent."

"Well, considering that it ain't yours to begin with, I reckon I can see the logic in that," I agreed.

"And now, Doctor Jones, it is best that we part company. I don't want anyone to know that we've been in contact since my release from jail." He stood up and walked me to the door. "Your remaining five hundred pounds will be delivered in an envelope to your hotel the morning after your arrest, and you will be contacted later in the week concerning our next venture."

"Sounds good to me, Brother Rupert," I said, shaking his hand. "It's always nice to do business with a Christian gentleman like yourself."

"We've lots more business to do when this sordid little affair is over," he said with a twinkle in his eye.

I kind of doubted it, since he never asked me what hotel he was supposed to deliver my money to. But with five hundred pounds in my pocket and Willie Wong on my side, I decided that things were definitely looking up for the Tabernacle of Saint Luke.

I had walked maybe half a mile from Cornwall's office when I saw two young Chinamen staring at me from a street corner, so I strolled over to them.

"Nine?" I said to the bigger one.

There was no response.

"Twenty-Six?" I said.

"Make it thirty and you've got yourself a date," he said with a giggle.

"Doctor Jones!" yelled a young man from across the street. "We're over here!"

I turned and saw two more Chinamen and made a beeline toward them.

"Are you Willie Wong's kids?" I asked.

The older one nodded. "We've got orders to take you to Dad."

"Lead the way," I said.

I followed them a couple of blocks to a dimly lit restaurant. They left me at the door, and as I entered it I saw Wong nod to me from a table in the back.

"You visit with Mr. Rupert Cornwall, yes?" he said, gesturing for me to sit down.

"Yeah. He doesn't like you much."

"Stitch in time save nine."

"You ever consider writing a Chinese proverb book?" I asked him.

"Please continue," he said, slurping his soup.

"Near as I can make out, he plans to steal the Empire Emerald around midnight tomorrow."

"Ah, so."

"Not only that," I added. "But he plans to make it look like *I* stole it, and while you're busy arresting me he's going to plant it on one of your sons."

"Very interesting," he said with no show of interest whatsoever.

"Well, that's it. I'm done now, right?" I said. "I mean, you'll be waiting for him at the museum, and I can go off converting all you godless yellow heathen—no offense intended—and maybe build my tabernacle."

"Not that easy," said Wong.

"Why not?" I demanded.

"Cannot make omelet without breaking eggs."

"What the hell is that supposed to mean?"

"So sorry," he said. "Wrong proverb." He paused and tried again. "Beauty only skin deep."

"Well, that explains everything," I said.

"Cannot capture Mr. Rupert Cornwall at museum where emerald reside," continued Wong as he finished his soup.

"I already told you what time he's going to show up."

"*He* will not steal emerald. He will have underling do so. I do not want little fish while big fish lead horse to water but cannot make him drink."

"So what *do* you plan to do?"

"Mr. Rupert Cornwall expect me to arrest you. I will not disappoint him."

"That may not disappoint *him*," I said, "but it'll disappoint the hell out of *me*."

He shook his head. "Just go through motions. Then catch him when he try to plant emerald on honorable son."

"What if he has a henchman do *that*, too?" I asked.

"Almost certainly will. After all, home is where heart is."

"I don't think you understand me, Brother Wong," I said. "What's the difference if you catch a henchman stealing the emerald or you catch one planting it on your kid?"

"Much easier to trace emerald back to Mr. Rupert Cornwall *after* he has stolen it than before," explained Wong.

"And what happens to me?" I asked.

"We arrest you with much fanfare in afternoon, release you when we apprehend henchman that night."

Then a particularly bothersome thought occurred to me.

"What if he changes his mind and decides to keep the emerald?"

"Then you have lied to me, I take full credit for capturing you, city give another medal to humble detective, and I apprehend Mr. Rupert Cornwall some other day." He smiled. "You see, either way it all work out."

Well, I could see it all working out for Willie Wong and Rupert Cornwall a lot easier than it all working out for me, so me and the Lord decided that it was time to take matters into our own hands, and what we did was this: I went out shopping at a bunch of costume jewelry stores, and when I finally came to a fake emerald about the size of the lump of coal I was toting around in the little cloth bag, I bought it for twenty pounds and tucked it away in my pocket.

Then I went over to Bonham Road and visited the Fung Ping Shan Museum a day early, found the Empire Emerald, and tried to figure out how to substitute my stone for the real one, but since I'm a God-fearing Christian missionary who ain't never had an illegal impulse in my life, I finally had to admit that while the trip wires and the lock on the front door wouldn't give me no problems, the alarm built into the case was a type I hadn't seen before and there was just no way I was going to be able to switch the emeralds without setting it off and waking up such dead as weren't otherwise occupied at the time.

One thing I did notice, though, was that the guards were Brits and not Chinamen, so I waited until they locked up the museum and followed one of them home. I got his name off the mailbox, and early the next morning, right after he'd left for work, I called his wife and told her that my laundry shop had inadvertently ruined her husband's tuxedo, but that we would be happy to make amends. She explained that he didn't *have* a tuxedo, and I told her I was sure it was his but just to make doubly certain I needed to know the name of the establishment she did her business with, and as soon as she told me I popped over there and informed them I was a visiting relative who had been sent by to pick up any uniforms he might have left there. Sure enough, they had one, all bright and green and neatly pressed, with shining · brass buttons. I tipped them a couple of pounds, took it to the men's room in the back of a nearby tavern, and slipped it on— and an hour later I was patrolling the corridors of the museum, nodding pleasantly to passersby and keeping a watchful eye on the emerald.

Then, when the museum hit a slow period and the room containing the Empire Emerald had emptied out, I walked into it with a beer in my hand, set it down atop the glass case that covered the gemstone, and tipped the bottle over. I pulled the phony emerald out of my pocket, lifted up the glass cover, and as the alarm went off I quickly exchanged it for the real emerald, got down on my knees, pulled out a handkerchief, and set about trying to clean the beer off the glass.

The room filled up to overflowing with guards about ten seconds later. A couple of them even covered me with their pistols until they saw the emerald where it ought to be, and then they helped me put the glass cover back on. I explained that I was new on the job, and that I was just trying to clean up after myself because I had spilled some beer, and after telling me what a clumsy fool I was, they told me to pack up my gear and go home, that my services were no longer needed. They managed to get the alarm turned off just about the time I was climbing down the museum steps to the sidewalk in front of the building.

I went back to my room at the Luk Kwok Hotel, where I had a little chat with my Silent Partner, explaining to Him that while what I did may have seemed a criminal act on the surface of it, if He would examine the consequences carefully He would have to agree that it was for the best all the way around. Willie Wong was still going to capture Rupert Cornwall, so *he* would be happy; the museum would never know they weren't displaying the real Empire Emerald, so *they* would be happy; Cornwall was going to go to jail anyway, so at least he wouldn't be any *less* happy for not having the emerald in his possession for a couple of minutes. And me, I finally had sufficient capital to build the Tabernacle of Saint Luke, which I promised the Lord I would do just as soon as I spent a few weeks scouting out the territory for the very best location.

Everything went pretty smoothly the next day. First thing I did was stop by the laundry and drop off the uniform, so no one would notice it was missing and maybe start thinking about *why* it was missing. Then I scouted up some lunch that didn't smell of fish, and wandered the streets a bit, and at about two in the afternoon I walked over to the museum, lingered there for an hour or two, had a very public misunderstanding with a blonde Frenchwoman, and then headed back toward the Luk Kwok.

Along the way, I picked up some chewing gum and stuck a wad of it into my mouth. Then I stopped by a little gift shop, and while the proprietor was speaking to another customer, I stuck the Empire Emerald on the back of his radiator with the chewing gum. Since it was midsummer, I knew he wasn't going to fiddle with the radiator for another few months, and I figured to be back for it within just a day or two. The very last thing I did was hide the cloth bag with the lump of coal inside the water tank behind the toilet once I returned to my room in the Luk Kwok. Then I lay back on my bed, pulled out the Good Book, and whiled the night away reading about Solomon's more exotic dalliances.

The police showed up right on schedule, at a quarter after two in the morning, and hustled me off to jail. I kept protesting my innocence, the way I figured both Willie Wong and Rupert Cornwall would expect of me, and then, just after daybreak, a guard came and unlocked my cell. As far as I was concerned he could have waited another couple of hours, since I hadn't yet got around to converting Mei Sung again, but given the circumstances I didn't think it proper to protest, so I let him escort me to freedom, which turned out to be Wong's little cubbyhole.

"Good morning, Doctor Jones," he said without getting up from his chair.

"Good morning, Brother Wong," I said. "How'd it go last night?"

"Apprehend whole gang," he said happily. "Rupert Cornwall in cell one flight up from yours."

"That's great news, Brother Wong," I said. "And did you get the emerald back?"

"Empire Emerald once again on display in Fung Ping Shan Museum."

"I guess that closes the case."

He nodded. "Cannot teach old dog new tricks."

"Well, I'll sure remember that the next time I run into an old dog, Brother Wong," I said. "I assume I'm free to go."

"Farther you go, the better."

"I beg your pardon?"

"It best you leave Hong Kong," said Wong. "Many friends and clients of Rupert Cornwall not very pleased with you."

"A telling point," I agreed. "Gimme just a couple of hours to get my gear together and I'll be off."

"Thank you for help, Doctor Jones," said Wong. "Knew you were right man for job."

"My pleasure, Brother Wong," I said.

Then I took my leave of him, went back to the Luk Kwok, and looked around to see if there was anything I wanted to take along with me. There were some old shirts and pants and socks and such, but since I was about to pick up the Empire Emerald on my way out of town, I decided that I really owed myself a new wardrobe, so I finally left empty-handed.

I moseyed over to the area where the gift shop was, did maybe an hour of serious window-shopping up and down the street for the benefit of anyone who might have been watching me, and finally entered the little store after I was sure I wasn't being observed.

"You are Lucifer Jones, are you not?" asked the proprietor the second I closed the door behind me.

"How did you know?" I asked. "I don't recall talking to you last night."

"I was given your description by Inspector Wong," he replied. "He left a note for you."

He handed me a folded-up piece of paper, which I opened and read:

> *Dear Doctor Jones:*
> *Had feeling all along you were perfect man for job. Had honorable Number Ten, Fourteen, Seventeen, and Twenty-Two sons observe you constantly since you left custody. Not only is Rupert Cornwall under arrest, but we now know weakness in museum security system, all thanks to you.*
> *Is old Chinese custom to exchange gifts. You will know where to look for yours.*
> *Your humble servant,*
Willie Wong,
Hong Kong Police
> *P.S. Money is root of all evil.*

I threw the paper down on the counter and raced over to the radiator. I reached behind it, found my gum and the stone, and pulled it out: it was the same lump of coal Rupert Cornwall had given me two days ago.

"Is something wrong, Mr. Jones?" asked the storekeeper.

"Nothing I shouldn't have expected from trusting someone who ain't a decent, God-fearing Christian," I said bitterly. "Give me a map, brother."

"A map?" he repeated.

"This town's seen the last of me," I said. "I'm heading to where a man of the cloth can convert souls in peace and quiet without being worried about getting flim-flammed by gangsters and detectives and the like."

He pulled a map out from behind the counter. I looked at it for a minute and then, with four hundred and fifty pounds of Rupert Cornwall's money still in my pocket, I lit out across the mouth of the Pearl River for Macao, where I hoped to find a better class of sinner to listen to my preaching.

2
The Sin City Derby

Macao didn't smell a lot better than Hong Kong, and it wasn't no cleaner, but it offered more opportunities to an enterprising Christian gentleman like myself. In fact, it offered more opportunities to just about everybody, since it was where all the young Hong Kong bucks went to do their gambling and find their short-term ladyfriends.

I got off the ferry, trying to figure out what to do next, when a young blond guy pulling an empty rickshaw stopped in front of me.

"Howdy, brother," I said. "Take me to wherever it is that the white folks stay when they're in town."

"That'd be the Bela Vista Hotel," he said in perfect American. "But you can do better at the Macao Inn, over on the Travesso de Padre Narciso."

"Sounds good to me," I said, climbing into the seat. "Let 'er rip."

"I can also get you into half a dozen high-class gambling clubs," he said as he began pulling the rickshaw down the street. "And if you've got an interest in the ladies . . ."

"Well, mostly I'm here to raise money for my Tabernacle," I said. "But I gotta admit it makes more sense to go where the money is than where it ain't. And of course, part of my calling is to show wicked, painted Jezebels the power and the glory."

He turned and grinned at me. "It sounds like you've got

yourself a mighty interesting religion, Preacher," he said. "I wouldn't mind joining up myself."

"How'd a well-spoken young feller like you come to be in the rickshaw trade thousands of miles from church and home in the first place?" I asked him.

"It's a long story," he said. "But the gist of it is that I hired on to work on an archaeological dig in the Gobi Desert. Our boat docked in Hong Kong on a Saturday afternoon, and a bunch of us came over to the Sin City of Macao for one last fling before going out in the wilderness."

"Makes sense," I allowed.

"They told us to be back at sun-up on Monday, which was when the truck was leaving. I guess I overslept a little."

"And they didn't wait for you?"

"I didn't get out of bed until half past Tuesday, and I figured they were all gone by then, so I looked around for some way to earn my passage back home. I thought I could be a croupier, or maybe a personal manager for some ladies of the evening, but all the good jobs were taken, and so I wound up pulling this goddamned rickshaw."

He took a hard left turn, and suddenly I could see the Macao Inn straight ahead of us.

"Here we are, Preacher," he said, sprinting the final fifty yards.

"Take it easy," I said. "We ain't in no race."

"Sorry," he said, coming to a stop in front of the hotel. "Sometimes I pretend I'm still outrunning tacklers on the football field back in high school. It helps to pass the time."

"You played football?"

"Sure did," he answered. "And being an ex-halfback gives me an edge on the competition. If we see a single customer stepping off the ferry or out of a hotel, I always get there first."

It was just about that instant that the Lord smote me right betwixt the eyes with a great big heavenly revelation.

"Are you telling me there ain't no coolie in town can match strides with you?" I said.

"Not a one," he said. "I even had a couple of Big Ten

scholarship offers—until they threw me off the team for a few minor infractions, that is.''

''What kind of infractions?''

''Oh . . . Zelda, Thelma, Patti . . . those kinds.''

''Brother,'' I said. ''How'd you like to get enough money for passage back to the good old U.S. of A. and have a little pocket money left over for an occasional infraction?''

''You've got a curious expression on your face, Preacher,'' he said. ''I can't quite tell if you're joking or not.''

''I never joke about money,'' I said. ''It's against the Third and Eighth Commandments. Come on inside and let's talk a little business.''

He pulled the rickshaw over to a side of the road and followed me into the Macao Inn. There was a great big fountain in the middle of the lobby, with about a dozen parrots dangling down from the ceiling in bamboo cages. There was a fat white man in a wrinkled suit and a fez talking to a couple of turbaned Indians in a corner, and an Englishman in tweeds was sitting on a leather chair, smoking a pipe and reading a copy of the *China Morning Post*. We walked past the check-in desk and turned left at the restaurant, which was just about empty, it being the middle of the afternoon.

''Have a seat,'' I said, escorting my rickshaw driver to a small table.

''Don't mind if I do,'' he replied.

''By the way, brother, I didn't catch your name.''

''Harvey,'' he said, reaching out and shaking my hand. ''Harvey Edwards, and before we discuss any further business, you still owe me for the ride.''

''How much?''

''Tell you what,'' he said. ''Buy me a couple of beers and we'll call it square.''

''I can't do that, Brother Harvey,'' I said, reaching into my pocket and pulling out a couple of coins. ''This ought to cover what I owe you.''

''You got something against beer, Preacher?'' he asked.

''Not a thing,'' I answered. ''Nothing slakes the thirst like a cold beer.''

"Then what's the problem?"

"*I* ain't got no problem, Brother Harvey," I said. "But *you*—you're in training."

"For what?"

"The rickshaw races."

He frowned. "What are you talking about? There *ain't* any rickshaw races in Macao."

I grinned at him. "Yet," I said.

Suddenly his eyes lit up like little candles. "Oh?"

"Brother Harvey, I been mulling on it, and I can't see no reason why I should risk the Lord's money playing fan-tan and other games of chance with these local sharks when we can invite 'em into *our* pool."

"You know," said Harvey with a great big smile, "I can't think of any reason either."

"Good!" I said. "Then we're in business."

"Fifty-fifty," he replied.

I shook my head. "One-third for you, one-third for me, and one-third for the Lord, which is only fair, since He's putting up the money."

"He ain't doing the running, though," said Harvey adamantly.

Well, we hemmed and we hawed and we haggled, and what it finally came down to was that Harvey and I would split the first ten thousand pounds we made down the middle, and the Lord got Himself a twenty percent option on the rest, provided He produced fair weather and a fast track. That settled, we indulged in a couple of grilled Macao pigeons, and then I started asking him where we were likely to find the biggest plungers.

"No question about it," he said. "They're all at the Central Hotel."

"Never heard of it."

"You're about the first person I've run across who hasn't," said Harvey. "It's the biggest building in town, even if it *is* only nine stories tall. You can see it from just about anywhere."

"Maybe I ought to rent a room there instead of here," I suggested.

He laughed at that. "They'll be charging you rent every twenty minutes, Preacher," he said. "It ain't exactly your run-of-the-mill hotel."

Which was an understatement if ever there was one.

We waited till the sun went down and then made our way over to the Central Hotel, which despite its name wasn't a hotel at all. We walked in the main entrance and found ourselves on the ground floor, which was crawling with coolies. There were small-stakes games of roulette and baccarat and fan-tan going on everywhere, and the girls were just about all in need of a little soap and water and a good dentist.

"These guys don't look like no high rollers to me," I said as we began walking across the room.

"They're not," replied Harvey.

"Well, then?" I asked.

"Follow me," he said, walking toward a huge, winding staircase.

The coolies were a little better dressed on the second floor, and the girls looked a mite healthier. By the third floor, they were playing with British pounds instead of Hong Kong dollars, and we ran into a bunch of Indians on the fourth floor. When we reached the fifth floor, most of the players were Europeans and well-dressed Chinamen, and the girls were so downright beautiful that I remarked to Harvey that I couldn't wait to see what they'd look like once we reached the penthouse.

"The gambling ends on the sixth floor," he answered. "The top three floors are just bedrooms."

So we made our way up one more flight, and the only difference between the sixth floor of the Central Hotel and the casino at Monte Carlo was that a third of the players here were Chinamen and the girls were all dressed for mighty warm weather.

"See that big Chinaman in the corner with his back to the wall?" whispered Harvey, gesturing to an ornery-looking feller sitting at a high-stakes poker table. "He's Lo Chung. He owns the place." He pointed to the others at the table. "That's Bet-A-Million Reynolds, over there is Sir Reginald Thurmand, and that little guy next to Lo Chung is Gerhardt Guenther, the German ambassador." He sighed. "Must be fifty million dollars sitting at that one table."

"They got a privy up here?" I asked as one of the hostesses passed by, and she pointed it out to me. I told Harvey to stay put, then went off by myself, pulled out a handkerchief, folded it into a nice neat square, folded Cornwall's money over it, and then slapped a rubber band around the whole thing, so it looked like I was walking around with maybe forty thousand pounds of cash rather than four hundred.

Then I went back out onto the floor and rejoined Harvey, who was getting a little nervous in the presence of all that money. We wandered around the room, exchanged pleasantries with a couple of hostesses, stopped to watch the action at the roulette wheel and the craps table, and finally wound up at the fan-tan game, where a Greek and a Korean were having a contest to see who could go broke first. I whispered to Harvey to go back to the rickshaw and that I'd meet him there in just a couple of minutes. He looked kind of curious, but he did what I told him.

"I *do* love the smell of money," I said, turning back to the fan-tan table.

"Perhaps you would like to join us," suggested the Greek.

I shook my head. "Too tame for me, brother."

He laughed so loud that everyone turned to see what was going on.

"You find fan-tan *tame*?" he said.

"Yeah. It's almost as dull as poker and craps," I said. I pulled out my bankroll, tossed it carelessly in the air and caught it a couple of times, and then stuck it back in my pocket. "Guess I'll go out looking for some *real* action."

At which point Lo Chung got up from his poker game and walked over to me.

"Good evening, Father," he said, bowing low.

"As a matter of fact, it's Reverend," I said. "The Right Reverend Lucifer Jones."

"It is not often that we play host to a man of the cloth," he said. "We have a reputation as the Sin City of the Orient."

"Well, I'm afraid it's gonna be even less often, brother," I said. "I like excitement when I bet." I reached into my pocket and fiddled with my bankroll again. "Nothing all that exciting here, except maybe for that little hostess with the green eyes and dress to match."

"We try to accommodate all our guests, Reverend Jones," he said, looking greedily toward my pocket. "Perhaps if you would tell me what type of gambling excites you . . . ?"

"Glad you asked, brother," I said, kind of gently shoving him aside and speaking to the room at large. "Ladies and gents, I came here by rickshaw, just like a batch of you folks did—and I got forty thousand pounds that says my rickshaw puller can whip any rickshaw puller you put up against him at any distance from fifty yards to six furlongs at equal weights."

"Now just a minute, Reverend Jones!" said Lo Chung. "This is *my* gambling establishment. You cannot arrange your own transactions with my customers!"

"Sorry, Brother Lo Chung," I apologized. "I certainly didn't mean to step out of line. I suppose I'd best take my leave of you."

I walked to the head of the stairs, and then stopped and turned back to the room. "The race starts in front of the Macao Inn at nine o'clock tomorrow morning," I said. "I'll cover any and all bets."

Then I ran down the stairs just before a couple of Lo Chung's bouncers could throw me down. I saw the cutest little lady serving drinks as I passed the third floor, but I didn't have time to start no conversations and I figured if I just grabbed her and carried her down the stairs with me the extra weight would slow me down enough so the bouncers could catch me, and so a brief and tender romantic moment went unrequited.

I yelled to Harvey to get ready to roll as I burst out through the front door with a couple of hundred coolies staring at me, but no one followed me, so thankfully he didn't have to use up no energy or calories or nothing getting us out of there, and ten minutes later we were back at the Macao Inn, sitting in the bar, him sipping an iced tea and eyeing my beer the way I had eyed that little hostess on the third floor.

"Have you given any serious thought to how you plan to cover all those bets tomorrow?" he asked.

"Me and the Lord'll think of something," I said. "After all, we got all night, ain't we?"

"All night isn't that long, Preacher."

"The Lord made the world in six days," I said. "That's one for each continent, the way I figure it. Now, if He could make Asia in a day and have time left over for creating the sun and the moon and swiping one of Adam's ribs, surely He don't need all night to solve this minor inconvenience." I finished up my beer. "You just make sure you don't bust no legs coming out of the starting gate."

"I could beat most of the local coolies on one leg," answered Harvey. "Don't worry, Preacher—it's in the bag."

"All right," I said. "It's about time you headed home and got a good eight hours, so you'll be all fresh and ready to go in the morning." Then I changed my mind. "You know, now as I come to think on it, it's probably better that you spend the night here. Can't chance you running into traffic and getting all tuckered out on your way here tomorrow morning."

"I don't have any money for a room."

I tossed him my room key. "Take mine," I said. "I'll get another. You can pay me out of your share of the winnings."

He picked up the key and headed off to the room. Then, just to make sure he didn't do nothing to damage his wind on the eve of the big event, I rounded up all the girls in the lobby, rented another room, and made sure that none of 'em were available just in case he came looking for a little infraction. It was a long and arduous chore, but I figured I owed it to him, and I was sure that my Silent Partner would understand that I was only doing it for the benefit of His tabernacle.

I got up a bit before sunrise, tiptoed out of the room, and went down to the front desk, where a young Chinaman was smoking a waterpipe and doping out the races.

"Got a safe deposit box for hire, brother?" I asked.

"Yes," said the clerk, pulling out a box and handing me the key. "That'll be one Hong Kong dollar."

"How'd you like to make some *real* money?" I said.

"I wouldn't be adverse to it," he admitted.

"Good," I said. "Comes nine o'clock, this place is gonna be crawling with rickshaws and big spenders. A lot of them are going to want someone responsible to hold their bets." I pulled a pair of hundred-pound notes off my roll, which was still wrapped around the handkerchief, and handed them to him. "This ought to make it worth your while."

"Yes, sir!" he said with a great big smile.

"Now, as you can see," I said, sticking the roll into the box, "I'm putting forty thousand pounds in here. You're my witness."

"Right," he said, barely taking his eyes off his own two hundred-pound notes, which was probably close to half a year's wages for him.

"Okay," I said, handing him the box. "Lock it up for safekeeping."

He put the box back in place, locked it, and returned the key to me.

"Now, just so you've got this straight: you're legally empowered to take bets up to forty thousand pounds. Once you've reached the limit, or there ain't no more money being wagered, stick it in another lock box and keep the key yourself."

"Then what?"

"The winner gets the contents of both boxes." I leaned across the counter and whispered in his ear: "And if things go right, this could be a daily chore for you—at the same rate of pay."

"I'm more than happy to be of service, sir," he assured me with a greedy grin on his face.

"Somehow I thought you might be," I replied.

Then I went off to wake Harvey, took him down to the restaurant for a breakfast of orange juice and tea, and walked back into the lobby at about a quarter to nine. It was filled to overflowing with coolies and their backers, all lined up to lay their bets with the clerk.

At nine o'clock sharp, we all walked outside, where Harvey and twenty-three other rickshaw pullers lined up across the broad street. Then it was just a matter of setting the conditions, which turned out to be twice around the block, or just under half a mile. Harvey was pawing at the ground with his feet, and his eyes were bright and excited, and I thought he might break out whinnying any second.

There must have been a good five hundred people crowded up and down the street, not all of them Chinamen, and finally we let Bet-A-Million Reynolds fire the gun that started the race.

Harvey opened up a quick two lengths on his field before they hit the first corner, and was leading by twenty yards when they passed the finish line the first time. They disappeared from sight around the corner a second time, and when they hit the homestretch Harvey was only leading by a length—but as he passed by he winked at me, and I realized he was just trying not to discourage the competition from trying him again. He won by about half a length, and before I could go to the desk to pick up our winnings, Sir Reginald Thurmond and Ambassador Gerhardt Guenther were demanding a rematch that night.

I hemmed and hawed as if I thought Harvey was too tuckered out to run again, and finally let them talk me into it, for midnight, sharp. We told the crowd when to come back, and then Harvey and me went to the desk and picked up thirty-seven thousand beautiful British pounds, counted it a couple of times and stood there admiring it for a few minutes, and then put it back in the safe.

"Easiest money I ever made for a rickshaw ride!" He laughed.

"We should just about double it tonight," I said, "and then we'll start running you in handicaps."

"Handicaps?"

"Yeah," I said. "After this weekend we'll never get another even race, so you'll probably have to tote weights in your rickshaw, just like a racehorse."

"Make the race downhill and the weights might actually help me go faster," he suggested.

"That little law of physics ain't exactly lost on me," I replied. "Ain't no rule says you have to run the same course every time out."

Well, we loafed around the hotel for most of the afternoon, but when I saw Harvey smiling at a couple of early-blooming flowers of the night I sent him to his room for a nap, and then, just to make sure that he couldn't give in to temptation, I took them off to my own room for the next couple of hours, where I got me an education in various Chinese arts that were even more complicated than fan-tan.

I could have spent another few hours saving Harvey from further temptation, and generous Christian gentleman that I am I was all set to do so, but at about seven o'clock he pounded on my door to say that he was going down to the restaurant to grab some dinner. I didn't want his stomach to go cramping up on him, so I took my leave of my lovely companions and went with him to supervise.

"I'll have a thick steak, and make sure that it's rare," said Harvey as the waiter approached us.

"Belay that order," I said. "He'll have two glasses of orange juice and a cup of coffee."

"Preacher," he said irritably, "sooner or later you got to let me eat something solid or I ain't gonna have the energy to run. I'm starving!"

"You can't run on a full stomach," I told him sternly.

"I can't run on one that's been empty for a day and a half, neither!"

"You're really all that hungry?" I asked.

"I am."

"Okay," I said, turning to the waiter. "Bring us a thick steak."

"Rare," added Harvey.

"Yes, sir," said the waiter, bowing.

"Does that come with a salad?" I asked.

"Yes, sir."

"Fine. Bring 'em out at the same time."

"And what will you have, sir?"

"I'm having the steak. My friend here gets the salad. No dressing."

"Preacher!"

"Ah, what the hell," I said, giving in to my soft Christian nature. "Bring him a half order of dressing, on the side."

"Thanks a heap," muttered Harvey.

He didn't say another word till the salad came, and then he wolfed it down so fast I thought he might take a couple of bites out of the plate by mistake, or maybe on purpose, and I noticed that he licked my steak plate clean while I was settling the bill, but when we left the restaurant I was satisfied that he was in perfect shape for the race.

The crowds started showing up at about ten o'clock, and by a quarter to midnight there must have been a thousand people, but the betting was going real slow since Harvey had impressed the hell out of 'em in the morning and they wanted to wait to see the opposition and have the odds posted before they started laying their money down.

Then, suddenly, everything got real quiet, and a big black limousine pulled up and Lo Chung stepped out. He looked like he'd had happier days.

"Howdy, Lo Chung," I said, stepping forward. "Welcome to the Sin City Rickshaw Racing Club. I thought you'd be tending to business over at the Central Hotel."

"All my customers have come *here*," he said grimly.

"Well, we'll shoot 'em right back to you once the race is over."

"You must not continue to interfere with my business, Reverend Jones," he said.

"Who's interfering?" I said. "You run roulette wheels and fan-tan games, I run rickshaw races."

"I warn you, Reverend. I am becoming seriously displeased with you."

"Six or seven weeks, and everyone'll get tired of trying to beat my champion and go back to blowing their paychecks over at your place, Lo Chung," I said. "You just gotta learn to be patient."

"Just remember, Doctor Jones, that my patience is not unending," he said, and got back into his limo and drove off to the Central Hotel.

Well, that kind of put a damper on things for a couple of minutes, but then Sir Reginald and the German ambassador showed up, each with what looked like a higher class of coolie, and a few minutes later the race was under way, and this time the coolies broke on top and Harvey just kind of lagged behind in third place, biding his time until the last hundred yards or so, where he came on to win by just under a length.

We cleared another twenty thousand pounds, stuck it with the rest of our money in the hotel safe, and went to bed, him alone and me with such temptations as I didn't want him to have no part of.

Next morning I woke him up again, and escorted him down to the restaurant.

"You know what I dreamed about last night?" he said after I'd ordered him a grapefruit juice and a cup of coffee.

"Women?" I suggested.

"Nope."

"America?"

He shook his head. "Food."

"Harvey, I'm your manager," I said. "You gotta trust me. Haven't I made us close to sixty thousand pounds already?"

"Sooner or later you gotta give me something to eat or I'm gonna be too weak to pull that damned rickshaw," he protested.

"After this morning's race," I said. "We'll give you an hour to cool out, and then you can have the biggest steak on the menu. That'll give you more than twelve hours to digest it and sleep it off before you run again at midnight."

"You promise?" he asked distrustfully.

"I swear it on my mother's grave," I said, which seemed to please him. At any rate, it had to have pleased him more than knowing that my mother was currently running an establishment for fallen women in Wichita, which was in fact the case, but somehow it just wouldn't have sounded as impressive to swear on my mother's sporting house.

Well, we finished breakfast and walked outside, shouldering our way through a few hundred Chinamen, and what we came to was Lo Chung, leaning against his limousine and doing his damnedest to look inscrutable.

"You're up early today, Lo Chung," I said by way of greeting.

"I finally decided that if I couldn't beat you, I should join you," he replied.

"Well, that's right thoughtful of you," I said, "but the Sin City Jockey Club ain't in the market for no partners."

"I meant that I intend to join you as a competitor," he explained. "Let me make sure I have the conditions correct. You state that your man can outpull any rickshaw in Macao?"

"That's right."

"And there are no other conditions?"

I shot a quick look at Harvey, figuring that Lo Chung was thinking of bringing in some Chinese track star who we hadn't never heard of, but he just gave me a confident nod.

"That's right," I said. "There ain't no other conditions."

He pulled a huge wad of bills out of his pocket. "I'll match whatever winnings you've accrued so far."

I looked at Harvey again. He looked fit and trim and confident, even if his stomach *was* rumbling to beat the band.

"Okay, Lo Chung, you got yourself a bet," I said, and escorted him to the desk while he placed his roll on deposit in the safe.

"Shall we outline the course?" he asked as we were walking back to the street.

"Well, usually they just run around the block a couple of times," I said.

"This may be the biggest wager ever made on a race in Macao," he answered. "I think more people should be able to see it. I suggest that we race from the ruins of the St. Paul Cathedral to the Temple of Kun Iam."

"That's pretty close to a mile," I noted.

"Isn't your man up to it?" he asked with a smile.

"Five yards, five miles, it makes no difference to me," said Harvey.

"Excellent!" said Lo Chung. "Shall we walk to the starting line?"

"Wouldn't you rather wait by the finish?" I asked.

"All in good time, Reverend Jones," he said. "I'll see the finish, too, never fear."

I figured that meant he planned to have his limo drive him to the finish line once the race was under way, and made up my mind to hop a lift with him since I didn't relish walking all the way to the Temple of Kun Iam in the morning sun.

The St. Paul Cathedral, which had fallen into a mild state of disrepair and now consisted of nothing but four walls, a staircase, and a lot of weeds, was about half a mile from the Macao Inn. Harvey, surrounded by a bunch of kids who all wanted his autograph, started toting the rickshaw there, with me and Lo Chung and a few hundred bettors tagging along behind. As we were walking I realized that I'd been so busy watching Harvey's diet that I'd neglected to eat breakfast myself, so I stopped by a local food stand and bought a couple of sandwiches and an apple, stuffed the apple and one of the sandwiches in my pocket, and munched on the other as we made our way to the starting line.

"By the way, I ain't seen *your* rickshaw yet, Brother Lo Chung," I said.

"It's waiting for us at the Cathedral."

When we got to within maybe fifty yards of the Cathedral, I turned to him. "You must be wrong, Brother Lo Chung," I said. "Ain't nothing there but a horse and buggy."

"A horse and *rickshaw*," he corrected me.

"Well, that's one way of getting it here," I said. "Where's your puller?"

"Right there, Reverend Jones," he replied.

"But that's a horse!"

"How clever of you to notice."

"That ain't in the rules! Get rid of it and get yourself a man to pull your rickshaw!"

"You explicitly stated that your man could outpull any rickshaw on Macao," said Lo Chung. "You never said that it had to be pulled by another man. *That* is my puller."

"No way!" I yelled. "You get a man in front of that rickshaw or the bet's off!"

"The bet is *on*, Reverend Jones," he said, and suddenly I was looking down the barrels of a couple of dozen pistols in the hands of his friends and relations, all of whom were dressed in black. "Perhaps next time you will think more carefully before cutting in on someone else's business."

"Well, maybe I'll just tie *our* rickshaw onto the back of a car," I said.

"That would be against the rules," said Lo Chung. "You've already named your puller. He's the one taking on all challengers, remember?"

"I'm gonna have to think about this," I said.

"Well, think quickly," said Lo Chung. "The race starts in seven minutes."

I walked over to Harvey.

"What about it?" I asked in low tones. "Think you can beat a horse?"

"Not a chance," he said dejectedly.

Then an interesting notion struck me. "Don't be so all-fired sure of that," I told him. "The horse don't know he's in a race, does he?"

"What are you driving at, Preacher?" asked Harvey.

"When the race starts, why don't you just walk calm and natural-like toward the Temple of Kun Iam? If he ain't got no reason to run, he'll either stay right where he is or fall into step behind you. Maybe we can win this thing without you breaking out of a walk."

"I think you've got something there, Preacher!" he said excitedly. "Let's give it a try!"

"Okay, Lo Chung," I said, walking back to the Chinaman. "We accept your puller."

"Good," he said, walking over to his rickshaw. "I knew you'd see the light of reason."

He began clambering up onto the seat.

"*Now* what the hell are you doing?" I demanded.

"I'm willingly giving my puller a handicap of one hundred and eighty-three pounds," he said.

"You can't do that!"

"There is nothing in the rules prohibiting me from sitting in my rickshaw during the race," he said as one of his henchmen handed him a whip and another began putting a bridle over the horse's head.

"I *made* the rules!" I shouted. "And I say that ain't legal!"

"Shall we put it to a vote?" asked Lo Chung.

"All right," I said furiously. "Let's just do that!"

Lo Chung nodded to his men, who turned their pistols on the crowd. "Will any man who thinks my actions constitute a breach of the rules please fall down with a bullet in his chest?" he said in a loud, clear voice.

Nobody fell down, or did much of anything else.

He smiled at me. "There you have it, Reverend. A unanimous vote. Now, if you have no further objections, I'll send some of my men ahead to make sure no one absconds with the money."

I had plenty of objections, but it didn't seem all that desirable to voice them at that particular moment. I suggested to my Silent Partner that time was running out fast, and that if He was going to intervene He'd better do it quick, and damned if He didn't come up with an idea.

I looked around until I found an old coolie with a bamboo fishing pole maybe ten or twelve feet long and asked if I could borrow it. I don't think he understood a word I said, but he just kept chattering and bowing until finally I took it out of his hands.

"Going fishing, Reverend?" asked Lo Chung with a chuckle. "I thought you were here to watch a rickshaw race."

"*You* got a whip," I said. "It's only fair that *I* should have a whip."

And with that, I climbed into the chair of Harvey's rickshaw.

"Are you crazy, Preacher?" he demanded. "I can't beat the damned horse *without* you!"

"Fair is fair," I said, smiling back at Lo Chung. "And when we win, I don't ever want anyone saying we done it because Harvey didn't have a passenger and the horse did."

Lo Chung busted out laughing at that, and Harvey kept muttering to himself, and a couple of minutes later we were lined up, nose to nose, in front of St. Paul's Cathedral, pointing toward the Temple of Kun Iam about a mile away.

"Are the contestants ready?" asked Sir Reginald, who had volunteered to be the official starter.

"Not quite," I said, fiddling with the wire on the end of the fishing pole.

"What are you doing, Reverend Jones?" demanded Lo Chung suspiciously.

"Just making sure my whip is in working order," I said.

"You whip me with that thing and I'll give you the beating of your life!" muttered Harvey under his breath.

"Okay, now I'm ready," I said after another moment or two.

"Splendid!" said Sir Reginald. He pulled out his little ivory-handled revolver. "On your marks, get set, go!"

He shot the pistol off just as I swung the fishing pole, with my apple attached to it, in front of the horse's face. He lunged at it, almost throwing Lo Chung out of the rickshaw, and Harvey got off to a quick lead.

"What's going on back there, Preacher?" he asked as he ran along. "Where the hell is the horse?"

"You worry about the running and leave the horse to me," I said, hanging over the side and dangling the apple just in front of the horse's nose. Whenever he reached for it, I flicked my hand and moved it a few inches away from him.

Lo Chung was beating the horse with his whip and cussing a blue streak, but evidently the poor animal hadn't had no more to eat than Harvey had, because he just ignored Lo Chung and kept his eyes peeled on the apple.

Well, we ambled along like that for almost three quarters of a mile, and I took a quick peek ahead and could see the Temple of Kun Iam maybe three hundred yards ahead of us. Then our rickshaw hit a big dip in the road and I almost fell out, and by the time I had regained my balance the horse had reached out and finally got his teeth into the apple and bit it off.

"Step it up, Harvey!" I yelled. "We got problems!"

The horse didn't speed up, but he didn't slow down none either, and I could see that he was going to be done with the apple before we crossed the finish line, and there wasn't no doubt in my mind that once that particular event came to pass he would finally respond to the whip that Lo Chung kept beating him with.

Then I remembered the other sandwich that I had tucked away in my pocket, and I figured what worked for one puller might work for another, so I quick tied it to the end of the fishing rod just about the time the horse downed the last of the apple and we had maybe forty yards to go.

I reached out and stuck it just out of Harvey's reach, and he took off with a burst of speed that would have done Jim Thorpe proud. Lo Chung's rickshaw was coming up fast on the left, but Harvey was inspired, and we crossed the finish line a good half length in front.

I let Harvey grab the sandwich then, and he kept running as he stuffed it in his mouth.

"You can stop now!" I said. "We won!"

"I saw fifteen of Lo Chung's friends and relations standing there in front of the Temple with their guns out and looking very upset for this early in the day," he hollered back at me.

"But we got all our money back at the Macao Inn!" I said.

"It's only money."

"What's so *only* about money?" I demanded.

"You do what you gotta do, Preacher," said Harvey, heading straight toward the dock. "Me, I'm getting out of town alive and intact. There'll be other rickshaw races, and I aim to have my legs still attached to the rest of me when I run in 'em."

I looked back and saw Lo Chung standing beside his rickshaw, raising all kinds of a ruckus, and then a few of his friends and relations looked after us and fired a couple of shots in our direction, and suddenly a boat trip to the mainland started looking better and better.

"After all," I said aloud, "what is a man profited if he wins a hundred thousand pounds sterling and loses his innerds?"

Harvey said "Amen!" and jacked up the pace as the Temple of Kun Iam faded into the distance behind us.

3
The Insidious
Oriental Dentist

Once we hit the mainland, Harvey and I parted company. He wanted to get right back into the rickshaw-racing business, but I decided to head off to Peking, which was the capital city of China and figured to have not only the most sinners in need of saving but the most opportunities to raise funds for my tabernacle.

Well, let me tell you something: it ain't no short hop from Macao to Peking. It took me six months to get there, during which time I picked up a smattering of the language, fell in love fourteen or fifteen times, and only got a personal tour of one calaboose. That was in a little town called Poshan, where the apple of my eye turned out to be the fruit of the local warlord's loins, but even that worked out for the good, because I lost a quick ten pounds on the prison grub and was more handsome than ever by the time I got the jailkeeper interested in a little game of chance involving the number twenty-one, and won my freedom.

By the time I finally got within hailing distance of Peking I wasn't looking my very best, not having changed clothes for the better part of half of a year, and despite taking a plunge into any river I passed by I wasn't on the verge of turning into any nosegay neither, so I started scouting around the countryside for some of the Christian missions I'd heard had been built in these parts. It didn't take too long to find one, where I stopped in for a meal and a little discussion of the Good Book—I'm kind of weak on the Sermon on the Mount, but I'll match my knowledge of the why and how of all the begattings with the best of 'em—and on the way out I borrowed a new set of missionary clothes that I found drying on a clothesline, since I knew these fellers wouldn't begrudge them to a fellow Christian, and besides, I figured an act of inadvertent charity would put them in real tight with the Lord, Who appreciates such things if not done to excess.

I was still some fifty miles out of Peking when I managed to land a ride in the back of a truck that was hauling bales of hay into the city. It was getting on toward winter, and I didn't have no overcoat, so I just kind of burrowed into the hay and decided to catch a quick thirty or forty winks.

I was awakened by a tall, thin Englishman jabbing me with his cane.

"You!" he said. "Get out of there, and be quick about it!"

I sat up, rubbed my eyes, and saw that he was pointing a revolver at my middle, which got my attention real fast.

"What were you doing in there?" he demanded, and as I climbed out I saw that he had the driver out of the cab, too.

"Mostly I was being woke up by an Englishman with a gun," I said. "If this is a holdup, brother, I got to inform you that I'm a man of the cloth who's taken a temporary vow of poverty. I ain't got nothing to my name but the clothes on my back and my copy of the Good Book."

He turned to the driver and jabbered something in Chinese so quick that I couldn't follow what he was saying. The driver, who looked scared to death, nodded his head and grunted.

"All right," said the Englishman. "You can go."

"Go *where*?" I said. "I don't even know where I am."

The driver said something else, and this time it was the Englishman who nodded and grunted, and a minute later the driver hopped back into the cab and took off.

"*Now* how am I gonna get into the city?" I said.

"I'll drive you," said the Englishman. "Where are you going?"

"Peking."

"I mean, where in Peking?"

"I ain't figured that out yet," I said. "Just getting here was effort enough."

He peered at me intently. "You've never been here before?"

"As God is my witness."

He kept on staring at me. "And you're really a man of the cloth?"

I held up two fingers and pressed them together. "Me and God are just like *that*," I assured him.

"Excellent!" He walked me over to his car, which we both got into. "What's your name?" he asked as we headed off toward Peking.

"The Right Reverend Honorable Doctor Lucifer Jones, at your service. Baptisms and funerals done cheap."

"How would you like the opportunity to help me defeat Satan Incarnate, Reverend Jones?" he asked.

"Satan Incarnate?" I repeated.

He nodded his head vigorously.

"He lives in Peking, does he?" I said.

"Peking is his headquarters, but he has residences all over the world."

"How many residences?"

He shrugged. "Fifteen, twenty, who can say?"

Which made the odds fifteen or twenty to one that he wouldn't be at home today, and I got to thinking that maybe I could appropriate a few Satanic artifacts for the local pawnshop.

"Sure," I said. "Standing up to Satan is one of the very best things I do, me being a man of God and all."

"Excellent!" said the Englishman. "It's been a long, lonely battle. But with you on our side, we just might win." He paused for a minute. "Allow me to introduce myself. I am Sir Mortimer Edgerton-Smythe."

"Pleased to meet you," I said. "Who else is on our side?"

"There's just you and me," he said.

"And how many are in the opposition?"

"Who can say? Surely thousands, possibly hundreds of thousands. Perhaps millions. Have you ever heard of Doctor Aristotle Ho?"

"Can't say that I have."

"He is the fiend who heads this secret organization," said Sir Mortimer, his eyes blazing with hatred. "His father was a Grecian ambassador, his mother the daughter of a Chinese warlord. Nothing is known of his childhood. We *do* know that he spent three years practicing dentistry in Hangchou before he began his nefarious career by taking over the leadership of the local tong. From there he spread out, assimilating one criminal organization after another, until today he is the most powerful villain on the continent. His tentacles are everywhere, Reverend Jones. They reach not only into Peking, but to the capitals of Europe itself. He dreams of worldwide conquest, and he is more than halfway to his goal, and yet so careful has he been, so circumspect, that almost no one has ever heard of him."

"You've met this Doctor Aristotle Ho?" I asked.

"Twice," said Sir Mortimer. "The first time was in England, where I prevented him from stealing the Crown Jewels. The second time was in Chunking, where I barely escaped with my life."

"I assume you're working for the British government?"

"That's correct."

"Why don't you guys just march in an army or two and blow him away?" I asked.

"We're operating in a foreign land, Reverend Jones," he said. "We can't just send our troops in and destroy him. Our only hope is to prove that he is guilty of breaking international law, and then arrest him."

"And how do you plan to do that?" I asked.

"The dragon is the key to it."

"Dragon?"

"Doctor Ho keeps an enormous dragon on his estate," began Sir Mortimer.

"There ain't no such things," I said. "They're just imaginary beasts, like dinosaurs and unicorns and honest redheads named Bernice."

"That's what I thought, too, until I saw it with my own eyes," said Sir Mortimer. "But it exists, and it's the way we shall bring him down."

"You plan to feed him to this here dragon?" I asked curiously.

He shook his head. "No," he said. "Britain is a nation of laws. I intend to use the law to put an end to his villainy."

"How is a dragon gonna help you do that?" I asked. "I thought they didn't do much except eat knights and virgins and things like that."

"This dragon eats just about anything that moves," answered Sir Mortimer. "The truck in which you were riding belongs to Doctor Ho; it was carrying hay and grain to fatten the cattle he feeds to the dragon. That's why I inspected it; I wanted to see if he was smuggling anything else into his fortress."

"You still ain't told me how the dragon is gonna cause Doctor Ho's downfall," I said.

"I'm coming to that," said Sir Mortimer. "Every year Doctor Ho ships the dragon to a different city for the Chinese New Year festival: Hong Kong, Shanghai, once even San Francisco. The dragon remains for a week, and is then shipped back. Last year he shipped it to Rio de Janeiro."

"So?"

"Reverend Jones," he said triumphantly, "*there are only seventeen Chinese in Rio de Janeiro—and eleven of them don't even celebrate the New Year!* The man is obviously smuggling something, and if we can just find out what it is, we can put him behind bars for life!"

"When's the next Chinese New Year coming up?" I asked.

"Soon! The dragon is due to be shipped out tomorrow."

"Exactly what do you think he's smuggling, Sir Mortimer?" I asked.

"That remains to be discovered."

"And just how do we plan to discover it?"

"Tonight, after dark, we'll sneak into the dragon's enclosure and examine both the beast and its cage. If there's any contraband there, from drugs to jewels, we'll find it—and that will be the undoing of the insidious Aristotle Ho!"

The only reason I didn't hop out of the car right then and there was because I didn't believe in dragons. I figured Sir Mortimer was like so many other Englishmen I'd met, who had a passion for foreign lands but never remembered to properly protect their heads from the vertical rays of the sun, and were now just a bit on the dotty side.

So you can imagine my surprise when we drove out to this huge estate after dark, and the first thing I heard was a roar that was like unto a volcano erupting.

"Good!" whispered Sir Mortimer. "We're in time! They haven't shipped him off yet!"

I opened the door. "Well, Sir Mortimer," I said, "it sure has been nice knowing you, and if you ever need spiritual comforting, why, you just be sure to look me up."

I started walking back in the general direction of Peking, but he ran around the car and grabbed me.

"Just where do you think you're going?" he demanded.

"Where's the dragon?" I asked.

"Right over there," he said, pointing to the left.

"Good," I said, heading off to the right. "I'm going *this* way."

"I need your help, damn it!"

"You need a short list of funeral prayers for crazy Englishmen," I said. "Little yellow guys who want to take over the world don't bother me none, but I ain't going into no corral with no dragon."

"I thought you were sworn to combat evil wherever you found it."

"I didn't swear to go hunting it up when it's peacefully minding its own business in its pasture."

"My people have posted a million-pound reward to the man who brings Doctor Ho to justice," he said desperately. "I'll split it down the middle with you!"

Which put a whole new light on things.

"Well, my tabernacle *does* need a new altar," I admitted, "along with walls and floors and pews and a steeple and a ceiling. You got yourself a deal, Sir Mortimer."

"Good! Let's get busy."

He led me over to a huge paddock with a high fence around it.

"He's inside, in the barn," whispered Sir Mortimer.

"How do you know?" I asked, kind of nervous-like.

"If he was outside, he'd have he____
roaring and spouting flames that w____
area."

"Just how big is this here dragon?" I ____

"Perhaps half a city block."

I was about to ask if that was a long New ____ or a
short Macao block when it suddenly occurred to n____ didn't
really make an awful lot of difference, given the curr_nt situation.

Sir Mortimer led me around the paddock to a broad driveway
that led to an oversized barn.

"You're *sure* this is the only way to get the goods on Aristotle
Ho?" I asked as he reached out for the door.

"Just don't make any sudden movements," he said.

"Uh . . . I don't wanna sound like I lack confidence in this
here operation, Sir Mortimer—but have you ever searched a
dragon before?"

"As a matter of fact, I've searched this dragon four previous
times," answered Sir Mortimer. "Each of the past four years,
just before he's shipped out, I've gone over him with a fine-
toothed comb. I've checked his harness for jewels, I've gone
over every inch of his cage, I've even gone through his stool in
case Doctor Ho is trying to ship some contraband *inside* him."

"And you ain't never found nothing?"

"Never," he admitted.

"Then why bother doing it all over again tonight?" I asked.

"Because I'm convinced that the answer lies with the
dragon." He frowned resolutely. "I'll just have to be more
thorough this time."

The building shook with another roar.

"If you've done this before, you don't really need *me*," I
suggested.

"Oh, I've always had help," he said.

"Yeah?"

He nodded. "Poor chaps."

He opened the door and pulled me inside before I had a chance
to ask what happened to them. Given the sight that met my eyes,
that was probably all for the best.

There was just one stall in the barn. It was made of steel bars, maybe two hundred feet long and a hundred feet wide, while it was filled with straw and food troughs and water drums, what it was mostly filled with was a dragon. He was green on top, bright yellow on the bottom, and scaly all over. The second I looked at him I decided he was big enough to eat a couple of dinosaurs for lunch and still be ready to polish off the Eiffel Tower or some similar tidbit for dinner. He had the longest, ugliest face I ever did see, with big red eyes the size of basketballs, and a nose that kept snorting smoke.

"Good evening, Cuddles," said Sir Mortimer gently.

"*Cuddles?*" I repeated.

"It's my pet name for him," said Sir Mortimer. "It makes him seem less formidable."

Cuddles roared again, and a flame a dozen feet long shot out of his mouth and barely missed us.

"They really shouldn't keep him on straw bedding," noted Sir Mortimer. "He's likely to set the place on fire." He paused. "Hmm . . . I suppose if we don't find the contraband, I could always report Doctor Ho to the local branch of the S.P.C.A."

"How in the world do they ship something like this?" I asked.

Sir Mortimer pointed to a number of barred cage sections piled up against the wall. "There's his traveling cage," he said. "They'll assemble it tomorrow morning and then drive him into it." He sighed deeply. "Well, I daresay we'd best get to work."

"Couldn't we just kind of examine him from right here?" I asked, positioning myself directly behind Sir Mortimer.

"No," he said. "If the contraband could be spotted from outside his cage, it *would* have been."

"What makes you so sure there *is* any contraband?" I asked.

"There *has* to be," answered Sir Mortimer firmly. "It's the only way Doctor Ho can finance his far-flung enterprises. I know all his other sources of income, and they simply don't amount to enough. No, Reverend Jones, it's *got* to be here!"

And with that, he opened the door to the stall, and, taking me by the arm, pulled me inside.

"I'll check out his feet," said Sir Mortimer, pulling out a flashlight. "You'd be surprised what can be hidden inside nails this size."

"What do *I* do?" I asked nervously as the dragon turned his head to face me.

"He's wearing a halter on his head," said Sir Mortimer. "Make sure there are no jewels attached to it."

"I can't see none."

"Check the underside of the leather."

"You're kidding, right?"

"I'm perfectly serious."

I took another look at the dragon, which looked like he was just itching for a little snack of charred missionary.

"You *got* to be kidding!" I insisted. "You don't expect me to—"

At that instant the dragon roared again, and I just barely ducked the flames that shot out at me.

"Ah! I see they've chemically treated the straw so it can't catch fire," said Sir Mortimer. "Too bad. So much for the S.P.C.A."

He went back to examining the dragon's toenails, and I took a tentative step toward the dragon's face.

"Nice Cuddles," I said. "Cute Cuddles."

Cuddles glared at me and growled. No fire came out, but I damned near choked to death on the smoke.

"Sweet Cuddles," I said, taking a couple of more steps that brought me right beneath his face.

"Careful now," said Sir Mortimer, pulling a hammer and an ice pick out of his pocket. "This may hurt."

He stuck the ice pick up against one of the dragon's toenails and banged on it. Cuddles let out another roar that could be heard all the way to Sioux City.

"Damn it, Sir Mortimer!" I yelled.

"Sorry. Just being thorough."

I turned back to Cuddles, who was still staring at me.

"Now, just take it easy, feller," I said. "I just want to look at your harness."

I reached up to let him smell the back of my hand, like you're supposed to do with dogs and such. He took a sniff and practically inhaled my whole arm.

"Sir Mortimer!" I hollered.

"Quiet, or you'll wake the whole fortress!" hissed Sir Mortimer.

"But my arm's stuck in his nose, and he won't give it back!"

Sir Mortimer nodded his head sadly, without looking up from the dragon's toenails. "Yes, that happened to poor Archie, too."

"Who was poor Archie?" I asked, trying to pull my arm loose.

"The assistant I lost on my second—or was it my third? No, definitely my second—inspection of the dragon."

I looked up at Cuddles, who was staring at me with a kind of stupid expression on his face.

"Okay," I said. "Fun's fun. Now leggo of my arm."

Cuddles just kept looking at me and not doing much of anything, and it occurred to me that dragons maybe didn't breathe more than once every ten or twenty minutes.

"Sir Mortimer, I really could use a little help here!" I said.

"Not now, Reverend."

I yanked once or twice more, to no effect. Then I started twitching my fingers, just to make sure they were still attached, and suddenly Cuddles let out with a sneeze that blew me halfway across the stall.

"Stop clowning around," said Sir Mortimer, taking a look at me as I rolled to a stop. "This is serious business."

Right at that second I would have been hard-pressed to tell you which of them I hated more, Cuddles or Sir Mortimer, but I think Sir Mortimer was in the lead. In fact, the only reason I approached the dragon's head again was because I knew Sir Mortimer wasn't going to let me out of that barn until we'd finished our search.

This time I knew better than to stick out my hand. In fact, the more I studied old Cuddles, the more I got to wondering how *anyone* approached him, and that led to my wondering how they got him into and out of the barn and into his cage, and that led me to think that someone had to have trained him to obey some simple commands. So I looked him right in his red eyes and said, in the sternest voice I could muster under the circumstances, "Sit!"

And damned if he didn't sit right down on his haunches.

"What did you do, Reverend?" asked Sir Mortimer, running to my side.

"I got a way with dumb animals," I explained to Sir Mortimer. "Now stand back and give him room. Down, Cuddles!"

Cuddles collapsed in a heap.

"Amazing!" said Sir Mortimer.

I started going over the harness, while Sir Mortimer examined whatever it was he was examining, but we had to admit after another ten minutes that there wasn't nothing hidden on Cuddles.

"I think I'd best examine his bedding next," said Sir Mortimer. "Do you think he'll be willing to follow you outside?"

"I can't see no reason why not," I said, sliding open the door to his pasture. "Come, Cuddles."

Cuddles almost trampled Sir Mortimer as he got to his feet and bounded out into the pasture behind me. He was feeling right frisky, and he galloped once or twice around it before I noticed that he was starting to spout a little fire and I told him to stop. Then I saw a couple of lights go on in the fortress up on the hill overlooking the pasture, which didn't bode no good, and I figured that if I was gonna get in any kind of a set-to with Doctor Aristotle Ho and his friends that the safest thing to have on my side was a dragon, so I told Cuddles to stand still, and then I ran to his south end and climbed all the way up his tail and back until I was sitting on top of his neck.

That made me feel a mite safer, even though he didn't smell none too good, and I waited for Sir Mortimer to finish going through the bedding and come out, but when he finally showed up he did so in the company of three or four mean-looking Chinamen who were pointing guns at him, and following them was a thin Chinaman with two-inch fingernails and a droopy mustache dressed all in black satin pajamas.

"Good evening, Reverend Jones," said the thin Chinaman.

"I don't know who you are, brother," I said, "but if you take one more step toward me I'm turning this here dragon loose on you!"

For some reason that seemed to strike his funnybone, because he kind of chuckled and didn't back off so much as a step.

"I am Doctor Aristotle Ho," he said, "and that is *my* dragon.

I raised him from an infant, and he would no more attack me than the sun and moon would veer from their heavenly courses.''

He uttered a couple of terse commands in Chinese, and Cuddles kneeled down and stretched out his neck flat on the ground. There didn't seem much point to staying on him when he was like that, so I climbed off. Doctor Ho said something else, and Cuddles got up and meekly went back into his stall.

Now the insidious Oriental dentist turned to Sir Mortimer with an amused smile on his face.

"Trespassing, breaking and entering, stealing dragons," he counted off. "What am I to do with you, Sir Mortimer?"

Sir Mortimer gave him a stiff upper British lip and didn't say a word.

"And *you*," he said, turning to me. "Why should you be conspiring against me, Lucifer Jones? What harm have I ever done to you?"

"How'd you know my name?" I asked.

"I know all about you," he replied. "Since the moment Sir Mortimer picked you up, I have had my minions tracing your every movement for the past five years. I know about your misadventures in Cairo and Johannesburg, about your arrests in Nairobi and Dar-es-Salaam and Mozambique, about your ivory poaching and slave trading, about the mutiny you led aboard a ship on the west coast of Africa, about your being banished from the continent forever . . ."

"A series of misunderstandings," I said. "Nothing more."

"About your theft of the Empire Emerald in Hong Kong," he continued, unperturbed. "I even know that Lo Chung has put a price on your head."

"He has?"

"And now here you are, invading my property, even riding my dragon. Frankly, Reverend Jones, I suspect that you are something less than a credit to your church."

"Let me tell you, one doctor to another, that I ain't never done nothing to be ashamed of," I said heatedly. "And if you got a couple of hours and maybe a cold drink with just enough alcohol to pound the germs into submission, I'll be happy to explain *my* side of all them incidents you just recited."

"Your explanation couldn't interest me less," said Doctor Aristotle Ho. "In fact, under other circumstances I could have used a man of your peculiar abilities on my payroll."

"Well, truth to tell, the facts didn't run all *that* far amok," I said quickly. "What kind of job did you have in mind?"

"Reverend Jones!" said Sir Mortimer sternly. "You are speaking to the most insidious villain in this part of the world!"

"I got nothing but your word for that, Sir Mortimer," I pointed out. "All I know about this here gentleman is that he treats his animals well and he probably ain't on speaking terms with the local manicurist."

"You interest me, Reverend Jones," said Aristotle Ho.

"Are you going to believe that foul demon, or are you going to believe *me*?" demanded Sir Mortimer. "I tell you, Doctor Ho is planning the conquest of the entire world!"

Doctor Ho turned and stared at Sir Mortimer for a minute. "More groundless accusations, Sir Mortimer?" he said.

"Microdots!" shouted Sir Mortimer suddenly. "That's it! He's hidden microdots on the dragon's scales!"

Doctor Ho shook his head sadly. "Poor deluded man."

"That's got to be the answer!" persisted Sir Mortimer. "We've searched everywhere else. Somewhere on that dragon's skin are some microdots that Doctor Ho is selling to our enemies in Europe. Probably the position of the British Navy!"

"If I let you examine every inch of my dragon, will that finally satisfy you, Sir Mortimer?" asked Doctor Ho.

"You haven't got the nerve!" said Sir Mortimer. "You know I'll find what I'm looking for!"

Doctor Ho turned to his men. "Make Sir Mortimer comfortable for the night, and when we ship the dragon tomorrow morning, make sure that Sir Mortimer accompanies him." He walked over to Sir Mortimer. "It will take approximately seven weeks for the dragon to reach its destination. You will be given free access to him all the way there and all the way back."

His men started dragging Sir Mortimer off.

"Well, that rids me of *his* unpleasant presence for the next few months," said Doctor Ho as he began walking back to his fortress.

"Hey!" I said. "What about *me*?"

"What *about* you?" asked Doctor Ho.

"I thought we were gonna talk a little business," I said.

"I don't believe we shall," said Doctor Ho.

"Why the hell not?" I demanded. "I took your side, didn't I?"

"The alternative would have been a swift and painful death."

"What's that got to do with anything?"

"Reverend Jones," he said, "you are perhaps the only man of my acquaintance with even less regard for the laws and morals of society than I myself possess. While I do not necessarily consider that a failing, it does make it difficult for me to trust you."

"Well, as I see it, Doctor Ho, you got two choices," I told him. "You can take me on as a partner, or have me as an enemy. Now, if we was to become partners and you really do take over the world, you could give me a little chunk of it, like, say, Australia, and we could plunder it six ways to Sunday and split the take right down the middle. If, on the other hand, you decide you'd rather have me as an enemy, you're not only taking on me but the Lord as well, and take my word for it, the Lord can whip you in straight falls without working up much of a sweat."

"There is a third alternative, you know," he said.

"Yeah? What is that?"

He pulled out a little pearl-handled revolver. "I can kill you right here and now."

Which, in my eagerness for gainful employment, was an alternative I had plumb forgotten to take into account.

"You look pale, Reverend Jones," said Doctor Ho. "And your knees are starting to shake. I fear you must be coming down with fever."

"Well, maybe I'll just mosey back into Peking and lie down for a week or two," I suggested hopefully.

He nodded. "It would be best." He reached out a bony hand and took mine in it. "Let us part friends, Reverend Jones."

"That suits me more and more as I come to think on it," I said sincerely.

"I am glad to have had this little chat with you," he continued.

"You are a most interesting man. I have the distinct feeling that our paths will cross again."

"You do?"

"Yes. And next time the outcome may not be so pleasant."

"You still plan to conquer the world?"

"That is a very indiscreet question, Reverend Jones," he said. "Let me answer it this way: whatever my plans may be, Sir Mortimer will never thwart them again."

"You mean there ain't nothing hidden on the dragon or inside his cage?" I said.

"That is correct."

"Then how come Sir Mortimer is dead convinced that you're smuggling something out every time you ship the dragon?"

"Sir Mortimer is right," said Doctor Ho with a smile. "The poor fool cannot see the forest for the trees."

"Doctor Ho," I said. "Whatever happens in the future, we're parting friends tonight. Just between you and me and the gate-post, no friend would keep another friend sleepless for days wondering what the hell he was shipping out in that cage."

He looked me up and down for a couple of minutes, and then shrugged.

"All right, Reverend Jones," said Doctor Ho. "This is the very last time I shall need this ploy, so your knowledge will never be able to be used against me. I will tell you the secret because it amuses me to do so, and because only a mind like yours can fully appreciate the subtlety of it." He paused. "Sir Mortimer will spend every day for the next seven weeks searching the dragon, the straw, the food, and the water for these imaginary microdots and nonexistent jewels and drugs. He will never find what he is looking for, and he will never prevent me from receiving the money I need to continue my operations—and yet, hundreds of times each day, he will be in physical contact with that which he seeks."

"I don't think I follow you," I said.

"The *cage*, Reverend Jones!" he said with a laugh. "The bars are made of pure platinum. For five years Sir Mortimer has microscopically examined everything within the cage, and has never thought to examine the cage itself."

"Well, I'll be damned!" I said.

"That is a foregone conclusion." Doctor Ho took me by the arm. "Now that you know, I'm afraid you must remain as my guest for a week, until the cage is well on its way. After that, you are free to go anywhere you wish."

Well, he took me up to this stone fortress of his, and gave me my own room and three squares a day, and every afternoon he stopped by to play chess with me until he caught me moving one of his pieces when I thought he wasn't looking, and after the week was up he gave me one final breakfast and had one of his men drive me into Peking.

I read a few weeks later that there was a real live dragon on display in Sydney, so I figured Doctor Aristotle Ho had gotten the funds he needed to conquer the world, but as you will see, I was just a little too preoccupied to worry much about it at the time.

4
The Great Wall

The very first thing I learned in Peking is that Chinamen like games of chance every bit as much as white Christian gents do. The very last thing I learned in Peking is that they are even quicker to spot a marked deck of cards than your average American or European. The two learning experiences came about twenty minutes apart, and before the morning was half over I was back on the road, looking for some new place to settle down and build my Tabernacle.

It was about this time that China was pretty much divided up into kingdoms, and each kingdom was ruled by a warlord, which may have been a little harsh on some of the local citizenry but sure saved a lot of time and effort at the ballot box, and it occurred to me that after all the time they spent fighting each other, at least some of the armies were probably in need of some spiritual comforting, such as could only be brung to them by a sensitive and caring man of the cloth, such as myself.

I'd picked up a smattering of Chinese while on my way from Macao to Peking, so once I was a few miles out of the city I stopped an old man who was taking his cow out for a walk, and asked him where the nearest warlord had set up shop.

He told me that a General Sim Chow's barracks were about forty miles south along the road we were on, but suggested that the warlord most in need of spiritual uplifting and best able to pay for it due to his propensity to trade in certain of his homeland's perishable commodities was General Ling Sen, whose headquarters were many days march to the west.

I thanked him for his time and trouble, and decided that I'd give General Sim Chow the first crack at my services, since he was so much closer. I began reappraising the situation when I came to a pile of bodies about ten miles later, and when I saw a Christian mission on fire a mile after that, I decided that General Ling Sen sounded so deeply in need of salvation that there wasn't no time to waste, so I took a hard right and started walking west.

I'd gone maybe seven or eight miles when I heard a drunken voice singing "God Save the King," except when I got close enough to make out the words it was more like "God Save the Liverpool Ruggers Team," which truth to tell made a lot more sense, as the Liverpool Ruggers Team was in fifth place in the standings the last time I'd seen a paper in Macao, whereas the King didn't have no serious competition for the throne that I was aware of.

I kept walking and came upon an English soldier, all dolled up in his parade best, with a bright red jacket and a pith helmet, sitting by the side of the road, drinking from a bottle of rice wine.

"Come join me, friend," he said when he looked up and saw me, and being the good-natured Christian that I am, I moseyed over and took a swig from his bottle.

"Are we still in China?" he asked after a moment.

"Unless they moved Peking when I wasn't looking, it's half a day's march from here," I answered.

"Damn!" he said. "I don't think the wine will hold out." He lowered his voice, and pointed to a backpack full of wine bottles. "I'm drinking my way back to jolly old England."

"Ain't you attached to some army unit or other?" I asked.

He shook his head unhappily. "They're all lost but me. I went out on a bit of a bender last month, and when I came back everyone was missing. So now I'm going back to England to report that my entire unit has gone A.W.O.L., and I alone am escaped to tell thee." He reached his hand out. "Merriweather's the name," he added. "Corporal Marmaduke Merriweather."

"The Right Reverend Doctor Lucifer Jones at your service," I replied, shaking his hand.

"Did you say *doctor*?" he said. "I've got a boil on my back that could use lancing."

"I ain't that kind of doctor," I answered. "I suppose I could recite some of Queen Sheba's racier amorous escapades over it, if you think that might help."

He considered it for a moment, then finally shook his head. "No, I think not. When all is said and done, it's the lot of the British soldier to suffer pain quietly and nobly."

"Well, you got the noble part down pat, Brother Merriweather, but I heard you singing from half a mile away."

"I keep hoping my army might hear me," he responded glumly.

Well, I took another drink just as a show of solidarity and sympathy, and then he took one, and before long we'd finished that bottle and another one, and then night fell and we slept beneath a tree alongside the road, and when morning came he decided to walk along with me until he came across his unit or England, whichever came first.

"Well, that's right neighborly of you," I said. "I always feel safer in the company of His Majesty's armed forces."

"And well you should," he replied. "Of course, I traded my rifle for the wine, and I seem to have misplaced my ammunition, but still, it's my function in life to protect all things British."

"I don't want to cause you no serious moral consternation, Brother Merriweather," I said, "but I ain't British."

"You speak British," he said. "That's enough for me." He paused for a moment. "By the way, Reverend Jones, I know where *I'm* going, but you haven't told me where you're heading yet."

"I'm seeking the headquarters of General Ling Sen," I said, "to offer them poor beleaguered soldiers a fighting shot at spiritual atonement."

"If you will accept a gentle word of advice," said Merriweather, "spiritual atonement probably does not rank very high up on General Ling Sen's list of priorities."

"Oh?" I said. "You know something about him?"

He shook his head. "I know absolutely nothing about him."

"Then how do you figure that he's not in the market for a preacher?"

"The mere fact that I haven't heard of him means that no one who has had any dealings with him has lived long enough to pass on that information to us." He shrugged. "Still, I suppose it's in our best interest to seek him out."

"It is?" I asked, since he had just loaded me down with a mighty tall heap of misgivings.

He nodded. "I'm already out of money, and I'll be out of rice wine in another few days. Possibly I can hire on as an adviser."

"What kind of combat do you specialize in, Brother Merriweather?" I asked.

"Combat?" he repeated. "Do you think I joined the army to *fight*? I'm an accountant."

"An accountant?"

"*Some*body has to pay for the uniforms and weapons and bullets and transportation and consumables," he replied. "I mean, Empire is all very well and good, Reverend Jones, but only if it can remain cost effective."

"And you figure this here General Ling Sen is in serious need of an accountant?" I asked him.

"He's got an army to run, hasn't he?" answered Merriweather. "Why, with the things I could teach him about double-entry bookkeeping alone, he could continue to devastate the countryside for an extra three or four months at no additional cost."

Well, we kept on walking and drinking from Merriweather's diminishing supply of rice wine, and he kept trying to explain the more esoteric principles of tax-loss carry-forwards to me, and one day kind of melted into another, until one morning about a month later we came smack-dab up against this great big wall and couldn't go no farther.

"Looks like General Ling Sen don't take kindly to visitors," I opined as I looked both right and left and couldn't see the end of the wall nowhere in sight.

"With a wall like this around his barracks, one might say that he seems absolutely hostile to them," agreed Merriweather.

"Still," I said, "a man who can build a wall this big probably ain't exactly destitute."

"True," added Merriweather. "In fact, he's probably more in need of an accountant than most."

"And if this here wall is half as long as it looks to be, I got a feeling General Ling Sen ought to be happy to pay for a little heavenly insurance to make sure it don't get wiped out by earthquakes or floods or other such disasters as God is inclined to bring to them who don't toss a few coins into the poorbox every now and then."

"I do believe we're in business, Reverend Jones," said Merriweather.

Just then I heard some feet shuffling, which one hardly ever tends to hear when standing on grass like we was, so I looked up and, sure enough, there were three Chinese soldiers looking down on us from atop the wall.

"What are you doing here?" asked one of them in Chinese.

"Just looking for General Ling Sen's headquarters," I answered.

"Why?"

"We've come all the way from across the sea to bring him spiritual and fiduciary comfort," I said. "If you guys work for him, why don't you run off and tell him his lucky day has arrived?"

The three of them conferred for a long minute, and then one ran off along the top of the wall and the other two trained their rifles on us.

"Do not move," said one of them. "We must decide what to do with you."

A minute later a door opened about fifty feet away, and the soldier who had run off stepped out of the wall and motioned us to come to him. When we got there, we found ourselves facing half a dozen armed soldiers, who escorted us up this winding staircase, and after we climbed up maybe fifty feet or so, we stepped out through another door onto the top of the wall, which was a lot broader than it looked from the ground.

I heard a motor off to my left, and when I turned I saw a brand-new Bentley sedan driving right toward us. I was still wondering how they managed to get it onto the wall in the first place when it came to a stop and a big fat Chinaman stepped out, his chest and most of his belly all covered with medals.

"I have been told that you wish to speak with me," he said in English.

"We do if you're General Ling Sen," I said.

"General Ling Sen is no longer in charge here," he said. "I am General Chang."

"Well," I said with a shrug, "it ain't like General Ling Sen was a close personal friend or nothing. This here is Corporal Marmaduke Merriweather of His Majesty's armed forces, and I'm the Honorable Doctor Jones, internationally known man of the cloth." Which was probably true, since there were still warrants out for my arrest in Illinois and Egypt and Morocco and Kenya and the Congo and South Africa, and I didn't suppose they could *all* have forgotten me so soon.

"Doctor *Lucifer* Jones?" he said.

"Now how'd you come to know that?" I asked, surprised.

He smiled. "Your reputation precedes you, Doctor Jones," he answered. "Already you have become something of a legend in Hong Kong and Macao."

"You don't say."

"I very much do say," replied General Chang. He turned to Merriweather. "And what have we here—a deserter from the British army?"

"*They* deserted *me*!" replied Merriweather. "*I'm* still here at my post."

"Why have you sought me out, Doctor Jones?" asked General Chang.

"I hear tell you run a territory of considerable size and complexity," I said, "so I just naturally figured that such a big bunch of ignorant yellow heathen—meaning no offense—would probably be in dire need of spiritual uplifting and maybe a nightly bingo tournament, the profits of which the Tabernacle of Saint Luke would be more than happy to split with the employer of these poor lost souls."

"And you?" asked General Chang, turning back to Merri-weather.

"I should like to enlist in your army," said Merriweather.

"Good. We can always use more men. I trust that you're accomplished at garroting and gouging out eyes?"

"Well, actually, my specialty is accountancy," said Merri-weather.

"*Our* specialty is conquest, pillage, and rape," said General Chang. "You'll just have to adjust." He turned to two of his men. "Take him away and see that he's properly equipped."

"But—" began Merriweather.

"No, please don't thank me," said General Chang as they began ushering Merriweather away. "All I ask is total, unques-tioning loyalty and obedience. You can keep your gratitude for another occasion."

"So, General," I said when Merriweather was out of earshot, "have we got a deal?"

"I think not, Doctor Jones," said General Chang. "Christian-ity is such a sterile, repressed religion."

"Not the way *I* practice it," I assured him.

"The answer is no," he said firmly. "Which is not to say that I might not have some other use for you."

"Long as the pay is good and it don't involve no heavy lifting, I suppose the Good Lord could spare me for a couple of weeks," I answered.

"Come with me back to my quarters," he said, signaling his car to turn around. "We'll talk as we drive."

"Suits me," I said, climbing into the Bentley. "By the way, just where is this kingdom of yours?"

"You're on it."

"I mean, how far does it extend?" I asked, looking off at the hills that rose up in the distance.

"Hundreds of miles," he replied.

"Really?" I said. "You must own half of China."

"Even better," he said with a smile. "I own a six-hundred-mile section of the Great Wall. Any traffic from one side to the other must pay me a healthy tribute."

"Yeah?"

He nodded. "And it just so happens that our most fertile poppy fields are on the west side of the wall, while our best markets for them are on the east side." He paused. "In truth, I cannot take credit for it. It was General Ling Sen who first saw the potential of taking control of the wall, and of course the wall itself was built to be easily defended." He lit up a cigar. "Yes, there's no question of it: General Ling Sen was a visionary of the highest order."

"What happened to him?" I asked.

"Ah, poor General Ling Sen!" said General Chang with feeling. "Surrounded by selfish, disloyal officers, he was betrayed by the most vicious of them."

"Who was that?" I asked.

"Me," said General Chang. "It was a dreadful, villainous, despicable thing to do, and if I had the slightest vestige of a conscience, I am quite certain I would be thoroughly ashamed of myself." He smiled at me. "However, to be perfectly candid with you, I must confess that I am enjoying the consequences of my unspeakable actions beyond my wildest expectations."

"Well, they say confession is good for the soul," I replied. "It strikes me that you're doing your poor blackened soul a heap of good just by telling me all this."

"You are a man after my own heart, Doctor Jones," said General Chang. "It is so rare that I meet anyone with whom I see eye to eye—and then, when I do, I am usually forced to kill him before he can do the same to me."

It seemed like a good time to change the subject, so I asked him exactly what kind of work he had in mind for me.

"As you know, Doctor Jones, my kingdom is some six hundred miles long."

"So you said."

"On the other hand, it is only sixty-five feet wide. That means that"—he pulled a pencil and paper out of a pocket and did some quick calculating—"the full extent of my kingdom is less than seven square miles."

"But as real estate goes, they're *prime* miles," I pointed out.

"Nevertheless, I have decided to expand my empire."

"Gonna take over more of the wall?" I asked.

He shook his head. "No matter how much of the wall we own, we remain at the mercy of anyone who wishes to lay siege to us. I have decided that it is time to take over General How Kung's territory."

"Where is this General How Kung located?" I asked.

He pointed out the window to the west. "He owns everything your eye can see, and beyond. If I had *his* territory, not only could I be assured of feeding my men, but I would never have to worry about fighting a two-front war." He smiled at me. "That's where *you* come in."

"Me?"

"Yes, Doctor Jones. For reasons I cannot fathom, General How Kung distrusts me; probably he is still carrying a childish grudge simply because I burned his village and stole his wife. At any rate, *you* shall be my emissary." He paused. "You will seek him out, guarantee his safety, agree to any conditions he sets, and get him to come and meet with me." Suddenly he smiled. "Then, after I murder him, I shall pay you the sum of one thousand British pounds."

"I don't want to throw no spanner in the works," I said cautiously, "but ain't this General How Kung likely to have some friends and relations that might consider such treatment unnecessarily harsh?"

"We live in a Darwinian world, Reverend Jones," replied General Chang. "To the victor belongs the spoils. How do you think How Kung *got* to be a general in the first place?" The Bentley came to a stop in front of a guardhouse that had been built into the wall. "Ah! Here we are. Would you care to join me in a drink?"

Plotting to kill Chinese warlords can be pretty thirsty work, so I got out of the car with him and followed him into his house, where he pulled out a bottle of whiskey while I was admiring all the treasures he had picked up during his travels. He poured us each a large glass, and we got to talking about this and that, and pretty soon he was asking me all about my adventures on the Dark Continent and I was asking him all about his wars of conquest, and suddenly it was getting on to midnight and we were on our third bottle.

"I'm feeling dizzy," said General Chang, getting kind of unsteadily to his feet. "I think I need a breath of fresh air."

"Sounds good to me," I said, getting up and following him out onto the wall.

"Lovely night," said General Chang, staggering just a bit. "It was on a night just like this that I killed General Ling Sen, poor fellow."

"How did you do it?" I asked.

He walked to the eastern edge of the wall. "I called him over to this very spot, told him I thought I saw someone prowling around on the ground, and then when he leaned over to look, I pushed him off."

I moseyed over to where he was standing and looked down. "That must be a good fifty feet or so," I said.

"It was a relatively painless death," said General Chang, starting to slur his words. "I don't believe he felt a thing for the first forty-nine feet."

"Maybe we ought to plant a cross or something to commemorate the unhappy event," I said.

"I like that," said General Chang. "Someday, hundreds of years from now, historians can come to the wall and see the very spot where I became a General. I like the way you think, Doctor Jones. Perhaps I shall permit you to become my biographer." He balanced himself precariously on the very edge of the wall and pointed down. "He hit the ground right there."

"By them little white flowers?" I asked.

"No," he said, peering into the darkness and swaying precariously. "It was right next to the bush."

"I can't see no bush," I said. "Maybe it's farther down the wall."

"Nonsense," said General Chang. "I know where I pushed him off."

"Well, maybe the bush died, then," I said. "But all I can see is grass and some flowers."

"You must be even drunker than I am, Doctor Jones," he said irritably. "It's right down *there*."

He leaned over the wall and pointed, and suddenly he wasn't

there anymore, and a second later I heard a yell of *"Oh, shit!"* and then a loud thud, and I looked down and there was General Chang lying flat on his back fifty feet below me.

"We were *both* right," he mumbled just before he died. "The bush is in blossom."

Well, this turn of events caused me no little consternation, as you might imagine, especially since I wasn't the only one who had heard him fall. Suddenly soldiers began approaching me from every direction, and I suggested to my Silent Partner that if He had stockpiled any miracles in my heavenly account, this might be a pretty good time for me to cash a couple of them in.

The soldiers came to a stop a few feet away from me, and a couple of them walked over to the edge of the wall and looked down.

"You have killed General Chang!" said one of them in a shocked whisper.

"I can explain everything," I said. "It ain't my fault."

"Do not be so modest, General Jones," said another.

"*General* Jones?" I repeated.

"To the victor belongs the spoils," he said.

"Yeah?"

"You defeated General Chang in personal combat. That makes you our leader—at least, until someone defeats *you*."

I looked around and saw at least half a dozen oversize Chinamen who looked like they were chomping at the bit to do just that.

"What would have happened if he'd just gotten drunk and fell off the wall?" I asked.

"Since he was in your company, we'd probably put you to death for not protecting him."

"Well, as long as we're being open and aboveboard," I said, "I got to admit that he put up one hell of a fight. Not that the outcome was ever in doubt," I added for the benefit of those who were thinking of moving up in the ranks.

"He was our greatest warrior," said the soldier. "Many of our strongest men have challenged him, but none was ever victorious."

"All in a day's work," I said with becoming modesty.

The soldier turned to his companions. "General Chang is dead!" he yelled. "Long live General Jones!"

"Long live General Jones!" they all shouted back.

"Well, now, that's a right touching sentiment," I said. "And me and the Lord will certainly do our best to lead you to victory after victory." When the cheering had stopped, I explained to them that I was going to set up housekeeping in General Chang's quarters while I plotted out our future conquests. That set off a whole new round of cheering, except for the five or six biggest of them, who had such lean and hungry looks whenever they stared at me that I decided it was time to leave the celebration and go to General Chang's guardhouse to consider my situation. A couple of minutes after I got there I heard a knock at the door, and then Marmaduke Merriweather let himself in.

"I heard the news," he said when he had closed the door behind him. "I suppose congratulations are in order."

"Thanks, Brother Merriweather," I said.

"If I may be so bold as to say so, I think a hasty retreat might be in even better order," he continued. "Somehow you don't seem to frighten them the way General Chang did."

"A couple of 'em are considering challenging me?" I asked.

"It's more like a couple of them *aren't*," he replied. "The rest are practically drawing straws to see who will be first."

"I was kind of afraid they might take that attitude," I said.

"It doesn't seem fair somehow," said Merriweather sympathetically. "I always thought that being a warlord was a lifetime position."

"Oh, it is, Brother Merriweather," I assured him. "The problem is that 'lifetime' seems to be a very elastic term in these here parts."

"What do you plan to do about it?" he asked.

"I'm still mulling on it," I said. "After all, I've only been the warlord for about twenty minutes. I ain't got all the nuances of the job nailed down yet."

"Well, as I see it," he said, "you've got two choices: you can flee to the east, or you can flee to the west."

"Running away is against my principles," I said. "Especially when there's a fortune in jade knick-knacks in the next room."

"But the only alternative is to fight every challenger," he pointed out.

"Well, I suppose that's what I'll have to do," I said, "me being the honorable Christian gentleman that I am."

"Meaning no disrespect," he said, "but if I were making book on the event, you'd be a fifty-to-one underdog against each and every opponent."

"That's what they said about old Jonah," I replied, "and he wound up harpooning the whale."

"I hate to correct you, Reverend Jones, but he wound up *inside* the whale," said Merriweather.

"Only in the British translation," I said. "Now, I appreciate your concern, Brother Merriweather, but my mind's made up. Get some of them soldiers in here so I can announce my intentions."

He shrugged and walked out onto the wall, then returned a minute later with a couple of soldiers in tow.

"You sent for us, General Jones?" asked one of them, snapping off a nifty salute.

"Yeah," I said. "It's come to my attention that some of the men think they can advance in rank pretty much the same way I did. Is that right?"

"I believe so, General Jones."

"I think we're gonna have to nip this in the bud," I said. "I want you to pass the word up and down the wall that I plan to take 'em all on, one at a time, comes morning."

"Our army extends for three hundred miles in each direction, General Jones," he replied. "It will take at least two days for word to pass up and down the ranks."

"All right," I said. "What's tomorrow?"

"Tuesday."

"Fine. You tell 'em that I'm going into training, and that on Thursday morning I plan to drive the Bentley to the south end of the army and work my way north, taking on all challengers one at a time."

"What about the ones who are outside right now?"

"They'll just have to wait their turn," I said. "After all, fair is fair. Tell 'em I should be able to get to them by Friday afternoon."

"You have that much confidence in your ability?" asked the soldier.

"I beat General Chang without working up a sweat, didn't I?" I answered.

Well, he didn't have no answer to that, so he just saluted and left and started spreading the word like I told him to.

"Is there anything I can do to help, Reverend Jones?" asked Merriweather when we were alone again.

"Well, I'd sure hate to be late for all these battles to the death," I said. "Why don't you spend the next couple of days making sure that the Bentley is all fueled up and in good working order?"

"I had in mind something more like lowering you down the side of the wall with a rope," he said.

"If Solomon had run from Goliath, where would we all be now?" I replied.

He just stared at me, sighed, shook his head, and walked out into the night. I locked the door behind him, spent the next couple of hours doing a quick inventory of General Chang's jade collection, and finally hunted up the bedroom and went to sleep.

I hung around the guardhouse for the next two days, finishing up General Chang's store of imported Scotch whiskey and watching Merriweather work on the Bentley. Just before sundown on Wednesday I wandered over to the building they were using for a mess hall, found an empty straw basket, and packed myself a big lunch so I wouldn't have to waste any time hunting up a restaurant between fights, and left a wake-up call for five in the morning.

I got up at about four o'clock, dumped the lunch under my bed, and filled up the basket with a pile of General Chang's better jade trinkets. Then I went out to where the Bentley was parked and put a couple of ten-gallon drums of gas into the trunk. Merriweather knocked on my front door at five on the dot, and

I loaded the straw basket into the back seat, saluted the row of soldiers that were lined up to see me off, and climbed into the car beside him.

"Wake me when we've got about ten miles to go," I said as he headed off down the middle of the wall.

"How can you sleep at a time like this?" demanded Merriweather. "I'm a nervous wreck."

"Just relax and trust to the Lord," I said, closing my eyes and leaning back.

I must have fell sound asleep then, because the next thing I knew the car had come to a stop.

"Reverend Jones?" said Merriweather, shaking my shoulder gently.

"Yeah, what is it?"

"You said to let you know when we were within ten miles of our destination."

"Thanks," I said. "I'm gonna stretch and get some of the kinks out."

I opened the door and stepped out into the morning air. Some soldiers had gathered around, so I popped open the trunk and asked one of 'em to load the canisters of gasoline into the tank while I walked over to the edge of the wall and attended to a call of nature.

"I'll drive the rest of the way," I told Merriweather when I returned to the car. "It'll help get my reflexes sharp."

He scooted over to the passenger's side, and I spent the next couple of minutes getting used to the Bentley, which was a mighty fine car except that someone had gotten all mixed up and put the steering wheel and pedals on the wrong side.

"I wonder how fast this baby can go?" I said as we got to within two miles of my first fistic encounter.

"The speedometer goes up to one hundred and fifty," he answered.

"Is that miles or kilometers?" I asked.

He shrugged. "I don't know."

"Let's open her up and find out," I said, pressing the gas pedal down to the floor.

"Careful, Reverend Jones!" he yelled as we barreled along the top of the wall, sending soldiers jumping for cover. "You'll get us killed!"

"Only if I stop or slow down," I said sincerely, and suddenly we were past the last of the soldiers and Merriweather finally figured out what was happening and started laughing his head off. We heard some gunfire behind us, but whoever built that wall just didn't know when to call it quits, and we drove another four hundred miles before we finally ran out of gas and had to get out and start walking.

We came to a pair of towers in about half a mile, one on each side of the wall, each with a staircase leading down to the ground.

"Well, it's been a fascinating experience, Reverend Jones," said Merriweather, walking over to the staircase that led to the west, "but I've really got to continue my journey to England. The sooner they know the army is missing, the sooner they can send out search parties."

Somehow the notion of foot-slogging across the Gobi Desert didn't seem as appealing to me as it did to him, so I bid him farewell and clambered down the stairs on the east side of the wall, all set to sell General Chang's jade baubles to the highest bidder so I could finally get around to building my tabernacle.

5
The Abominable Snowman

I spent the next week walking south, since I had the Gobi to the west and a bunch of warlords to the east. I kept thinking that a town ought to pop into view any minute, but I didn't see anything except a bunch of farm fields and an occasional former warlord being hung out to dry, and I began thinking that my picnic basket could have used a little less jade and a little more lunch.

I was sitting down in the shade of a tree, thinking that whoever had called China a crowded country hadn't actually tried walking across it, when I heard a familiar voice coming from behind me.

"Well, I'll be damned if it ain't the Reverend Lucifer Jones!"

I got to my feet and turned around and found myself facing Capturing Clyde Calhoun, decked out in his usual khakis and pith helmet and leading a safari column.

"Well, howdy, Clyde," I said. "I ain't seen you since Mozambique. What are you doing in these here parts?"

"Same as usual," he said, walking up and shaking my hand. "Collecting animals for my circus—them what survives getting captured, anyway. The rest go to museums and gourmet chefs and other interested parties."

"I ain't seen hide nor hair of any animals since I got here," I said.

"Well, they take a heap of finding," he said. "But I just picked up seventy-three giant pandas from the bamboo forest up north."

"That's a lot of pandas," I said. "I hear tell they're an endangered species."

"They are *now*," he agreed, patting his rifle fondly.

"Maybe you should have left some for the Chinese," I suggested.

"Oh, I left 'em enough to breed," he assured me. Suddenly he frowned. "Unless both of 'em was females." He took a swig from his canteen, and then offered it to me. "How about yourself, Lucifer?" he continued as I took a long drink of water. "What are you doing out here in the middle of China?"

"Mostly looking for a way out," I admitted.

"Well, I'm headed for Tibet," he said. "Why don't you come along with me? I could use a little companionship; none of my bearers speak any American."

"What's so special about Tibet?" I asked.

"That's where we'll find the Abominable Snowman," he replied.

"Sounds ugly," I said. "Or at least sadly lacking in manners."

"He's worth a pretty penny back in the States," confided Calhoun. "Fifty grand stuffed and mounted, and at least twice that much if he's still mildly alive and twitching." He paused for a minute. "Tell you what: you come along with me, and I'll not only give you three squares a day, but I'll split the take with you if you find him first."

Which suddenly made Tibet start looking a whole lot more interesting.

"Clyde," I said, "you got yourself a deal. What's for lunch?"

He had a couple of his people set up a table and his chef whipped us up some panda sandwiches, and we washed 'em down with a few beers and got to reminiscing about old times, and before we knew it it was getting dark, so we wound up spending the night right there. We were up bright and early the next morning, and we made pretty good time, especially considering that Clyde had this habit of stopping every couple of minutes to shoot birds or squirrels or anything else that had this regrettable tendency to breathe in and out. I kept expecting to run into some warlord or other, but Clyde kept shooting so much that all the local warlords must have figured the Imperial Army was on the march and hightailed it out of our path, because we didn't see nary a one during the whole trek.

After a couple of months it started getting right chilly at night, and pretty soon the days weren't much warmer, and finally we had to stop long enough to make us a pair of fur coats out of panda skins. When we finally hit the Kunlun Mountains, Clyde paid off about eighty of his bearers and skinners and sent 'em packing, and just kept a cook and a couple of trackers with us.

Now, it's entirely possible that there's a piece of level ground somewhere in Tibet, but if there is, I never did see it. We started following footpaths up the mountains, hunting for a pass to the other side, where Clyde was sure he could get a line on the Abominable Snowman in a little town called Saka, but once we found the pass all it did was lead us out of the Kunlun Mountains into the Tangkula Mountains, which were even higher and colder, and before long we were sitting in a cave at about ten thousand feet in the middle of a howling blizzard, warming our hands next to a fire he'd built and trying real hard not to listen to our teeth chattering.

The weather had cleared by morning, and as we wandered out of the cave we came upon some tracks in the snow.

"Looks like we had some polar bears hanging around last night," I said.

"Ain't no polar bears in Tibet," answered Clyde, squatting down and examining them. "These here tracks was made by something what walks upright, and stands maybe eight feet tall." He looked up at me with a great big smile. "I don't think we're gonna have to go to Saka after all. I think maybe we just lucked out and are sharing this mountain with the Abominable Snowman."

"Yeah?"

He nodded vigorously. "Let's split up forces and go out searching for him. I'll follow his tracks, and you go the other direction just in case he circled around, and we'll meet back at the cave at nightfall."

He started walking off.

"Ain't you gonna take your gunbearer or your tracker with you?" I asked.

"Too dangerous," he shouted back. "Best to leave this kind of work to experienced hunters."

"I don't want to cast no pall of gloom on the proceedings, Clyde, but I ain't an experienced hunter, or even an inexperienced one if push comes to shove."

"Then wait in the cave with the others. I'll be back in a few hours."

Which made excellent sense, and which is what I did.

Clyde piled in at twilight, with little icicles hanging down from his mustache, and immediately sat down by the fire.

"How'd it go?" I asked, since I didn't see no snowman, abominable or otherwise, in tow.

"The tracks vanished about a mile from here," he said, holding his hands out to warm them. "I spent most of the afternoon hunting for his lair, but I couldn't find it." He paused thoughtfully. "I think tomorrow I'll lay some traps for him."

"Tell me more about this here Snowman," I said.

"Ain't that much to tell," answered Clyde. "The locals call him the Yeti, and near as I can figure out he spends most of his time hanging around the mountain doing abominable things."

"Anybody ever seen him?"

"Probably," said Clyde, "but I get the distinct impression that them what's actually encountered him have passed on to the next plane of existence with remarkable alacrity."

"I wonder what he eats?" I mused, hoping that he hadn't developed a taste for Christian missionary somewhere along the way.

"Beats me," said Clyde. "If it's anything but snow and rocks, he must be one hungry snowman." Suddenly he looked up. "Say, you gave me an idea, Lucifer. I think I'll bait some of them traps with the last of the panda meat."

I told him I thought it was a good plan, especially since I'd had my fill and then some of panda steaks, and then we turned in, and the next morning Clyde was out laying his traps as soon as the sun came up.

I asked Kim, our cook, to fix me up some coffee. He came back a couple of minutes later with a pot of tea.

"I said I wanted coffee," I told him.

"Coffee all gone," he said. "You drink tea."

I didn't think no more of it, but when Clyde went out the next morning to bait more traps, I asked for tea, and this time what I got was a pitcher of hot water.

"Tea all gone, too," explained Kim.

"Just how much tea did Clyde drink last night?" I asked.

"Him no drink tea at night. Just whiskey."

"Maybe he took it with him this morning," I suggested.

"Twenty pounds of it?" replied Kim.

That did seem like a lot of tea, no matter how eleven o'clockish Clyde might feel, so I got to thinking, and it didn't take me long to figure out that someone was swiping our supplies. And since the bearer and the tracker hadn't gone out in two days and there wasn't no place inside the cave to stash it, I figured it had to be someone else.

And since there was only one other person who was crazy enough to be wandering around on the mountain in this weather, I decided that things were suddenly looking up for my bank account.

Clyde returned at sunset, and immediately started warming himself by the fire.

"How'd it go?" I asked.

"Oh, he's out there all right," answered Clyde. "And he's a smart one, too."

"How so?"

"He managed to pick up one of the panda steaks without getting snared. I'll have to camouflage my traps better."

We talked for a while, settled down for a hard evening's drinking, and fell asleep just about the time the nightly blizzard started blowing.

The next morning I waited until Clyde had left, then told Kim to fix me up a dozen sandwiches. While he was busy making them, I got into my panda coat and picked up one of Clyde's auxiliary rifles. When Kim was done, I put the sandwiches into a backpack, and then, as an afterthought, I added twelve bottles of beer, and told him I was going out for a little exercise and to maybe hunt up a grocery store.

I saw Clyde's footprints heading off to the left, so I turned right and began following a narrow ridge that wound its way down the mountain. I stopped about every half mile, took a sandwich and a beer out of my backpack, and placed them on the snow. After about three miles the path I was on started branching every which way, but that didn't bother me none since all I had to do to get back was turn around and follow my footprints, so I just kept on wandering and setting down sandwiches and beer.

The snow was right deep, and the altitude wasn't exactly a boon to serious breathing, and by the time I'd emptied my backpack I figured it was getting on toward midafternoon, so I turned around and started heading back to the cave.

I'd gone about half a mile, and was just turning a corner around a big boulder, when I saw this huge shaggy figure, maybe eight feet high, standing about two hundred yards away with its back to me, eating a sandwich and washing it down with a beer. I figured the safest course was to fire a warning shot, just to kind of get its attention and let it know I was armed, so I pointed the rifle straight up at the sky and pulled the trigger.

I think I ought to break into my narrative at this point to make a suggestion born of bitter experience: if you ever find yourself on a narrow ledge of a snow-covered mountain in Tibet, firing a .550 Nitro Express into the air probably ain't the smartest course of action available to you.

When I woke up, I felt kind of constricted. I thought I heard the sounds of digging, but I couldn't move, or even turn my head, to see what was happening. Then, after a couple of minutes had passed, I felt two huge hands grab me by the shoulders and pull me up through the snow, and suddenly I was facing this great big guy who was wearing a shaggy coat made out of sheepskin.

"All right," he said, holding me off the ground by my shoulders and shaking me. "Who are you?"

"The Right Reverend Doctor Lucifer Jones."

"You're from Guido Scarducci, right?" he said, finally putting me down.

"I ain't never heard of him," I said, brushing myself off.

"Then why did you shoot at me?" he demanded.

"I thunk you was the Yeti."

"What's a Yeti?" he asked.

"Well, as near as I can tell, a Yeti is you," I said. "Except it sure sounds to me like you're speaking one hundred percent pure American."

"Of course I am," he said. "I was raised in Butte, Montana."

"What's a fellow American doing on a mountain in Tibet?" I asked.

"It's a long and tragic story, Doctor Jones," he said, sitting down on a big rock. "My name is Sam Hightower. By the time I was fifteen years old I was seven feet tall and still growing, so I figured that playing basketball was my calling in life, and as soon as I got out of high school I latched onto a semi-pro team called the Butte Buccaneers. About a week before we were scheduled to play the Great Falls Geldings for the championship, for which we were a real big favorite, a gambler called Guido Scarducci came up and offered me five thousand dollars to make sure we didn't win by more than ten points."

"No sense embarrassing the other team," I said sympathetically.

"Those were my feelings precisely," said Hightower. "The problem is that the next night, another gambler named Vinnie Bastino offered me twenty thousand to make sure we won by fifteen points or more."

"I can see where that might present a serious moral and economic dilemma," I said.

"Well, I was young and innocent and didn't view it as such," said Hightower. "I just figured I'd pay Mr. Scarducci his five thousand back out of my earnings and we'd be all square and there'd be no hard feelings and we might even have a laugh about it over a drink or two."

"I take it he didn't quite see it that way?" I said.

"I realized he and I had a little communications problem when he blew up my car and set fire to my apartment that night,'' said Hightower. ''And when he missed me and shot six of my teammates during the victory parade the next day, I figured it was probably time to take my leave of the fair city of my birth, so I hopped the first train heading east, and wound up in New York.'' He paused. ''Problem is, he found me there, too. And in London. And in Rome. I finally decided that it's not all that easy to disappear in a crowd when you're eight feet two inches tall, so after he found me again in Athens, I made up my mind to go where there weren't any crowds at all, and I've been living on this damned mountain for six years now, waiting for Guido Scarducci to hunt me down.''

''You hang around here much longer and you're gonna get yourself hunted by a lot more people than Guido Scarducci,'' I told him.

''Why?'' he asked. ''Surely borrowing a little coffee and tea isn't a capital offense even in Tibet.''

''This ain't got nothing to do with coffee or tea,'' I said. ''You ever hear of the Abominable Snowman?''

''I heard legends when I was growing up, just like I heard about Bigfoot and Paul Bunyon.''

''Well, most folks in these parts think you're him.''

''Why on earth should they think that?'' he asked, kind of bewildered.

''Well, the notion of an eight-foot basketball player hiding out from gamblers on top of a mountain in Tibet probably ain't had time to take root yet,'' I explained.

''Yeah,'' he said thoughtfully. ''Now that I come to consider it, I can see your point. I assume that's why you were shooting at me?''

I nodded. ''After all, you did go for my bait.''

''You know how hard it is to find food up here?'' he replied. He rubbed his jaw. ''And I damned near broke a tooth on that frozen meat you put out yesterday.''

''*I* didn't put it out,'' I said. ''Which reminds me—we'd better get back to my cave so I can tell Capturing Clyde not to shoot you.''

''Capturing Clyde *Calhoun*?'' he said excitedly.

"You've heard of him?"

"I've seen all his movies and read all his books," said Hightower. "He's one of my boyhood heroes."

"I'm sure he'll be mighty glad to hear it," I said.

"But surely I'm not in any danger from him," continued Hightower. "I mean, doesn't Capturing Clyde always bring 'em back alive?"

"Well, now, that's subject to various delicate shades of interpretation," I said. "But I think it's fair to say that them what he brings back without eating or skinning first is generally alive. Still," I added, "if I was you, I'd introduce myself to him right quick, and preferably when he wasn't carrying his gun."

He stood up and looked up the mountain.

"I'm afraid that won't be possible, Doctor Jones," he said.

"Why not?" I asked.

"Because when you fired your rifle you started an avalanche that seems to have brought down half the mountain. We could be days or even weeks getting back to your cave."

"What are we going to do in the meantime?" I asked.

"I've got shelters hidden all over the mountain," answered Hightower. "We'll find one that hasn't been covered by the avalanche and use it for a headquarters while we try to clear the trail to your cave."

Well, I couldn't think of no better alternative, and so I followed him to one of his shelters, where he had a fire going and an old hand-cranked Victrola and lots of Rudy Vallee records, which weren't really to my taste but were a lot better than just sitting there listening to the wind whistle by.

He was real interested in finding out what events of earthshaking import had transpired since he'd left the States in rather a hurry, so I told him about how the Red Sox had traded Babe Ruth to the Yankees, and how Clara Bow had encouraged the Southern California football team to win the Rose Bowl, and that one of our Presidents had died but I couldn't remember which one. He was especially glad to hear that Morvich had won the 1922 Kentucky Derby.

"I put all my money on him just before I took off," he explained.

"Well, you ought to have a tidy nest egg waiting for you when you finally go home," I said.

"I doubt it," he replied with a sigh. "My bookie was Guido Scarducci."

"Maybe there's some subtle little nuance I'm missing here," I said, "but ain't Guido Scarducci the fellow that's out to kill you?"

"Yes."

"Then why on earth did you bet your money at his particular establishment?"

Hightower shrugged. "He was the only bookie in Montana."

I suddenly found myself silently agreeing that Tibet was probably just the place for him to hang out while his survival skills were catching up with the rest of his growth, but I kept these sentiments to myself since I make it a practice never to offend anyone over eight feet tall unless it ain't avoidable.

The nightly blizzard came and went, and we were out at sunrise the next morning, digging a path up to Clyde's cave. It wasn't all that hard to dig through the snow, but every half hour or so we'd come to a boulder that we couldn't climb over or walk around, and as you might imagine it kind of slowed our progress. Hightower was afraid Clyde might be trapped in his cave, but I figured that Clyde was used to taking care of himself in strange lands and ticklish situations, and in truth the one thing that kept me going through all them days of digging and shoving boulders down the mountainside was the thought of all that jade sitting there in my picnic basket.

After a week we ran out of food and had to change shelters, and after two more weeks *all* the shelters were plumb out of food, and we figured if we didn't reach Clyde in another day or two we were going to have to climb down the mountain and borrow a little food from some of the locals. Hightower assured me that it wouldn't be no problem, since whenever they saw him they started screaming and running the other way, which up to now had made him think he should maybe have packed some deodorant when he left Athens, but which he finally realized was just their reaction to him being the Abominable Snowman.

Anyway, we finally cleared the way to Clyde's cave on the twenty-second day, and much to our surprise we found that it was deserted, except for a note and some kind of printed ticket that he'd stuck onto the wall right near the entrance, and which I picked up and read as follows:

> Dear Lucifer:
> I went out looking for you after I heard the shot, but I soon saw that you were probably buried under half the mountain. If that is true and you are dead, then read no further, but if you are alive and manage to make your way back here, I should tell you that after waiting a week for you to show up I have figgered that you and the Yeti are both dead, and have therefore decided to make tracks for Australia, where I got me a commission to hunt down a few hundred koala bears. At least they figure to make better eating than panda meat. (Ho ho.)
> It seems a shame to leave all your jade doodads to rot here in the cave, so I am taking them with me back to civilization and will buy a drink to your sainted memory with some of the profits when I sell them. And just in case you ain't dead, I want you to know that I am a honorable man what would never rob a friend, and I am leaving you a lifetime pass to Capturing Clyde's Circus and Wild Animal Show in exchange for taking the trinkets with me.
>
> > Your Pal (or Rest in Peace,
> > whichever is applicable),
> > Clyde Calhoun

I crumpled up both the letter and the lifetime pass and threw them to the floor of the cave.

"The son of a bitch ran off with my jade!" I said.

"You can't eat jade," said Hightower unhappily. "He might at least have left us some food."

"Well, we got no money and we got no food," I said. "I reckon it's time we took our leave of this here mountain."

"Where will we go?" asked Hightower. "I'm still a wanted man, you know."

"Well, there's no sense going back north into China," I said. "They'd probably just ask a bunch of bothersome questions about General Chang's knick-knacks. I figure our best bet is to head south."

"If we go south we'll run into the Himalayas," said Hightower.

"Religious sects don't bother me none," I replied confidently. "I'll convert 'em in no time flat."

I walked out of the cave and started heading south, having wasted the better part of three months and a modest fortune in jade while wandering around the countryside with Clyde, and I promised my Silent Partner that the next time I took charge of a wall or an army or anything big like that, I was setting up shop and finally building my Tabernacle.

But as you will soon see, it wasn't quite as easy as it sounds.

6

The Land of
Eternal Youth

It took Hightower and me another month before we hit anything resembling civilization, at which time we found ourselves in Katmandu, which has a real exotic name but truth to tell ain't a lot different from Boise or Dubuque, except that it's a hell of a lot colder in the summers, and hardly any of the locals speak English.

Still, mathematics is a universal language, and I soon replenished our coffers in a series of friendly little contests involving pasteboards and various combinations of the number twenty-one. It was only after a couple of disgruntled losers started complaining that *my* deck added up to a lot more twenty-ones than *their* decks did that I decided it was time to hit the road again.

"Where are you heading?" asked Hightower.

"Someplace warm," I said. "What's south of here?"

"India."

"Then that's where I'm heading."

"I can't go with you," he said.

"Why not?" I asked.

"From everything I hear, India's a pretty crowded place," he answered. "And the bigger the crowd, the more I stand out. I'll be much safer finding a nice little village in Nepal and settling down here."

"Guido Scarducci's probably forgot all about you by now," I said.

"Have you ever known a bookie to forget a debt?" he asked.

Well, I didn't have no quick and ready comforting answer to that, so I bid him good-bye, packed enough food for a month, and lit out of Katmandu just in time to avoid a tedious discussion about the laws of statistical averages with some of the locals. I made pretty good progress for a week or so, but then a major league blizzard came up, and by the time it ended two days later all the roads and trails were covered, and within another week I was forced to admit that I was about as lost as people ever get to be.

Then one day I came to a pass that led to a winding trail down a mountainside, and suddenly it wasn't so cold anymore, and before long the snow vanished and I was walking on grass. I could see a great big green valley stuck smack in the middle of the mountains, and I decided to head on over to it to see if I could rustle up a hot meal and maybe a friendly game of chance or two.

Just before I reached the valley I came to a rickety wooden bridge leading over a stream, and on the other side of it were a bunch of guys who looked kind of Chinese lining a path that led up to this enormous white temple, which in turn was surrounded by a batch of little white houses.

Well, they just stared at me without saying nothing, so I put on my friendliest smile and crossed the bridge and was about to introduce myself when the strangest damned thing happened: the second I got to their side of the creek, they all got to their knees and bowed their heads, which could have meant anything from them all being ready for a friendly game of craps to this being the quickest mass conversion in my experience as a man of the cloth.

Then a tall thin man came out of one of the houses and walked up to me.

"Greetings," he said. "I am Tard."

"Me, too," I said. "This place take a heap of getting to."

"You misunderstand me," he said. "Tard is my name."

"And I'm the Right Reverend Doctor Lucifer Jones at your service," I said. "Group weddings and funerals done cheap."

"We have been waiting for you, Doctor Jones," said Tard.

"You have?" I said.

"Yes," he replied. "Welcome to the kingdom of Shali-Mar."

"I don't recall seeing anyplace called Shali-Mar on any of the maps of the area," I said.

He just kind of chuckled at that. "You must be tired and hungry after your journey. I will have your rooms prepared while you are eating."

"Well, that's right neighborly of you, Brother Tard," I said.

"It is my job to serve you," he answered. "If there is anything you want, anything at all, you have but to tell me, and it shall be arranged."

"You act like this to all your guests?" I asked.

"You are our first visitor in almost two hundred years," he replied.

"Probably just as well," I said, admiring the sight of some young ladies walking through the fields with water pitchers on their heads. "If the travel agents ever find out about this place, they'll ruin it. Still," I added, "I don't know how you could have been expecting me. This little stopover wasn't exactly on my itinerary."

"Nonetheless, we have been expecting you, Doctor Jones." He paused. "Doesn't it strike you as unusual that everyone has knelt down the instant they have seen you?"

"Truth to tell, I been mulling on it, Brother Tard," I admitted. "I finally figured that they'd just never seen such a good-looking white man before, and didn't know quite what else to do about it."

He shook his head. "This is their traditional way of greeting the High Lama."

"He looks a lot like me, does he?" I asked.

"He has been dead for one hundred and thirty-four years," answered Tard. "But according to our legends, the day would come when a pale man from a distant land would cross over the bridge to Shali-Mar, and he would become the High Lama." He turned to me. "And now the legend has come true."

"Well, now, that's right interesting, Brother Tard," I said. "What does the job pay?"

"I don't think you understand, Doctor Jones," said Tard.

"The High Lama is the absolute ruler of Shali-Mar. He is our physical master, and our conduit to God."

"The absolute ruler, you say?"

"That is correct."

I looked at a couple of nubile young maidens who were coming out of the temple and winked at one of 'em, who blushed and got down on her knees right quick. "The High Lama is your conduit to God?"

"That's right."

"And anything the High Lama says goes?"

"Of course."

"Well, Brother Tard," I said, shooting him a great big smile, "your prayers have been answered. Talking to God is one of the best things I do, me being a man of the cloth and all." I pulled a cigar out of my pocket and lit it up while surveying my kingdom. "Why don't you join me for lunch and explain some of the intricacies of the job?"

"I am merely your chief administrator," said Tard. "It would be better for the High Priestess to discuss the more esoteric details of your position with you."

"Sounds good to me," I said. "I've always had a soft spot in my heart for High Priestesses."

We entered the temple, and I found myself face-to-face with a big golden statue of a lion which had rubies the size of golf balls for eyes and a bunch of diamonds for teeth. As I looked around, I saw a bunch of other little gem-covered trinkets that put General Chang's collection of jade knick-knacks to shame.

"Doctor Jones?" said Tard, after I'd spent a proper amount of time appreciating them. "Please follow me."

He led me through a batch of rooms, each bigger and finer than the last, and finally we came to one that had a huge table in the middle of it. At the center of the table was an ornate silver bowl filled with fruit.

"Please make yourself comfortable," said Tard. "I will go fetch the High Priestess." He walked to a doorway and turned to me. "She will be so happy to know that you have finally arrived, Doctor Jones. She has been waiting seventy years to instruct you."

"She's seventy years old?" I asked.

"No, she's much closer to one hundred and ten," answered Tard. "But she's only been the High Priestess for seventy."

Well, as you can imagine, this kind of dampened my enthusiasm, but I didn't see no way out of meeting with her, so I just pulled an apple out of the bowl and started munching on it, and about the time I was done I looked up and there in the doorway was this voluptuous young lady with long black hair and big brown eyes, all done up in a white silk outfit that didn't hide anywhere near as much as she seemed to think it did.

"Good afternoon, Doctor Jones," she said in the sweetest voice I ever did hear.

"It's getting better by the minute," I agreed. "What's your name?"

"Lisara," she said, giving me a great big toothy smile.

"Well, Lisara, honey," I said, "I got to meet with some wrinkled old High Priestess in the next couple of minutes, but once I get rid of her, what do you say to coming up to my room for an intimate little dinner for two?"

"I *am* the High Priestess, Doctor Jones," she said.

"I guess the thought of meeting with the High Lama was too much for the last one, huh?" I said. "Send my regrets to her family, and remind me to bring a wreath to the funeral."

"I have been the High Priestess for seventy years," she said.

"Come on," I said. "You can't be much more than nineteen or twenty years old."

"I am one hundred and eleven."

"You're kidding, right?"

"No, I truly am one hundred and eleven years old."

"Then how come you look like you do?" I asked.

"I avoid all fats and starches," she said, "and I jog five miles every morning."

"And that's all there is to it?"

"Well, that's why I look *fit*," she explained. "As for why I look *young*, it is because I live in Shali-Mar. This is the Land of Eternal Youth: no one ever ages here."

"Come to think of it, I didn't see no old codgers on the path up to the temple," I said.

"There aren't any," said Lisara. "The oldest of us all is Tard; he was alive when the last High Lama died." She paused. "It is something in the air, I think."

"Then why do you keep this place such a secret?" I asked. "You could put Miami Beach and the Riviera out of business."

"We have everything we need," she replied. "We have no desire to be overrun by outsiders."

"You could at least send a team to the Senior Olympics and clean up making side bets on 'em."

She shook her head sadly. "Once a citizen of Shali-Mar leaves, the aging process accelerates. Before he passes beyond the mountains that surround us, he is a gnarled and withered travesty of a human being."

"Yeah, I can see where that might present a problem or two," I said. "Especially in the sprints and high hurdles."

"But we have no wish to leave," she continued. "Our life here has been idyllic, and now that we once again have a High Lama, it will be perfect."

"Well, now that you brought the subject up," I said, "just what does the High Lama do?"

"You are our spiritual leader," she explained. "It is your job to probe the eternal verities."

"I can think of a lot of 'em that need probing," I agreed, getting into the spirit of it. "Like why do elevators all arrive at the same time? Or why does it always rain right after you wax your car? Why does traffic always move faster in the other lane?"

"Those are not precisely the ones I had in mind," she said.

"Why don't you come up to my room tonight?" I said. "We can discuss what you got in mind, plus a couple of things *I* got in mind."

"Oh, I couldn't do that, Doctor Jones," she said.

"Well, if it's a problem, *I* could come to *your* room," I said agreeably.

She shook her head. "The High Lama must avoid even the appearance of impropriety."

"What's the point of being the High Lama in the first place if I can't pay a social call on a lovely young lady when I'm of a mind to?" I asked.

"It simply isn't done," she said. "You are our spiritual leader."

"No reason why I can't do both," I said. "I always set aside Sunday mornings for saving souls."

"You do not understand, Doctor Jones," she said. "The High Priestess must forsake all earthly pleasures."

"That's kind of a rigid job qualification, ain't it?" I said.

"No one ever said that being the High Priestess was easy," she answered.

I made up my mind then and there to issue an executive order, or whatever it was High Lamas did, to the effect that it was okay for the High Priestess to indulge in a little hanky-panky from time to time, and was about to mention it to her when a couple of Lesser Priestesses arrived with lunch, and since I hadn't seen no cooked food for almost a month I sat right down and started eating away.

Tard came in just when I was finishing up dessert, and told Lisara that he had to prepare me for the inauguration or coronation or whatever gets done to them what is elected High Lama, and that she could continue talking to me at dinnertime. She bowed and left the room, and Tard sat himself down next to me.

"You will officially become our High Lama in a ceremony this afternoon," he said. "I think it would be best if you shaved and bathed before it begins. I'll have a couple of servants prepare your bath."

Well, you can imagine my disappointment when I found out that the servants were of the masculine persuasion, so I scrubbed right quick, shaved off three weeks growth, and got into this white robe they'd laid out for me. I'd barely had time to light up a cigar when Tard came by and ushered me down to a huge open courtyard in the middle of the temple. It seemed like the whole town was there to greet me, all of 'em young and beautiful except for them what was young and handsome, and pretty soon Lisara showed up, looking better than ever, and started talking at me in some unfamiliar language, and then she and everyone else seemed to be waiting for an answer, so finally I said "I sure do!" and she put this gold amulet around my neck and then everyone knelt down again and suddenly I was the High Lama.

I figured at least we'd have a few drinks to celebrate, and maybe do a little serious dancing, and I was already preparing a speech about how I was gonna clean up all the mistakes of the previous administration and lower taxes and put a chicken in every pot, when they all kind of wandered back to their houses, and I was left alone with Tard and Lisara.

"That's it?" I said.

"It is accomplished," said Tard.

"Ain't there even no Inauguration Ball?" I asked.

"It would be anticlimactic after your investiture," said Tard.

"Are you trying to tell me that there little ceremony was the high point of the day?"

"For most of our people, it was the high point of their lives," said Lisara.

"Well, I can see we're gonna have to make some changes around here," I said.

"That might not be a wise idea," said Tard.

"I'm the High Lama, ain't I?" I said.

"Yes."

"As I undesrtand it, that means that any idea I got is a quality idea."

"But you are supposed to spend your life in serene contemplation," said Tard.

"I been contemplating nonstop since I got here," I said. "I spent half the afternoon contemplating what that gold lion would be worth on the open market, and I spent the rest of it contemplating how much rent I could save the government by having Lisara move in with me."

"I don't think you understand your position, Doctor Jones," he said. "You are the High Lama of Shali-Mar."

"Right," I said. "And that means what I say goes."

"Within limitations," said Tard.

"Nobody ever mentioned no limitations for me when I applied for the job."

"Aren't you aware of the fact that you just took vows of poverty and celibacy in front of the entire community?" said Tard.

"I did *what*?"

"It's true, Doctor Jones," said Lisara. "That's what you agreed to at the end of the ceremony."

"I thought I was agreeing to be the High Lama!" I said.

"You were," she said. "And the High Lama is penniless and celibate."

I took off the amulet and handed it to Tard. "That being the case, I hereby resign from the High Lama business."

"You can't," he said.

"I just did."

"I urge you to consider the consequences of your actions," said Tard. "If you are not the High Lama, then you are just an intruder from the Outside World, and it is our obligation to kill you."

"Why?" I demanded. "What have I ever done to you?"

"We must keep our location secret, or we will be overrun with adventurers who will steal our women and loot our treasures."

"Let's calm down and be reasonable, Brother Tard," I said. "I can see why you don't want no foreign devils messing with your women or your trinkets, but it seems to me that a naturalized devil who also happens to be the High Lama ought to have a little more leeway."

"That's out of the question," he said, and then held out the amulet in one hand and drew his sword with the other. "You can be the High Lama, or you can be put to death. The choice is yours."

"Well," I said, staring at his sword, "I can see now that I may have been a little hasty in my previous decision. I suppose there's worse things than being the High Lama." First and foremost of which was the thought of getting cut up into fishbait.

Tard reached over and placed the amulet around my neck again. "You are young and hot-blooded and impetuous, as I once was," he said, putting his sword back in its sheath. "Fortunately, it's a phase that only lasts for two or three centuries."

"Well, that's a definite comfort, Brother Tard," I said glumly. "I think I'll take a walk around the kingdom and mull over everything you've said."

"Certainly, Doctor Jones," answered Tard. "Dinner will be served at sunset."

"Lisara, why don't you come with me to make sure I don't get lost?" I said.

"I am yours to command," she said. I must have looked right approving of that, because she quickly added, "Within limitations."

We started walking through the fields, and everywhere I went people kept kneeling down the second they saw me, and I tried to imagine a couple of centuries of seeing nothing but the tops of people's heads.

"Try not to be disappointed, Doctor Jones," said Lisara. "You will soon adjust to the contemplative life."

Well, truth to tell, for the past five minutes the only contemplating I'd been doing was how to get out of Shali-Mar with maybe a few diamonds and rubies for my trouble, and perhaps a handful of Lesser Priestesses for warmth and companionship of a cold winter's night, but Lisara was going on so rhapsodically about the pleasures of the mind that I figured that this probably wasn't the most propitious time to share my thoughts with her.

We got back to the temple just in time for dinner, and afterward Lisara went off to wherever it was that the Priestesses hung out, and Tard came up and asked me if there was anything he could do for me before I turned in.

"Well, now that you come to mention it, Brother Tard," I said, "I still got some questions about this whole set-up."

"Yes?"

I nodded. "Like, for example, nobody ever grows old or gets sick here, right?"

"That is correct."

"Then what did the last High Lama die of?"

"He tried to cross the bridge and leave Shali-Mar, and so I was forced to kill him," answered Tard.

"Was he a visitor, like me?" I asked.

He nodded. "So were the three before him."

"Let me guess: you killed them all for trying to leave?"

"Curious, isn't it?" said Tard. "That so many High Lamas would want to leave our little paradise?"

"Beats the hell out of me," I said.

"Was that all you wished to know, Doctor Jones?"

"I got a few more questions, if you got the time to answer them."

"Certainly," he said.

"Just out of curiosity," I said, "is there anything a High Lama can do that constitutes a firing offense, as opposed to a killing offense?"

"Absolutely nothing," he said. "As long as you obey your vows, you are virtually all-powerful in Shali-Mar."

Which was like telling me that as long as Exterminator didn't break no legs, he was a fair-to-middling racehorse.

"Is there anything else you wish to know, Doctor Jones?" he asked.

"No, I guess that's about it."

"If you need anything, just send for me," he said, bowing. "I am your servant."

Which was just when the Lord suggested to me that there was more than one way to skin a cat.

"Just a minute," I said.

"Yes, Doctor Jones?"

"Who appointed you my servant?"

"We are *all* your servants."

"Okay, then—who made you the chief administrator?"

"I have been chief administrator for more than three hundred years."

"But if I was to make an official pronouncement that you'd be better fit to clean the royal stables, you'd show up for work there tomorrow morning with a broom and a shovel, right?"

"Have I displeased you in some way, Doctor Jones?"

"Not a bit, Brother Tard," I said. "But I just did my first serious visualizing of the Cosmic All tonight, and for some reason I keep seeing you sweeping up behind horses."

"Why am I being demoted?" he asked.

"Don't view it as a demotion at all," I said. "If I was you, I'd consider it an opportunity to get back in touch with the common people—them what don't hold their noses and run the other way when you approach."

"Is this change in my status temporary or permanent?" he asked, kind of frowning.

"Well, seeing that no one ever gets old here, I think you can view it as temporary," I said. "I figure six or seven hundred years ought to do the trick."

He swallowed hard.

"One more thing," I said. "As your last official duty, pass the word that I'll be interviewing potential chief administrators tomorrow morning."

He stared at me and didn't say nothing, and since I'd said everything I had to say, I gave him a friendly pat on the shoulder and went up to my room.

Tard showed up maybe half an hour later. "Perhaps I was mistaken," he said.

"Yeah?"

"The High Lama is incapable of making an unwise decision," he said. "And since it is patently unwise to send such a qualified person as myself to work in the stables for the next five hundred years, you perforce cannot be the High Lama."

"I do believe you've hit the nail on the head, Brother Tard," I said.

"Therefore," he continued, "the best thing to do is sneak you out of here under cover of night."

"I was wondering how long it would take you to come around to that conclusion," I said.

"How soon can you be ready to leave?" he asked.

"I've been all packed for the past twenty minutes," I told him.

"Where is your luggage?"

"Right there on the bed," I said, pointing to my backpack.

"Excuse me for a moment," he said, and started rummaging through it. It was after he'd pulled out the fifteenth and last of the statues that he turned to me and said, "Did you plan to leave us *anything*?"

"These are just little keepsakes to remind me of the pleasant hours I spent here as the High Lama," I said. "I mean, it ain't as if you got any picture postcards I can take with me."

"The amulet," he said, holding out his hand.

Well, his other hand was perched on the handle of his sword, so I sighed and took it off from around my neck and tossed it onto the bed.

Then I followed him down to the main level of the temple, out the door, across the fields, and over to the bridge. All the guards took one look at me and immediately knelt down and bowed their heads, and I was across the bridge before anyone looked up. They hooted and hollered a lot, but I knew none of 'em would cross the stream to come after me as long as doing so would qualify 'em for a quick trip to the old-age home.

As I headed toward India, I decided that the Land of Eternal Youth wasn't all it was cracked up to be, especially since it seemed to go hand-in-glove with eternal poverty, and I redirected all my more serious contemplating toward rounding up a grub-stake and building the Tabernacle of Saint Luke.

7
Secret Sex

There are worse things than walking down the streets of Delhi on a hot summer day.

For one thing, you could be walking down the streets of Delhi on a hot summer day with a bunch of knife-wielding gamblers hot on your trail for trying to pay off your losses with a pandaskin coat.

Or you could be walking down the streets of Delhi on a hot summer day with half the British Raj hunting for you because you figured that white men ought to stick together in foreign climes and you borrowed a few thousand rupees from the local church and left an I.O.U. in its place so that you could pay off all them disgruntled gamblers.

Or you could be walking down the streets of Delhi on a hot summer day with the Royal Governor's private guards searching for you after you figured you'd raise a little capital by selling tours of the executive mansion to a group of British clergymen, and when you got a mite confused and turned right instead of left, you came across the Royal Governor and a pair of chambermaids reenacting a solemn biblical scene that probably took place on a regular basis between Solomon and a couple of his more athletic wives.

Or you could be walking down the streets of Delhi looking out for the father and eight burly brothers of one of the city's fairest flowers, who in their enthusiasm to welcome a little fresh blood into the family seemed totally unable to differentiate between a declaration of eternal love and a bonafide proposal of marriage.

All of which happened to me through a series of innocent misunderstandings, but which nonetheless imbued me with a pretty strong desire to take my leave of Delhi until everyone calmed down and was willing to listen to reason.

It was when I saw a handful of the Royal Governor's men standing in the middle of the road, comparing notes with a couple of gamblers, that I decided it might be a good idea to duck into a nearby building and wait for nightfall before clearing out, so I walked through the nearest door and found myself in the lobby of the Victoria Hotel, which looked like it had been sadly in need of a spring cleaning for the better part of half a century or so.

"May I help you, Sahib?" asked the desk clerk, who was a skinny little Indian with a dirty turban.

"Yeah," I said, looking out the window as the Governor's men started looking into all the shops and stores. "I need a place to stay, kind of short term."

"We have a number of empty rooms," he said.

"I don't need nothing for the whole night," I said. "Five or ten minutes should do the trick."

He frowned. "We have never rented a room for less than the night, Sahib," he said.

"I ain't got no time to haggle," I said, flashing my last fifty rupees and walking around behind the desk next to him. "I'll just rent this here floor space for half an hour. Payable when I get up and leave."

I sat down about ten seconds before a couple of soldiers entered the lobby and walked over to the clerk.

"We're looking for an American masquerading as a minister," said one of them. "Have you seen him?"

I shoved half the rupees into the clerk's hand.

"No, Sahibs," he answered. "No one has come in here all day."

"Well, if he should, let us know."

"Certainly, Sahibs," he said.

He waited until they walked out and closed the door behind them, then turned and looked down at me.

"You can stand up now," he said. "They're gone."

"It's kind of comfortable down here," I said. "Besides, they were just the first wave of an unending ocean of misfortune."

"There are more people looking for you?" he asked.

"No more'n eighty or ninety of 'em," I answered.

"What did you do?"

"Hardly anything at all," I said. "These English fellers just can't stand the fact that we whipped 'em at Bunker Hill. All I can figure is that they're still carrying a grudge."

"I hate the English, too," he said. "Even now we are planning to drive them from our country as you Americans did."

"You don't say?"

"I do say," he replied. He paused and stared at me for a minute or two. "Would I be correct in assuming you plan to leave Delhi when night falls?"

"I got to admit that sticking around waiting to get tarred and feathered ain't real high on my list of priorities," I answered.

"They will be watching all the major roads and train stations," he said. "If you try to get out by foot or car or train, they will stop you."

"That's right depressing news," I said.

"But *I* can get you out," he added.

"Well, as one revolutionary to another, let me say that that's mighty neighborly of you."

"I will be happy to help you thwart the British," he said. "And once you are safely away from Delhi, I hope you will do me a favor in return."

"Doing favors for ignorant brown heathen is part of my calling," I assured him. "No offense intended."

"None taken."

"Exactly what kind of favor did you have in mind?"

"I will tell you when the time comes," he said, handing me a room key. "In the meantime, I have arrangements to make. Wait for me in this room. I will knock three times at midnight."

"Sounds good to me," I said, getting up onto my feet. "By the way, I never did catch your name."

"Gunga, and no bad jokes, please."

"Why would I make a joke, Brother Gunga?" I asked.

"The British seem to find it hilarious," he said bitterly.

"It don't bother me none," I said.

"I take it you don't like Kipling?"

"It ain't never been one of my favorite sports," I replied. "And by the bye, I'm the Right Reverend Honorable Doctor Lucifer Jones, at your service."

"You'd better get to your room now, before anyone else comes looking for you," suggested Gunga.

Well, I did like he said, and spent a few minutes finding solace for my present situation in the Good Book before I drifted off to sleep. I must have been tireder than I thought, because the next thing I knew Gunga was knocking at the door.

"Are you ready, Sahib?" he whispered.

"Ready and rarin'," I said, opening the door.

"Everything has been prepared," he said, walking into the room.

"Sounds good to me," I said. "How am I getting out—by car or by train?"

"Neither," he answered. "Take off your clothes."

"I can hardly blame you for being smitten by my manly good looks," I said sternly, "but us men of the cloth don't go in for no degenerate activity."

"Get into this," he said, tossing me a white loincloth. "It's part of your disguise."

Now that I knew he wasn't gonna attempt no unnatural perversions, I got undressed right quick and clambered into the loincloth. Then he walked over and tied a turban around my head.

"How do I look?" I asked.

He studied me thoughtfully for a moment. "Like an American in a loincloth and turban," he said. "Still, it will have to do. Follow me, please."

He walked out the door and down the stairs, with me right behind him, and then we went through the kitchen and out the back door, where I bumped smack-dab into an elephant.

"Say hello to Akbar," said Gunga. "He will take you out of Delhi."

"I don't know how to tell you this, Brother Gunga," I said, staring at Akbar, of whom there was an awful lot to stare at, "but I ain't never rode no elephants before."

"The British will never be looking for a coolie atop an elephant," said Gunga. "You should pass by unnoticed."

"That's a powerful lot of elephant to pass by anything unnoticed," I said.

"Trust me, Reverend Jones," said Gunga. "It is your only chance."

"You I trust," I said. "Akbar I got my doubts about."

"He is trained to respond to whoever is his mahout."

"His what?"

"His rider," said Gunga. He handed me a stick with a metal hook at one end. "To make him go, just say 'Kush.' Use the stick to turn him." He looked up and down the alleyway. "I must leave shortly."

"How do I get on top of him?"

"Just stand in front of him and tell him to lift you up."

"That's all there is to it?" I asked dubiously.

"Trust me, Reverend Jones."

"Well, I suppose I ought to thank you for going to all this trouble, Brother Gunga," I said.

"You can repay a favor with a favor," he replied.

"Just name it," I said, keeping my fingers crossed behind my back in case it involved giving money to one of his pet charities.

"Take Akbar to the town of Khajuraho, which is south and east of here. Once you arrive there you will be contacted by our leader, Rashid Jahan." He looked around nervously. "Now I must leave before my absence is noticed."

He darted back into the hotel, and I was left alone with Akbar, who looked like he didn't trust me a whole lot more than I trusted him, which was not at all. Still, I couldn't just stand there in the alley forever, so I finally walked around to his front end and said "Lift." His trunk snaked out and wrapped itself around me, and before I could scream for help or ask my Silent Partner to intervene I was sitting on top of his head. I tucked a leg behind each ear, said "Kush!" and off old Akbar went. When we came to a corner I jabbed him with the stick, and sure enough, he turned just the way he was supposed to.

We made it to the edge of town in less than an hour, and the British soldiers just waved me past without even looking at me, and then we started kushing south. Akbar wasn't the type to travel on an empty stomach, and he ate on the march, so to speak, and by the time morning rolled around I decided that maybe he had the right idea about things, so I steered him to a nearby apple orchard and told him to stop, but evidently he didn't speak no American because he just kept on plodding along at the same brisk pace. I managed to grab a couple of apples off a low-hanging branch or I could have starved for all Akbar gave a damn.

About noon we hit a forest, and started plowing through it, and then suddenly old Akbar's trunk shot straight out and his ears stopped flopping and started listening, and a minute later he began trumpeting to beat the band, and just about the time I was sure he was trying to warn me that the Royal Governor was waiting in ambush I heard an answering trumpet and then a wild elephant broke into a clearing. I started whacking Akbar with my stick to make him turn around, because even though this wild elephant was a couple of feet smaller than him I still didn't relish sitting on his head while he indulged himself in a friendly little fight to the death, but he just kept walking forward, and at the last second I realized that the wild elephant was of the female persuasion and I was about to become an inadvertent participant in an affair of the heart.

Well, Akbar stopped when he was maybe two feet away and trumpeted again, and she trumpeted back, and pretty soon you could have sworn that a brass band was giving a concert of John Philip Sousa marches what with all the trumpeting that was going on. Then the lady elephant gave Akbar a playful shove that could have brought a house down, and Akbar started prancing around like a puppy, and then suddenly there was a great crashing of bushes and trees and another elephant broke into the clearing some forty yards away. This one was bigger than Akbar, and he had a jealous husbandly look about him, and Akbar right quick decided he had urgent business elsewhere, because he took off like a bat out of hell and didn't slow down until we reached the end of the forest and broke out into the open once again.

Losing the love of his life seemed to take all the zip out of Akbar's stride, but it didn't affect his appetite none, so he munched and plodded his way across the countryside for the rest of the day and all the next night.

It was dawn when we hit the outskirts of Khajuraho, and the first thing I saw was this temple, which wasn't like no other I had ever seen, and truth to tell reminded me a lot more of the Rialto Burlesque Theater back in Kansas City than a house of worship. There were a bunch of figures, carved all over the walls of the temple, most of 'em dressed for extremely warm weather, and all of them doing exactly what Akbar had planned to do with his lady elephant.

We went a little farther, and came to another temple with even more enthusiastic figures on the walls, and by the time we hit a third temple that was just like the first two only more so, I figured I had finally found the perfect community to build my tabernacle.

I turned Akbar toward town, and when we came to a run-down hostelry called the Janata Hotel, I pointed him toward a brick wall since I didn't know no other way to stop him, and while he was pushing against it I took a stroll down the middle of his back and slid off when I came to his tail. Then I walked around to the front and told the desk clerk to give me a room with a bath, and tend to my elephant for me.

"I'm sorry," he said, staring at me, "but we do not cater to the native trade."

Which was when I remembered that I was all done up like a coolie.

"Don't pay no never-mind to these duds," I said. "I was just out getting a suntan."

"You sound like an American," he said. "I thought only we British ran around naked in the midday sun in tropical climes."

"I ain't so much running around as trying to rent a room," I pointed out.

He got out the register right quick, and I signed in, and a few minutes later I was sitting in my bathtub washing off the smell of elephant, of which I'd acquired an awful lot, when there was a knock at the door.

"Come on in," I hollered. "It ain't locked."

A little Indian feller walked into the room and headed over to the tub.

"You are Lucifer Jones?" he asked.

"The Right Reverend Honorable Doctor Lucifer Jones, at your service," I said.

"I have been waiting for you ever since I got a telegram from my cousin Gunga," he said. "I am Rashid Jahan."

"You hunted me up kind of fast, Brother Rashid," I remarked.

"Well, we knew we were looking for a white man wearing a loincloth and riding an elephant," he replied. "You'd be surprised how very few of them come through town in a day."

"So what can I do for you, Brother Rashid?"

"I understand from my cousin Gunga that the two of you discussed expelling the British from our country."

"Yeah, I recall his mentioning something about it," I said.

"And I further understand that you share our philosophy."

Now, I couldn't figure out how Gunga had known that, since I hadn't seen any of the temples until I hit Khajuraho, but I allowed that he was dead right.

"Excellent!" said Rashid. "He also mentioned that you had promised to do us a favor in exchange for his help."

"True enough," I said.

"Then I wonder if you would be willing to visit our secret sex tonight?" he said.

"Your secret sex?" I said.

He nodded. "We could draw enormous inspiration from an American like yourself."

I thought for a moment about the temples I had passed by on my way into town, and I figured that if that was their notion of public sex, I couldn't wait to see what kind of secret sex they practiced.

"I consider it a debt of honor, Brother Rashid," I said. "I'll inspire the hell out of 'em."

"Excellent," he said. "I shall tell them that you will join us."

"As often and as vigorously as I can," I promised. "Where do I find this here secret sex?"

"Wait until ten o'clock tonight, and then come south of town to the Temple of Kali."

"I'll be there with bells on," I assured him.

He bowed and left, and I spent the next couple of hours just soaking in the tub. Then, just after sunset, I got out and changed into my best Sunday go-to-meeting clothes, after which I shaved and slapped a bunch of grease on my hair to slick it down. I didn't have no file to clean the dirt out from under my fingernails, so I bit 'em off instead. I didn't have any cologne either, so I wandered down to the bar and slapped a little Napoleon brandy on my face when the barkeep wasn't looking.

Then, since I had high hopes of meeting a lady of quality at this secret sex affair, I moseyed out into the hotel's garden and picked a couple of dozen flowers which I wrapped in a copy of the *Bombay Times* that someone had left in the lobby.

Finally I went looking for Akbar, and found him munching peacefully on some greenery down the street.

"Lift," I said, and he did, and soon we were heading down the road to the Temple of Kali. I still hadn't figured out how to make him stop, so I just aimed him up against a huge pillar, and while he was pushing away at it I climbed down and walked around to the front door, holding the flowers behind my back since I didn't want to give 'em to the first lady I saw, just in case a prettier one was hanging back just waiting for a handsome young buck like me to sweep her off her feet.

I knocked on the door, and Rashid opened it.

"You're right on time, Reverend Jones," he said.

"Well, I didn't want no one to start without me," I said. "Which way to the secret sex?"

"Follow me," he said, walking me past a couple of dozen statues that looked so acrobatic that the models could probably have gotten jobs with the Ringling Brothers if they'd put their clothes on.

We took a hard left, and then went down a flight of stairs

to this big ornate door, where Rashid stopped and turned to me.

"You are a Westerner," he said, "unused to our ways. I warn you that you may be shocked by some of the things that you will see before the evening is over."

"Different strokes for different folks," I said.

"I admire your open-mindedness, Reverend Jones."

He reached out for the door and was just about to open it when a figure darted out of the shadows and cracked him over the head with a blackjack, and he just kind of smiled and blinked once or twice and then collapsed on the floor.

"Reverend Jones!" whispered the figure, which was dressed all in black. "What in blazes are *you* doing here?"

I turned to face him, and realized that I was looking at Sir Mortimer Edgerton-Smythe.

"Howdy, Sir Mortimer," I said. "Last time I saw you you were heading into the sunset with Doctor Aristotle Ho's dragon. What happened?"

"That foul fiend duped me," said Sir Mortimer. "But now I've gotten wind of his latest plot to take over the world, and I plan to bring him to justice."

"And you figure hitting my friend Rashid on the noggin is going to have a deleterious effect on a Chinaman who's four thousand miles away from here?" I asked.

"I did it to save *you*, Reverend Jones," he said. "Now I must have an answer to my question: what are you doing here?"

"I been invited to participate in some secret sex," I said. "And while I don't mean to be critical or nothing, you're putting a real damper on the festivities."

"You fool!" he snapped. "You have no idea what's going on behind that door!"

"I'm a quick study," I assured him.

"You're totally unprepared for this."

I considered what he said and looked down at my flowers. "You think I should have brung candy instead?"

"You shouldn't have come at all," he said. "Take my advice and go right back to your hotel."

"Now just a minute, Sir Mortimer," I said. "I'm glad to

share some of this here secret sex with you, you being a fellow white man and all, but I'll be hanged if I'm gonna leave and let you have it all to yourself.''

"What's going on behind that door is a meeting of secret *sects*, you blithering idiot!'' he said.

"Secret sects?'' I repeated.

"Doctor Aristotle Ho has resurrected the Thuggees and other ancient sects with the purpose of overrunning India and eventually all of Asia, with himself as their leader. Tonight is the night that they have all gathered under one roof so that he can address them and spell out his plans. *Now* do you understand what you have blundered into?''

"You mean there ain't no women in there?'' I asked.

"That's what I've been trying to tell you!''

"And I got all decked out in my Sunday best for nothing?''

"Don't you understand anything I've said?'' demanded Sir Mortimer.

"I understand that Doctor Aristotle Ho has got a lot to answer for,'' I told him. "This was a downright cruel and unfeeling trick to play on a Christian missionary who never did nobody no harm.''

Sir Mortimer stared at me for a minute. "I don't suppose it matters what your motive is, as long as you're against him. What do you say, Reverend Jones—will you throw in with me and bring this insidious villain to justice?''

"I should consider my answer very carefully before I gave it, Doctor Jones,'' said a familiar voice, and we turned to find ourselves facing Doctor Aristotle Ho and maybe a dozen of his henchmen, all of 'em with their guns drawn.

"You!" hissed Sir Mortimer.

"Our paths cross once again, Sir Mortimer,'' said Doctor Ho. "You are becoming a serious annoyance to me. I should have killed you the last time we met; this time I will correct that oversight.''

"Well, I can see you two have lots to talk about,'' I said, "so if you'll excuse me, I think I'll be on my way.''

"Not so fast, Doctor Jones,'' he said, as a couple of his men blocked my path. "Why are you here in the first place?''

"It's a Saturday night, and I was looking for a little female companionship," I explained.

"At a meeting of the Thuggees in the Temple of Kali?" he said, kind of arching an eyebrow.

"I was the victim of false doctrine," I said. "Everybody kept talking about all this secret sex that was going on, and I thought I'd partake of some of it."

He stared at me for an awfully long and uncomfortable minute.

"Nobody can be that foolish, Doctor Jones," he said. "Not even you. Therefore, I must conclude that you are working in concert with Sir Mortimer."

"I didn't even know he was gonna be here!" I protested. "I even brung these flowers along for the lucky lady of my choice."

"An excellent disguise," said Doctor Ho, nodding approvingly. "Who would suspect such a naive, bumbling idiot of being a master spy?"

"I ain't no master spy," I said. "I'm just an innocent man of the cloth, bringing spiritual comfort across the face of Asia to all you unwashed heathen."

"Please do not insult my intelligence, Doctor Jones," said Aristotle Ho. "Do you think I am unaware of your exploits since last we met? You killed one of my most trusted agents, General Chang, in hand-to-hand combat atop the Great Wall, and then made off with *my* jade." He paused and glared at me. "You fooled me the first time we met, but now I know just how dangerous you are."

"Sir Mortimer," I said, "tell him I ain't working for you!"

"You know, you fooled me, too, Doctor Jones," said Sir Mortimer admiringly. "Who *are* you working for—the United States government or some private organization of super assassins?"

"Thanks a heap, Sir Mortimer," I said glumly.

"Enough talking," said Doctor Ho. "Now you shall see what happens to those who are foolish enough to attempt to hinder me in my goal of world conquest! Open the door!"

One of his henchmen pulled the door open, and we marched into this huge chamber that had about three hundred men in it, all of 'em wearing red robes with weird designs on 'em. A couple of men were lying on stone altars, but since their heads were missing I figured they weren't in any real serious pain at the moment. The second the guys wearing the robes saw us they pulled out their swords and knives, but then Doctor Ho raised his hand and everyone stood stock-still.

"I have captured these two spies," he announced. "What shall we do with them?"

Well, just about everyone in the room screamed "Death!" but I did hear one voice say "Let's rape them first!", which implied to me that at least one other person had come looking for a little secret sex himself.

"How shall we kill them?" demanded Doctor Ho.

"The Death of a Thousand Cuts!" yelled a batch of 'em.

"Do you know what the Death of a Thousand Cuts is?" Doctor Ho said to me.

"Sounds like trying to shave with a hangover," I opined.

"I am afraid not, Doctor Jones," he said. "First, we will string you up and hang you a few feet above the floor. Then we will start slicing you to ribbons, but we will not deliver the fatal blow until the thousandth cut. The pain will be exquisite, I assure you."

"I got a better idea," I said. "If you really want to string this out, why not give me one cut tonight? Then I could go back to my hotel and sleep it off, and I promise to show up each of the next nine hundred and ninety-nine nights."

"What kind of fool do you take me for?" demanded Doctor Ho.

"Do your worst!" bellowed Sir Mortimer. "I will show you how an Englishman dies."

Well, I wasn't anxious to show *anyone* how an American died, so I turned back to Doctor Ho again.

"This is silly," I said to him. "I ain't no spy, and you probably ain't got no followers what can count all the way up to a thousand. Why don't we just shake hands and let bygones be bygones? I'll even buy you a drink back at the Janata Hotel."

"You have heard the verdict of my Thuggees," replied Doctor Ho sternly. "They demand blood."

"As long as Sir Mortimer seems bound and determined to

bleed, why not settle for him?" I suggested. "I'll even do some of the cutting, just as a gesture of Christian goodwill."

"I admire your coolness in the face of an excruciatingly painful death, Doctor Jones," said Aristotle Ho. "Under other circumstances we could have been great friends."

"It still ain't too late," I said. "I feel a burst of friendship coming over me right this second."

He shook his head. "You are much too dangerous to be allowed to live." He turned to his men. "Prepare them both for the Death of a Thousand Cuts."

"Remember," said Sir Mortimer as they dragged us to the center of the room, "we represent the civilized world. Don't give them the plesaure of screaming in agony no matter how terrible the pain. Keep a stiff upper lip."

I was about to point out the difficulty of keeping a stiff upper lip once they chopped it off, but by then we were surrounded by Thuggees who placed us on a large platform and ripped our jackets and shirts off and started to tie our hands behind our backs when Doctor Ho stepped forward again.

"One moment," he said, and everything came to a stop. "I know you think me a barbaric fiend, Sir Mortimer," he continued, "but actually I am one of the more civilized fiends I know. To that end, I will allow you to make a last statement, if you so desire."

Sir Mortimer was already getting into his impersonation of the strong, silent type, and he just glared at Doctor Ho without saying a word.

"Doctor Jones?" said Aristotle Ho. "Have you any last words?"

I looked up toward the ceiling. "Lord," I said, "pay attention now: this is your friend and admirer Lucifer Jones suggesting that if you ever plan to manifest yourself, you couldn't pick a much more opportune time than this here moment to bring the temple crumbling down."

Doctor Ho threw back his head to laugh, but before a sound had a chance to come out we heard a great crashing noise and the whole temple started shaking. A couple of seconds later the ceiling started caving in, and half the Thuggees were buried under it while the rest lit out for the hills with a speed and grace that would have done Jim Thorpe proud.

Suddenly there was no one left except me and Sir Mortimer and Aristotle Ho, and he just glared at us furiously for a second, and then said, "You have thwarted me today, Lucifer Jones, but you haven't heard the last of me!" And then, before we could say anything, he melted into the shadows.

"Thanks a lot, Lord!" I shouted. "Now I owe *you* a favor."

Then we heard a mournful trumpeting, and we raced up what remained of the stairs, and there was old Akbar beating his head against a wall of the temple. He'd been pushing against the pillar where I left him until it finally collapsed on top of the Thuggees' private meeting room, and since nobody had told him to stop he'd just proceeded forward a few feet until he came to the wall, which wasn't near as thick and was already starting to buckle.

"Well, Doctor Jones," said Sir Mortimer. "Once again we've put a crimp in that insidious fiend's plan to conquer the world! Well done, sir!"

"Well, that's what he gets for leading an innocent gentleman on with promises of secret sex," I said righteously.

"I must be on my way, to report the night's proceedings to my government," he said. "It was nice collaborating with you again." He paused. "Allow me to give you one last piece of advice: do not return to your hotel tonight. There's always a chance that Aristotle Ho will be waiting there for you."

Well, I hadn't planned on returning anyway, since there was a dead certainty that the desk clerk and the hotel manager would be waiting there for me, and I had a feeling that they wouldn't accept payment in elephants, so I bade Sir Mortimer good-bye, got atop old Akbar again, and making a vow not to be duped by Doctor Aristotle Ho ever again, I headed off in search of fame, fortune, and maybe a little secret sex with an obliging lady of quality.

8

The Flame
of Bharatpur

Twenty-five rupees didn't buy a lot of food, even back in 1930, so Akbar and I kept pretty much to the countryside, eating whatever we could find in the fields, and heading in a kind of westerly direction. After a couple of weeks we hit the Rajasthan province, and the landscape got a little prettier, and we started passing an occasional old temple, and here and there we came to deserted cities, but since I still didn't know how to make him come to a stop I didn't get no chance to examine them.

It was when we were nearing Jaipur, where I had every hope of finding a used elephant lot and trading old Akbar in for a grubstake and maybe finding a friendly little game of chance, that we came across a field of tall grasses backing up to a forest. I was about to head for the trees in the hope that some of 'em might have something nourishing hanging down from their branches when I saw a movement in the grass off to my left, and I heard this voice whispering "Help me!" so I steered Akbar in that direction.

Then, when we were about twenty yards away, I heard a great big *"Oof!"* kind of sound, like something had had all the air squoze out of it, so I jumped off Akbar to see what was the matter, and what I found was that he had accidentally stepped on this tiger and crushed it flatter than a board.

I walked over to where the voice had come from, and found a white man, all torn up and bleeding, lying in the grass.

"Thank God!" he whispered when he saw me.

"What seems to be the problem, Brother?" I asked, kneeling down next to him.

Well, he was kind of delirious, and he kept mumbling about a tiger hunt and jealous lovers and murder and some kind of flame or fire, and finally I figured I'd better get him to a doctor right quick, so I called Akbar over and told him to lift us up, and once I laid the man across Akbar's neck and perched myself on his head, we made tracks for Jaipur, where we went to the nearest hospital. I left Akbar pushing his head against the wall of the emergency room, while I turned the patient over to a couple of doctors who carted him off and went right to work on him. I decided to hang around for a while, inasmuch as I didn't have no place better to go anyway, and before long I made fast friends with a pretty little nurse who rustled up some hospital grub for me, and then after a couple of hours one of the doctors hunted me up to say that the patient was going to live and wanted to see me, and not to do anything to wear him out, as if he was expecting me to arm-wrestle him or something.

I entered the room and walked over to the bed, where the fellow I had saved was all covered in bandages.

"I'm told that I owe you my life," he said weakly.

"All in a day's work," I said, "me being a servant of the Lord and all."

"Well, your intervention was divinely inspired," he said. He reached out a hand to me. "My name is Geoffrey Bainbridge."

"The Right Reverend Doctor Lucifer Jones, at your service," I replied, taking his hand kind of gingerly. "Just out of idle curiosity, Brother Bainbridge, what in tarnation were you doing, alone and unarmed, in tiger country?"

"It's a complicated tale of desire and deceit, Doctor Jones," he said.

"That's my very favorite kind of tale, Brother Bainbridge," I said. "Take all the desire and deceit out of the Good Book and you wouldn't have more than a handful of chapters left."

"It all revolves around the Flame of Bharatpur," he said.

"Yeah?"

"Maybe I should begin at the beginning," he said. "I'm a bachelor, Doctor Jones. Some months ago, while judging a livestock show, I made the acquaintance of Lady Edith Quilton, the widow of Lord Randolph Quilton, who owns the largest estate in all of Rajasthan. We struck up a friendship, and shared many an afternoon tea together, and finally I proposed marriage to her.'' He paused. ''I shall be perfectly honest with you, Doctor Jones. While I enjoy her company and admire her adventurous spirit, the real reason I wanted to marry her was to gain possession of the Flame of Bharatpur.''

''I take it this Flame of Bharatpur is worth a bundle of money?'' I said.

''The Flame of Bharatpur is perfection itself,'' he said. Suddenly he frowned. ''But even as I was pressing my suit, another gentleman entered her life.''

''He wanted the Flame of Bharatpur, too?'' I asked.

''He wants everything she owns,'' replied Bainbridge. ''She is quite the wealthiest woman in the province, and he is a low, deceitful fortune hunter.''

Well, truth to tell, I couldn't see much difference between a selective fortune hunter and a generalized one, but I just sat there and listened to Bainbridge pour out his story.

''We disliked one another at first sight, although we continued to behave in a civilized manner toward each other. But things reached a head this morning. Lady Edith organized a tiger hunt, and I found myself sharing a howdah with this villain. Feigning enthusiasm, he drove our elephant far ahead of the others, and when the beaters flushed a tiger, he grabbed my rifle and pushed me out of the howdah, racing off and leaving me to face the tiger's charge unarmed and on foot. The brute knocked me down and raked me with its claws, and was about to finish me off when you providentially arrived.'' He leaned his head back against the pillow, all wore out from telling his story. ''And now, although I owe my life to you and can never repay you, I must nevertheless ask you one last favor, Doctor Jones.''

''What did you have in mind, Brother Bainbridge?'' I asked, just kind of figuring to humor him until he drifted off to sleep.

''I realize that it was wrong of me to propose a loveless marriage simply to gain possession of the Flame of Bharatpur,'' he said. ''But I cannot leave poor Edith to the mercies of her current suitor, and I will be in no condition to confront him for weeks or possibly even months. *You* must prevent that filthy fortune hunter from possessing the Flame of Bharatpur, even if it means marrying her yourself.''

"Well, now, that's a right interesting proposition, Brother Bainbridge," I said. "And now that I come to mull on it, I can see that it's my Christian duty to save this poor woman from such a scoundrel, even if it means I got to spend the rest of my life helping her manage her fortune rather than bringing the word of the Lord to these poor deprived brown heathen."

"Then you'll do it?" he said.

"Brother Bainbridge," I said, "it's as good as done."

"You are truly one of Nature's noblemen," he said, and suddenly he was sound asleep, and I kind of tiptoed out of his room before he could wake up and change his mind, and a couple of minutes later me and Akbar were headed off to Lady Edith's estate on the edge of town.

I didn't know her exact address, but when I came to a house that was just a little bit smaller than Buckingham Palace and had even nicer gardens, I knew I'd hit paydirt, so to speak. I figured Akbar might prove to be a bit of a social handicap, especially since he'd recently developed a taste for flowers, so I pointed him down the road, wished him well, and took my leave of him. Last I saw of him he was just vanishing over the top of a small hill, and with no one to tell him to stop, I figured he'd keep going until he hit the Indian Ocean, by which time he could probably use a little seaside vacation.

Then I wandered up the long, winding driveway and knocked on the front door. A couple of Indians, dressed all in white, let me in, and one of them escorted me to the drawing room while the other went and fetched Lady Edith. While I was waiting for her I decided to take a look around and see just what I was marrying into. I knew right off that Lady Edith liked the ballet, because there were a bunch of paintings of ballerinas hanging on the wall, all done by some Frenchman, and I could see that her late husband had an eye for the ladies, because there were also a few paintings of half-naked island girls by yet another French-man, which were so racy I would have thought she'd toss 'em out once her husband departed this mortal coil, but I couldn't see no signs of conspicuous wealth until I noticed a little glass case in the corner. I walked over to it and there, setting on a little gold pedestal, was the biggest, reddest ruby I ever did see, and I knew right off that this had to be the Flame of Bharatpur that all the fuss was about.

I heard a little feminine cough behind me, and turned to find myself facing a vigorous-looking woman of about fifty years. She was decked out in riding togs, and she held a leather crop in her hand.

"Just admiring your taste in gemstones, ma'am," I said. "You must be Lady Edith."

"I'm afraid you have the advantage of me, Mr. . . . ?"

"Reverend, ma'am," I said. "The Right Reverend Doctor Lucifer Jones at your service, fresh from risking life and limb to save Geoffrey Bainbridge from a tiger attack."

"My goodness!" she said. "Is he all right?"

"The doctors say he'll be up and around in a couple of months," I said.

"How did it happen?"

"Well, it's a long story, ma'am, and being the modest Christian gentleman that I am I hate to set myself up as a fearless hero what dragged poor Geoffrey from the jaws of death and dispatched a tiger with my bare hands, so it's probably best left untold." I paused. "I do bring a message from him, though."

"What is it?" she asked.

"Due to the delicate nature of one of his injuries, he regrets to inform you that he's no longer on the marriage market, and he hopes you'll understand and won't think no less of him for it."

"The poor man!" she said. "We wondered what happened to him when he didn't show up for lunch after the hunt."

"He was probably preoccupied with bleeding to death at the time," I said. "It was just a stroke of providence that I came by when I did."

"You must tell me all about it," she said.

"Well, I'd enjoy doing so, Lady Edith, but Geoffrey ain't the only one what missed out on lunch, and I think now that I've delivered his tragic message to you, I'd best be getting back to town to hunt up some grub.''

"Nonsense," she said. "You will have dinner here, with us, Reverend Jones. It's the very least I can do for such a noble and courageous man.''

"Well, I'd surely like to, Lady Edith," I said, "but I also ain't got no place to stay, and I'd better scare me up a room before all the hotels are sold out for the night.''

"I won't hear of it," she said. "I'll have my servants make up a room for you right now.''

"I couldn't impose on you like that, ma'am," I protested. "Even though I give all my money to the poor, I usually hold enough back to rent a cot in some flophouse.''

"You're staying here, and that's all there is to it," she said firmly.

Well, I spent a couple of more minutes letting her argue me into it, and then I went up to my room and freshened up a bit. When my stomach told me that it was dinnertime, I opened the door and started walking down the hall to the big winding staircase that led to the main floor and the dining room, when I bumped into a familiar-looking figure coming out of his own room.

"Doctor Jones!" said Rupert Cornwall. "What the hell are you doing here?"

"Howdy, Brother Rupert," I greeted him. "You still on the run from Inspector Willie Wong?"

He put a finger to his lips. "I must ask you to be more discreet," he said, which I took to be an affirmative.

"No problem at all, Brother Rupert," I said. "But just out of curiosity, what's Hong Kong's most notorious criminal kingpin doing hiding out in Lady Edith's house?"

He grabbed me by the shoulder and pulled me into his room, then closed the door behind us. "I'm not hiding out, Doctor Jones," he said. "In point of fact, I'm here to press my suit upon her.''

"Sounds painful," I said. "Wouldn't an ironing board do just as well?"

"You misunderstand," said Rupert. "I'm courting Lady Edith."

"So *you're* the guy who pushed Geoffrey Bainbridge out of the howdah," I said.

"How did you know that?" he demanded.

"I happened along just in time to save him from getting et by a tiger."

"You mean he's here right now?" asked Rupert, a kind of wild look about his eyes.

"No, he'll be indisposed for the next couple of months."

Rupert kind of chuckled at that. "Good!" he said. "I'll have her married long before then."

"Well, now, I sure wouldn't count on it, Brother Rupert," I said.

He stared at me kind of suspiciously. "Why not?"

"You might say that another player just entered the game," I answered.

"You?" he sneered. "You haven't got a chance with her."

"Well, that remains to be seen, don't it?" I said.

"I want you to know that I resent your intrusion, Doctor Jones," he said. "I'm the one who found this setup. I think it's very unfair of you to come along now and try to horn in after I've laid all the romantic groundwork."

"Before you get to feeling too righteous, Brother Rupert," I said, "let me remind you that I'd still be in Hong Kong spending our ill-gotten gains if some criminal kingpin had played square with me."

"That was just business," he said innocently. "Surely a man of the world like yourself doesn't hold that against me."

"*This* is just business too, Brother Rupert," I said. "I'll make you a deal, though: I won't tell her how and where we met if you don't."

"I agree," he said. "And may the best man win."

"Especially if he's a handsome, God-fearing Christian missionary," I added.

We left his room then and went down the stairs to dinner, where we were joined by Lady Edith and maybe a dozen other house guests, most of them titled and all of them very old and very British. Afterward I recounted how I had pulled this raging tiger off poor Geoffrey Bainbridge's torn and tattered body and choked the life out of it, and when Lady Edith insisted that I stay over for a week or two, I shot Rupert a triumphant grin and figured that the Flame of Bharatpur was as good as mine.

We were up bright and early the next morning, and Lady Edith offered to show me around the place. She was dressed in her walking britches, and looking vigorous as all get-out, and she set a mighty fast pace, pointing out all her various flowers that had won prizes in flower shows. Then we visited the stables, and I saw her prize-winning horses, and after that we went to the kennels, where I saw her prize-winning dogs, and by the time we got to the barn to look at her prize-winning cattle and her prize-winning pigs I began to get the impression that Lady Edith was more than a little bit on the competitive side.

"I show them all over the Continent," she said, pointing to a pair of bulls who were snorting to beat the band and looked like they wanted nothing more than a matador breakfast. "This one even took a first in England last year before I imported him."

One of the pigs started squealing, and she walked over and petted him. "This is Sylvester, my pride and joy," she confided to me. "He's won prizes in five different countries."

Well, I looked at Sylvester, and Sylvester looked at me, and all I could think was that he'd go mighty well with fried eggs and maybe some hash-brown potatoes, but I didn't want to offend Lady Edith, so I allowed that Sylvester was about the prettiest pig I'd ever seen. That seemed to satisfy her, and we moved along past the ducks and the chickens, most of which had blue ribbons tacked up next to their coops, and finally we finished the tour and returned to the house. "It's such a lovely day, why don't we have breakfast on the terrace?" she suggested.

Well, that suited me fine, since it meant I wouldn't have to share her company with my rival, and I followed her to a glass table with an umbrella over it. We sat down, and a couple of servants appeared from nowhere to serve us tea and little biscuits, and then they vanished again, and just as I was trying to figure out the best way to start charming her, she turned to me and reached her hand out for mine.

"I'm so glad you decided to stay, Lucifer," she said.

Well, I'd had ladies fall in love with me before, but never quite that fast, and I figured this was going to be even easier than I'd thought.

"Well, that's perfectly understandable, you being the vigorous and attractive woman you are, in the prime of life so to speak, and me being a dashing Christian gentleman of noble mind and bold spirit."

"You are the answer to my prayers," she continued.

"Yeah?" I said, wondering whether to pop the question now or wait a respectable amount of time, like maybe another five minutes. "Tell me about 'em."

"I've been so worried, what with all the tigers in the area," she said.

"Tigers?" I said, surprised. "Who in tarnation is talking about tigers?"

"*We* are," she replied. "That's why I'm so thrilled that you're here, Lucifer. As long as there are tigers in the area, all of my prize livestock is at risk, and to be perfectly honest, Mr. Cornwall, while a fine and thoughtful gentleman, really isn't the sort to comb the countryside looking for tigers—whereas you, the man who killed the tiger that attacked Geoffrey Bainbridge with your bare hands . . ."

"Well, it wasn't quite with my bare hands," I interrupted her uneasily.

"Don't be so modest, Lucifer," she said. "One of the local natives found and skinned the tiger, and the shopkeeper who bought the pelt said that there wasn't a bullet hole or even a knife wound anywhere on it." She paused and stared at me. "Will you agree to lead a tiger hunt this afternoon?"

"I'd sure like to, ma'am," I said, "but usually I set afternoons aside for prayer and meditation, me being a man of the cloth and all."

"Couldn't you forego your meditation this one time, Lucifer?" she said. "You would have my undying gratitude."

Well, it wasn't quite the same as her undying love, but it was a step in the right direction, and besides, I suddenly had a notion of how to impress the bejabbers out of her and make Rupert Cornwall look feeble by comparison.

"Well, God is a pretty understanding critter," I said. "I suppose He wouldn't mind if I took an afternoon off to clear up your tiger problem."

"Thank you," she said with a great big smile.

"Of course, you understand that I don't make a point of rasslin' tigers hand-to-hand," I continued. "It takes too much time, and it's right hard on my clothes."

"We have all the guns you could possibly need," she assured me. "I can supply you with beaters, trackers, gunbearers, elephants, anything you want."

"Well, I thank you for the offer, ma'am," I said, "but I couldn't risk the lives of the very heathen that I came to India to save. No, I think it'd be best if I just go out alone and match my wits and skills with the fearsome beasts of the jungle."

"What a remarkable man you are, Lucifer!" she said. "I didn't know such brave, adventurous spirits still existed!"

"That's because you been associating with men like Rupert Cornwall too long," I said. "Nature ain't run totally out of noblemen just yet."

"You may just have a point, Lucifer," she said, and I figured that I had just pulled ahead of Rupert right then and there.

Well, I spent the rest of the morning loafing around, and by noontime most of Lady Edith's guests were up and around, and even Rupert wandered downstairs looking for a little grub, so we all had lunch together while Lady Edith told 'em what a brave and fearless deed I was about to do on her behalf, and I modestly explained that it wasn't nothing special and indeed was all part of a day's work for a Christian gentleman of high moral standards what was intent on serving his fellow man, or woman as the case happened to be.

Rupert just kept looking at me like I was crazy, but everyone else was right impressed, and when it came time for me to pick up a gun and head out the door, all of the guests came up and hugged me one by one, which was a most fortuitous thing since it enabled me to lift a couple of the old gentlemen's wallets. Once I got outside I pulled about five hundred pounds out of 'em, then went back and announced that I was feeling mighty lucky this afternoon and thought I'd probably better take some extra ammunition along. We all hugged each other again, which allowed me to replace the wallets, and then I was out the door and walking boldly into the wild fields that surrounded Lady Edith's estate.

I walked for nearly a mile, and when I was sure no one was following me I took a hard right and headed off to Jaipur. It took me the better part of an hour to get there, and once I arrived I went right up to the first Indian I saw on the street and asked him where the local taxidermist was. He pointed out a shop down the block, and I went over to it and opened the door.

"Good afternoon on you, Sahib," said a pudgy Indian with a neat little beard. "How may I be at your service?"

"I'm in the market for tiger skins," I said. "You got any for sale?"

"How many do you want?" he asked.

"I dunno," I replied. "How many have you got?"

"You come back and see," he said, escorting me through a door to his workshop.

Well, there were skins galore back there, everything from tigers to leopards to deer to what-have-you, along with a fair sampling of elephant tusks and rhinoceros horns. He pulled out a tigerskin rug and held it up for me.

"Very nice rug, very nice price, Sahib," he said. "Forty pounds."

"I don't want no rugs," I said. "Just skins."

He ran over to another pile and held up a skin. "Beautiful tiger skin, this one, Sahib. The notorious Maneater of Dindori. For you, twenty-five pounds."

"What about those over there?" I asked, pointing to a pile of skins that had flies buzzing around them.

He shook his head. "Oh, you do not want these, Sahib," he said. "I have not had time to prepare them yet. They just arrived this week."

"How many of 'em are there?" I asked.

"Seven."

"Tell you what," I said. "I'll take 'em all off your hands for fifty pounds apiece."

His jaw dropped so far I thought it was going to hit the floor. Then he gave me a great big smile and nodded his head.

"You drive a hard bargain, Sahib," he said. "But what is a poor shopkeeper to do?"

"I'll tell you what he's to do," I said.

"Sahib?" he said, looking kind of puzzled.

"For another hundred and fifty pounds, he's to keep his mouth shut about this little transaction."

For just a minute there I had the feeling that he was going to get down on his knees and kiss my feet, but he showed admirable restraint and a few minutes later I had loaded all seven skins into a cart he loaned me and started back toward Lady Edith's estate.

When I was maybe three miles away I made a big semicircle and wound up in the fields where Akbar had accidentally saved Geoffrey Bainbridge's life the day before, and I took my rifle and fired seven quick shots into the air. Then I sat down and smoked a cigar, hid the cart in the woods, and started lugging the tiger skins up to Lady Edith's house.

Just about the time I hove into view a bunch of her servants ran out to greet me, screaming and cheering wildly, and took the skins from me, and then all the guests started yelling "Hip hip hooray!" and Lady Edith ran up and planted a great big kiss on me, and Rupert looked like if someone had given him a shovel he'd have dug a hole and crawled right into it.

About an hour later we all sat down for dinner, and I recounted the story about how I'd wiped out all the tigers in the neighborhood, adding a number of properly heroic embellishments, and Lady Edith couldn't take her eyes off me, and everyone kept asking me to tell it over and over again, and Rupert just sat and looked like something he'd et had disagreed kind of violently with him.

We adjourned to the drawing room, where I gave 'em a few last thrilling details of the hunt, and then they started heading off to their bedrooms, and Lady Edith gave me another kiss and shook Rupert's hand goodnight, and finally I didn't have no one left to tell my story to, so I went up to my room.

I hadn't been there more than a minute or two when Rupert came in and closed the door behind him.

"All right, Doctor Jones," he said. "I don't know how you did it, but you've managed to turn her head. Temporarily."

"Well, it's mighty decent of you to acknowledge that, Brother Rupert," I said.

"I didn't come here to flatter you," said Rupert. "I came here to talk business. What will it take to buy you off?"

"What makes you think I want to be bought off?" I asked.

"Why spend the rest of your life in a loveless marriage when I can make you independently wealthy?" he said.

"Ain't that what *you* plan to do?" I replied.

"That's beside the point," said Rupert. "Name your price."

"Okay," I said, after mulling on it for a minute or two. "I want the Flame of Bharatpur."

He looked at me kind of funny-like. "That's *it*?" he asked.

"Well, not quite," I said. "I hate farewell scenes with love-crazed women, so I'm going to leave tonight while everyone's asleep, and I want you to give her a note from me saying that I was called away because my wife is having a baby, which should help ease her sorrow. I'll take the Flame of Bharatpur with me on the way out."

"That's impossible," he said. "She has guards posted everywhere. There's no way you can take the Flame tonight without being caught out."

"Well," I said, "then I guess I'll just have to stick around and marry her."

"No, wait," said Rupert, lowering his head in thought for a minute. Finally he looked up. "I'll tell you what. Leave in the middle of the night like you planned, and go to Geoffrey Bainbridge's house. I'll remove the Flame of Bharatpur tomorrow when security isn't so tight, and have it delivered there before dark."

"I trust in human nature as much as any man," I said, "but I'd rest a mite easier if you'd write me a letter saying that you gave me the Flame of Bharatpur in exchange for ending my courtship of Lady Edith. Just in case something happens to the Flame in the meantime.''

Well, he hemmed and hawed, but finally he sat down and wrote the letter, and I jotted down a note to Lady Edith, and a few hours later I was walking down the road to the hospital, which I reached just after daylight. They didn't want to let Bainbridge out, but when I told him that the Flame of Bharatpur was being delivered to his house that day nothing they could say could make him stay there, and finally his chauffeur drove up and packed us into the car.

"I can't believe you got the Flame of Bharatpur in just one day!" said Bainbridge as we drove down the road toward his house.

"Well, it's our little secret," I said, after I'd told him the deal I'd made with Rupert Cornwall. "Lady Edith don't know nothing about it yet."

"I fully understand," he replied. "What I plan to do is keep the Flame against the day when she regains her senses and sends the rascal packing."

"That's all well and good for you," I said, "but what about *me*? After all, I'm the one who got Rupert to part with it."

"You will not go unrewarded, Doctor Jones."

"Good," I said. "Because I figure half of the Flame of Bharatpur belongs to me, and that probably translates into three or four million pounds on the open market."

He turned and stared at me. "Are you crazy?" he said.

"Okay," I said agreeably. "I forgot there's a depression on. I'll settle for a million."

We reached Bainbridge's house, and suddenly the car screeched to a halt just before it ran into a pig that was munching some flowers at the edge of the driveway.

"Looks like Rupert ain't been here yet," I said, but I suddenly found I was talking to an empty seat, because Geoffrey Bainbridge had gotten out of the car and was kneeling, bandages and all, next to the pig, running his hand lovingly over its head.

"Nice Sylvester," he was crooning. "Sweet Sylvester."

"You know," I said, climbing out of the car, "Lady Edith's

got a pig called Sylvester that looks just like this one. Ain't that a striking coincidence?''

"This is him," said Bainbridge.

"Yeah? What's he doing here?"

"It means that Rupert Cornwall kept his word."

"What are you talking about?" I demanded.

"Sylvester," he said. "Champion The Flame of Bharatpur. He's won prizes in five different countries. Isn't he gorgeous?"

"The Flame of Bharatpur is a *pig*?"

"He's not merely a pig," said Bainbridge. "He is the greatest swine I have ever seen!"

Well, right at that moment I had my own opinions about the greatest swine I had ever seen, and Rupert Cornwall and Geoffrey Bainbridge were running neck-and-neck for the award. I couldn't go back and rekindle my romance with Lady Edith, because by now she'd read my note, and I didn't see Sylvester bringing no multi-million-dollar price on the black market even if I could convince Bainbridge to part with him, and I'd spent every penny I had on tiger skins, so I decided then and there that I would take Bainbridge's reward and go to some country where folks wasn't so all-fired deceitful and an honest man of God could build a tabernacle and finally get around to doing some serious preaching.

9
The Scorpion Lady

I'd pretty much had my fill of India, and I figured that I'd use Bainbridge's reward to get as far away from it as I could. It turned out that his notion of "generous" and mine differed considerably, and when the dust had cleared I found I only had enough money to fly to Siam.

I landed in Bangkok, found out that most of the white folks stayed at the Oriental Hotel, checked into a room there, and then set out to find some sinners that were more in need of redemption than most.

This led me to the Lumpini Stadium, where they were holding their nightly kick-boxing tournament, and when I heard that one of the combatants was named Moses I figured it was a signal from my Silent Partner and I put all my remaining money on him with one of the local bookmakers, and sure enough Moses kicked the bejabbers out of his opponent, and suddenly I had about six hundred dollars in my pocket, and I figured as long as God was looking over my shoulder there was no reason why I shouldn't let my money keep working for me.

A couple of discreet inquiries led me to the Scorpion Club a few blocks away. It had an exotic-looking doorway, and inside there was a long bar, a bunch of itinerant belly dancers, and a few gaming tables, and before trying my luck I decided to slake my thirst on something with just enough alcohol to kill any germs I might have picked up during the day.

"Good evening, Father," said a voice at my left, and I turned to see that a nattily dressed Englishman had sat down next to me.

"It's Reverend," I said. "The Reverend Lucifer Jones, at your service."

"Reginald McCorkle," he said, extending his hand. "It's very rare that one meets a man of the cloth in these surroundings."

"Trolling for sinners is a lot like trolling for fish," I explained. "You got to go where they congregate."

"Makes sense, at that," he agreed. "Will you allow me to buy you a drink?"

"I suppose I could hold my natural generosity in check long enough to accept your kind offer," I allowed. "You work around here, Brother McCorkle?"

He nodded. "And yourself?"

"I just stepped off the plane this afternoon," I said.

"You're staying at the Oriental, I presume?"

"Yeah," I said. "It's a nice enough temporary residence, until I decide where to build my tabernacle."

"It's about three miles away from here," he noted. "How did you happen to find this place?"

"It was highly recommended as a prime source of lost souls," I answered.

I was about to tell him about the kick-boxing, but just then the door opened and the most beautiful lady I ever did see walked in. She was Eurasian, and dressed in a slinky black gown, and she was wearing a necklace made of enormous pink pearls, and she had a huge jeweled scorpion pinned to her dress right between her lungs, and she had so many rings on her fingers that I figured it must have kept a diamond mine working all year around just supplying the stones for them. She glanced at me and Reginald McCorkle for just a second, and then walked over to a staircase and up to the second floor.

"Close your mouth, Reverend Jones," said McCorkle. "You never know what might fly into it in a place like this."

"I don't want to cut short an enjoyable conversation, Brother Reginald," I said, "but I think I've just been smitten by Cupid's capricious arrow."

"She does have that effect on people," said McCorkle.

"You know her?" I asked.

"I think just about everyone in Siam knows her, or at least knows *of* her," he replied.

"What's her name?"

"She has more names than you can shake a stick at," said McCorkle. "In this part of the world she's known as the Scorpion Lady."

"She gets around a lot, does she?" I asked.

"Quite a lot."

"Good," I said. "We can compare travel notes once we get to know each other."

"You don't want to get to know her, Reverend Jones," continued McCorkle. "She's the most dangerous woman in all of Southeast Asia."

"A pretty little lady like that?" I said disbelievingly.

He nodded. "She runs the biggest smuggling operation in Siam, and is probably responsible for half the murders in Bangkok. She's so powerful that even the notorious Doctor Aristotle Ho gives her territory a wide berth."

"So what you're saying is that she's probably *not* responsible for half the murders in Bangkok," I said, trying to look on the bright side.

"She owns this club," added McCorkle. "It's her headquarters whenever she's in the country."

"How do *you* know all this, Brother Reginald?" I asked him.

"It's common knowledge. Ask anyone—or read a newspaper."

"Well, I thank you for all this advice," I said, "and for the drink as well, but my heart's been overcome by the siren song of true love."

"I warn you, Reverend," he said. "She's more than just a pretty face."

"I know," I said. "She's got one of the finest sets of lungs it's ever been my rare privilege to encounter."

I figured any further conversation would just delay me, so I took my leave of him then and headed over to the stairway, and when no one tried to stop me, I climbed up to the second floor.

There was a door opposite the stairs with a light coming out from under it, so I walked up to it and knocked.

"Enter," said the most melodious voice I ever heard, and I pushed the door open.

She was sitting in front of a mirror, kind of admiring herself, which is just what I'd have done if I was her, and suddenly she spotted me in the mirror and turned to face me. "Who are you?" she demanded.

"I'm the Right Reverend Honorable Doctor Lucifer Jones, Miss Scorpion Lady, ma'am, and I've come to tell you that you are the most beautiful sight to grace my eyes since I landed on this continent some four years ago, and also to inquire delicately as to your current marital status."

She just stared at me for a minute without saying a word. Then she smiled. "How flattering, Doctor Jones."

"Ma'am, you got a voice like unto a symphony," I said. "Every word is a thing of undying beauty."

"Won't you have a seat, Doctor Jones?" said the Scorpion Lady.

"Thank you, ma'am, I sure will," I said, plopping myself down on a dainty little chair that had all kinds of mother-of-pearl designs inset in it. "And you can call me Lucifer."

"Thank you, Lucifer," she said. "And you may call me the Scorpion Lady."

"Just as a nonsequitur, ma'am, ain't it scorpions that eat their husbands at a most indelicate point in their connubial relationship?"

"No, those are black widow spiders, Lucifer," she replied. "Why?"

"Oh, no reason in particular, ma'am," I said. "I was just kind of curious why such a gorgeous little lady with a face like an angel and a tiny waistline and all other kinds of attributes would call herself the Scorpion Lady while some real high-class names like Fifi and Fatima are going begging."

"I have a passion for scorpions," she replied. "As you can see, most of my jewelry is shaped into facsimiles of them."

"And mighty fine jewelry it is, ma'am," I said, "though it pales into insignificance compared to your own beauty."

"I do believe you are trying to make me blush, Lucifer," she said with a smile.

"I ain't never seen an Oriental lady blush before," I answered. "It might be a pretty interesting and educational experience."

"Some other time," she said.

"Your wish is my command," I said. "You just name that other time and I'll be here with bells on."

"Why in the world would you want to wear bells?" she asked.

"That's just a figure of speech, ma'am," I explained. "Actually, what I'm trying to say is that you've won me over heart and soul."

"What if I don't *want* you, heart and soul?" she asked.

"That ain't my problem, ma'am," I said. "I had enough trouble just finding you and falling in love. I don't hardly see that making *you* fall in love too can rightly be considered my responsibility."

"You have an interesting notion of romancing a woman, Lucifer," she said.

"I'm just here to announce my feelings and intentions," I said. "The romancing comes a little later, after I've run my bankroll up at your tables downstairs. Though," I added, "if you want to get a head start on the romancing, I got no serious objections to that. I could bring us up a couple of beers and lock the door behind me."

"I'm afraid I'm a bit busy right now."

"No problem," I said. "I can come back in an hour or two, after you've slipped into something more comfortable, like maybe the bedroom."

"Is this the way you sweep them off their feet in America?" she asked with a smile.

"Well, truth to tell, ma'am, I ain't been back to America in quite some time, and I ain't never encountered an American girl with your virtues. Or if she had 'em, they sure as hell weren't in the same places."

"I assume that's a compliment," she said.

"No, ma'am," I said. "It's a statement of absolute fact. I know you got your detractors here in Bangkok, but I ain't one of 'em."

"Oh?" she said. "And who *are* my detractors?"

"Well, one of 'em is an English feller named Reginald McCorkle, who was buying me drinks down in the bar until I was smitten by your rare and exotic beauty."

"What did Reginald McCorkle tell you?"

"Nothing important," I said. "Probably he just wants you for himself, which is an understandable but unacceptable position."

She stared at me for a long moment, while I stared right back, my attention kind of torn betwixt her jewelry and her lungs.

"You are the most interesting man I have encountered in years, Lucifer," she said at last. "I do believe I shall let you pay court to me."

"I *knew* you couldn't say no to a good-looking young buck like me!" I said happily. "And being as how I'm a man of the cloth, it'll likely do wonders for your reputation too."

"There are a few ground rules we have to agree to, Lucifer," she said.

I wasn't aware that sex had any different ground rules in Siam than anywhere else in the world, but I perked up and paid attention, just so I wouldn't break no local taboos and wind up in the hoosegow while the Scorpion Lady wasted away grieving after me.

"I do not tolerate any competition," she said. "If you make a commitment to me, you make it willingly and totally."

"You got it," I said. "Should I get the drinks now?"

"I'm not finished," she said. "I also pledge to make a total commitment. If we are to become romantically involved, everything I have is yours." She paused. "That includes my nightclub, my house, my business interests, everything."

"I suppose I could adjust to that," I allowed.

"From this moment on, you are a full partner, Lucifer," she said. "In fact, I think that, starting tomorrow morning, I will turn my import-export business over to you."

"Well, that's mighty generous of you, Scorpion Lady," I said. "And I promise you won't be sorry you done it."

She got to her feet. "As I said, I have business to attend to tonight, but why don't you come back at, shall we say, six o'clock in the morning?"

"I'll bring my toothbrush, my pajamas, and me," I promised.

She walked me to the door, then grabbed me and gave me one of the more memorable kisses I'd ever got from a gorgeous lady smuggler, and then I was out in the hall and I heard the door lock behind me.

I climbed down the stairs, and walked over to the bar for a celebratory drink, and found Reginald McCorkle still sitting there.

"Well?" he said.

"Brother Reginald," I said, "you were dead wrong. She's the sweetest, prettiest, friendliest flower in all of Siam's gardens."

"I take it you hit it off with her?"

"You might say that."

"It's too bad," he said.

"You may have seen her first," I said, "but I spoke up first. Try to be a good loser, Brother Reginald."

"I don't plan to be any kind of loser at all, Reverend," he replied.

"You're too late," I said. "She's head over heels in love with me."

He pulled out his wallet and flashed a couple of official-looking cards at me. "Do you know what this means?" he said.

"It means you're a civil service employee," I answered.

"Read it carefully, Reverend Jones," he said. "I work for the British Embassy in Siam. We've been after the Scorpion Lady for three years."

"That ain't none of my concern," I said.

"I hope to make it your concern," he said. "I want to enlist your help."

"Out of the question, Brother Reginald," I said. "I love her wth a mad and all-encompassing passion."

"I just want you to consider it."

"Never," I said. "She's the heart of my heart and soul of my soul."

"I should add that there's a million-pound reward for any information leading to her capture and conviction," he said.

"On the other hand, she's just a woman," I said. "I can always get more."

He grinned. "I knew I could appeal to your better nature. When are you seeing her again?"

"Six in the morning."

"I'll tell you what," he said. "I'll be waiting in that little restaurant across the street. As soon as you leave here, come over and we'll discuss what you've learned."

Well, I figured the best he could expect was a lecture on whatever Oriental love techniques I learned, but I agreed to meet with him, and then I started walking back to the hotel, but a couple of ladies of the evening stopped me and struck up a conversation, and I decided that by the time I got to the hotel I'd just have to turn around and walk right back to the Black Scorpion, and besides I couldn't see that my pledge of eternal fidelity officially took effect until six in the morning, so one thing kind of led to another, and I left their company at about five o'clock, feeling mightily refreshed and ready to seize the day at such time as it should make an appearance.

I was banging away at the door to the Black Scorpion at six on the dot, and the Scorpion Lady clambered down the stairs and let me in.

"Here I am in all my masculine glory," I told her. "You ready to play Romeo and Juliet, or have you got something more exotic and Oriental in mind?"

"Ah, Lucifer," she said sadly, "I wish that I had time to introduce you to the more esoteric delights of the flesh, but we have a business to run. It will simply have to wait."

"It will?" I said.

She nodded. "You are in charge of my import-export business, remember?" she said.

"I had in mind something more in the way of importing a little ecstasy to you and exporting the memories of a brief but happy encounter with me when I left here," I said.

"Tonight," she promised me. "But for now, you have work to do."

"Tonight for sure?"

"For sure," she said.

"Okay," I said. "What do I have to do?"

"In the alley behind the Black Scorpion you will find an empty truck with the keys in the ignition,'' she said. ''I want you to take it to the Acme Fertilizer Company on Phaya Tai Road and pick up a shipment from them.''

''A shipment of what?''

''Fertilizer, of course,'' she said. ''Then drive to the river and pull up to the Scorpion Freight Company.''

''And then what?'' I asked.

She smiled. ''That's all. Just leave the truck there and come home. They'll unload it and return it tonight.''

''Let me get this straight,'' I said. ''I pick up a load of fertilizer from Acme, I drive it over to your shipping company, and that's *everything*?''

''That's right.''

''Son of a gun,'' I said. ''I thought there was more to running a million-dollar business than that. I'll be here by noontime.''

''*You* may be,'' she said, ''but I won't be back until nine in the evening. I'll be waiting for you then.''

''You won't have long to wait,'' I promised her.

''All right,'' she said, starting to shut the door. ''I'll see you then, Lucifer.''

''As long as I got all day, I don't suppose there's no harm in my going across the street and grabbing a little breakfast first,'' I said.

''None at all,'' she said. ''Until tonight, my love.''

''Till tonight, my . . . uh . . . scorpion,'' I replied, and then I moseyed across the street and sat myself down at a table. Reginald McCorkle pulled up a chair a minute later.

''Well?'' he said.

''I got to pick up a shipment of fertilizer at the Acme Fertilizer Company and deliver it to the Scorpion Freight Company,'' I told him.

''When?'' he asked.

''No particular time,'' I said. ''Long as I deliver it before dark, there ain't no problem.''

''That's it?'' he said. ''No other pick-ups, no stops in between?''

''That's it.''

"Then we've got her!" he exclaimed. "You'll drive directly to Acme, fill up the truck by seven o'clock, and then take it to a secret warehouse that I've leased on Set Siri Road. We'll have almost ten hours to discover what she's smuggling before you have to drive to her freight office. This is the break we've been waiting for, Reverend Jones!"

"I got a special request, Brother Reginald," I said.

"What is it?"

"Whatever we find, don't arrest her before midnight."

"Oh? Why not?"

"I got a romantic assignation arranged for nine o'clock tonight, and I'd hate to see the love of my life get marched off to the hoosegow without a chance at one last fling with a handsome and caring young man like myself."

"All right, Reverend Jones," he said. "It's a deal. We've been trying to arrest her for three years; I suppose an extra few hours won't make all that much difference. Now we'd best be started."

"After I eat breakfast," I said. "And since I'm working for the British Embassy, I think it's only fair and fitting that you pick up the check."

"All right, but be quick about it."

Well, so as not to cause him undue consternation, I ate a light breakfast consisting of nothing but orange juice and oatmeal and steak and eggs and hash browns and toast and biscuits and a few cups of coffee, and then I went into the alley behind the Black Scorpion and found this beautiful brand-new truck waiting for me. Sure enough, the keys were in the ignition, just like the Scorpion Lady had promised, and I drove out to Phaya Tai Road and cruised up and down it till I finally found the Acme Fertilizer Company. I backed up to one of their shipping docks, and before I could even tell 'em who I was or what I wanted, they began loading the truck up with bag after bag of fertilizer, and after about twenty minutes, when it was filled to the brim, they had me sign for it and then I was on my way again.

I spotted Reginald McCorkle's car waiting for me just outside the fertilizer factory, and I followed him to the warehouse he had leased on Set Siri Road, and pulled into it behind him. He closed the door and turned on the lights while I climbed out of the cab of the truck.

"What now?" I asked him.

"Now we start examining your cargo and see what she's trying to smuggle out of the country."

"Surely you got a staff to do that kind of menial labor, ain't you?" I asked.

"No," he said. "There was no one I could be sure I could trust. There's just you and me, Reverend." He unbuttoned his shirt cuffs and rolled up his sleeves. "Let's get to work."

We each pulled a bag of fertilizer out of the back of the truck, and he tossed me a knife.

"Open them very carefully along the tops," he said, "so that we can close them when we're through and no one will know that they've been examined."

I did as he said, and poured the contents out on the dirt floor.

"What have you got there?" he asked while working on his own bag.

"Looks like about fifty pounds of elephant shit to me," I said. "Smells like it, too."

"Sift through it carefully," he told me. "There could be a bag of drugs or diamonds in the very middle of it."

"Sift through it with *what*?" I asked.

"Your fingers, of course," he said, kneeling down and going to work on his own pile.

After five minutes we had both determined that the bags contained exactly what they were supposed to contain, and nothing else.

"Ah, she's a sly devil, that one!" said McCorkle, never losing his enthusiasm. "Probably only one or two bags contain the goods."

"You ain't seriously suggesting that after we pick all this stuff up and throw it back into the bags and seal 'em up that we do the same thing all over again with the other seventy or eighty bags?" I said.

"Do you know a better way?" he demanded.

"Not offhand," I said. "But that don't mean there ain't one."

"More work and less talk," he said, pulling another bag off the truck. "Just keep thinking of the reward."

Well, I spent the next five hours thinking of the reward, and the three hours after that thinking of a bath, and by the time four o'clock rolled around we had to admit that what I had in my truck was a few tons of elephant shit and nothing else.

"Probably this was just a test run," he said when we'd gotten 'em all loaded back into the truck. "Once you deliver it and show up back at the Black Scorpion, she'll know she can trust you. Tomorrow you'll pick up the real stuff. I'll be waiting for you in the restaurant again."

Well, I drove on down to the river, and spent about an hour hunting up the Scorpion Freight Company, and then I left the truck there like she had told me to, and walked the four or five miles back to my hotel. I'd done more lifting and working than I'd done in years, and I ached everywhere, and I took a long hot bath and finally stopped smelling like an elephant about halfway through it.

I showed up at the Black Scorpion club a little after nine, and dragged myself up the stairs to the Scorpion Lady's room.

"You look terrible, Lucifer," she said.

"It's been a long, hard day," I said. "We'll get around to the hanky-panky in a couple of minutes, but first I just gotta lie down here for a second."

I walked over to her bed and collapsed on it, and the next thing I knew she was shaking my shoulder and telling me that it was six in the morning and it was time to take the truck back to the Acme Fertilizer Company and make another pick-up.

I walked over to the restaurant, all bleary-eyed, had my usual modest breakfast with a little more coffee than usual, and an hour later Reginald McCorkle and me were sifting through another five tons of elephant shit, looking for the elusive contraband that the Scorpion Lady was smuggling out of the country. Once again we didn't find it.

Well, this went on for the better part of two weeks, us examining tons of elephant shit every day, and me falling sound asleep on the Scorpion Lady's bed every night before we could get around to consummating our romance, and just about the time I was ready to call it quits and give up on the reward and just spend the next few years enjoying a little pre-connubial bliss, she told me that I was all through going to Acme Fertilizer Company and would now be making my pick-ups at the Prime Fish Hatcheries.

"Excellent news!" said Reginald while I was eating my breakfast. "Now we're getting somewhere! I had thought that the first day was a test, but obviously she is a very careful woman. She sent you there fourteen days in a row before she knew she could trust you, and now we're finally going to pick up her contraband goods."

The truck was waiting for me in the alley, all cleaned and polished and looking like new, as usual, and I drove it over to the Prime Fish Hatcheries, where they loaded it up, and half an hour later me and Reginald were in his warehouse, looking at maybe twenty thousand dead fish.

"Damn, but she's a clever one!" he muttered.

"She is?"

"Obviously she's put the goods inside one or more of the fish, but only her contact can tell which ones. We'll just have to cut them open one by one until we come to whatever it is we're looking for."

Well, we spent ten hours looking through fish guts for diamonds or microfilms or opium, and mostly what we found were fish guts. I smelled worse than ever when I left the truck at her freight office and trudged back to the hotel, and it took longer than usual to wash all the odors away, and as a result I didn't have no time for dinner before I showed up at the Black Scorpion, and I was so tired and weak from hunger that this time I didn't even climb the stairs and fall asleep in her bed, but instead I sat down at the bar to catch my breath and the next thing I knew the sun was shining in and the Scorpion Lady was shaking me awake, and then I gobbled some breakfast and me and Reginald spent another day cutting fish open with no hint of success.

Two weeks later the Scorpion Lady told me to skip the Hatchery and go back to the Acme Fertilizer Company, and Reginald attacked the elephant shit with the same enthusiasm he had attacked it a month earlier. As for me, I was discovering that the life of a millionaire businessman wasn't all it was cracked up to be, and I made up my mind that the next morning at breakfast I was calling it quits and spending the next few years romancing the true love of my life.

That night I was so tired that I didn't even make it out of my hotel. I fell asleep in the tub, woke up when the water got cold, and barely made it to my bed before I fell asleep again. I got up at about five-thirty in the morning and hopped a cab over to the Black Scorpion. It was locked, and I figured the Scorpion Lady must have had a pretty hard night, too, because no matter how much I banged on the door nobody came down the stairs to let me in.

Finally I decided to go across the street and grab some breakfast and give Reginald my notice, but when I got there I couldn't spot him, so I just sat down and had the waiter bring me the usual.

I was just polishing off the last of my steak and eggs when a well-dressed Englishman walked over and sat down across from me.

"Are you Lucifer Jones?" he asked.

"The Right Reverend Doctor Lucifer Jones," I corrected him. "And who are you?"

"My name is Winston Spiggot," he said. "I work for the British Embassy."

"Did Reginald McCorkle send you?" I asked.

"Reginald McCorkle is in no position to send anyone anywhere," he replied. "In fact, even as we speak he is being sent home in black disgrace."

"You don't say," I said. "What all did he do?"

"He bungled his assignment and let the Scorpion Lady escape."

"Escape?" I said. "What are you talking about?"

"She fled the country during the night, when she got word that I had replaced McCorkle. I missed her by no more than an hour."

"I don't suppose she left no forwarding address?" I said, trying to soothe my broken heart.

"Don't be foolish, Doctor Jones," he said. "A number of

people at the Embassy wanted me to take you into custody, but as I see it you were simply an unwitting dupe.'' He paused. ''Nonetheless, you have caused us a great deal of trouble, and I think it might be best for all concerned were you also to leave Siam.''

''Well, with the love of my life on the lam, I can't see no compelling reason to stay here,'' I said. ''But I think you guys have got her figured all wrong. Me and Reginald went over every truckload of fertilizer and dead fish with a fine-tooth comb, and I guarantee she wasn't smuggling nothing out of the country.''

''Certainly she was,'' said Winston Spiggot. ''I wouldn't expect you to have figured it out, but McCorkle was a professional. He should have known.''

''What was it?'' I asked. ''Something in the fish or something in the elephant shit?''

''Neither.''

''You mean it was the fish and the fertilizer themselves?''

''Idiot!'' he said. ''You helped her smuggle twenty-nine brand-new armored trucks to Doctor Aristotle Ho's army!

It was with a heavy heart that I took a boat down the Chao Phraya River to the ocean that afternoon and hopped the next ship north for Japan, where I planned to forget the duplicitous love of my life in the arms of as many Geisha girls as my anguished soul and bankroll could mutually accommodate at one time.

10
The Other Master Detective

It took the ship the better part of five days to reach Japan, by which time I was more than happy to take my leave of it, especially since the cabin girl with whom I whiled away a couple of pleasant afternoons happened to have a brother on the crew who took an instant dislike to me for no discernible reason and spent half of the last evening hunting for me with a Samurai sword while I huddled in a lifeboat and counted off the last few hours until we hit shore.

Tokyo was one of the more crowded cities I ever saw. I've been mulling on it all these years now, and I think the reason is that they've got too many people crowding into too few streets, and if I ever go back I plan to tell the Emperor, or whoever's in charge these days, that it'd be a good idea to move some of 'em out to the suburbs.

Still, I was young and adventurous back then, and it didn't bother me none, because the more people there were, the more likely I was to find some who didn't mind sharing their money with an upstanding man of the cloth who was all ready to settle down and build his tabernacle and get to work on his life's calling.

There wasn't a lot of white folks in Japan in those days, and them that found themselves there split their loyalties between the Imperial Hotel and the Nikkatsu Hotel, and since the Nikkatsu was closer to the Ginza and had the biggest gaming room in town, I made a beeline toward it.

"Have you any luggage, Mr. Jones?" asked the desk clerk after I'd signed in.

"That's *Reverend* Jones, and no, I ain't got naught but the clothes on my back, me being a servant of God and all," I said.

"Then I am afraid I must ask if you can afford to pay for your room," he said.

I flashed him my six hundred dollars, which I hadn't touched since the kick-boxing matches in Siam, and he looked much relieved.

"Excellent, Reverend Jones," he said. "Will you be wanting a room with or without?"

"With or without what?" I asked.

"With or without a Geisha."

"With, I think," I said. "They tend to brighten up a room, don't you agree?"

He marked something down on my form. "Do you want a single or a double?"

"I didn't know Geishas came in different sizes," I replied. "I'll have to spend a moment or two considering it."

"I meant a single or a double room, Reverend Jones," said the desk clerk.

A single room sounded like I'd expend less energy chasing her around it, so that was what I asked for.

"Fine," he said. "A bellboy will be by to show you to your room in just a moment. And if you would like anything at all, just ask."

"Well, you might recommend a good restaurant," I said.

"I'd be happy to," he answered. "The Momonjiya, just across the street, specializes in monkey brains. If you find that too exotic for your taste, then go to the Taiko down the block."

"The Taiko, huh? What do *they* serve?"

"The sexual organs of oxen, highly spiced."

"Don't anyone around here cook no hamburgers?" I demanded.

He looked shocked. "Please, not so loud, Reverend Jones. We don't wish to offend the clientele."

Well, I'd kind of lost my appetite during the conversation

anyway, so I followed the bellhop to the staircase and up two flights to the third floor, where we walked down to the end of the hall, and he unlocked my door and kind of stood there jingling his change in his pocket, but since I hadn't had any luggage for him to tote I just laid my hand on his head and blessed him, and he walked off muttering to himself in Japanese.

I entered my room and took a look around. The bed wasn't much—it was a pile of silks on a wood board—but it beat the hell out of the furniture, which was more to look at than sit on. There was a knock at the door, and I figured it was the bellhop back to argue about the tip, but when I opened it the cutest little Geisha girl I ever set eyes on entered the room and minced over to the window.

"You have a beautiful view here," she said in a voice that was a lot deeper than anyone looking at her would have expected.

"Well, now that you're here, I got *two* beautiful views," I said. "What's your name, honey?"

"Miyoshi," she said, turning around and facing me.

"Well, that's a right pretty name," I said. "And you can call me Lucifer."

"Would you perhaps like a massage before your bath?" said Miyoshi.

I walked over to her. "How's about we indulge in a little mutual massaging?" I said.

I think I reached out to her to demonstrate what I meant, but things happened awfully fast then and it's kind of hard to remember. All I know is that about two seconds later I was flying through the air, and I landed on my back with a thud, and Miyoshi was kneeling on top of me with her fists doubled up and growling kind of deep in her throat.

"I guess I got to work on my timing, huh?" I muttered.

"I'm sorry," said Miyoshi, and now her voice was yet another octave lower and most of her accent was gone. "It was a reflex action."

"You got the healthiest reflexes I ever encountered, Miyoshi," I said. "Now how's about hopping off my chest? I'm having trouble breathing."

"My name isn't Miyoshi," said the Geisha, standing up and removing her wig, and I saw now that she was a man. "I am sorry for the deception, but it was necessary."

"You're a Geisha *boy*?" I said, getting painfully to my feet. "I didn't know they came in both flavors."

He shook his head. "I am Toshiro Mako of Interpol," he said. "Perhaps you have heard of me?"

"I'm afraid not," I said. "The only Oriental detective I know is Inspector Willie Wong of the Hong Kong Police."

"That bumbling incompetent, with his stupid platitudes and his legion of ape-like children!" said Mr. Mako contemptuously.

"You ain't on real good terms with him, I take it?"

"*I* am a master of disguise," said Mr. Mako. "I speak seventeen languages, possess a black belt in karate, and hold the Chair of Antiquities at Pacific University in my spare time, but do *I* ever get any publicity? No, it's always that Hong Kong clown with his pidgen English and his idiot parables! He always gets the best cases!" Suddenly his eyes flashed with triumph. "But *this* time will be different! This time *I*, Mr. Mako, will make headlines the world over!"

"For impersonating a Geisha girl?" I said. "Them ain't exactly the kind of headlines designed to endear you with the public, Mr. Mako."

He shook his head. "This is just a disguise, Doctor Jones," he explained. "My quarry has a room down the hall, and I am keeping him under surveillance, just waiting for the opportune moment to strike."

"Who are you after?" I asked him.

"Have you ever heard of Doctor Aristotle Ho, the Insidious Oriental Dentist?" he said.

"The name ain't totally unfamiliar to me," I said. "Is *he* staying here at the Nikkatsu?"

Mr. Mako nodded his head. "Yes. He's got some criminal coup in mind. I haven't been able to determine what it is, but I plan to dog his steps night and day, and when he makes his move, I shall make mine."

"He's already wanted all over Asia," I said. "Why don't you just arrest him now and cart him off to the calaboose?"

"I want his entire organization," said Mr. Mako as a kind of fanatical glow spread across his face. "*Then* let them talk about Willie Wong!"

"Well, I wish you all the luck in the world, Mr. Mako," I said. "But I think I'm gonna move over to the Imperial Hotel just to get out of the line of fire, so to speak." I reached out a hand. "It's been nice meeting you."

"I'm afraid I can't permit that, Doctor Jones," he said. "Any sudden unexplained activity could draw Doctor Ho's attention."

"I'll explain it at the desk," I said. "I'll just say that I was looking for something in the way of a blonde Geisha girl."

He shook his head. "I can't run the risk of alerting him. You will have to stay here." He paused. "In fact, I may have to impress you into service."

"What are you talking about?"

"I can't keep watching him every moment of the night and day," said Mr. Mako. "Even *I* have to sleep and eat and answer calls of Nature. Yes, the more I think about it, the more I see that I need your help."

"I don't know about this . . ." I said reluctantly.

"Think of the publicity, Doctor Jones!" he said. "Not only will we rid the world of this vermin, but we'll push Inspector Willie Wong off the front page!"

"I ain't got nothing against Willie Wong," I protested. "And now that I come to think of it, I ain't got nothing against Doctor Aristotle Ho, neither."

"Do you have anything against rewards?"

"I got a lot against risking life and limb for 'em," I said.

"That won't be necessary," said Mr. Mako. "You just follow him when I'm unavailable. Take notes of where he goes and who he meets, and keep out of sight. I'll take over from there."

"You're *sure* that's all I gotta do?" I said.

"Absolutely," said Mr. Mako. "I'm willing to share the reward with you, but I want the glory of capturing him myself. I'll show the world you don't need twenty-eight sons and a handful of trite aphorisms to be Asia's finest detective!"

Well, he seemed pretty sincere to me, so I finally agreed, provided that when it was all over he'd also tell the world that he was just in disguise as a Geisha girl and he and I didn't have no degenerate relationship going on behind the scenes, and then he went to sleep on the couch and left the bed for me, but about two in the morning I finally decided that I had to get something to eat even if it meant eating at the Momonjiya or the Taiko, so I climbed into my clothes and tiptoed out into the hall so as not to wake the sleeping Mr. Mako, and then I climbed down the stairs and headed out the door of the hotel into the street, figuring I'd just walk up and down the row of restaurants until I came to one with some civilized food in the window, and then suddenly I saw a familiar-looking figure walking ahead of me, and I realized that it was Doctor Aristotle Ho.

I hid in the shadows until he got a little farther away from me, and then fell into step behind him and followed him for about a mile, and suddenly we were in the Ginza, and every building was either a casino or a bar or a drug den or a whorehouse, and while it made me feel right at home, I didn't dare relax or partake in none of the entertainments with the Insidious Oriental Dentist just ahead of me. Finally he turned into a small tavern, and I stopped about fifty feet away and decided to wait till he came out rather than go in after him.

Suddenly I heard some gunshots coming from the tavern, and then there was a scream, and then a whole bunch of little yellow fellers raced out, and a crowd started gathering around the place, and then Doctor Ho walked out, calm as you please, with a smoking pistol in his hand. He tucked it into the belt of his brocaded robe, looked contemptuously at the crowd, all of whom backed away, and then turned to his right and started walking away.

One little old gray-haired Japanese feller stepped out of the crowd and started following him, and I walked over and grabbed him by the shoulder.

"Hey, neighbor," I said, "you don't want to get involved. That's the notorious Doctor Aristotle Ho."

He yelled something in Japanese at me, and I hung on to his arm.

"He shoots people for a livelihood," I explained. "Leave this to the authorities and maybe you won't get your damnfool head blown off."

Well, by now Doctor Ho had heard the commotion, and he turned and recognized me, and pulled out his pistol and fired twice, just as I pulled the old Japanese guy to the ground. When I looked up again, he was gone.

"Fool!" muttered the old guy. "I had him within my grasp!"

He started pulling off his mustache and wig, and suddenly I was looking at Mr. Mako.

"Why the hell didn't you tell me it was you?" I demanded.

"He would have overheard."

"What are you doing here in the first place?" I said. "I left you sleeping back at the hotel."

"I heard you leave," said Mr. Mako, "and since I couldn't be sure that Doctor Ho hadn't seen through my Geisha disguise, I thought I'd better come along to protect you."

"Don't you ever go anywhere as just plain Mr. Mako?" I asked.

He shook his head. "I am much too famous. Only my ability as a master of disguise allows me the freedom of movement."

A couple of bystanders had been watching him as he plucked off his mustache and wig and got rid of his cane, and one of them walked up.

"May I have your autograph?" he said.

"You see?" said Mr. Mako to me. "It happens everywhere I go."

"I've followed all your cases from Honolulu to Tokyo, Inspector Wong," continued the man. "What brings you to our fair city?"

Mr. Mako started cursing a blue streak, and didn't stop until the autograph seeker had run off in fear of his life.

"Come on, Mr. Mako," I said when he had finally run out of breath. "It's just been one of those days. I'll buy you a beer."

"Saki," he said.

"What's that?" I asked. "A Japanese brand?"

He just glared at me and walked into the nearest bar, and he didn't start loosening up until he'd had his fourth or fifth saki, which is this Oriental beer with no head on it that they serve in tiny little glasses.

"I was so close," he murmured. "So close!"

"Well, the thing to remember, Mr. Mako," I said, "is that Doctor Ho was just as close to you, and he was the one with the gun. Besides," I added, "he was all alone, and you said you wanted his whole gang."

"His *whole* gang encompasses entire armies and governments," said Mr. Mako. "What I meant was that I wanted his Japanese operatives."

"What's he doing here anyway?" I asked. "I thought he operated on the mainland."

Mr. Mako shrugged. "That is something else we have to discover, but I suspect that it involves our pearl industry."

"You grow a lot of pearls in Japan, do you?" I asked.

"You make it sound like you think they grow on trees, Doctor Jones," he said, amused.

"Nonsense," I said. "Everyone knows you dig for 'em in mines."

He just stared at me for a minute and then continued. "Recently we heard through the underworld grapevine that a criminal mastermind was planning to steal our entire supply of pearls. Doctor Ho's presence here would seem to confirm it."

"Where do you keep all your pearls, Mr. Mako?" I asked.

"In a building—a fortress, really—called the Pearl Exchange, on the edge of Shiba Park, right next to the ancient Buddhist temple. It is there that Doctor Ho will strike."

"Well, then, it's just as well he got away tonight, ain't it?" I said.

"You are quite right, Doctor Jones," he said. "In my enthusiasm I moved too soon. I owe you an apology."

"Happily accepted," I said. "Now why don't we get on back to the hotel and grab forty or fifty winks?"

"You go ahead," he said. "I am wide awake now, and perhaps it would be best for me to do some reconnoitering."

I didn't put up no objections, especially since he had left his Geisha duds back in the hotel, and I figured it wouldn't enhance neither of our reputations to be seen going into my room together, so I left him there and returned to the Nikkatsu Hotel and was sound asleep and snoring to beat the band a couple of minutes later.

The room was still empty when I got up at noon, so I shaved and dressed and went out hunting for a little breakfast that didn't have no monkey brains or ox organs or dead fish in it, but I found that I couldn't read the menus, which were all printed in Japanese, so after walking into and out of three or four restaurants I finally sat myself down and pointed to a pot of tea, and settled for drinking my breakfast with a bit of milk and sugar.

It was only as I was pouring my second cup that I realized that the place suddenly seemed a lot less crowded than it had, and as I looked up I saw all the customers and waiters and cashiers running for the door, and I figured the place must have caught fire or something, and I jumped to my feet to join them when a heavy hand landed on my shoulder and shoved me back down, and then the proud owner of the hand sat down and I found myself staring across the table at Doctor Aristotle Ho.

"We meet again, Doctor Jones," he said.

"Look," I said, "I'm right sorry that your temple collapsed and it put your plans of worldwide conquest on hold, but it wasn't my fault."

"Why do you continue to torment me, Doctor Jones?" he said. "No sooner do you leave Sir Mortimer's company in India than I find you in Tokyo, working in concert with Mr. Mako. What have you got against me?"

"Nothing," I said. "Cross my heart and hope to die."

"Be careful what you wish for, Doctor Jones," he said. "It may come true sooner than you think."

"The only reason I was with Mr. Mako was because I thunk he was a Geisha girl." He just stared coldly at me and didn't make no reply. "I guess that requires some further explanation, right?"

"I am in no mood for your drolleries, Doctor Jones," said Doctor Ho. "I have come here to ask you to deliver a message for me."

"A message?"

"I want you to tell Mr. Mako that if he persists in trying to thwart me, he will not survive the week."

"You'd make him a lot madder if you told him you were an admirer of Inspector Willie Wong's," I said helpfully.

"Just deliver the message."

"Right," I said.

"As for yourself," he continued, "this is the third time our paths have crossed."

"Well, it's the fourth time, actually," I said. "There was your farm in China, and then the secret sex ceremony in India, and then last night, and now this afternoon."

"Silence!" he snapped. "Do not contradict me when I am about to deliver an ultimatum."

"Okay," I said. "We just won't count last night, since it was an accident anyway."

"*Shut up!*" he screamed.

"Whatever you say."

He took a deep breath and continued. "That was the first time I have lost my temper in fifty-three years. You have a strange effect on me, Doctor Jones."

"You probably just ain't used to dealing with Christian gentlemen that was brung up to respect the Ten Commandments and the Bill of Rights and such," I said sympathetically.

"*Be quiet!*" he snapped, and then started blinking his eyes right fast. "I quite forgot what I was going to say."

"Beats me," I said. "So if you'll excuse me, I think I'll just be moseying back to my hotel now and—"

"Sit down and be still!" he said, still fighting to control his temper. "I have remembered what I had to say to you." He leaned across the table and stared into my eyes. "The next time our paths cross will be the last time."

"Well, I sure am relieved to hear that, Doctor Ho," I said. "I was afraid we were going to keep bumping into each other every few months for the rest of our lives. You planning on taking an extended trip somewhere?"

"You don't understand what I am saying to you," he said with a frown.

"Sure I do," I said. "You figure we're only gonna meet once more, and then I said that—"

"Can you possibly be this stupid, or is it all an act?" he interrupted.

"I resent that!"

"Never mind," he said wearily. "Just see to it that Mr. Mako receives my message."

"Happy to, Doctor Ho," I told him.

He got up and walked out of the restaurant, and suddenly all the customers and crew came back in, and the manager tore up my bill and just asked me to leave real quick, which I thought was a right gentlemanly thing of him to do simply because I'd attracted a local celebrity to his establishment, and I walked back to the hotel to deliver Doctor Ho's message to Mr. Mako, but the room was still empty.

I was about to go out in search of a friendly little game of chance, or maybe a Geisha who didn't change genders every time I turned around, when I saw a piece of paper lying on the table next to the phone, so I picked it up and read it:

> Doctor Jones:
> Pearl Exchange, 5:00 P.M. The net is closing!
> Mr. Mako

This put me in a bit of a quandary, since I knew Mr. Mako didn't want no help apprehending Doctor Ho, but on the other hand I thought the very least I should do as a law-abiding Christian gentleman was deliver Doctor Ho's message to him, so he could reconsider his plans if he was of a mind to protect life and limb and other vital organs.

I mulled on it for a couple of minutes, and finally went down to the front desk and asked where the Pearl Exchange was, but the directions were so complicated that I finally gave up and hired a rickshaw to take me there. It was maybe 4:30 when I arrived, which meant I had half an hour to find Mr. Mako before he went up against Doctor Ho.

The Pearl Exchange was a huge building that looked like it had withstood a lot of charges and sieges over the centuries before someone got the bright idea of stashing all of Japan's pearls there. There were bars on all the windows, and soldiers standing guard all around the place, and a bunch of English and American and Chinese and Arab merchants kept coming and going, and since I knew Mr. Mako was a master of disguise I scrutinized each and every one of them, trying to spot him, but within ten or fifteen minutes they had all left the building, and suddenly there wasn't no one left inside but me and an old Indian gentleman in a wheelchair and a uniformed Japanese feller standing guard on one of the balconies.

I checked my watch and saw that the doors were due to close in another few minutes, and then I finally realized that I was watching the Master of Disguise in action, and that the old Indian in the wheelchair was really Mr. Mako. I was about to walk up and congratulate him on his get-up, but I didn't want to give him away to Doctor Ho, who was probably lurking in the shadows somewhere, so I just stood back and admired him for a minute or two.

Then I saw a flash of motion out of the corner of my eye, and I looked up and saw that the uniformed guard was walking along the balcony to where he could get a clearer view of Mr. Mako, and that as he did so he unsnapped the leather cover on his holster and wrapped his fingers around the handle of his pistol.

I raced up the stairs just as he pulled his pistol out and was taking aim, and hit him with a tackle that under other circumstances would have got me a contract to play for the Chicago Bears.

"No!" I hollered. "You can't shoot him! That's Mr. Mako!"

We rolled along the floor a bit, and his gun got jarred loose, and then Mr. Mako jumped up out of his wheelchair and looked up at us and shook a fist in the air and ran out of there hell for leather, and suddenly I listened to the guard cursing and hollering at me and his voice sounded awfully familiar.

"Fool!" he screamed. "Idiot! Imbecile!" He ripped his eyebrows and beard and mustache off. "*I* am Mako! *That* was Doctor Aristotle Ho!"

"Well, how the hell was I to know?" I said.

"He is getting away, and it is all your fault!" yelled Mr.

Mako. "Worse still, our informants tell us that his next port of call is Hong Kong. Now Inspector Willie Wong will get all the glory again!"

"It ain't my fault," I said. "I was just trying to protect you."

Well, poor Mr. Mako just broke down and cried, and I did my best to comfort him and explained that even though he'd lost Aristotle Ho he had saved the country's pearls, but he wouldn't have no part of it, and finally he got control of himself and insisted that I come with him to his car, and then he drove me to his office and told his secretary to bring him any file Interpol might have on me, and wouldn't let me light up a cigar or have a beer or nothing until she returned lugging this huge folder.

"You have been a busy man since you arrived in Asia, Doctor Jones," he said after he'd spent a few minutes reading what she'd brought him.

"Well, I try to keep active," I said.

" 'Active' is an understatement," he said, still thumbing through the folder. "Not only did you help Doctor Aristotle Ho escape from me today, but it seems that you are wanted for setting up an illegal gambling operation in Macao."

"I didn't make a penny on that," I said defensively.

"Let me continue. The Chinese government has issued a warrant for your arrest for the murder of a General Chang."

"A simple misunderstanding," I said.

"Tibet is after you for absconding with a national treasure," he continued.

"He wasn't no national treasure," I protested. "He was just a basketball player on the lam from the mob. He wasn't even a Tibetan!"

"The government of India wants you for your complicity in the destruction of a national shrine, as well as killing eight tigers without a license," he said.

"I didn't kill 'em, I just sort of *appropriated* 'em," I said. "Well, seven of 'em, anyway."

"And the government of Siam has charged you with smuggling armored vehicles."

"I can explain all that," I said.

"And worst of all," he said, glaring at me, "when you were

in Hong Kong you helped Willie Wong grab yet another headline!'' He got to his feet and walked around to the front of his desk. ''Speaking in my capacity as the chief representative of Interpol on the Asian continent, I must inform you that your presence here is no longer tolerable, Doctor Jones. I could, of course, turn you over to any of the governments that seek to bring you to trial, but relations between your country and my own have become strained recently, and I do not wish to exacerbate an already tense situation. Therefore, if you will sign a pledge agreeing never to return to Asia, I will put you on the Trans-Siberian Express and let you become Europe's headache.''

''And if I don't sign it?'' I asked.

''Then I will have to devise a series of coin tosses to determine which government gets to incarcerate you first. The choice is yours.''

Well, it wasn't all that much of a choice that I could see, and I figured that if all my efforts to bring the word of the Lord to these brown and yellow heathen were that unappreciated, it was probably time for me to pull up stakes and take my leave of the place anyway, so I signed his paper and he flew me to Siberia, where I really could have used my panda-skin coat, and placed me on the train and pointed me to the West, and that was the end of my attempt to civilize the barbaric hordes of Asia.

Which ain't to say that my preaching days were over. During the next few years I came to grips with some mighty interesting folks and critters in the glittering capitals of Europe, and made and lost a fortune or two, and discovered a lost continent, and fell hopelessly and eternally in love fifteen or twenty times, and even was king of my own country for a spell.

But that is another story, and writing is mighty thirsty work.

PART II

ENCOUNTERS

(1931–1934)

11
The Home-Made Man

Europe is a lot different from Africa and Asia.

For one thing, it's got a lot more Europeans living there. For another, it's got better roads and it's a little more built-up. For a third, having been told by a batch of governments that totally misunderstood my motives that my presence was no longer desired on those first two land masses, I was in some danger of running out of continents while still in the prime of my young manhood.

Therefore, I made up my mind that this time I was going to keep out of trouble and obey all the nuances of the law while seeking to establish my tabernacle and pursue my vocation (which was preaching, no matter what Interpol and some of them other biased institutions said). So when the train that took me out of Asia and all the way through Russia finally came to a stop in Bucharest, I was determined that *this* time I wasn't going to spend my first night on a new continent in the local jail.

Of course, I hadn't really counted on the fact that my Silent Partner was out to test me the way He'd tested Job in times past, and that I'd lose my bankroll in the first twenty minutes of a friendly little game of chance with a pack of Gypsies just outside the railroad station. I was sorely tempted to even the odds by insinuating my own dice into the contest, but they were a swarthy-looking lot who spoke in tongues and carried an awful lot of knives and didn't look like they'd appreciate an effort to bring the laws of statistical probabilities under my more direct control, and so I took my losses like a man and wandered off, looking for some place to hole up for the night.

Well, you'd be surprised how many Romanian hotels wouldn't take an I.O.U. from a man of the cloth, and eventually I wandered out toward the edge of the city, and just after it got dark I found a quiet little park, and figured I'd catch a quick forty or fifty winks there before hitting all the major banking and brokerage houses with a request for donations to my tabernacle.

Well, I was just lying there, snoring kind of gentle-like and minding my own business, when all of a sudden I opened my eyes and looked up and realized that either the stars were moving awful fast across the sky or someone was dragging me along the ground by my feet, and I looked ahead and sure enough this little hunchbacked guy was pulling me across the grass toward a wooden wagon that was attached to an old swaybacked horse.

"Hey!" I said. "What in tarnation is going on here?"

He dropped my feet like they were on fire and turned to look at me.

"You're alive!" he said.

"Of course I'm alive!" I said. "What kind of country are you running here, anyway? Can't a man take a little nap in a public place without getting hauled off to jail?"

"This isn't a park," he said. "It's a cemetery."

"I'm the Right Reverend Honorable Doctor Lucifer Jones, and if I've busted any laws by camping out here, I'm sure we can work something out."

"It makes no difference to me," he answered. "I am Ivor. I serve the Baron Steinmetz."

"Then if you ain't some kind of night watchman, why were you dragging me off to that there wagon?" I demanded.

"I thought you were dead," said Ivor.

"The Baron pays you to go around tidying up the cemetery, does he?" I asked.

"Not exactly," said Ivor. "He sent me here to bring him back a better brain."

"He ain't pleased with the one he's got?"

Ivor sighed. "It's all very complicated, Doctor Jones."

"Yeah, it sounds a mite complicated," I allowed. "I mean, a lot of folks wish they were a little smarter, but this Baron of yours is the first one I ever heard tell of who's actually trying to do something about it."

"You don't understand, Doctor Jones," said Ivor. "He doesn't want the brain for himself."

"He's stealing it for a friend?"

Ivor shook his head. "It's for his work. He has long sought to create a living man. For years he has labored to reanimate dead tissue, putting together spare body parts in the laboratory he has built in the basement of his castle."

"Seems to me that the standard way of creating new men is cheaper and easier, not to say more fun," I said.

"He is a brilliant man," said Ivor. "A great scientist. He is on the verge of a major breakthrough."

It sounded to me like anyone who wanted to build a man in his basement was more on the verge of a major break*down*, but I just smiled and nodded sagely.

"After more than a decade of trial and error, of experiment after experiment, he had reached the final stage of his work," continued Ivor. "All he needs now is the proper brain."

"And he wanted mine?" I said. "Well, I'm flattered, Brother Ivor, but if it's all the same to you, I ain't done using it myself yet."

"I didn't know you were alive, Doctor Jones," said Ivor apologetically. "I heard that a major bookseller had died yesterday, and I thought: what a wonderful present that would make for my master—a brain that had spent its entire life immersed in literature. It's his birthday, and the brain would be such a nice surprise for him."

"Well, it seems to me that if you just stick around long enough, Brother Ivor, they'll bring this here bookman to the cemetery and plant him, and then all you got to do is mark the spot and dig him up at your leisure."

"It's not that easy," he said. "They have already arrested me twice for grave-robbing. I can only sneak in here at night, and by then the day's corpses have already been buried."

At which point my Silent Partner, who had returned from sabbatical, smote me right betwixt the eyes with another of His great big heavenly revelations.

"That ain't no problem at all, Brother Ivor," I said.

"It isn't?" he asked.

"For a small retainer, I'd be happy to hang around here till they brung this guy in, and mark the spot where they bury him."

"Oh, the Baron will be so happy!" said Ivor, clapping his little hands together.

"And for a further consideration, I'll give you a hand digging him up and delivering him to your boss."

"You have no moral compunctions about digging in hallowed ground?" he asked.

"Who better to dig in it than a man of the cloth?" I said.

"It's a deal, Doctor Jones!" he said excitedly. "I will return every night at midnight until they have brought him here and buried him."

"Sounds good to me, Brother Ivor," I said as he took his leave of me, and a couple of minutes later I was sound asleep again.

When I woke up in the morning I took a little stroll around the cemetery and found an apple orchard at the far end of it, which took care of my meals for the rest of the day. I spent the bulk of the morning and afternoon attending maybe half a dozen graveside services, and I was so moved by the sad story of a lovely young milkmaid who died of bloat after drinking her employer's entire wine cellar that I even stepped up and said a few words on her behalf myself.

Then, at about twilight, they lugged in another casket, and I moseyed over to find out the identity of the deceased.

"I don't think anyone knew his real name," said one of the gravediggers. "His headstone says he's Gustave Book."

"Where are all the mourners?" I asked.

"He didn't seem to have any friends or family, so we're burying him right now," was the answer.

"That's kind of tragic, a man devoted to books like poor old Gustave," I said.

"Well, it's not a profession designed to make you a lot of

lasting friends," said the gravedigger. "A lot of people went broke at old Gustave's place of business."

I never knew anyone to go broke buying books before, but I figured Gustave must have been a dealer in rare antiquarian stuff and maybe some illuminated manuscripts and the like, and I figured he must have had a very unhappy missus, because with all the money he left her she could at least have bought him a bigger headstone and put his right name on it, but that wasn't none of my business. I just thanked the gravediggers for their information, sat down on a bench and watched 'em plant old Gustave, and then took a little constitutional around the cemetery while waiting for Ivor to show up.

He was there right at midnight, just like he'd promised, with his old swaybacked horse and his wooden cart.

"Did they bury him today, Doctor Jones?" he asked eagerly.

"You're in luck, Brother Ivor," I said. "He's been resting peaceably for the better part of six hours now."

"Excellent!" said Ivor. "Where is he?"

I led him over to the grave. "He showed up kind of late, and they barely had time to bury him before dark," I explained. "Evidently they aim to plant the headstone tomorrow."

"Let's get busy," said Ivor, tossing me a shovel.

"What's *this* for?" I asked.

"You're going to help me dig, aren't you?"

"Well, actually, I had in mind something more in the line of offering you encouragement and giving the Baron the benefit of my sage advice and worldly experience," I said.

"Ten extra American dollars," said Ivor.

"Fifty," I said.

"Fifteen," he countered.

"Tell you what," I said. "We'll split the difference. Make it an even forty and it's a deal."

Well, we haggled for another five minutes, and I finally agreed to apprentice at the grave-robbing trade for $34.29. It took us the better part of two hours to dig down to old Gustave, and then we found that we weren't strong enough to pull his casket out of the hole, so we unlatched it and I kind of climbed in with him and handed him up to Ivor, who dragged him by the feet over to the cart and loaded him up. Then we spent another hour putting all the dirt back and patting it down nice and neat, and finally we climbed into the cart and the old horse started trotting along the empty streets.

"He sure looks calm and peaceful, lying there staring up at the moon like he is," I said, turning in my seat to get my first real good look at Gustave.

"I wonder what he died of," said Ivor. "I hope it wasn't anything catching."

I opened Gustave's formal jacket and took a quick peek. "Looks like he was shot to death," I said.

"It sounds painful," said Ivor with a shudder.

"I don't believe he felt the last twenty or thirty bullets at all," I said, buttoning his coat back up.

"Why would anyone want to kill a bookseller?" mused Ivor.

"Beats the hell out of me, Brother Ivor," I admitted. "I know you Europeans are degenerate and sadly lacking in Christian virtues, but that seems an awfully stern punishment for overcharging."

Well, he didn't say nothing to that, and we rode in silence for about half an hour, till we left the city limits and got out into the suburbs, and pretty soon we came to a rocky hill, and there on top of it was this huge castle.

"The Baron will be so happy to meet you!" said Ivor. "I told him how you had agreed to help us."

"I'm always happy to help advance the cause of science," I said modestly.

"Tonight we will witness the culmination of his life's work," continued Ivor. He leaned over and added confidentially. "He is delighted that you are a man of the cloth. He wants you to baptize his creation."

"Well, a critter what's made of twenty or thirty other men ain't the easiest thing in the world to baptize," I said. "I figure we'll have to baptize each part separately, at maybe five dollars a shot, just to be on the safe side. Can't have his left elbow doing evil things when the rest of him is trying to serve the Lord, if you see what I mean."

"Money is no object to the Baron," answered Ivor.

"You don't say?" I replied. "I don't suppose he wants his castle blessed too, just to cover all the bases?"

"You'll have to speak to him about it," said Ivor as the horse started climbing a little path in the hill. "We're almost there."

We reached a huge wrought-iron gate and Ivor got out and rang a bell, and a moment later the gate opened inward just long enough to let us through, and then slammed shut behind us. Ivor guided the horse up to the huge front door, and then we stopped and climbed down off the wagon, and the door opened, and out stepped this real skinny guy with wide staring eyes. He was wearing some kind of a laboratory coat, and he was smoking a Turkish cigarette that was stuck in a long gold holder.

He walked over to the back of the wagon and looked at Gustave.

"Excellent, excellent," he murmured. "You have done well this night, Ivor." Then he turned to me. "You are Doctor Jones?"

"The Right Reverend Doctor Lucifer Jones, at your service," I said.

"I am Baron Steinmetz," he said. "Ivor has told me how you have aided my cause. I wish to thank you."

"Well, I had in mind something just a tad more substantial than a handshake," I said.

"I quite understand, and you will not find me ungrateful, Doctor Jones. But first let us bring the body inside and prepare for the final transformation."

The three of us lifted old Gustave out of the wagon and carried him into the castle, which was huge and cold and kind of damp and made of stone and lit by candles.

"This way," said the Baron, heading off for a staircase that led down to the basement. We almost lost Gustave a couple of times as the stairs kept curving around corners, but finally we made it to the next level, and found ourselves in a big laboratory, filled with all kinds of gizmos that didn't make no sense to me but were humming and glowing to beat the band.

We laid Gustave on a wood table and then the Baron took me by the arm and led me over to another table, which was covered with a big blanket. He reached down and pulled the blanket off, revealing a huge body lying there. Parts of it didn't seem to quite fit, and there were stitches and electrodes everywhere, and the top of its skull was missing.

"Well, Doctor Jones," said the Baron. "What do you think?"

"You wouldn't happen to have something in a blonde of the female persuasion, would you?" I said. "Maybe a size eight?"

"All in good time," he said. "One day I shall turn out beauty queens galore, but first we must complete the prototype. He lacks only a brain to be a completely functioning human being."

"That ain't never stopped certain select politicians and constabularies I've known," I offered.

"This one will be a worthy representative, I assure you," said the Baron. He turned to Ivor. "*If* you got the right brain this time."

"*This* time?" I asked.

"I don't know how it keeps happening, but the first four brains he obtained were abnormal."

"Just poor luck," said Ivor.

"It not only held back my moment of triumph, but it played hell with my fire insurance premiums."

"How can an abnormal brain affect your fire insurance?" I asked.

"The locals keep trying to burn the castle down," answered the Baron. "They simply cannot comprehend the importance of my work." He paused. "Of course, I can see their side of it, too. Number Three *did* kill seventeen of them and tear down the local church, right after Number Two destroyed the school."

"Don't forget Number One," said Ivor.

"He simply lacked empirical knowledge," said the Baron. "I mean, how was he to know that all those people couldn't survive after he threw them off the belltower? He himself was incapable of feeling pain."

"I almost hate to ask," I said, "but what happened to Number Four?"

"I don't want to talk about it," said the Baron, and walked over to begin work removing Gustave's brain.

"He's kind of sensitive about Number Four," whispered Ivor.

"How come?" I asked.

"It ran off with his wife," said Ivor. "Last postcard we got from them, they were living it up on the Riviera." He paused. "But this time will be different. This time we've got the brain of a man who spent his whole life with books, who even took literature itself as part of his name."

"Done!" announced the Baron after another couple of minutes. "Now we simply transfer the brain to my creation, attach all the ganglia and synapses, and it is accomplished."

"What do you plan to call this critter?" I asked as he placed the brain in a metal pan and carried it over.

"I really hadn't considered that," said the Baron. "I just assumed we'd call him The Monster, just like the other four."

"Ain't that likely to upset his delicate bookish feelings?" I said.

"You're quite right, Doctor Jones," said the Baron. "Ivor, what shall we call him?"

"Creature Number Five?" suggested Ivor.

"Why not just call him Gustave?" I said. "After all, that's the name he's responded to all his life."

"Gustave?" repeated the Baron distastefully. "What a dreadful name!"

"What's wrong with it?" I asked.

"I've only known one Gustave in my life, and if I never see him again, it will be too soon."

"Why not wait till you bring him back to life and ask him what he wants to be called?" said Ivor.

"A capital suggestion!" said the Baron. He turned to me. "I'll be at least half an hour transplanting and connecting the brain, Doctor Jones."

"That long, huh?"

"Well, it *is* delicate surgery," he said. "Why don't you freshen up and have Ivor get you some food in the meantime?"

"Sounds good to me," I said. "Ivor, where's the kitchen?"

"Right above us," said Ivor. "I hope you like apples."

"Why?"

"The Baron is a vegetarian. That's all we have in the house."

"Maybe I'll just settle for a quick shave and shower," I said.

"Well, that poses another problem," said Ivor apologetically. "This is an *old* castle. We don't have any running water."

"Perhaps none of that will be necessary," said the Baron, working away at the top of the monster's head. "If I just take *this* shortcut, and bypass these two synapses . . . Yes! It's done!"

"You got him all hooked up that fast?" I said.

"Well, he'll be tone-deaf, and I rather suspect he won't be able to play rugby, but except for that, he should function just perfectly."

"I hope so," said Ivor. "Remember Number Three? He kept smelling colors and stuffing candy bars into his ear."

"We learn from our mistakes," said the Baron, starting to connect a bunch of wires to all these metal bits and pieces that were sticking out of the monster. "That is how we avoid making them again and again."

Well, I couldn't see that a batch of brand-new mistakes in a ten-foot-tall monster was all that preferable to the same old ones, but it wasn't none of my business, so I just kept quiet and watched while the Baron finished wiring his creation.

"All is in readiness," he said after another minute or two, and walked to a big metal switch on the wall. "Ivor, Doctor Jones—please stand back."

He didn't have to ask me twice, and I backed up against the wall, which had a damp and chilly feel to it, and then he pulled the switch and every gizmo in the place started buzzing and whistling, and just about the time I was sure he was gonna blow every fuse in the castle he pushed the switch back to its starting position.

All three of us walked over to the table, and son of a gun if the monster wasn't breathing. The Baron disconnected all the wires and pulled out a stethoscope and listened to its heart for a while, and the critter's eyelids kind of fluttered a bit and suddenly I was staring into its wide, wondering eyes, one brown and one blue.

"Where am I?" asked the monster.

"You're perfectly safe," said the Baron. "You are the late

Gustave Book, and I am the Baron Theodore von Steinmetz. I have reanimated you here in the lower recesses of my castle.''

"I'm not Gustave Book," said the monster. "I'm Gustave *the* Book." It paused while the Baron suddenly turned white as a sheet. "Steinmetz, Steinmetz . . ." it muttered, and suddenly it sat up. "Steinmetz, you owe me three hundred pounds sterling!''

"What are you talking about?" demanded Ivor.

"Nobody welches out on a bet with Gustave the Book," said the monster. "Let's have it.''

Suddenly the Baron turned to Ivor and started hitting him on the top of his head.

"Idiot!" he screamed. "Fool! I ask for a dealer in literature, and you bring me the local bookmaker! I *thought* he looked familiar!''

"You," said Gustave to me. "Tell me what the hell is going on around here! Why is my voice different? Why does everyone look so small? Since when does my left hand have six fingers? What has happened to me?''

"You were dead, and the Baron brung you back to life," I said.

"Well, a form of pseudo-life, anyway," corrected the Baron.

"I don't believe it.''

"Maybe we could all sing you a rousing chorus or two of 'Happy Birthday,' to kind of put you in the mood," I said.

"Just a minute," said Gustave. He closed his eyes, then opened them again. "The last thing I remember was seeing a car go by, and then a tommy gun was pumping bullets into me, and then everything went blank. How come I'm not dead and buried?''

"Well, actually you were," I said. "Until we unburied you a couple of hours ago. In fact," I added, "there's probably them what would say you still are.''

"Buried?''

"Dead," I said.

"I'm going to need some time to consider all this," said Gustave.

"You have all of eternity," said the Baron. "Being dead already, it is impossible for you to age."

"Don't bet on it," muttered Gustave. "I think I've aged thirty years in the past three minutes."

"I must write this up in my journal," said the Baron. "Ivor, you and Doctor Jones stay with him, and don't let him get excited."

He left the laboratory, and Gustave turned back to me.

"Do I look as terrible as I think I look?" he asked.

"Well, that all depends," I said.

"On what?"

"On what you think you look like."

"Like the ugliest living thing on the face of the earth," he said.

"Worse," I answered.

"Well, I suppose I haven't got too much to complain about," he said at last. "I could be back in that grave you dug me out of."

"That's the spirit, Brother Gustave," I said. "Look on the bright side. The ladies may not beat a path to your door, but at least you ain't still pushing up daisies."

"But what am I to do with myself?" he asked.

"Seems to me like you're in prime shape to become a professional rassler," I said.

"He could be a weight lifter or a basketball player," suggested Ivor.

"Right," I said. "You been looking at this through jaundiced eyes, Brother Gustave. There's no end of things you can do when you're ten feet tall and weigh six hundred pounds."

He shook his head. "I can't let anyone see me looking like this."

"Actually," said Ivor, "I believe that the Baron plans to put you on exhibition."

"I'm not going to play the freak just to satisfy his ego," answered Gustave. "I'll kill myself first."

"It's too late for that," said Ivor sympathetically. "You're already dead."

"Right," he said. "I keep forgetting." He paused. "On the

other hand, if I'm already dead, he can't threaten or force me to do anything.''

"Mighty few people of your particular physical attributes get forced to do anything they don't want to do," I agreed.

"Why did he use so many spare parts?" asked Gustave. "Doesn't he realize how much a new wardrobe will cost me?"

"I don't think that was among his primary concerns," said Ivor.

"I might have guessed as much from a man who won't pay off his gambling debts," muttered Gustave. "He walks into my establishment, loses three hundred pounds playing poker, writes an I.O.U., and then refuses to honor it."

"There was a reason for that," said a voice from behind us, and we all turned to see that the Baron had reentered the laboratory.

"Let's hear it," said Gustave. "I could use a good laugh after the day I've had."

"The game was rigged."

"I've never run a rigged game in my life!" said Gustave.

"Do you know the odds against someone beating me in a five-man game with the hand I held?" said the Baron.

"Yeah," said Gustave. "32,457 to one."

"How did you know that?" asked the Baron.

"Numbers are my business."

"Really? I'm terrible with them myself."

"I can tell," said Gustave, holding his arms out in front of him. One was a good six inches longer than the other.

"Quick," said the Baron. "How much is 358 times 409?"

"146,422," said Gustave.

"How are you at calculus?" asked the Baron.

"I've done my fair share of it in school."

"Have you studied any other higher mathematics?"

"Oh, not really," said Gustave modestly. "I helped Einstein a bit when he passed through here. And Shwarzchild wanted to call it the Gustave Radius, but I told him that he had done most of the initial work and it should really be the Shwarzchild Radius." He sighed. "I never could help Schroedinger understand those damned cats, though."

"My God, man!" said the Baron, his eyes wide. "Why have you been hiding in a bookie joint?"

"I haven't been hiding," answered Gustave. "It's just dead-beats like you who can't find me."

"But why aren't you a scientist?"

"I had to loan Einstein rent money last month," said Gustave. "Does that answer your question?"

"But think of the inestimable service you could be to humanity!" said the Baron.

"That didn't interest me even when I was human," said Gustave. "So why should I care now?"

"Don't you understand?" said the Baron. "I want you to work with me! I'll make you a full partner!"

"You mean you'll give me half of a run-down castle?" said Gustave. "Don't make me laugh."

"What do you want to come to work with me?"

"First," said Gustave, "I want to start my business up again. We'll run it out of Castle Steinmetz."

"What else?"

"I want my three hundred pounds."

"Done."

"One more thing," said Gustave. "The next thing we work on is a wife for me."

"Certainly," said the Baron. "With your input, I should be able to create an exact replica of Mary Pickford."

"I'll settle for Mabel Normand," said Gustave.

"Here," said the Baron. "Go over my notes while I get your money."

He tossed a stack of papers onto the table next to Gustave and raced from the room. Gustave started going over them, making little corrections here and there and muttering to himself. The Baron returned a minute later and handed him three hundred pounds.

"Well?" said the Baron eagerly. "What do you think?"

"We have a lot of work to do," said Gustave.

"Oh?"

Gustave pointed to a line on the paper. "Either five times

seven equals thirty-eight, or Mary Pickford is going to have feathers.''

"But if you change this notation *here*," said the Baron, pointing to another of Gustave's scribblings, "she not only won't have feathers, she'll be bald as an egg.''

"It's only fitting," said Gustave, "since *this* equation will eliminate her arms and legs.''

Ivor kind of signaled to me, and I walked over to him.

"I know better than to interrupt the master when he's like this," he said, "so I will pay you what we owe you." He slipped me a wad of bills. "Thank you for your help, Doctor Jones."

"Any time, Brother Ivor," I said, counting the money and then putting it away in my pocket.

"Will you be staying in Bucharest?" he asked.

"No, I don't think so," I said. "From what I can see, the Baron's got the god biz pretty well under control without no help from me, so I'd best be off to seek fame and fortune elsewhere."

I followed him to the stairs, and was just starting to climb up out of the laboratory when I heard the Baron say, "So what's *wrong* with giving her three of them?''

And then Gustave paused for a moment and said, "Not a damned thing, now that I come to think of it.''

I left the two of them plotting out the shape of things to come, and that was the last I ever saw of Baron Steinmetz and his home-made man . . . but I guess they got along pretty well together, because I did hear a couple of years later of a Romanian bur-leyque dancer who had three of what most women generally settle for two of.

12
Doubled and Redoubled

You know how some people are connoisseurs of fine art or rare books or gourmet food?

Well, I seem to have become a connoisseur of jails.

The jailhouse back in Moline, Illinois, is kind of a community gathering place on Saturday nights. The Johannesburg jail is pretty friendly, but the food lacks a little something. The Cairo jail is noisy and crowded. The Nairobi jail is hot and stuffy. The jail in Beira, over in Mozambique, is kind of cramped and smells of raw sewage. The Hong Kong jail smells of dead fish. The jail at Poshan is well-appointed, and the jailor's got a weak spot for games of chance, but if you can't eat with chopsticks you're out of luck.

But the strangest jail I ever spent a night in was unquestionably the jail in Sylvania, a tiny kingdom which probably ain't on any map printed in the past half century. It seems they'd built this particular hoosegow with the thought of filling it to the brim with criminals, but the people of Sylvania were a pretty law-abiding lot, and although the jail had been standing for seven years, I was its first customer. The jailor was so glad to have a little company that he moved a four-poster bed into my cell, and his wife started fixing me a six-course meal every three hours.

How I came to be in the Sylvania jail was a matter of some mystery to me, because I was still bound and determined not to break no laws or otherwise impede my progress toward constructing my tabernacle and bringing all these degenerate Europeans back to the straight and narrow path. So when I hit Sylvania, with Baron Steinmetz's money still pretty much intact, I disdained all games of chance, and instead moseyed over to the Royal Hotel and ordered up the biggest suite in the house, intent on washing the dust from my body and grabbing a good night's sleep before I went out looking for donations or shapely female assistants or whatever else I thought the tabernacle might need.

I probably should have figured something was a little strange when the desk clerk looked at me with wide, staring eyes, gulped a couple of times, and said that of course I didn't have to pay for the room, but I make it a point never to look no gift horses in the mouth. And when a passel of waiters brung up some pheasant under glass and caviar and champagne and wheeled it into my lounge with the compliments of the house, I just assumed they were being polite to a man of the cloth.

Still, since everyone was being so all-fired nice to me, I decided to test the waters, as it were, and ask one of the waiters to send up a friendly young Sylvanian lady to help me pass the long lonely hours of the night. He just took it right in stride and asked me if I preferred blondes or brunettes or redheads, and I allowed that I was equally fond of all of 'em, and about half an hour later in came one of each.

And just as the four of us were getting to know each other and I was thinking that Sylvania was about the most hospitable country that I ever did visit, in burst two guys in tuxedos and two more in military uniforms, and they chased the young ladies out and told me to get dressed and carted me off to the calaboose without so much as a by-your-leave.

But like I said, the jail was well-appointed and the service was better than I'd paid for in a batch of hostelries, so except for lacking a little company of the female persuasion and wondering what particular laws I had broken, I wasn't exactly discommoded at my current situation, and truth to tell I was eating better than I'd et since I'd arrived in Europe.

Then, at about noontime, two of the guys who'd arrested me the night before came to pay me a visit. One of 'em was still in his military uniform, all glittering with medals and sporting a general's insignia, and the other was dressed in a dour gray business suit. They nodded to the jailor, who let them into the cell with me and then left the building.

"Well, Heinrich," said the General, "what do you think?"

Heinrich peered intently at me through a monocle. "It's remarkable," he said at last. "Absolutely remarkable."

"I agree," said the General. "Even here, in the light of day, no one could tell the difference."

"But it's such an audacious scheme," protested Heinrich.

"It will work," said the General adamantly.

"Excuse me for interrupting," I said, "but would you gents like to tell me what I'm doing here, a clean-cut God-fearing Christian who ain't never broke a law in his life?"

"My apologies," said the General. "But it was absolutely essential that we speak to you before anyone else laid eyes on you."

"It wasn't exactly the laying on of eyes that got so rudely interrupted last night," I pointed out.

"We forgive you for that," said Heinrich.

"Well, I'm sure that's right generous of you," I said, "but I hadn't quite got around to doing anything I need to be forgiven for, if you understand my subtle but outraged meaning."

"Forget all that," said the General. "We have important business to discuss with you."

"Yeah?" I said.

He nodded. "You could be the answer to our prayers."

"Well, you're in luck, General," I said. "Answering prayers is one of the very best things I do, me being a man of the cloth and all."

"You may be in luck, too, Reverend Jones," said the General. "We have a job for you. It's dangerous, but the pay is excellent, and you'll know that you are serving the cause of Right and Justice."

"Uh . . . back up a couple of steps to the dangerous part," I said.

"I won't deceive you," said the General. "Your life will be constantly at risk."

"Well, it sure has been nice chatting with you fellers," I said, getting to my feet and walking to the door of my cell. "But I think it's time for me to hit the road."

"A quarter of a million dollars," said the General.

"On the other hand," I said, walking back to my bed and sitting down on the edge of it, "it would be rude to leave without at least hearing you out."

"I don't know," said Heinrich. "Are you *sure* this is our only option?"

"We both know it is," answered the General. He turned to me. "We've yet to be formally introduced. I am General Gruenwald, head of Sylvania's army, and this is Lord Mayor Heinrich Rembert."

"Pleased to meet you," I said. "Let's talk about the quarter of a million dollars."

"All in good time, Reverend Jones," said the General. He pulled a photograph out of his pocket and handed it over to me. "Do you recognize the man in this picture?"

"It's me," I said. "But I sure can't remember posing in all them fancy duds. It must have been took at a carnival or something when I was on a bender."

"It is *not* you," said General Gruenwald. "It is a photograph of King Philbert of Sylvania, and it was taken two weeks ago."

"You don't say?"

"We *do* say," replied Lord Mayor Rembert. "You could be his double, Reverend Jones. The same weak chin, the same unkempt hair, the same look about the eyes that inspires instant mistrust, even the same slovenly way of walking."

"All right," I said. "I look like King Philbert. So what?"

"An attempt was made to assassinate Philbert the night before last," said General Gruenwald. "He still lives, but he is in the hospital, and will be confined there for at least a month. We believe that the attempt on his life was made by Wilhelm Von Sykoff, the leader of the opposition party. Von Sykoff is an evil man, totally opposed to everything King Philbert stands for. He has begun spreading the rumor that Philbert is dead, and if the people start to believe him, it will totally destabilize the kingdom. Yet the doctors will not permit Philbert any visitors, not even the members of our press, nor would it do any good, since he is swathed in bandages from head to toe and cannot possibly be recognized even by those nearest and dearest to him." He paused. "Do you see where this is leading, Reverend Jones?"

"You want to pay me a quarter of a million dollars to say a prayer for him?" I asked.

"We want you to impersonate him," said Mayor Rembert. "To *become* King Philbert for the next four weeks. To wear his clothes, make his speeches, eat his meals, sleep in his bed."

"If you can carry off this illusion until Philbert is healthy enough to resume his duties, you will save the kingdom," added General Gruenwald. "And for this we are prepared to pay you the sum of two hundred and fifty thousand American dollars."

"Of course," continued Lord Mayor Rembert, "we would be less than candid if we did not warn you that Wilhelm Von Sykoff will probably redouble his efforts to kill you."

"Why don't you just lock him away in some dungeon somewhere?" I asked.

"He is not without his followers," said General Gruenwald. "Any such action would instantly precipitate a civil war."

"Well, Reverend Jones," said Lord Mayor Rembert, "will you do it?"

I mulled on it for a minute, and decided that even if I couldn't lock Von Sykoff away, maybe I could make him my ambassador to Tasmania or Fiji or some place like that and be rid of him for the month I had to pretend to be Philbert.

"Well," I said at last, "I ain't never been king of my very own country, and my tabernacle could sure use that money. Put half of it up front and you got yourself a deal."

"In King Philbert's—ah, *your*—bedroom there is a metal box in the top drawer of your dresser," said General Gruenwald. "The down payment will be there waiting for you by this evening."

"Perhaps you should tell him that's not *all* that will be waiting for him," suggested the Lord Mayor.

The General nodded. "I'd almost forgotten about Princess Griselda."

"Princess Griselda?" I repeated.

"She is your—um, *Philbert's*—betrothed. The wedding is scheduled for next spring."

"*That* will be your most severe test as Philbert's impersonator," said the Lord Mayor. "Do you think you can handle it?"

"I'm quite a hand with the ladies," I said. "Except for the improvement, she'll never know the difference."

"Then I suppose we'd best get to work," said General Gruenwald. "We'll have to sneak you into the palace and get you dressed in Philbert's clothes. Since everyone knows Philbert was shot two days ago, it might be best to keep one arm in a sling, or perhaps affect a limp." He paused. "I'll be at your side night and day to point out who you know, what their names are, what Philbert would do in given situations.".

"Well, I appreciate that, General Gruenwald," I said. "Especially during the days. But," I added, thinking of Griselda, "I got a feeling that I can handle the nights on my own."

"As you wish," said General Gruenwald. He led me to the door of my prison cell. "The sooner we begin, the sooner we'll know if this audacious impersonation will work."

"Sounds good to me," I said, falling into step beside him.

We walked out to a car that had all its back windows covered up, and then climbed into it and began driving through the winding, stone-covered streets of Sylvania, passing a number of churches and taverns along the way, until we pulled up to this huge palace with gargoyles peering down at the liveried doormen. We zipped around to the servants' entrance just next to the kitchen, and they snuck me up the stairs before anyone even knew we were there.

A minute later I was standing in this room that was only slightly smaller than Lumpini Stadium back in Siam. Almost all the furniture was painted gold along the edges and covered with velvet, and the walls were loaded with paintings by some Dutchman who I figured was a friend of the family since I'd seen dancing hall posters that had more accurate renderings of what people looked like. There was a mahogany table that could have sat the whole of the Chicago White Sox, along with their manager and coaches, for dinner. Off to one side was a private cinema theater, but since General Gruenwald hadn't never heard of

Theda Bara or Clara Bow, I figured I'd give it a pass. And finally there was a bedroom, with a huge four-poster bed that Solomon and all his wives could have bounced around on at the same time. The bathroom held a tub you could go sailing in, and a shower with five nozzles for them what didn't have time for a long, leisurely wallow.

"Well?" said General Gruenwald.

I allowed that I could get used to my surroundings without putting forth an enormous effort.

"Let's get you dressed properly," said the Lord Mayor, walking to a closet in which Baron Steinmetz could have stashed a couple of hundred of his home-made men. He pulled out an outfit and tossed it over to me. "Here," he said. "Change into this."

When I was done, I looked at myself in one of the dozen or so mirrors and I must admit that I was mightily impressed. My jacket, which stopped at the waist, had gold epaulettes and braid, and maybe five pounds' worth of medals, and the shiniest brass buttons I ever did see, and my pants were deep blue with a gold stripe down the side. My boots were soft and polished within an inch of their lives.

"And now your sword," said the General, attaching it around my waist.

"Uh . . . this Philbert ain't prone to sword-fighting when he has too much to drink or loses his temper, is he?" I asked.

"Certainly not," said the General. "It's merely for show. Although he *is* a master swordsman."

"And now," said the Lord Mayor, "it's time to go downstairs for dinner."

We walked out the door of my suite and down a huge winding staircase. There was a little guy in glasses waiting at the bottom.

"Am I supposed to know him?" I whispered.

"He's a reporter," answered the General.

"What do I say to him?"

"Be vague and noncommittal."

When we reached the end of the staircase, the little feller walked up to me.

"How are you feeling, King Philbert?" he asked.

"I'm fit as a bull moose," I said.

"I had heard you were badly wounded," he said.

"Well, let me amend that," I said. "I'm fit as a bull moose what's been gut-shot."

"I thought you were shot in the leg."

"I was," I said quickly.

"Then why do you compare yourself with a bull moose that has been gut-shot?"

"Because I ain't never made the acquaintance of a moose that's been shot in the leg," I said. He just kind of stared at me, so I figured I'd change the subject. "Lovely day, ain't it?" I asked him.

"What do you plan to do about Wilhelm Von Sykoff's tax bill?" he said.

"Think it may rain, though," I said.

"All right, King Philbert," he said with a sigh. "As long as you feel compelled to discuss the weather, what do you think of it?"

"Oh, I approve of weather," I said. "And as long as I'm the King, we're gonna have it."

He was about to ask me something else when the General led me into the dining room.

There were a bunch of people there, all decked out to the nines, and the minute I entered the room they all bowed. I didn't quite know what to do, so I bowed back, which set 'em all to bowing again. I figured maybe we could just keep doing it all night long and not have to get around to talking at all, but the General nudged me and whispered that I should sit down, so I did, and then everyone else sat down too.

"I am pleased to see Your Majesty looking so well," said a large, burly man with a black mustache and lamb-chop sideburns.

"Well, I could stand to lose maybe a pound and a half," I said modestly.

"I mean, you seem to have recovered from your unfortunate accident."

"It takes more than forty or fifty bullets to keep a good man down," I answered.

"Careful," whispered the General. "That's Von Sykoff."

"Have you any idea who was behind this heinous act?" asked Von Sykoff.

"Oh, probably some disgruntled retard who envies my manly good looks," I said. "It ain't worth worrying about. Now let's all dig in and grab some grub."

"Such quaint Americanisms," chuckled a lady, and I turned to see I was sitting next to one of the prettier females it had ever been my privilege to see. "You are such a wit, Philbert!"

"The Princess Griselda," whispered the General.

"Why, thanks, Griselda honey," I said.

She shot me a smile that made me right anxious for dinner to end, and then Von Sykoff spoke up again.

"Has Your Majesty given any further consideration to my tax bill?" he asked.

"Not really," I said. "How much do you owe?"

Everyone kind of laughed at that, except for Von Sykoff, who turned a bright red.

"Your Majesty is in a rare humor this evening," he said through gritted teeth.

"You think that's funny?" I said. "Have you ever heard the one about the dancing girl and the Albanian priest?"

Well, I shared that little drollery with them, and then I told 'em about the traveling salesman and the architect's daughter, and then I topped it off with the tale of the airplane pilot and the Chinese virgin, and even though I forgot the punch line everyone laughed fit to kill, and it suddenly occurred to me that I *liked* being King, and that if old Philbert wanted to spend an extra couple of months recuperating it wouldn't bother me none at all.

"This is a side of you I've never seen before," said Griselda when I was all done telling my stories. "Where did you ever learn such risqué tales?"

"Griselda, honey," I said, "you wouldn't believe how many sides of me you ain't seen yet. After we get rid of all these here guests, I'll take you upstairs and show you some of them."

She just giggled like I was telling another joke, and then the waiters brought out dessert, and eventually we were all through eating, and then the General got up and proposed a toast to me, and everyone stood up and yelled "Long live Philbert!" and we all drank up, and then the Lord Mayor did the same, and then Griselda got up and drank to my health, and I began to see that even if the people weren't a hundred percent in favor of having a king instead of a president, it could break every liquor company in Sylvania if they ever changed the political system.

"Suggest that we repair to the drawing room," whispered the General after eight or nine more toasts.

"Folks," I said, getting kind of shakily to my feet, since I'd been matching 'em all toast for toast, "I just been informed that the drawing room's broke and in need of repair. Let's all mosey over there and see if we can fix it."

Everyone chuckled again, and I could see that Philbert never had to worry about people laughing at his jokes, even when he wasn't necessarily making 'em, and then I stared at everyone and they all stared back at me, and finally the General jabbed me in the short ribs and I jumped up, and then everyone else got up and we all wandered over to the drawing room, which was filled with fancy chairs and dinky little tables but didn't have no drawing materials or even pencils that I could see.

I was about to amuse the guests with some more stories, but a bunch of guys with violins started strolling around the room. They finished when they were right in front of me, and I figured I should probably reach into my pocket and tip 'em for their trouble, but they just bowed and thanked me for letting 'em perform and walked off to the kitchen or wherever it was they'd come from.

One by one the guests started leaving, until there was no one left except Griselda and Von Sykoff, and he came over and stood in front of me and stared at me.

"You seem somehow different tonight, Your Majesty," he said kind of suspiciously.

"Yeah?" I asked. "In what way?"

"Your manner of expressing yourself, for one thing."

"It's all the rage in Moline, Illinois," I said.

"How very witty," he said with an oily smile. He bowed, and suddenly lowered his voice to a whisper. "You may fool the others, but not Wilhelm Von Sykoff. Your days are numbered, imposter.''

Then he turned on his heel and left before I could tell the General what he'd said.

"He's right," said Griselda.

"You know it, too?" I asked.

"That you're witty?" she said. "Absolutely. It was a very pleasant change, Philbert. You seemed so tense and stern last week."

"Probably my boots were too tight," I said.

She stood up and walked over to me. "There's a beautiful moon out tonight," she said. "Shall we go for a walk?"

"Why the hell not?" I agreed.

"Philbert, you never used vulgarisms before," said Griselda.

"Well, they came cheap and they played nice music," I said, taking her arm and heading for the front door.

"I think I'd better accompany you, Your Majesty," said the General, joining us.

"I got the situation well in hand," I said.

"It is my job to protect you."

"You protect me from Princess Griselda and you just might find out what it's like to be a private again," I said.

"But . . ."

"I'm the King, ain't I?" I said. "And the King says scram."

He backed away, and we went outside, and Griselda turned to me. "You seem so different tonight, Philbert," she said. "So forceful."

"What's the point of being King if I can't voice a few terse commands as the mood strikes me?" I said.

"But you've never behaved like that to General Gruenwald before."

"Let him get his own Princess," I said, giving her a friendly little pinch in a delicate area.

She shrieked. "Philbert!"

"Just being boyishly playful, my love," I said.

"You mustn't do that again until we're married," she said severely.

Which was when I began to see that old Philbert's love life hadn't yet left the starting gate.

"Refresh my memory," I said. "Just how long have we been engaged?"

"Since you were five and I was two," she answered. "But you know that."

"I also know it's about time we brung this here courtship into the Twentieth Century."

"What's come over you, Philbert?" she demanded.

"Probably it was getting shot by all them bullets," I said. "It makes a man realize just how fleeting life is."

"I *knew* there was some reason for this strange behavior," she said. "Does it hurt much?"

"Only when I breathe in and out," I said.

"You poor man!" she said. "And here I am, thoughtlessly making you walk around the grounds and expend your energy only two days after that frightful experience."

"Now as I come to think on it," I said, "I probably would feel a mite better if I went up to bed."

"Certainly," she said. "Let's turn around and go right back inside."

"I don't want to disturb General Gruenwald and the Lord Mayor none," I said. "Why don't we mosey around to the back entrance?"

"If you wish," she said.

We reached the stairs in the back a couple of minutes later, and I turned to her and shook her hand.

"Thanks, Griselda," I said. "You've been right understanding about my condition."

"Can you make it up the stairs yourself?" she asked.

"I made it up to the seventh stair this afternoon before I collapsed," I said. "I feel a lot stronger now. I can probably make it to the tenth or even the eleventh before I have to crawl the rest of the way."

She put my arm around her shoulders. "I'll help you," she said.

"No," I said. "Fun's fun, but I can't have a full-blooded

Princess compromising her reputation on my behalf, even though there ain't no one here to see us."

"Just be quiet and save your strength," she said, helping me up the first stair.

Well, it took some work, but we made it up to the second floor, where I dropped to my knees and told her I'd make it the rest of the way without her.

"I won't hear of such a thing," she said, helping me to my feet and letting me lean on her until we reached the bedroom.

"I'll be all right now," I said.

"You're sure?" she asked.

"Yeah," I said. "I'm supposed to bathe my wounds every two hours, but that can wait till morning."

"And risk infection? Nonsense!"

"I don't know what we're gonna do about it," I said. "If I can't give you a friendly little pinch, I hardly figger I can take my clothes off in front of you." I paused for a moment. "Of course, I could turn the lights out and have you swab my wounds in the dark."

"Well . . ." she said hesitantly, "I *suppose* that would be all right. After all, they *do* have to be cleaned."

Modesty and a sense of literary decorum forbids me from relating the rest of the scene, except to say that after she couldn't find no wounds on me I started pointing out where they were on her so she would have a firmer grasp of the situation, and pretty soon we were grasping each other so firmly that both of us plumb forgot about my wounds, and we might have stayed like that forever except that about four in the morning I woke up and started feeling kind of eleven o'clockish a good seven hours early, so I climbed back into my clothes and moseyed on down to the kitchen to see if I could scare up a little snack, and ran smack-dab into General Gruenwald and Lord Mayer Rembert, who were there sipping glasses of brandy.

"You took an enormous risk," said the General. "You should never be alone with anyone who knows Philbert."

"There are certain circumstances under which three is a crowd," I answered. "Or at least a mighty peculiar arrangement."

"Has she guessed who you are yet?"

"No," I said. "But Von Sykoff has. Or, at least, he's guessed who I ain't."

"Damn!" muttered the General. "We'd better triple the guard around Philbert. If Von Sykoff can't get to him, he'll have to come after you."

"Me?"

The General nodded. "Absolutely."

"I don't know how to tell you this gently," I said, "but from my particular point of view, that ain't a consummation devoutly to be wished."

"One can't always have what one wants," said the General.

Well, as you can imagine, I wasn't in no mood to sleep after this particular conversation, and Griselda was in no mood to wake up, so I finally took to wandering through the palace, absently pocketing such little *objets d'art* as caught my eye.

By sun-up the palace was bustling with activity, and I grabbed some breakfast, and then I figured it was time to wake Griselda and send her home, so I went up to the bedroom, but she had other ideas, most of which I'd given her the night before, and it was another hour before I made it back downstairs, where the General and the Lord Mayor were waiting for me.

"It's time for you to make a speech to Parliament," said the Lord Mayor.

"What about?" I asked.

"The economy," said the General. "We've written it down for you. All you have to do is read it."

It sounded easy enough, so I took a quick look at it while we were driving over to the Parliament building, and then, after waiting in the wings to be introduced, I walked up behind a podium and started reading it, but when I came to the part about how we were going to raise the peasants' taxes again I got a better idea, so I just put the speech aside and suggested that maybe we should just let Wilhelm Von Sykoff and his cronies pay for the government, since they were trying to steal it anyway, and suddenly Von Sykoff was on his feet cursing a blue streak and demanding satisfaction, and I explained as patiently as I could that if he hadn't gotten no satisfaction last night I felt right sorry for him, but we didn't want to hear about his sexual problems on the floor of the Parliament.

Then he walked up to the podium and took his glove off and kind of waved it at my face, so I took it from him and tried it on, and explained it was a mite large for me and did he have anything in the next smaller size, and suddenly he was cursing again and carrying on something awful, and insisting that we have a duel.

"Some other time," I said. "I'm busy giving this here speech now."

"You *must* face him, Your Majesty," said one of the members of the Parliament.

"I *am* facing him," I said. "I just ain't gonna fight him."

"The honor of Sylvania demands it," said another.

"He's no Sylvanian!" shouted Von Sykoff. "He's an imposter!"

"Don't pay him no never-mind," I said. "He's been out in the sun too long."

"Would King Philbert behave like this?" demanded Von Sykoff. "He has many faults, but cowardice isn't one of them!"

I turned to General Gruenwald, who was still standing beside me.

"What happens if I admit he's telling the truth?" I whispered.

"You lose the quarter million, and the mob tears you apart."

"And if I don't admit it?"

"Then you have to accept his challenge."

"What weapons is he good with?" I asked.

"All of them."

"Let me re-word that just a bit," I said. "Is there anything he *ain't* good at?"

"Losing," said the General.

Well, I figured as long as I was probably going to die anyway, I might just as well die fighting for a quarter of a million dollars, so I turned back to Von Sykoff and said, "Okay, if you want a fight, you got one."

Everyone stood up and cheered, and Von Sykoff just grinned at me and bowed.

"I choose swords," he said. "Everyone knows that Philbert is a superb swordsman. If I am wrong, he will make short work of me."

The Lord Mayor stepped between us and turned to me.

"What type of sword do you select, Your Majesty?"

"There are types?" I asked.

"Certainly," said the Lord Mayor. "There are foils, epees, sabres, scimitars, broad's swords . . ."

I thunk about it for a moment, and I figured that from the sound of it a broad's sword was probably a dinky little weapon that might not draw much blood, and that maybe we could all shake hands and have a drink when the fight was over.

"I choose broad's swords," I said.

There was a gasp from the audience.

"But we haven't used broad's swords this century!" exclaimed Von Sykoff.

"Well, if you want to call the thing off, I got no serious objections," I said.

"No!" he snapped. "Broad's swords it is."

Well, they cleared a huge area in the middle of the floor, and we each took off our fancy coats and rolled up our sleeves, and then two big burly guys walked out with a long box that looked like it weighed a ton, and they set it on the edges of two chairs and took the top off, and there were the two biggest, heaviest swords I ever did see, and I couldn't help but wonder what kind of broads had been able to fight with them.

Von Sykoff walked over, placed both his hands on the handle of one broad's sword, and dragged it away to where he had been standing. I tried to lift the other one and couldn't, and finally the two guys who had carried 'em out gingerly hefted up the point and helped me take it back to where I was supposed to start.

"Are you ready, Wilhelm?" asked the Lord Mayor.

"Ready," muttered Von Sykoff.

"Are you ready, Your Majesty?"

"Ready?" I said. "Hell, I can't even pick the damned thing up."

"It was *his* choice," said Von Sykoff. "He can't back out now."

"I'm afraid he's right, Your Majesty," said the Lord Mayor. "You will begin on the count of three: one, two, three!"

Well, Von Sykoff somehow or other managed to raise his broad's sword over his head while I was still trying to lift mine off the ground, and he kind of staggered over to where I was. I could see he was about to take a mighty big swing with it, so I made one last effort and pulled on the handle with all my might, but the damned sword was so heavy and my hands were sweating so badly that I lost my grip on it and fell backward just as Von Sykoff's sword came down on where I had been.

It hit the marble floor with the loudest *clang!* I ever did hear, and suddenly Von Sykoff shrieked and dropped his sword and fell to his knees.

"I think I broke both my hands!" he said.

He tried to pick his sword up, screamed again, and let go of it.

"Your Majesty is free to administer the *coup de grace* at your leisure," said the Lord Mayor.

"What in the world do I want a cup of grass for?" I asked.

"He meant you may deliver the death blow whenever you wish," said the General.

"I can't even lift my sword," I said. "Besides, the Good Book tells us never to smite a helpless opponent, especially when he's got a lot of friends and relations watching. Why don't you just cart him off to the calaboose and give him a couple of months to think about whether he really wants to kill the King?"

"I haven't broken any law!" protested Von Sykoff.

"Well, there's another alternative," I said agreeably. "We can all hang around here until I figure out how to lift my sword and finish the fight."

"No," said Von Sykoff. "You win."

So they took him away, and everyone cheered, and even his followers figgered I was a pretty nifty King for letting him live, and the General was pleased as all get-out and said that he'd make sure that Von Sykoff stayed in jail until Philbert was back in shape, and the Lord Mayor said that things would be so peaceful for the next month that they could announce I had taken a vacation to the Alps and no one would try to overthrow the government, so I could take my money and leave if I was of a mind to.

It was a mighty tempting proposition, but being the noble and decent Christian gentleman I am I just couldn't bring myself to break poor Griselda's heart, so I hung around for another few weeks, and when Philbert finally got back on the job he found himself a mighty changed and friendly fiancée.

As for me, I finally had enough money to build my tabernacle, and I figured it was time to go scout out the proper location for it—and besides, I'd made it almost a month without running into one of the ladies whose sword I'd used, and the Good Book tells us not to press our luck when we're on a winning streak.

13
Treasure Hunting

I figured that if I was finally going to settle down and build my tabernacle it made a lot of sense to do it where the weather was pleasant all year around and the people had been sinning for a good long time, so I headed south to Greece to scout out properties.

I wanted something with a nice view, maybe on a hillside or something like that, but all I could find in Athens were a bunch of real old buildings that were falling apart. So I went farther out to the countryside, where the buildings weren't a lot newer but the land was cheaper, and finally found myself in a little town called Tinos, overlooking the Aegean Sea. I decided to put off looking for a room until I stopped off at a local bar for a little something to quench my thirst with maybe just enough alcohol in it to whip the tar out of the germs.

I took my glass to a table in the corner and sat down to drink it in peace and quiet, when suddenly a familiar-looking figure sat down next to me.

"Well, fancy meeting you here, Doctor Jones!"

"You got me mistook for someone else," I said as soon as I recognized him. "I ain't never heard of no Doctor Jones."

"Nonsense!" he said with a smile. "This is me, Erich Von Horst, you're talking to."

"Every other time I ever talked to you I wound up dead broke and usually in the hoosegow," I said sullenly.

"Let's let bygones be bygones," he said amiably. He signaled for two more drinks. "I'm buying."

"You ain't never bought nothing in your life," I said.

"You mustn't be so bitter, Doctor Jones," he said. "In the end, all it will do is get you an ulcer."

"Why ain't you still back in Africa, cashing in on elephants' graveyards and lost diamond mines and the like?" I asked.

"Because I found something better here in Greece," he said.

"Well, I wish you luck with it, and don't call me, I'll call you," I said.

"Is that any way to speak to an old friend?" asked Von Horst with a hurt expression on his face.

"Show me an old friend and I'll think about it," I said.

"I see you still have your delightful sense of humor."

"Look," I said. "The first time I laid eyes on you you robbed me of two thousand pounds in Dar es Salaam."

"I paid you back," he said.

"With counterfeit money," I said. "That was the time we met in Algeria."

"You *did* try to swindle me out of the Jacobean Red Letter edition of the Bible," he pointed out.

"There ain't no such thing as a Jacobean Red Letter edition of the Bible!" I shouted at him.

"Ah, but you didn't know it when you tried to cheat me out of it."

"All I know is you wound up with the biggest ruby in Africa and I wound up with a bunch of money that wasn't worth the paper it was writ on!"

"That's all in the past," said Von Horst with a shrug. "I'm a changed man. I'll be happy to make amends."

"I'll just bet," I said.

"If you'd like, we can go to my hotel room just as soon as we've slaked our thirst, and I'll pay you the seven thousand pounds I owe you—the two thousand from Dar es Salaam and the five thousand from Algeria."

"Fine," I said, as the waiter brought us our drinks. "And in the meantime, don't say a word."

"Why on earth not?" he asked.

"Because every time I listen to you it costs me money."

"Doctor Jones, you cut me to the quick!"

"It's a pretty tempting thought," I said.

"Truly, you misjudge me," said Von Horst. "I wish there was some way to make up for all the trouble I seem to have caused you."

"Just give me my money and get out of my life, and we'll call it square," I said.

"I said I would, and I will," replied Von Horst. He peered across the table at me. "Have *you* got any money?"

"That's none of your business."

He grinned. "*That* much?"

"I don't want to hear this," I said.

"Forget the seven thousand pounds, Doctor Jones," he said. "How would you like to make some *real* money?"

"With you?" I asked.

"Yes."

"I'd hate it."

"You could triple your investment in a week."

"You want me to start quoting psalms at you," I asked, "or should I just hold up a cross to make you go away?"

"There's absolutely no risk involved."

"Go away."

"I just want to make amends for our prior misunder-standings," he said.

"Shut up," I said.

He shrugged. "As you wish."

I finished my drink and sat there staring at my glass for a few minutes.

"I could triple my money in a week?" I said at last.

"At the very least."

"I don't want to hear about it," I said. "Just leave me alone."

"Certainly," he said.

I lit a cigarette and smoked it all the way down.

"No risk?" I said.

"None at all."

"Then what do you need *me* for?"

"I don't," he said. "I'm simply trying to make restitution for my past indiscretions."

"Let's hear it," I said.

"Not here," said Von Horst. "Too many interested ears are listening. Let's go back to my hotel, and I'll lay it out for you."

He got up and I followed him out.

"Beautiful place, Greece," he said as we walked down the pavement. "Far more opportunities for entrepreneurs like you and me than there were in Africa, eh, Doctor Jones?"

"You seemed to find more than your share in Africa," I said.

"Do I detect a trace of bitterness?" he said.

"Von Horst, I trust you about as far as I can spit with my mouth closed," I said. "I'll listen to you until I spot your scam, and then I'm taking my seven thousand pounds and leaving."

"That's all that I ask, Doctor Jones," he said. "By the way, since we're such old friends, may I call you Lucifer?"

"No."

"As you wish," he said with a sigh. "But after I explain this deal to you, you're going to realize that I'm truly doing you an enormous favor."

"The next favor you do anyone will be the first," I said. "Let's just get this over with."

"Ah, here we are," he said, stopping in front of a little waterfront hotel.

"You're making seven thousand an afternoon and you're staying *here*?" I asked.

"I don't want to attract undue attention to myself," he said. "Come on in."

He waved to the desk clerk, and we climbed up to the fourth floor, where he opened a door and led me into a suite of rooms.

"I've rented the entire floor," he said. "Have a seat, Doctor Jones. Can I get you something to drink?"

"Not a thing," I answered him. "Just say what you've got to say and then fork over my money."

"All right," he said, sitting down on a sofa and lighting a thin cigar. "Look out the window and tell me what you see."

"The Aegean Sea," I said.

"Wrong, Doctor Jones," he said enthusiastically. "It's a bank, and there's no door on the vault."

"What the hell are you talking about?" I said.

"I'm saying that we're in similar lines of business these days, Doctor Jones," he replied. "You're in salvation, and I'm in salvage."

"I don't think I follow you."

"You save souls. I save treasures."

"Treasures?" I repeated.

"Do you know how many ships lay beneath that calm surface, Doctor Jones?"

"A few," I said.

"*Hundreds!*" he said, leaning forward. "Warships, trading ships, pirate ships. The treasure they carry runs into *billions*!" He walked over to a desk, took a diamond necklace out of the top drawer, and tossed it to me. "I picked this up yesterday morning. Take a good look at it."

"It looks real," I said.

"It *is* real!"

"Okay," I said. "It's real. So you're a rich man. So what do you need *me* for?"

"It's not that simple," he said with a heavy sigh.

"Somehow it never is," I said.

"Let me lay the situation out for you," he said. "I came here with a lot of money to invest. Some fool bought the elephants' graveyard from me"—I decided not to tell him that the fool was my former partner, Colonel Carcosa, who was probably still gathering dust in a Mozambique jail—"and I was seriously considering retiring. Then I heard about Mazarati's map."

"Mazarati's map?" I asked.

"Enrico Mazarati, a nineteenth-century Italian sailor, spent his entire adult life making a map that marked the location of every wrecked ship in the Aegean, going back to Pericles' time. At first I thought it was a myth, but it piqued my curiosity, and the more I looked into it, the more I became convinced that the map existed. It took me almost five years to hunt it down, and it took every penny I had to purchase it—but it's *mine* now! In the two months I've had it, you wouldn't believe what I've pulled out of the sea!''

"I repeat: what do you need *me* for?''

"Well, there's a little problem with the authorities," he said. "They seem to believe that anything taken out of the Aegean belongs to them, whereas I personally have always believed that possession is one hundred percent of the law.''

"Not totally unreasonable," I allowed.

"Since I haven't been able to win them over to my position, I am unable to sell the treasures I've accumulated until such time as I can . . . ah . . . *covertly* remove them from the country," continued Von Horst. "I'm finding more every day, but given the situation, my cash flow isn't quite what it should be.''

"You're broke," I said.

"Well, not entirely," he replied. "I can afford my rooms at the hotel, and I have a small boat—but with a major infusion of capital, I could hire the best boat and equipment for the job, and pull these treasures up by the carload rather than one at a time.'' He looked at me. "Do you see where this is leading?''

"Let me see the map," I said.

He walked over to a painting of a seascape that was hanging on the wall, turned it over, and there, taped to the back of it, was Enrico Mazarati's map, showing the exact locations of maybe four hundred sunken ships.

"How do I know this isn't just another scam?" I asked.

"I show you Mazarati's map and you *still* distrust me?" he demanded.

"Anyone can draw a map," I said.

"Take the necklace to any jeweler in town and have it evaluated," he said. "If it's not legitimate, I'll pay you double what I owe you and never darken your door again.''

"Let's leave it at that," I said, getting up and stuffing the necklace in my pocket. "I'll take it around in the morning, and if it's legit, I'll be back here at noon.''

"Fine," he said, standing up and walking me to the door. "Once you find out what it's worth, I'm sure you will be tempted to take it and simply leave the country. If you do that, two things will happen: first, I will inform the authorities that you have stolen a priceless relic belonging to the Greek government, and second, you will not be allowed to share in the vast treasure that I've yet to recover.''

"What a thing to suggest about a man of the cloth!" I said, working up a good head of outrage and wondering how he'd figured out my plans so fast.

I found myself a nice old rooming house with lots of character, and the more I thought about it, the more I decided that future generations of tourists would never forgive me if I gave them enough money to cover those beautiful old stucco walls with ugly-looking wallpaper, so I kind of tiptoed out while the desk clerk was on the phone, and then I took Von Horst's necklace up the street to the first jeweler I could find.

The man looked at it, then blinked a couple of times, looked again, and offered me ten thousand dollars if I could prove I was the owner. I thanked him for his time, told him I'd consider it, and then, because I knew just how sly Von Horst was, I took it to three other jewelers, just in case he'd paid a couple of 'em off. Every one of them assured me that it was authentic.

This wasn't exactly what I had expected to hear, and it put a whole new light on things. Obviously the Mazarati map was the pure quill, and Von Horst would never have trusted me with real diamonds if he hadn't been sure I'd come back . . . which meant that he really did have a cash flow problem.

And suddenly I saw a way to make enough money to put me and God on Easy Street while paying Erich Von Horst back for all them times he'd duped me back in Africa.

My mind made up, I grabbed some breakfast, waited until noontime, and moseyed over to his hotel.

"Well?" he said.

"It's real," I said, handing the necklace back to him.

"Are you in or out?" he asked.

"In," I said.

"Excellent," he said, shaking my hand. "We'll begin this afternoon."

"Well, we got a little problem there," I said. "My money ain't where I can lay my hands on it. It'll take me a couple of days to move it to Tinos."

He frowned. "I hate to wait," he said. "Every day we sit here is another day that someone else might discover some of the treasure. How much money are we talking about?"

"Maybe a quarter of a million," I said.

"Pounds?"

"Dollars."

"That's fabulous!" he exclaimed. "For that kind of money, we can buy every boat in Tinos. We'll lock the competition out!"

"They can always go to some other town and buy boats," I said.

"By the time they do that and get back here, we'll have pulled up the treasure from all the nearby wrecks," replied Von Horst, "and without the Mazarati map they'll never find the rest . . . and that alone will pay for the boats twenty times over."

"Sounds good to me," I said.

"In the meantime," he added, "there's no reason why we shouldn't pull a quick ten or twenty thousand dollars out of the sea this afternoon. I've got until sundown on the boat I've been using before the lease runs out."

"Sounds good to me," I said. "Just give me some time to send for the money."

"Fine," he said. "I'll meet you at the docks in, shall we say, an hour?"

"Make it two, just to be on the safe side," I said.

The first thing I did when I left his hotel was go to a local map shop and buy a map of the area just about the same size as the Mazarati map. Then I took it to the library, where no one would bother me, and traced it onto a sheet of blank paper I had bought, so it would look like the authentic Mazarati map. Finally, I marked about four hundred shipwreck locations, just making little X's like the Mazarati map had done. When I was through, I threw the original map into the garbage and folded up the map I'd just made and stuck it into one of my pockets. Then I went to the dustiest, emptiest section of the library, pulled out my wad of money, and stuck it behind a huge copy of *Eighteenth Century British Maritime Rules and Regulations*, which looked like it hadn't been touched since Queen Victoria was in bloomers.

I checked with the head librarian on the way out and found that the place was open until six o'clock. Then I went on down to the docks, where I found Von Horst waiting for me by a beat-up fishing boat with a motor that looked like it had seen a lifetime's worth of better days.

"*This* is what we're going out in?" I asked.

"It's seaworthy, and it doesn't attract attention," he said. "I've got the diving gear hidden under the canvas." He tossed me a fishing rod. "Here. Let people see you holding this so they think we're just a pair of tourists going out for a little sport."

Well, I spent a couple of minutes playing with the rod for the benefit of any onlookers, and then we hopped into the boat and Von Horst started the motor, and when we were maybe a mile off the shore he pulled out his map and checked his compass, then turned about two hundred yards to his left.

"We should be right over the wreck of the *Isadora*," he said.

"Never heard of it."

"It's an old Spanish galleon that theoretically carried grain and fabrics, but actually trafficked in stolen gemstones." He pulled back the canvas to reveal a deep-sea diving suit. "I'm afraid all I could afford was one. We'll take turns using it. You can go first."

"Me?" I said. "I ain't never been in nothing like that. How do I breathe?"

"The same as always," he said. "I'll pump the air while you're beneath the surface."

"Just a minute," I said. "Who pumped the air for *you* before I showed up?"

"A lovely young lady of my acquaintance who thought we were looking for shells," he said. "The diving outfit was too heavy for her to manipulate, so she never dove down and hence never knew about all the sunken ships."

I climbed into the deep-sea suit, and as Von Horst was adjusting my helmet, I said, "You realize that if you stop pumping air, two things are gonna happen: first, I'm gonna die, and second, you ain't never gonna see a penny of that quarter million."

"I swear I never met such a distrustful man," he said.

Well, he lowered me down, and I turned on the light at the top of my helmet. There were enough fish to feed the whole of Hong Kong with maybe enough left over for Tokyo, but finally they cleared away and suddenly I could see this old, rotting Spanish ship. It took awhile to learn how to maneuver, but eventually I landed on the deck and walked into a couple of the rooms, which didn't have nothing in them except old rotting furniture.

But when I hit the third room, I tried the top drawer of a dresser that hadn't rotted apart yet, and inside it was a bunch of bright, glittery stuff. I picked it up, stuck it in a pouch on my outfit, walked back out to the deck, and signaled that I wanted Von Horst to pull me up.

"Did you find anything?" he asked when I was finally back on the boat.

I reached into my pouch and pulled out one of the objects.

"A diamond tiara!" he said. "Fit for a queen—or a reputable fence. What else do you have?"

I emptied the pouch, and we counted up two sets of diamond earrings and a pearl necklace.

"Not bad, partner," he said. "Did you ransack the whole boat?"

"I just tried three or four cabins," I said. "There must be fifty of 'em."

"I think I'll go down and have a look for myself," he said. "If you don't mind climbing out of the suit."

It took about ten minutes for me to get out of the outfit and him to get back in, and then he was down inspecting the ship and I was pumping air to him. I figured an experienced treasure hunter like him would stay down half an hour or so, but less than a minute later he jerked on the line, the signal that he wanted to come up. I hauled him to the surface, and then, just before dragging him up out of the water and onto the deck, I took the phony map out of my pocket and substituted it for the Mazarati map, which I removed from his coat and tucked inside my shirt.

"That was mighty fast," I said.

"Sharks," he said, removing the helmet and starting to climb out of the outfit. "One of them looked like he was thinking of biting right through the air hose."

"Well, we made a pretty decent haul anyway," I said. "I suppose we can come back when my money arrives."

"Still," he said, "it seems a shame to waste the rest of the afternoon. I can find another location on the map."

"It ain't necessary," I said.

"It's no problem," he insisted. "The map's right here."

"I'm all tuckered out," I said, since I didn't want him doing no close inspection of the map. "I ain't used to walking around underwater like unto a fish."

"You're sure?" he said, walking over to his jacket. "It's no trouble to find another ship."

I grabbed my stomach and moaned. "I think I'm getting a case of the folds."

"You mean the bends?"

"Whatever," I moaned. "Let's just pack it in and go on home."

"Whatever you say," replied Von Horst, turning his attention from the map to the engine, and about half an hour later we were parked at one of the docks.

"How are you feeling?" he asked when we got back on dry land.

"Better," I said.

"If you're up to dinner, we'll celebrate today's finds with the best meal in town. My treat."

"I don't think I could look at food tonight," I said. "I'll just go back to my room and lay down. I should be fit again by the morning."

"Take all the time you need to recuperate," he said. "As long as your money won't arrive for a couple of days, and my lease on the boat has run out, you might as well spend tomorrow in bed regaining your strength. I'll meet you the day after tomorrow."

"Sounds good to me," I said.

"Take care now," he said. "I'd hate to lose you before the money arrives."

Well, that sounded like the Von Horst I knew, so I bade him good-bye and started staggering off, with the Mazarati map, the tiara, the necklace, and the earrings all safely tucked away on various parts of my person. When I was sure I was out of sight, I straightened up and resumed my normal gait and rushed over to the library, where I retrieved my money.

Then, while Von Horst ate his fancy dinner and went back to his suite to relax, I went down to the docks and bought every boat in town. Most of these here sailors and fishermen drove mighty hard bargains, but by dawn I owned every boat in Tinos and still had about two thousand dollars left, which as far as I could see left Von Horst out in the cold and made me the sole owner of the treasures on Mazarati's map.

Then, bright and early the next morning, while Von Horst was still asleep, I went down to the docks, found the boat Von Horst had leased, and hired a little Greek feller to pump my air for me. I pulled out Mazarati's map, pinpointed the *Isadora*, and steered the boat until we were directly over it. Then I changed into the deep-sea gear and went down to find some treasure.

Well, I must have spent three hours going over the *Isadora*, and I couldn't find so much as a tie pin. Finally I went back up to the surface and took the boat back to shore, where I figured on having lunch before setting out to spend the afternoon going over the rest of the *Isadora*.

I was sitting down eating a sandwich in a little *taverna* when a heavyset, bearded feller who smelled of fish walked up to me.

"You are Lucifer Jones, are you not?" he asked.

"The Right Reverend Lucifer Jones at your service," I said.

He pulled up a chair and sat down across the table from me. "I wonder if you could answer a question, Reverend Jones," he said.

"If it's within my power, I'd be right happy to, brother," I said. "What particular question did you have in mind?"

"What is so valuable about our boats that you paid so much for the entire fleet?"

"Let's just say I'm a kind of collector," I told him.

He leaned back and scratched his head. "I didn't know anyone collected old fishing boats," he said. "I guess Mr. Von Horst was right."

"Von Horst?" I said. "What's he got to do with anything?"

"When he bought our fleet two days ago, he told us that if we were patient, a collector would come by sometime within the next week and buy the whole fleet for at least ten times what he paid for it."

"But I didn't buy the boats from *him*," I said with that old familiar sinking feeling in the pit of my stomach, "I bought 'em from *you* guys."

"Oh, no," he corrected me. "They have been Mr. Von Horst's boats for two days. But he was very generous: he paid us each a fifteen percent commission to sell them for him."

"Where is he now?" I demanded.

The man shrugged. "I don't know. He collected his money while you were out fishing this morning, and that was the last I saw of him."

I raced out of the restaurant and didn't stop until I came to a jeweler, one of the few I hadn't visited with the diamond necklace the day before.

"Quick," I said, slapping the tiara, the earrings, and the pearls down on the counter. "What are these worth?"

He just looked at them without even putting on his little eyepiece, and then turned to me. "The same thing they were worth when I sold them to Mr. Von Horst last week," he said. "About three dollars. Well, make that two—they almost look like someone has been keeping them in salt water. See how the gold paint is pitted here?"

"You mean you only deal in costume jewelry?" I demanded.

"Of course not," he replied. "I deal in whatever the market will bear. In fact, if you'd like a truly beautiful piece of authentic jewelry, perhaps I can interest you in this diamond necklace that Mr. Von Horst just returned after renting for a week."

He held up the same necklace I'd had appraised the day before, and I screamed a couple of things I hoped my Silent Partner didn't overhear, and rushed off to Von Horst's hotel. As I was heading to the stairway, the desk clerk looked up and called over to me.

"Doctor Jones?"

"Yeah?"

"I'm afraid your friend has checked out. Something about an illness in the family. He left you this note."

I walked over to the desk, opened the envelope, and read as follows:

> *My dear Doctor Jones:*
>   *How very fortuitous it was to meet you once again. Very few people, having been burnt once, will willingly stick their hands in the fire a second time,*

and yet here you are, after three unfortunate experiences on the Dark Continent, once again attempting to swindle me.

Still, some people are slower learners than others, and while I was not waiting specifically for you, you can imagine my surprise and delight when you showed up in the bar the other night.

By now you have doubtless figured out that there never was an Enrico Mazarati. He is one of my, shall we say, business names, and I hereby will him to you, along with the map that took me the better part of an afternoon to draw. (It won't do you much good, alas; I have been assured that the Isadora is the only wreck within fifty miles of here.) Nor are there any sharks in the vicinity; I knew you couldn't switch maps while you were pumping air, so I decided that the sooner I came back to the surface, the sooner you would be free to steal my map and begin bringing this affair to a satisfactory conclusion.

Still, you might look at the bright side: you are now the commander of your very own fishing fleet. I trust this pleases you, as I am afraid you are stuck with it, since you paid approximately one thousand percent of market value for the boats, and the commissions I handed out this morning have all been earmarked for new boats.

Oh, and keep the pearls and the tiara: there's always a chance you may run into a young lady who is as greedy and gullible as you yourself are.

> *Yr. Obdt. Svt.,*
> *Erich Von Horst*

Five seconds later I got a case of the bends.

14
The Lost Continent

After my unfortunate treasure hunting experience off the coast of Tinos, I decided to head back to Athens. I couldn't see no sense purchasing a first-class compartment that might better go to visiting royalty, assuming any such was in the area and hankering for a night on the town in Athens, so I moseyed up the track about a mile, figuring to hop a lift in a freight car and save the price of a ticket.

Well, it turns out that I wasn't the only guy with that idea, because I found an old feller sitting next to a small fire, warming up a cup of coffee in an empty tin can.

"Howdy," I said. "You mind if I join you?"

"Help yourself," he said in perfect American. "You sound like a countryman."

"The Right Reverend Doctor Lucifer Jones at your service," I said, shaking his gnarly old hand.

"Pleased to meet you," he said. "I'm Zachariah MacDonald, from West Allis, Wisconsin."

"We're practically neighbors," I said. "I hail from Moline, Illinois—though I ain't been back there, or even to America, in many a year."

"Me neither," said MacDonald. "What are you doing here in Tinos?"

"Mostly looking for a way out," I said.

"I mean, what are you doing abroad in the first place?" he asked.

"I heard the siren song of romance, mystery, and adventure," I said. "As well as the footsteps of various biased and misguided prosecuting attorneys coming up behind me."

"Where are you off to?" he asked.

"Oh, it don't make much difference," I said. "Athens seems as good a place as any."

"You don't sound wildly enthused," said MacDonald.

"One place is pretty much like another," I said. "It all depends on the opportunities."

"Now there we disagree," he said. "I find all places absolutely unique and different from each other. For example, have you ever been to Africa?"

"Yeah, I spent a few years there."

"And you've no desire to go back?"

"Desire ain't got nothing to do with it," I said. "I been invited to keep off that particular land mass due to a series of innocent misunderstandings by the local authorities."

"How about Asia?"

"Same problem," I admitted.

"Can you go back to America?"

"Well, I *think* I'm still allowed in Montana and Arkansas," I said.

"It sounds like you've led a most interesting life," he said, backing off just a bit.

"I'm just a God-fearing man of the cloth who's trying to establish a tabernacle and bring the word of the Lord to all these depraved Europeans." I paused. "How about you, Brother Zachariah? What brings a Wisconsin man to this here forsaken little spot in the Greek countryside?"

"The culmination of my life's work," he said.

"You been working all your life just to sit here and hop a freight for Athens?" I asked.

He shook his head. "Of course not."

"Well, then?"

"I was a professor of geology at the University of Wisconsin for close to thirty years," said MacDonald. "My special field of study was lost continents: Lemuria, Mu, Gondwanaland, and the like."

"Yeah?"

He nodded. "Most of them are myths, of course—but about twenty years ago I became convinced, from certain hints both in Plato and elsewhere, that Atlantis actually existed, that it was not merely a myth."

"And you think it's somewhere near this here railroad track?" I asked.

"No, of course not. Over the years I pieced together every bit of data I could get my hands on. Then, when I was sure I was right, I quit my job, cashed in my life savings, and went hunting for it." Suddenly he smiled triumphantly. "And four months ago I found it!"

"Funny how that little piece of news didn't make the papers," I said.

"I haven't made it public yet," he said. "There are others who are also searching for it, who would gladly kill me if they knew I had found it first. I'm on my way to stake my claim right now."

"If you can't afford to buy a ticket on the train," I said, "how do you figure to pay for a whole lost continent?"

"Oh, I've got the money," he said. "It's safely tucked away in a bank in Athens. But my competitors—no cretins, they—have finally figured out that I found what I was looking for, and there have been a series of attempts on my life. I'd have been a sitting duck at the Tinos train station."

"Well, if they know that Atlantis is near Tinos, ain't they likely to buy it out from under you anyway?" I asked.

"It's nowhere near here. I've been in Tinos for a month to throw them off the scent." He frowned. "The problem is, I did *too* good a job of it. I convinced them so thoroughly that it's near Tinos that they now feel free to kill me." Suddenly he stared at me. "You seem like a man of action, Doctor Jones. How would you like to hire on as my bodyguard?"

"Well, the Tabernacle of Saint Luke *is* a mite short of funds these days," I allowed. "What's the job pay?"

"Five thousand dollars, for a week's work."

"Brother Zachariah," I said, "you got yourself a body-guard."

"Excellent!" he said, shaking on it. "By the way, I don't believe I've ever heard of the Tabernacle of Saint Luke."

"It ain't real well established around these here parts," I admitted.

"In fact," he continued, "I'm not aware of *any* church or tabernacle named after Saint Luke."

"Well, it seemed more modest than calling it the Tabernacle of Saint Lucifer," I said, "me not yet having been canonized or nothing."

"You're a very enterprising young man," he said.

"Well, the Lord teaches us to grab what's there."

"He does?"

"I practice an exceptionally aggressive form of Christianity," I explained.

"Where did you learn it?" he asked.

"Oh, it's just something me and the Lord worked out betwixt ourselves of a Sunday afternoon back in Moline," I replied. "So far it's served me pretty well, except for them occasions when it hasn't."

Well, we chatted for a few more minutes, and then the train came along, and we hopped into an open cattle car and slid the door shut. The train stopped at Tinos for about five minutes, no one looked into our car, and then we took off again, hitting Athens about six hours later.

We waited till the station was pretty much deserted, then caught a cab and went straight to the Grande Bretagne Hotel, where MacDonald had an account, and they gave us a pair of connecting rooms on the sixth floor, overlooking Constitution Square. He was afraid to go down to the restaurant, so we had room service deliver us a dinner of *dolmades* and *moussaka* and *pastitso* and *saganaki* and all kinds of pastries, and by the time we were done I was wondering why I hadn't discovered the bodyguard business a long time ago.

Then a shot rang out and the window shattered and we both hit the floor, and I realized that there was more to bodyguarding than met the eye.

"Get out your gun!" he whispered.

"I don't know quite how to tell you this, Brother Zachariah," I said, "but I ain't got no gun."

"What kind of bodyguard are you?" he snapped.

"Right now I'm concentrating real hard on being a live one," I said. "Beyond that, I ain't too particular at this here point in time."

"Did you at least see where the shot came from?" he asked.

"Well, if it didn't come from outside, we're in a lot more trouble than I hope we are," I answered.

"What use are you?" he demanded.

"Well, I never claimed to be a bodyguard by trade," I said. "On the other hand, if they manage to kill you, I'll give you the best send-off any funeral's ever seen."

"Let's crawl to the door," he said. "We'll be safer in the corridor."

I didn't necessarily agree with that, since I didn't know who might be waiting in the corridor to greet us, but then another shot came through the window and we high-tailed it to the door and raced out of the room. The corridor was empty, and we decided that trying to leave the hotel wouldn't be the brightest course of action, since someone on the outside already knew we were there, so instead we climbed down to the third floor and found a real small broom closet without no windows.

"I'll wait here," said MacDonald. "You go down to the desk and have them phone the police."

That didn't have no more appeal to me than returning to the room to finish up the pastries.

"Maybe you'd better go, Brother Zachariah," I said. "I don't speak Greek."

"The desk clerk speaks English."

"He'd probably be more inclined to believe a regular customer of good standing in the community," I said.

"Just *do* it!" he said, shoving me out into the corridor and locking the door behind me.

Well, I couldn't see no point to standing out there all night, so I walked over to the elevator and pushed the button, and a minute later I was down on the main floor, walking over to the desk, when a couple of well-dressed gentlemen walked over and grabbed me by each arm and escorted me out the door and to a black car that was waiting at the curb. Then they frisked me and had me climb into the back seat between them.

"What is your name?" demanded the taller one, shoving a pistol into my short ribs.

"The Right Reverend Honorable Doctor Lucifer Jones at your service," I said.

"I hope so," he said.

"Just check my passport if you doubt me, brother."

"I meant that I hope you will be at our service," he said. "What is your exact relationship to Professor Zachariah Mac-Donald?"

"I'm kind of a paid traveling companion," I said.

"Enough talk!" snapped the shorter man. "Has he found it?"

"Has *who* found *what*?" I asked.

"You know precisely what I'm talking about: has MacDonald found what he's been looking for?"

"Last I saw of him, he was mostly looking for a place to hide," I said.

"Listen to me, Reverend Jones," said the taller one. "I don't know what your involvement is, but whatever he's paying you, we'll triple it."

"Let me get this straight," I said. "He's paying me five thousand dollars to keep him alive for a week. You're saying that *you'll* pay me fifteen thousand to keep him alive?"

"Don't play the fool with me, Reverend Jones!" said the taller man. "We'll pay you fifteen thousand to come over to our side."

"You want me to protect *you* from *him*?"

I thunk the tall guy was going to hit me with his gun, but the short one reached over and stopped him.

"What he means, Reverend Jones," he said, pronouncing each word real slow and careful-like, "is that we will pay you to keep us informed of Professor MacDonald's plans—and if you can tell us where Atlantis is before he stakes his claim and makes the news public, we'll pay you a bonus of another fifteen thousand."

"Well, that seems right generous," I said. "But you got to promise me that you won't kill him."

"Why not?" demanded the tall guy.

"He's paying me to keep him alive," I explained. "That would be a breach of faith."

"But telling us his plans isn't?" he asked, surprised.

"He just hired me to guard his body, not his secrets," I said. "Have we got a deal?"

The two looked at each other, and then nodded.

"What are your names, and how do I contact you?" I asked them.

"You may call us Mr. Tall and Mr. Short, and we'll contact *you*," said Mr. Short. "From this moment on, you'll never be out of our sight."

They opened the door and sent me back into the hotel. I didn't see much sense stopping at the broom closet to tell MacDonald that the coast was clear, since he was bound to ask why, and I figured he wouldn't see the situation quite the same way I did, so I went up to his room, finished off the *baklava* and a bottle of *ouzo*, and then sacked out in my own room right next door.

When I woke up I checked the clock and saw it was about noontime, so I opened the connecting door to MacDonald's room to see if he was ready to go to the bank yet, but he wasn't nowhere to be seen. I went down to the lobby looking for him, but although Mr. Tall and Mr. Short were there waiting for us, the desk clerk told me that MacDonald hadn't come down yet.

I figured the only place left that he could possibly be was the broom closet on the third floor, so I went up there to open it, and found it was still locked.

"Come on, Brother Zachariah!" I shouted, pounding away on the door. "It's almost noon. You can't stay in there forever."

Well, I must have kept it up for a good ten minutes with no answer, and suddenly Mr. Tall and Mr. Short were standing beside me, and finally Mr. Tall pulled out a little piece of wire and picked the lock and opened the door, and there was poor Zachariah MacDonald, sprawled out on the floor.

"Dead?" asked Mr. Short.

Mr. Tall felt for a pulse. "Definitely. It must have been all these ammonia fumes in a closed room."

Which brought my one and only attempt at bodyguarding to a sorry end.

"Well, Doctor Jones," said Mr. Short, "you're working exclusively for us now. We won't pay you the fifteen thousand for telling us the dear departed's plans, of course, but we'll pay you the other fifteen if you can figure out where Atlantis is."

"In the meantime," said Mr. Long, "let's carry poor Professor MacDonald up to his room so that he doesn't disturb the hotel guests, and we can go over his pockets and such without any untimely interruptions."

Well, the three of us didn't have much trouble carting Brother Zachariah, who wasn't all that big or tall, up to his room, where Mr. Tall and Mr. Short stripped him down to the buff looking for clues.

"Damn!" said Mr. Tall when they were done. "There's nothing but his bank book—and now that he's dead, that won't do us any good."

"Did he have any luggage, Reverend Jones?" asked Mr. Short.

"Not a thing," I said. "He was traveling just as light as I was."

"*Think*, Reverend Jones!" said Mr. Tall. "Did he say anything, anything at all, that might give you a hint as to where Atlantis is?"

"Nothing. Just that it wasn't nowhere near Tinos, that he'd wasted a month there to throw you off the trail."

"Did he tell you where he'd been before going to Tinos?"

"Not as I recall."

"Then that son of a dog died with the secret intact!" said Mr. Tall.

"Hey, that's no way to speak of the dead," I said. "Especially since he always spoke kindly of you."

"He did?" said Mr. Short sharply. "I thought he held all competitors in complete contempt. *What* did he say?"

"He allowed as to how you were pretty bright fellers."

"That hardly sounds like MacDonald," said Mr. Short.

"Maybe not," I said. "But he kept saying that you weren't no cretins."

"That's *it*!" screamed Mr. Short.

"What are you talking about?" I asked.

"He didn't say cretin!" said Mr. Short. "He said Cret*an*! It was his way of having a little joke!"

"I don't follow you," I said.

"He found Atlantis off the coast of Crete!" exclaimed Mr. Short excitedly. "And when he said that we were not Cretans, he meant that we could never be expected to find it!"

"It makes sense," agreed Mr. Tall, studying the bank book. "His bank has a branch on Crete, and that's where he made his last two transactions."

"So all we have to do is buy the submerged land around Crete and we'll be rich beyond our wildest dreams!" said Mr. Short.

"Excuse me for interrupting," I said, "but getting rich beyond my wildest dreams is one of my favorite conversational subjects. What has Atlantis got that makes it so valuable?"

"Artifacts from a civilization that existed a millennium before Christ!" said Mr. Tall. "Artifacts that no one has ever seen before. By the time we finish selling them to museums and collectors, we can practically buy our own country!"

"What makes you think the government of Crete is gonna be real anxious to sell it to you?" I asked.

"They won't *know* they're selling us Atlantis," said Mr. Short. "We'll merely buy dredging rights for a few miles in each direction."

"I don't want to sound ungrateful or nothing," I said, "but fifteen thousand dollars seems a small price to pay me for helping you becoming billionaires."

"We're not through doing business with you yet, Reverend Jones," said Mr. Tall.

"No?"

"Unfortunately, Mr. Short and I have had certain . . . ah . . . technical disagreements with the authorities on Crete."

"It's true," added Mr. Short. "They would be most unhappy to see us show up there."

"They might even ask how we came by the money we plan to use to purchase Atlantis," chimed in Mr. Tall.

"In fact," said Mr. Short, "there are probably fifty or sixty customers of the Bank of Crete who would be more than happy to tell them."

"It's our own fault for leaving so many witnesses alive," added Mr. Tall, "but how were we to know the bank would be that crowded?"

"We simply didn't have enough bullets for them all," explained Mr. Short. "It was most unprofessional of us, and I assure you it will never happen again."

"But in the meantime," concluded Mr. Tall, "it would probably be best if someone else were to purchase Atlantis—someone totally unknown to the Cretan authorities."

"You're looking at him," I said proudly. "I don't even know where Crete is."

"Fine," said Mr. Tall. "Then it appears that we will be able to do some more business, Reverend Jones."

"I'm all ears," I said.

"We don't know how much money it will take to purchase Atlantis, so we may have a momentary cash flow problem," said Mr. Short. "But if you will forgo your fifteen thousand dollars now, we will give you five percent of everything we recover, which should come to considerably more. A thousandfold, at the very minimum."

"Well, that's right generous of you gentlemen," I said. "But if you will allow me an indiscreet question, how can I be sure you'll give me a fair accounting of what you owe me—not that I think for a single moment that you'd ever cheat a partner. View it as an academic question."

Mr. Tall chuckled. "In point of fact, Dr. Jones, it's *we* who have to make sure that *you* don't cheat *us*. Everything will be registered in your name, so all the revenues will come to you."

"Now," added Mr. Short, "can *we* be sure that you'll give *us* a fair accounting of what you owe us?"

"You'd ask that of a man of the cloth?" I said.

"We'd simply like to hear your reassurances."

"Brother Short," I said, "I wouldn't never cheat no partner. That's contrary to the Seventh and Twelfth Commandments."

"Then we're in business," said Mr. Tall. "Let's stop wasting time here and catch the next plane to Crete."

"What about poor Brother MacDonald?" I asked. "Seems we ought to give him some kind of a send-off, long as he's the one who's making us all rich."

"Well, we'd like to," said Mr. Short uneasily. "But unfortunately, should the Athens police see us at his graveside, they might ask some embarrassing questions."

"That ain't no problem," I said. "I'll vouch that he died by accident."

"Oh, they won't ask about Mr. MacDonald," said Mr. Short. "Not at first, anyway."

"But when they finish asking about the other seventeen misunderstandings, they might well want to know about poor Mr. MacDonald as well," added Mr. Tall.

"Well, the Good Book teaches us to be adaptable, so why don't we all just observe a moment's silence right now?" I suggested.

Which we did.

Then we went down to the black car, which was parked by the curb, and headed out to the airport, where we found that there weren't no scheduled flights to Crete for the next four days, so Mr. Tall chartered us a plane—leastwise, I *think* he chartered it, though the pilot didn't seem none too happy about the proceedings—and a few hours later we landed on Crete.

It was too late in the day to visit the government offices, so we spent the night in the El Greco Hotel, which took in tourists, roaches, and rats with equal hospitality, and in the morning we headed on over to the Iráklion Public Works Building. Just before we got there, Mr. Small handed me a thick envelope and told me that it contained all the money he figured I'd need for dredging rights, and that he planned on getting a strict accounting the minute I came out.

Well, it took me a good hour and a half to get to the right department, and then another hour to make myself understood, but by noon I was the proud owner to the dredging rights to Atlantis for a mere thirty-two thousand dollars, which was two thousand more than was in the envelope, so I used my last two grand to cover it, and I walked back out carrying the certificate that made it all legal. Then we celebrated with lunch, and in the afternoon Mr. Tall and Mr. Short hired a mighty impressive-looking boat and we all went out to pull a few rare pots and pans out of the ruins of Atlantis.

We sent down half a dozen divers, all loaded with sacks and pouches to pull up their treasure. What they brung up was three sea shells and a blowfish.

"Where are the artifacts?" demanded Mr. Short.

"I keep telling you," said the captain of the ship, "we have sailed this sea all our lives, and we have never seen a trace of this lost continent or city or whatever it is."

"Maybe we're not looking in the right place," said Mr. Tall. "Let's head south."

The captain shrugged. "It's your money."

Well, we looked south and east and north and west. We looked right off the shore, and twenty miles out to sea, and eighty miles out to sea. We looked halfway to Italy and all the way back to Greece, but after a month we had to conclude that we had guessed wrong, and that there wasn't no lost continent, or even a lost suburb, off the island of Crete.

"I suppose in every enterprise there comes a time to pull up stakes and call it a day," said Mr. Short while we were eating dinner at a little waterfront *taverna*.

"That's what happens when you put your faith in an academic," said Mr. Tall distastefully. "Obviously the late lamented Professor MacDonald really *did* mean cretin, and now the secret of Atlantis has gone to the grave with him."

"We'll head back to the mainland tomorrow morning," said Mr. Short.

"Since you guys are quitting and there ain't no million dollars' worth of old ashtrays and such to be dug up out of the sea," I said, "what about my fifteen thousand dollars?"

"You stood to make a fortune if we had succeeded," said Mr. Tall. "I see no reason why we should bear the brunt of our failure alone."

"Well, at least give me five thousand," I said. "If you guys hadn't been after him, poor Brother Zachariah would have lasted out the week and I'd have earned my bodyguard money."

"Nonsense," said Mr. Short. "You're the legal owner of Atlantis, such as it is. Go sublease the dredging rights."

"That's *it*?" I demanded. "You're just gonna get up and walk away?"

"Well, if you feel we've been unfair to you in any way, we could shoot you first," suggested Mr. Tall.

The conversation kind of flattened out and lay there like a dead fish after that, and the next morning Mr. Tall and Mr. Short were gone, leaving me with nothing but my last fifteen dollars and the ownership of a continent that was so lost nobody could find it.

I figured I might as well head back to the mainland, too, but when I went to the airport I found out that I didn't have enough money to pay for a plane ticket, and they wouldn't extend me no credit even though I was a man of the cloth. Then I moseyed over to the docks, and discovered that there weren't any boats leaving for the next three days.

So since I was stuck there, I got to thinking about what Mr. Short had said about my being the legal owner of Atlantis, and suddenly the Lord hit me between the eyes with one of His better revelations, and I walked over to the telegraph office and got ahold of the biggest newspaper in Athens and spent all but my last seventeen cents placing an ad.

I had given my address as the El Greco Hotel, so I spent my nights sleeping on a park bench and my days hanging around the lobby, and sure enough, in three days the money started pouring in, and within a week I'd made a quick forty-two thousand dollars and had barely scratched the surface of my potential market, and just when it seemed like me and God were finally gonna get our tabernacle, a bunch of Cretan police officers entered the El Greco's lobby and had a quick conversation with the desk clerk, who pointed to me, and a minute later I was being dragged, none too gently, to a squad car, and a couple of minutes after that we pulled up at the police station and they escorted me into a room with a single chair and damp white walls.

"Is anyone gonna tell me what's going on?" I demanded. "I'm a peaceful law-abiding businessman what ain't been bothering no one, and suddenly you guys drag me off like I was some kind of undesirable or something."

"You are Lucifer Jones, are you not?" said the captain of the squad.

"The Right Reverend Lucifer Jones," I corrected him.

"The same Lucifer Jones who placed an advertisement last week in *The Daily Athenian*?"

"Yeah, that's me."

"I hate to think of how many laws you have broken, Reverend Jones," said the captain.

I pulled out my certificate of dredging rights. "I stand on the law," I said. "I got every legal right to subdivide what I own and sell it off."

"You do understand, do you not, that every square centimeter of land you own is under the water?"

"So what?"

"Then how can you possibly sell lots with, as the ad says, 'a Mediterranean view'?"

"I didn't never say what angle the view was from," I replied. *"Caviar empire."*

He shook his head. "I am afraid we will have to confiscate any money you have appropriated and return it to the poor dupes who answered your advertisement," he said. "And of course," he added, taking my certificate away, "your dredging rights have been revoked."

"Then give me my thirty-two thousand dollars and we'll call it square," I said.

"Your fine comes to thirty-one thousand nine hundred dollars or fifteen years in jail," he said calmly. "The choice is yours."

Well, I growled and I grumbled, but finally I didn't have no choice but to pay the fine.

"Now give me my hundred dollars and let me out of here," I said.

"First you must sign over all claims to dredging rights," he said. "Then it will be my pleasure to place you on a plane that is leaving for Rome in less than an hour."

"Who do I sign the rights over to?" I asked, looking at the certificate.

He frowned. "The Iráklion Public Works Building is closed today. To facilitate matters, you can sign them over to me—Captain Hektor Papadoras—and I will conclude the paperwork tomorrow."

I did what he said, and they put me on the plane—which cost sixty of the hundred dollars they owed me—and a few hours later I was in Rome, chastising my Silent Partner for turning His back on me just when things were going well for the two of us.

I ate something I hadn't never heard of called a pizza pie for dinner, which I decided was okay for Italy but would never catch on in the States, and then I found a cheap hotel and took a room there.

The next morning I picked up a newspaper and read a feature about how an enterprising Cretan policeman named Hektor Papadoras was selling private fishing concessions off the coast of his island.

I gave my Silent Partner a serious talking-to, explained that He'd been falling down on the job and that I expected better of Him in the future, and then I set out afresh to make my fortune and bring His word to the degenerate heathen of the Roman Empire, or such portion of it as I could snugly fit in the Tabernacle of Saint Luke once it got itself built.

15
Exercising Ghosts

For a city that all roads were supposed to lead to, Rome wasn't exactly the most dazzling municipality I'd ever encountered. Of course, it may well be that I was somewhat hampered in my ability to enjoy its sights and sounds by the fact that I only had seventeen cents in my pocket, all that remained from my unfortunate ventures into treasure hunting and buying lost continents (which in this case was so lost that nobody ain't found it to this very day).

Still, it takes more than poverty and a string of bad luck to keep a good Christian down, especially a man of the cloth, so I headed on down the Via Veneto looking for some way to replenish my funds, which was when I realized that even though the Vatican was right next door I was surrounded by a bunch of pagans, because even though I hunted up three different craps games on street corners, none of the participants was willing to take my marker, even after I explained that I was toiling in the personal service of the Lord.

Never one to be downcast by cruel turns of Fate, I hung around the bus terminal until a batch of Americans got off about noontime, introduced myself as their guide, and collected a quick three dollars a head from all seventeen of 'em. Fortunately they didn't know Rome any better than I did, so nobody objected as I led 'em through town pointing out Buckingham Palace and the Louvre and other such historic sights as I reckoned were towering about the countryside somewhere. It was when I was explaining to them how the Sistine Brothers had hired Leonardo da Vinci to give their chapel a couple of coats of paint that I began to detect unhappy stirrings in my little group, and by the time I got around to trying to collect some more money for a gondola ride to the Tower of Pisa they all just up and left.

Still, fifty-one dollars for two hours of work wasn't bad pay, though it only took me ten minutes to lose half of it once I scared up another game of chance. I figured my Silent Partner had His attention directed elsewhere for the time being, and I was seriously considering taking a little fling at the guide business when I heard the worst kind of shrieking and wailing coming from a nearby house, and then the door opened and a priest walked out, followed by a pudgy-looking woman.

"I told you this would be a waste of time, signora," he said. "Probably you need an exterminator."

"I need *you*!" she hollered.

"You are a superstitious old woman," he said. "Your church has more important things to do. You must stop bothering us with these foolish requests."

He turned on his heel and walked away, and she started weeping and wailing to beat the band, so I moseyed on over and asked her what the problem was.

"Ghosts!" she said, answering in heavily accented American.

"Ghosts?"

"In my attic," she said, crossing herself. "Every night I hear them, pacing the floors and rattling their chains. So I asked the church to send someone to exercise the ghost, and instead they sent that . . . that *buffoon*, who wouldn't know a ghost if it jumped up and spit on him!"

"Well, I'm right sorry to hear it, ma'am."

"I even offered to pay a million lira to the church if they would just exercise my ghosts."

I couldn't figure out why she was so all-fired anxious to have someone take her ghosts out for a walk, but suddenly I thought I saw a way to raise a little grubstake for me and my Silent Partner.

"Uh . . . how much is a million lira in real money, ma'am?" I said.

She didn't know, but she told me what it bought, and I figured we were talking close to a thousand dollars.

"Well, ma'am, I don't want to say nothing bad about our competitors, me being a decent Christian, but it appears to me that you've been dealing with the wrong church."

"What are you talking about?" she said.

"I'm the pastor of the Tabernacle of Saint Luke," I said, "and it just so happens that exercising ghosts is one of the very best things we do."

"Where is this tabernacle?" she asked suspiciously.

"Well, truth to tell, it ain't quite built yet, but your kind donation could buy us the first cornerstone."

"I don't give money to any charlatan who comes around making promises," she said. "First you exercise my ghosts. *Then* I'll pay you."

"Ma'am, you got yourself a deal," I said with my very best Sunday go-to-meeting grin. "I'll exercise the tar out of the critters."

"They're never around in the daytime," she said. "Come back after dark."

"Sounds good to me, ma'am," I said. "I'll see you then."

I shook her hand, and went off to buy myself some lunch with the money I'd gotten from the tourists, and with what was left I stopped by a pet store and bought a couple of leashes so these here ghosts wouldn't try to get away from me while I was exercising 'em. Then I bought a flashlight, and a nice black bag to hold everything, and I spent the rest of the afternoon testing out half a dozen fine Italian wines, all of which had been aging at least since midmorning, and finally the sun set and I went back to the lady's house and knocked on the door.

"I really didn't think you would come back," she said, and now that it was dark out her whole manner was different, like she was scared to death or something. If it had been me and I felt that way about ghosts, I'd have wanted 'em permanently removed from the premises instead of just given a workout, but there ain't no accounting for the peculiarities of the female mind, even though it's frequently attached to other parts that seem to make a lot more sense, so I just walked into the living room and asked her where the ghosts were at.

"Upstairs," she said with a shudder. "In the attic."

"Thanks a lot, ma'am," I said. "Just go about your business. I'll have 'em exercised in no time at all."

"What is that?" she asked, pointing to my black bag.

"It's got all my exercising equipment in it," I explained.

"You are the bravest man I have ever met," she said. "What is your name?"

"The Right Reverend Doctor Lucifer Jones at your service, ma'am," I said.

She stared at me for a good long time. "Are you married?" she said at last. "I have this beautiful young niece in Florence . . ."

"Well, actually, ma'am, I'm kind of married to the Lord, though He gets a mite fidgety when I refer to it that way." I looked around. "Which way to the attic? The sooner I get these here ghosts up and exercised, the sooner I can put your kind donation to use."

She pointed to a staircase. "Go up two flights, to the third floor," she said. "Then you will see a bolted wooden door leading up to the attic."

"Well, at least *I'm* gonna get exercised," I said, but she didn't understand my joke, leading me to conclude that middle-aged Italian widows ain't got no sense of humor, so I just smiled at her again and started climbing up the stairs. When I came to the wooden door on the third floor I slid back the bolt, opened it, and went up this narrow set of creaky stairs leading to the attic.

I pulled out the flashlight and turned it on. I hadn't never seen a ghost before, but I figured it'd be wearing a white sheet and floating a little bit off the floor, unless Italian ghosts were a lot different from American ones, but before I could look into every nook and cranny of the attic a huge unghostly hand reached out and grabbed me from behind.

"What are you doing here?" demanded a low voice.

"I ain't armed and I don't mean you no harm!" I said. "I'm just here to take you out for a little walk."

"Your voice sounds familiar," said whatever was holding me.

"Now as I come to think on it, so does yours," I said. "Let go of me so's I can get a look at you."

I twisted around and found myself facing this eight-foot-tall guy with brown hair and blue eyes. He hadn't shaved in a few weeks, but I didn't have no trouble recognizing him.

"Sam Hightower!" I exclaimed. "What in blazes are *you* doing here?"

"Lucifer Jones!" he said. "I was about to ask the same thing of you."

"I been commissioned to exercise such ghosts as may be setting up shop in this here attic," I said. "How about you? The last time I saw you, you'd given up the Abominable Snowman business and were hiding out from Guido Scarducci's friends and relations in Nepal."

"They found me," he said.

"He still ain't forgiven you for not shaving points in the big basketball game like you agreed to, huh?" I said.

"The man is totally without compassion," he answered. "I barely escaped with my life. They chased me all across Asia and into Europe, and I finally wound up in Rome."

"But why are you hiding out in an attic?"

"Well, it's mighty difficult to hide out in a crowd when you're eight feet two inches tall," he said. "I've been keeping to myself by day, and sneaking out to steal food at night."

"You know," I said, mulling on his situation, "I think I see a way for the two of us to make a profit out of your unhappy plight. Maybe even enough so that you can finally pay Guido Scarducci off and go back home without worrying about what might be gaining on you."

"Yeah?" he said. "What's your plan?"

"The old lady what owns this place is paying me a million lira to exercise you," I said, "but even a compassionate woman like her ain't likely to pay me to take you out for a walk each and every day. But," I added, "if you was to move down the block, or maybe around the corner, and do some serious moaning and wailing at night, I could probably get another million to turn you out into the street, and we can keep doing it as long as you can keep finding attics."

"It does have possibilities," he admitted thoughtfully. "And the best part of it is that no one would have to see me."

"Getting seen wouldn't exactly work to our advantage," I agreed.

"How will we manage it?" he asked.

"We'll just wait until the widder lady's gone to sleep, and sneak on down the stairs," I said, "and then you can point out the next house you plan to haunt. I'll stop by in the morning to collect my fee and explain that the ghosts ran off while I was exercising 'em and at least she ain't gonna be troubled by 'em no more. Then I'll give you a couple of evenings to stir up the owners of your next attic, after which I'll come by and offer my services again."

"Sounds good to me," he said. "We split all the fees fifty-fifty, right?"

"Wrong," I said. "One-third for me, one-third for you, and one-third for the Lord."

He kept insisting that this was really a two-for-one split, so finally we struck a deal that he and I would split the first fifty million lira down the middle, and then the Lord had an option on the next ten million, at which point the three of us would renegotiate the contract.

Well, we sat around in the attic for a few hours, reminiscing about Tibet and Nepal, and he told me all about how he got chased through Russia by Guido Scarducci's gunmen, and I told him all about the Land of Eternal Youth and the Scorpion Lady and the home-made man and all the people and places I'd seen since we parted, and then it was close on to three o'clock and we could hear the widder lady snoring up a storm, so we gently and quietly descended the stairs and let ourselves out, and just before we parted company Sam Hightower pointed out the next attic he planned to haunt, and I took my last few dollars and rented a room for the night.

I came by in the morning and explained that the ghosts had all run off and hid once I got 'em outside, and before I could apologize or make excuses or nothing the lady had thrown her arms around me and kissed me and started thanking everyone from God to the Madonna to half a dozen local saints, although it was me and me alone what removed the ghosts, and then she paid me my million lira and kissed me again, and ran off to tell her neighbors the good news while I moseyed over to the Via Veneto and rented a suite at the Excelsior, which was the poshest hotel in Rome back in them days.

I figured to give Sam three nights to get the owners of his new domicile used to the idea that they had more than mice in their attic, but the very next afternoon a little Italian feller with glasses and an umbrella came calling on me while I was grabbing some espresso at a local streetside cafe.

"You are Lucifer Jones, are you not?" he asked.

"The Right Reverend Lucifer Jones, at your service," I said, gesturing for him to join me, but he just stood there looking kind of nervous.

"Thank God I have found you!" he said. "Signora Mondedori described you to me, but nobody knew where you lived. I have been searching for you all day."

"Who's this Signora Mondedori?" I asked, wondering if I'd made any romantic promises that had slipped my mind in the past few hours.

"You removed the ghosts from her house."

"Oh, *that* Signora Mondedori," I said, much relieved.

"She lives across the street from us, and told us of your faith and your bravery," he said.

"Well, it comes from living a clean life and thinking nothing but pure thoughts," I said modestly. "And now that you've found me, what can I do for you, Signor . . . ?"

"Signor Palusco," he said. "Enrico Palusco. I will come right to the point. I have lived in my house all my life. My father lived there for his entire life, as did my grandfather. Never have we had a cause to regret this. Never has there been any reason not to be content."

"I'm sure glad you're getting right to the point," I said.

"But last night," he continued, "I heard things in my attic!"

"What kind of things?" I asked.

"Unholy, supernatural things!" he said, his voice shaking. "Ghostly things! Horrible moaning and hideous screeching!"

"I'm right sorry to hear that, Brother Palusco," I said. "Sounds like your neighborhood has caught itself a plague of ghosts."

"Will you remove them from my house?" he asked.

"Well," I said, "I got a lot of exercising jobs lined up. To be truthful, I don't think I could get to your house much before next week. My best advice is to put all your affairs in order and scout out a reputable funeral parlor. These ghosts don't ordinarily devour a whole family at a single sitting, so there ought to be at least one survivor to see to the burials."

"I will pay you ten million lira if you come tonight!" he said. "I beg of you, Signor Jones!"

"Well, I really shouldn't sneak you in ahead of all these other needy families," I said, "but somehow you've touched my compassionate Christian heart. I'll be there with my exercising gear just after dark. Why don't you wait out front for me, to make sure I got the right address? I'd hate to wind up in the wrong house, since in my experience goblins and leprechauns don't take as well to exercising as ghosts do."

He kissed my hand and started muttering in Italian.

"And don't forget to have the money ready, Brother Palusco," I said as he began walking away.

Well, when I showed up, there must have been fifty people from the neighborhood all wanting to shake my hand and bless me and such, and I thanked 'em and told 'em to go back to their houses because exercising ghosts was a delicate and tricky business and could well take the whole night, and then I went up the stairs with my little black bag and found Sam wailing and moaning into a heating vent. I gave him a sandwich that I'd brung along, and then pulled a couple of beers out of my bag, and we sat around until we figured the rest of the world was asleep, and then we snuck on down the stairs and back into the street, and Sam chose his next attic, and the next day, even before I could come back for my money, Signor Palusco showed up at my hotel and paid me, and it was all I could do to get him to leave before he started kissing me so much that people began looking kind of strange at us, and one very clean-cut young man stopped by to tell me his name was Damon and he could usually be found hanging around the lobby in late afternoons.

Then a strange thing happened. Even though I knew Sam was only haunting one house at a time, word of my success at exercising spooks and spirits started making the rounds, and before evening I'd had another half a dozen requests from people that was sure they had ghosts in the attic, though after talking to 'em I figured what they mostly had was bats in the belfry.

Still, business looked so good that I figured I might as well rent out an office. I found myself a nice one over near the Spanish Steps, all furnished and everything, and even though the sign painter couldn't spell and wound up painting "Ghosts Exorcised" on the door, I was pretty well-satisfied with the way things were going.

I exercised Hightower out of five more houses in the next two weeks, and we began thinking about expanding the business and maybe hiring a few more ghosts and a few more exercisers. We were still mulling it over when I escorted him out of yet another house in the middle of the night, and we decided that before we committed to taking on more help we ought to make sure that the market could bear it, so we decided to have him move his base of operations and start haunting a brand-new neighborhood, just to see if we got the same reaction.

Well, we walked through the residential sections of Rome for maybe an hour, and finally, when we figured we'd put enough distance betwixt ourselves and our former stamping grounds, we turned onto the Via Aurelia. Hightower studied the area for a minute or two, then pointed to a house about halfway down the block and told me that was where he planned to set up shop. I couldn't see what it was about that particular house that attracted him when they all looked so much alike, but I figured that haunting was his business and unhaunting was mine, and I didn't want to make no intrusions in his area of professional expertise.

I spent the next day visiting my competition at the Vatican, mostly because I'd heard that they had a really fascinating collection of pornography, but evidently they didn't feel the need to share it with no outsiders, because I was told it was kept under lock and key and no one was allowed to see it, which struck me as just plumb wasteful, but even though I put up a fuss and asked to see the head man they wound up escorting me out the door, and I returned to my office just in time to get a phone call from a Signor Crosetti who lived on the Via Aurelia and had just come down with a bad case of ghosts. I scribbled down his address and negotiated a fee, then promised him I'd be there an hour after sundown.

In the meantime, I had myself a nice dinner at the Sans Souci, where I'd took to reserving a regular table, and then picked up a couple of sandwiches and some beers to bring along for Hightower. Since it wasn't quite dark yet, I returned to the office to spend a few happy minutes counting our money and arranging it into artistic stacks and the like, and somehow or other I must have fallen asleep because the next thing I knew Signor Crosetti was on the phone, telling me that it was after midnight and his ghost was haunting up a storm.

When I showed up, Signor Crosetti was waiting for me out in front of his place with a lantern in his hand, all red of face and covered with sweat. He told me he'd sent his family off to spend the night with his brother, and he planned to join 'em just as soon as he let me into the house, and that nothing would ever get him to go inside again until I assured him that I'd whipped his ghost in straight falls and sent it packing.

This struck me as right considerate on his part, since it meant that Hightower and me could enjoy our beers in comfort in the living room before making our departure a few hours later, so I waited until he unlocked the front door and told him to show up at my office in the morning and I'd give him a blow-by-blow account of what went on.

Then I was inside the house, and the door slammed shut behind me, and I walked over to the staircase and pulled out my flashlight and shined the beam up to the next floor, where Hightower was moaning like there was no tomorrow.

"Hey, Hightower," I called out. "Come on down and have a beer. The coast is clear."

Nothing much happened except that he stopped moaning and started rattling a batch of chains that he must have found up there, or maybe swiped off someone's bicycle and brought along for the effect.

"Come on, Hightower!" I yelled. "This is me, Lucifer, calling to you. The house is empty!"

Hightower started making noises like unto a bull moose calling for his ladyfriend, and I started getting a little hot under the collar.

"Are you gonna make me climb all the way up there?" I said. "I keep telling you, there ain't no one else in the whole house except you and me!"

He got to moaning and wailing again, really sorrowful-like, and after a couple of minutes I gave up yelling at him and climbed up the stairs.

"Okay, Hightower," I said, shining the light around. "Where the hell are you hiding?"

He started moaning louder, and now I could tell he was up in the attic, and I figured that probably he just hadn't been able to hear me, and even though I was annoyed at having to climb all them stairs, I made up my mind to praise him for the way he was devoting himself to his work.

Problem was, when I finally reached the attic, there wasn't no one there. There was a heap of wailing, and I could hear some chains rattling in the corner, but I couldn't see hide nor hair of Hightower, and at eight feet two inches tall that was a lot of hide and hair to hide all at once.

"Come on now, Hightower," I said. "Fun's fun, but the beer's getting warm and I'm getting tired. Let's go on downstairs."

"Go away!" he whispered.

"What do you mean, go away?" I demanded. "Here I am being considerate enough to bring you some grub and some beer to wash it down with and you're getting temperamental?"

"Leave me to my misery!" he whispered.

"Your misery?" I said. "Look, I may have took a little more out of your half than mine for expenses, but that ain't no reason to—"

"Go away!" he whispered again.

"You tell me to go away once more and I just may do it!" I snapped. "I can always hire me another ghost, you know."

"Who are you talking to up there, Lucifer?" said a familiar voice.

I looked back down the stairs and saw this eight-foot-tall figure climbing up to join me.

"Hightower?" I said.

"I was in the attic next door, and I saw you come into the wrong house," he said. "When you didn't come right back out, I figured I'd come over to see what was going on."

"You mean you're just getting here this second?" I said.

"That's what I just told you," he answered.

"And I suppose you ain't never studied to be a ventriloquist?"

"It ain't ever been one of my major ambitions," he said.

"Then I think we got a serious problem on our hands," I said.

"What are you talking about?"

"I'm all through talking," I said, heading down the stairs. "What I'm about to start doing now is beating a tactical retreat."

"What's so all-fired frightening about an attic?" he yelled after me.

"Attics don't scare me none," I hollered back. "It's what's *in* the attic that I don't want no part of!"

"I've been living in these old attics for months," he said, walking in. "I'll show you there's nothing to be afraid of."

"You do whatever you think's best," I said as I reached the front door. "Me, I'm high-tailing it out of here."

I had just made it to the street when I heard a scream that would have woke such dead as weren't otherwise occupied, and a second later Hightower burst out of the house, yelling that he was heading for home and all Guido Scarducci and his friends and relations could do was kill him, and that wasn't nothing compared to what could happen to him in the attic. The last I saw of him he was running on a true course for Butte, Montana, and something about his manner implied that he wasn't gonna let a little thing like an ocean stand in his way.

As for me, I figured if I stayed in Rome people would keep asking me to get rid of their ghosts for them, and I had permanently retired from the exercising business the minute I ran out of Signor Crosetti's house, so I cleaned out the office, stuck all the money into my little black bag, and set out to find a suitable site to build my tabernacle.

16

The Werewolf

After I left Italy I wandered north and west. A couple of months later I found myself in Hungary, which ain't never gonna provide the Riviera with any serious competition for tourists. Each town I passed through was duller than the last, until I got to Budapest, which was considerably less exciting than Boise, Idaho, on a Tuesday afternoon.

I passed by an old, run-down arena that did double duty, hosting hockey games on weeknights and dog shows on Saturdays, then walked by the only nightclub in town, which was featuring one of the more popular lady tuba soloists in the country, and finally I came to the Magyar Hotel and rented me a room. After I'd left my gear there I set out to scout out the city and see if there were enough depraved sinners to warrant building my tabernacle there and setting up shop in the salvation business. My unerring instincts led me right to a batch of them, who were holed up in the men's room of the bus station, playing a game with which I was not entirely unfamiliar, as it consisted of fifty-two pasteboards with numbers or pictures on 'em and enough money in the pot to make it interesting.

"Mind if I join you gents?" I asked, walking over to them.

"Either you put your shirt on backward, or else you're a preacher," said one of 'em in an English accent.

"What's that got to do with anything?" I asked.

"We'd feel guilty taking your money," he said.

"You ain't got a thing to worry about," I said, sitting down with them.

"Well," he said with a shrug, "you've been warned."

"I appreciate that, neighbor," I said, "and just to show my goodwill, I absolve everyone here of any sins they committed between nine o'clock this morning and noon. Now, who deals?"

The game got going hot and heavy, and I had just about broken even when the British feller dealt a hand of draw, and I picked up my cards and fanned 'em out and suddenly I was looking at four aces and a king, and two of my opponents had great big grins on their faces, the kind of grin you get when you pick up a flush or a full house, and one of 'em opened, and the other raised, and I raised again, and it was like I'd insulted their manhood, because they raised right back, and pretty soon everyone else had dropped out and the three of us were tossing money into the pot like there wasn't no tomorrow, and just about the time we all ran out of money and energy and were about to show our cards, a little Hungarian kid ran into the room and shouted something in a foreign language—probably Hungarian, now as I come to think on it—and suddenly everyone grabbed their money and got up and started making for the exit.

"Hey, what's going on?" I demanded. "Where do you guys think you're going?"

"Away!" said the British feller.

"But we're in the middle of a hand," I protested.

"Lupo is coming!" said the Brit. "The game's over!"

"Who the hell is Lupo?" I demanded.

"He's more of a what. You'll leave too, if you know what's good for you!"

And suddenly, just like that, I was all alone in the men's room of a Hungarian bus station, holding four totally useless aces and a king, and thinking that maybe Hungarians were more in need of a shrink than a preacher. Then the door opened, and in walked this thin guy with grayish skin and hair everywhere—on his head, his lip, his chin, even the backs of his hands.

"Howdy, Brother," I said, and he nodded at me. "You better not plan on lingering too long," I added. "Someone or something called Lupo is on its way here."

He turned to face me and stared at me intently.

"*I* am Lupo," he said.

"You are?"

"Count Basil de Chenza Lupo," he continued. "Who are you?"

"The Right Reverend Doctor Lucifer Jones at your service," I said.

"Do you see any reason why you should run at the sight of me?" he continued.

"Except for the fact that you got a predatory look about you and probably ain't on speaking terms with your barber, nary a one," I answered.

"They are fools," he said. "Fools and peasants, nothing more."

"Maybe so," I said, "but you could have timed your call of Nature just a mite better, considering I was holding four bullets and the pot had reached a couple of thousand dollars."

"*Bullets?*" he said, kind of growling deep in his throat. "What kind?"

"Well, when you got four of 'em, there ain't a lot left except clubs, diamonds, hearts and spades," I said.

"But not silver?" he said.

"Not as I recollect."

"Good," he said, suddenly looking much relieved. "I am sorry I have caused you such distress, Doctor Jones."

"Well, I suppose when push comes to shove, it ain't really your fault, Brother Basil," I said.

"Nevertheless, I insist that you allow me to take you to dinner to make amends."

"That's right cordial of you," I said. "I'm a stranger in town. You got any particular place in mind?"

"We will dine at The Strangled Elk," he said. "It belongs to some Gypsy friends of mine."

"Whatever suits you," I said agreeably.

We walked out of the station, hit the main drag, and turned left.

"By the way, Brother Basil," I said, "why *were* all them men running away from a nice, friendly gent like you?"

He shrugged. "They are superstitious peasants," he said. "Let us speak no more of them."

"Suits me," I said. "People what entice a man of the cloth into a sinful game like poker and then run off when he's got the high hand ain't headed to no good end anyway."

I noticed as we walked down the street that everyone was giving us a pretty wide berth, and finally we turned down a little alleyway where all the men were dark and swarthy and wearing shirts that could have been took in some at the arms, and the women were sultry and good-looking and wearing colorful skirts and blouses, and Basil told me we were now among his Gypsy friends and no one would bother us, not that anyone had been bothering us before, and after a little while we came to a sign that said we'd reached The Strangled Elk, and we went inside.

It wasn't the cleanest place I'd ever seen, but I'd been a couple of weeks between baths myself, so I can't say that I minded it all that much. There was nobody there except one skinny old waiter, and Basil called him over and said something in Gypsy, and the waiter went away and came back a minute later with a bottle of wine and two glasses.

Well, we filled the glasses and chatted about this and that, and then we drank some more and talked some more, and finally the waiter brought out a couple of steaks.

"Brother Basil," I said, looking down at my plate, "I like my meat as rare as the next man, but I don't believe this has been cooked at all."

"I am sorry, my friend," he said. "That is the way I always eat it, and the cook simply assumed you shared my taste." He signaled to the waiter, said something else in Gypsy, and the waiter took my plate away. "It will be back in a few moments, properly cooked."

"You *always* eat your steak like that?" I asked, pointing to the slab of raw meat in front of him.

"It is the only way," he replied, picking it up with his hands and biting off a goodly chunk of it. He growled and snarled as he chewed it.

"You got a bit of a throat condition?" I asked.

"Something like that," he said. "I apologize if my table manners offend you."

"I've et with worse," I said. In fact, if push came to shove, I couldn't remember having dined with a lot that were much more refined.

Well, my steak came back just then, and after covering it with a pint of ketchup just to bring out the subtle nuances of its flavor, I dug in, and just so Basil wouldn't feel too conspicuous I growled and snarled too, and we spent the next five or ten minutes enjoying the noisiest meal of my experience, after which we polished off a couple of more bottles of wine.

"I have truly enjoyed this evening, my friend," said Basil after we were all done. "So few people will even speak to me, let alone join me in a repast . . ."

"I can't imagine why," I said. "You'd have to search far and wide to find a more hospitable feller."

"Nonetheless," he said, "it is time for you to leave."

"It's only about nine o'clock," I said. "I think I'll just sit here and digest the repast and maybe smoke a cigar or two, that is if you got any to spare, and then I'll mosey on back to my humble dwelling."

"You really must leave *now*," he said.

"You got a ladyfriend due any minute, right?" I said with a sly smile. "Well, never let it be said that Lucifer Jones ain't the soul of understanding and discretion. Why, I recall one time back in Cairo, or maybe it was Marrakech, that I . . ."

"*Hurry!*" he shouted. "The moon is rising!"

"Now how could you possibly know that, sitting here in the back of the room?" I asked.

"I *know*!" he said.

I got up and walked over to the doorway and stuck my head out. "Well, sun of a gun, the moon *is* out," I said. "I don't see your ladyfriend nowhere, though."

I turned back to face him, but Count Basil de Chenza Lupo wasn't nowhere to be seen. In fact, there wasn't no one in the room except the old waiter and an enormous wolf that must have wandered in through the kitchen door.

"Well, I've heard of restaurants that got roaches," I said, "and restaurants that got rats, but I do believe this is the first eatery I ever been to that was infested by wolves." I turned to the waiter. "What happened to Basil?" I asked. "Did he go off to the necessary?"

The waiter shook his head.

"Then where is he?"

The waiter pointed to the wolf.

"I don't believe I'm making myself clear," I said. "I ain't interested in no four-legged critters with fleas and bad breath. Where is Basil?"

The waiter pointed to the wolf again.

"I don't know why it's so hard to understand," I said. "That there is a wolf. I want to know what became of Basil."

The waiter nodded his head. "Basil," he said, pointing at the wolf again.

"You mean the wolf is named Basil, too?" I asked.

The waiter just threw his hands up and walked out of the room, leaving me alone with the wolf.

Well, I looked at the wolf for a good long while, and he looked right back at me, and as time went by it occurred to me that I hadn't seen no other wolves in all my wanderings through Europe, and that some zoo ought to be happy to pay a healthy price for such a prime specimen, so I walked over kind of gingerly and let him smell the back of my hand, and when I was sure he wasn't viewing me as a potential appetizer, I slipped my belt out of my pants and slid it around his neck and turned it into a leash.

"You come along with me, Basil," I said. "Tonight you can sleep in my hotel room, and tomorrow we'll set about finding a properly generous and appreciative home for you."

I started off toward the door, but he dug his feet in and practically pulled my arm out of the socket.

"Now, Basil," I said, jerking on the leash with both hands, "I ain't one to abuse dumb animals, but one way or the other you're coming with me."

He pulled back and whimpered, and then he snarled, and then he just went limp and laid down, but I was determined to get him out of there, and I started dragging him along the floor, and finally he whined one last time and got to his feet and started trotting alongside of me, and fifteen minutes later we reached the door of the Magyar Hotel. I had a feeling they had some policy or other regarding wild critters in the rooms, so I waited until the desk clerk went off to flirt with one of the maids, and then I opened the door and me and Basil made a beeline for the staircase, and reached the second floor without being seen. I walked on down the corridor until I came to my room, unlocked it, and shagged Basil into it. He looked more nervous and bewildered than vicious, and finally he hopped onto the couch and curled up and went to sleep, and I lay back down on the bed and drifted off while I was trying to figure out how many thousands of dollars a real live wolf was worth.

Except that when I woke up, all set to take Basil the wolf off to the zoo, he wasn't there. Instead, lying naked on the couch and snoring up a storm, was Basil the Count, with my belt still around his neck.

I shook him awake, and he sat up, startled, and began blinking his eyes.

"You got something highly personal and just a tad improbable that you want to confide in me, Brother Basil?" I said.

"I *tried* to warn you," he said plaintively. "I told you to leave, to hurry."

"You considered seeing a doctor about this here condition?" I said. "Or maybe a veterinarian?"

He shook his head miserably. "It is a Gypsy curse," he said at last. "There is nothing that can be done about it. I am a werewolf, and that's all there is to it."

"And that's why all them guys were running away from you at the station and looking askance at you on the street?"

He nodded. "I am an outcast, a pariah among my own people."

"Yeah, well, I can see how it probably hampers your social life," I opined.

"It has hampered *all* aspects of my life," he said unhappily. "I have seen so many charlatans and *poseurs* trying to get the curse removed that I am practically destitute. I cannot form a lasting relationship. I dare not be among strangers when the moon comes out. And some of the behavior carries over: you saw me at the dinner table last night."

"Well, it may have been a bit out of the ordinary," I said soothingly, "but as long as you don't lift your leg on the furniture, I don't suppose anyone's gonna object too strenuously. Especially since if they object at the wrong time of day, there's a strong possibility they could wind up getting et."

"You are the most understanding and compassionate man I've ever met, Doctor Jones," he said, "but I am at the end of my tether. I don't know what to do. I have no one to turn to. Only these accursed Gypsies will tolerate my presence, because it amuses them. I think very soon I shall end it all."

At which point the Lord smote me with another of His heavenly revelations.

"Seems to me you're being a mite hasty, Brother Basil," I said.

"What is the use of going on?" he said plaintively. "I will never be able to remove the curse."

"First of all, you got to stop thinking of your condition as a curse," I continued. "What if I was to show you how the werewolf business could be a blessing in disguise?"

"Impossible!"

"You willing to bet five thousand dollars on that?" I asked.

"What are you talking about?" he demanded.

"You see," I said, "the problem is that you ain't never really examined yourself when the moon is out. You ain't simply a werewolf, but you happen to be a damned fine-looking werewolf."

"So what?"

"On my way into town, I passed an arena that holds a dog show every Saturday. The sign said that the prize money was ten thousand dollars."

"You just said five," he pointed out.

"Well, me and the Lord have got to have a little something to live on, too," I said.

"What makes you think a wolf can win a dog show?" he said dubiously.

"Why don't you just concentrate on being a handsome, manly type of critter and let *me* worry about the rest of it?" I said.

Well, we argued it back and forth for the better part of the morning, but finally he admitted that he didn't see no better alternatives, and he could always commit suicide the next week if things didn't work out, and I went off to buy a leash and some grooming equipment at the local pet store, and then stopped by the arena for an entry form. I didn't know if he had an official werewolf name or not, so I just writ down Grand International Champion Basil on the form, and let it go at that.

The biggest problem I had the next two days was finding a vet who was open at night, so I could get Basil his rabies and distemper shots, but finally I convinced one to work late for an extra fifty dollars, which I planned to deduct from Basil's share of the winnings, since the shots didn't do me no good personally, and then it was Saturday, and we just stuck around the hotel until maybe five in the afternoon, Basil getting more and more nervous, and finally we walked on over to the arena.

Basil's class was scheduled to be judged at seven o'clock, but as the hour approached it began to look like the moon wasn't going to come out in time, and since I didn't want us to forfeit all that money by not showing up, I quick ran out into the alley, grabbed the first couple of cats I could find, and set 'em loose in the arena. The newspaper the next morning said that the ruckus was so loud they could hear it all the way over in Szentendre, which was a little town about forty miles up the road, and by the time everything had gone back to normal Basil was about as far from normal as Hungarian counts are prone to get, and I slipped his leash on him and headed for the ring.

There were three other dogs ahead of us, and after we entered the ring the judge came over and looked at Basil.

"This is a class for miniature poodles," he said severely. "Just what kind of mongrel is *that*?"

"You know this guy, Basil?" I asked.

Basil nodded.

"He one of the ones who's mean to you when you walk through town?"

Basil growled an ugly growl.

"*Basil?*" said the judge, turning white as a sheet.

Basil gave him a toothy grin.

"Now, to answer your question," I said, "this here happens

to be a fully growed miniature poodle what takes umbrage when you insult its ancestry.''

The judge stared at Basil for another couple of seconds, then disqualified the other three dogs for not looking like him and handed me a blue ribbon.

Well, to make a long story short, old Basil terrorized the judges in the next three classes he was in and won 'em all, and then the ring steward told me that I had five minutes to prepare for the final class of the day, where they would pick the best dog in the show and award the winner the ten thousand dollars.

Suddenly Basil started whining up a storm. I couldn't see no ticks or fleas on him, and he couldn't tell me what was bothering him, but something sure was, and finally I noticed that he was staring intently at something, and I turned to see what it was, and it turned out to be this lovely-looking lady who was preparing to judge the Best in Show class.

"What's the problem, Basil?" I asked.

He kept whining and staring.

"Is it *her*?"

He nodded.

I racked my mind trying to figure out what it was about her that could upset him so much.

"She's been mean to you before?" I asked.

He shook his head.

"She's got something to do with the Gypsies who cursed you?"

He shook his head again.

"I can't figure out what the problem is," I said. "But what the hell, as long as we let her know who you are, it's in the bag."

He pointed his nose at the ceiling and howled mournfully.

"She's from out of town and doesn't know you're a werewolf?" I asked with a sinking feeling in the pit of my stomach.

He whimpered and curled up in a little ball.

"Will the following dogs please enter the ring?" said the announcer. "Champion Blue Boy, Champion Flaming Spear, Champion Gladiator, Champion Jericho, and Grand International Champion Basil."

Well, we didn't have no choice but to follow these four fluffy little dogs into the ring. The judge just stared at us for a minute with her jaw hanging open, and I figured we were about to get booted out, but then she walked over and knelt down and held Basil by the ears and peered into his face, and then she stood up and stepped back a bit and stared at him some more, and finally she walked over to me and said, "This is the most handsome, rugged, masculine dog I have ever seen. I have a female I'd love to breed to him. Is he for sale?"

I told her that I was just showing him for a friend, and that she'd have to speak to the Count de Chenza Lupo about it later. She scribbled down her address, and it turned out that she was staying three rooms down the hall from me at the Hotel Magyar.

Finally she examined the other four dogs briefly and with obvious disinterest, and then she announced that Grand International Champion Basil was the best dog in this or any other show and had won the ten thousand dollars.

Well, Basil and me stuck around long enough to have a bunch of photos taken for the papers and then high-tailed it back to the hotel, where we waited until daylight and he became Count Basil again and we divvied up the money. Then he walked down the hall to talk to the judge about selling himself to her, and he came back half an hour later with the silliest grin on his face and announced that he was in love and she didn't mind in the least that he was a werewolf and all was right with the world.

I read in the paper that the other dog owners were so outraged about losing to a wolf that they tore the building down, and with the dog shows canceled for the forseeable future I couldn't see no reason to stick around, so I bid Hungary farewell and decided to try my luck in Paris, where I'd heard tell that the sinners were so thick on the ground you could barely turn around without making the real close acquaintanceship of at least a couple of 'em.

I never saw old Basil again, but a few months later I got a letter from him. He'd married his lady judge and left Budapest for good, and was living on her country estate managing her kennel—and he added a proud little postscript that both his wife and her prize female were expecting.

17
The Clubfoot of Notre Dame

If you wander down the Champs-Élysées today, or mosey over to Montmartre or the Trocadero or the Latin Quarter, you can still find a few people who remember me, even though I haven't been there since 1933.

Therefore, I think it's only fair that I tell you *my* side of the story.

I hit Paris in late afternoon of a lovely spring day in April, and even before I had time to line up a hotel and hunt up a place to eat, I found myself in a mild disagreement with some of the locals concerning exactly how many aces there were supposed to be in the deck I was dealing from, and just as things were starting to get ugly, the local constabularies rescued me and thoughtfully lined up my room and board for the next week, all at public expense.

Now, while I wouldn't never want to complain about such generous treatment, I'd be less than my usual forthright and honest self if I didn't point out that the prison fare in Paris don't quite measure up to the quality of grub you get at Maxim's or the Tour d'Argent, and the beds weren't quite as luxurious as you might expect at the Plaza-Athenee or the Ritz. But given the price, I didn't have no real serious objections, and I was almost sorry to leave when they gave me my walking papers a week later.

I stopped at a sidewalk cafe, which didn't cater to no locals but was filled to overflowing with bearded American writers, all of 'em with tortured artistic eyes, and after I'd et some snails and washed them down with a bottle of wine, I realized that I still didn't have no place to stay.

I couldn't see no sense wasting any money on one of the more expensive hotels, so I started wandering around, kind of testing the waters to see if I could rent a room and a companion of the female persuasion for the price of a room alone, and pretty soon I found myself in an alley, and I came to this big door, and I could hear all kinds of laughing and clapping on the other side of it, like folks were having a real good time, so I opened it and stepped inside.

It was dark, and there were all kinds of theatrical-type props lying around, and about twenty yards off I could see a light, so I went in its direction, and suddenly I found myself face-to-face with this beautiful blonde lady who had evidently dressed in kind of a hurry, because she wasn't wearing nothing but a pair of high heels and a bunch of feathers in her hair.

"Howdy, ma'am," I said. "I heard the sound of merrymaking out in the alley, and I just followed my ears."

She looked kind of startled, and shot me a quick grin, and whispered, "Who are you?"

"The Right Reverend Doctor Lucifer Jones at your service, ma'am," I said. "If you ain't got no serious plans for the rest of the evening, I'd be happy to escort you to some of the finer night spots in town."

Suddenly I heard a roar of laughter off to my left, and I turned and saw a bunch of people sitting at tables, all of 'em laughing their heads off.

"Am I intruding in some kind of private party, ma'am?" I asked.

"You are intruding on the stage of the Folies Bergere, you fool!" she snapped.

"Does that mean you *ain't* available for an evening of fun and frolic?" I asked.

"Don't you understand?" she hissed. "You're interrupting a performance!"

"Where I come from, ladies don't perform wearing nothing

but a smile,'' I said. Then I mulled on it a bit, and added, ''Maybe that's why I left, now that I come to think on it.''

The audience laughed again, and then I was surrounded by maybe two dozen more ladies who weren't wearing no more than the first, and it seemed that as long as I was there, and a stranger in town, the least I could do was introduce myself to each of 'em. I'd gotten about halfway down the line when they all started dancing across the stage, and I was left standing there all alone, so I figured I might as well dance after 'em. Now, the waltz is just about the only dance I know, and it's right difficult to do without a partner, but I done the best I could, and just as I caught up with them a bunch of gendarmes started walking toward the stage, and even though I knew I was innocent of all wrongdoing, I didn't like the look in their eyes, so once I got near the curtain I just kept on waltzing, but the second I was offstage the audience started screaming something in French, and a minute later the stage manager ran up to me.

''They want more of you!'' he said breathlessly.

''Well, of course they do,'' I said. ''With all the old guys who stare at 'em night after night, it's probably been years since they was approached by a good-looking young buck like myself.''

''I don't mean the girls,'' he said. ''I mean the audience!''

''I don't think I follow you, brother,'' I said.

''They think you're a clown, that you're part of the act. They want an encore!''

''An encore?'' I repeated.

''What else can you do?''

''I'm a preacher by trade,'' I said. ''I suppose if push came to shove I could give 'em a rouser about the Song of Solomon.''

''Just get out there and do *something*!'' said the stage manager, shoving me out into the spotlights.

The audience stopped yelling then, and settled back into their chairs.

''Howdy, folks,'' I said. ''I'm the Right Reverend Lucifer Jones, and I've come to bring the word of the Lord into your dull, lackluster lives.''

Well, for some reason or other, that brought forth a burst of chuckles, and I figured as long as they seemed to be in a partying mood, I'd warm 'em up with the story about the peg-legged whaler and the fireman's daughter before I got down to serious business, and they liked that one so much I followed it up with the one about the schoolmarm and the left-handed plumber, and by this time even the gendarmes were having a good time, and I figured I might as well put off any serious sermonizing till Sunday morning rolled around, and I told 'em a couple of more tales I'd accumulated during my travels to distant and exotic lands, and even though they didn't understand the one about the bowlegged jade merchant and the mandarin's daughter they laughed anyway, and we were having a high old time when the manager slipped me a note saying the girls were in serious danger of catching cold if they didn't start generating a little body heat, and I writ back that I may well have had the strength of ten because my heart was pure but I had counted twenty-five of 'em and he'd have to send fifteen of 'em home, and he wrote back to say I'd misunderstood him and what he meant was that he wanted me to get off the stage so they could go back to dancing.

Well, I didn't want none of them frail flowers coming down with a cold because of me, so I thanked the audience for being so friendly to a foreigner, and told them to stop by my tabernacle if they ever felt in serious need of salvation.

"Where is it?" asked one old geezer.

"I ain't had time to set up shop yet," I said. "But if any of you gents or ladies can suggest a good location, I'm willing to listen."

"Notre Dame!" said another, and everyone guffawed, and then I left the stage and the girls started working up a sweat, and the manager walked over to me.

"I don't know whether I should arrest you for interrupting the show, or offer you a long-term contract," he said. "I think I shall settle for politely showing you the door."

"Well, you *could* do me one favor, Brother," I said.

"And what is that?"

"Tell me about this Notre Dame," I said. "I always knew they played football. I didn't know they saved souls, too."

"It is the greatest church in the world," he said, looking at me like I had some kind of rare tropical disease. "How can you not know of it?"

"I know of it," I said with some dignity. "But I was under the impression that it was somewhere in Indiana."

He shook his head. "It is at the Île de la Cité." I asked him to tell me how to get there, since I figured if I could get in tight with Knute Rockne or whoever was coaching the team these days I might get a little inside information that would help me beat the point spread, and then I thanked him for his help, bade him a fond farewell, and started walking down the lonely, deserted streets of Paris.

It must have been close to four in the morning when I got there, and let me tell you, it was one mighty impressive sight, even if I couldn't spot the stadium in the dark. There were gargoyles galore, one in particular bringing back memories of Honor Weinberger, a girl I'd known back in Moline, Illinois, and all kinds of stained-glass windows, including a big rose-colored one, and finally I opened the door and walked inside. Someone was playing some mighty mournful music on the pipe organ, but I couldn't see who it was. In fact, it was so dark in there that I couldn't even see the ceiling, and after I'd looked around a bit and drunk in the architecture, of which there was an awful lot to drink in, I decided to see if I could hunt up the locker room, so I opened a door and started moseying down this corridor, which led to a batch of other corridors and doors, and pretty soon I couldn't hear the music no more and I was pretty well-nigh lost, so I figured I'd retrace my steps and wait until daylight and maybe hunt up Knute and the gang at their practice field, but as I turned I saw this ugly little feller kind of shuffling after me. He looked like he knew his way around a lot better than I did, so I walked over to him on the assumption that he might be able to help me.

"Good evening, Brother," I said. "Was that you playing on the organ?"

He nodded. "I do it to relax, when nobody's around."

"You're right good at it."

He smiled a homely kind of smile. "Thank you very much." He paused. "Who are you, by the way?"

"I'm the Right Reverend Lucifer Jones, and I'm looking for the team's headquarters."

"Team?" he repeated. "What team?"

"The varsity, of course," I said. "Can't make no money betting on freshman games."

"We don't have any teams here," he said. "This is Notre Dame."

"I'm afraid that you been misinformed," I told him. "It just so happens that you got a top-notch football team."

He smiled. "That is the Notre Dame in America."

"You mean there's more than one of you?" I said.

He nodded.

"You know," I said, "I been thinking all night that it seemed like you guys scheduled an awful lot of road games. I guess that explains it."

"Well, now that you're here, why don't you join me in a glass of wine?" he said.

"That's mighty neighborly of you," I replied.

"It gets lonely here at night," he explained. "You're the first person I've seen in weeks."

"Well, you must see 'em when you go home in the mornings."

"I live here," he said. "My room is over by the belltower. I haven't set foot outside the church in, oh, it must be close to thirty years now."

We reached this little room that had a table and four chairs, and while I sat down, he limped over to a cabinet and pulled out two glasses and a bottle of red wine.

"Looks like you twisted your ankle," I said.

"It is a permanent condition," he said. "I'm a clubfoot."

"Well, I don't suppose it makes much difference, as long as no one's kicking field goals around here."

"I *like* you, Reverend Jones," he said, filling the glasses. "You are a very understanding man."

"And you are a very generous host," I said. "I want to thank you for the wine, Brother . . . ?"

"Quesadilla."

"Brother Quesadilla," I concluded.

"You didn't laugh," he noted.

"Did someone tell a joke?"

"No," he said. "But my name . . . the Spanish seem to find it amusing."

"Well, the Spanish are easily amused," I said. "Usually a dead bull will do the trick."

"I like you more and more," he said. "No one has ever conversed so freely with me."

"Why not?" I said. "You seem like a friendly enough feller."

"Who knows? They hear the rumors, and . . ." He spread his hands and shrugged.

"Uh . . . just what kind of rumors are you referring to, Brother Quesadilla?" I asked.

"Oh, that I kidnap women and do grotesque things to them in the belltower," he said with a shrug.

"Sounds noisy," I allowed.

"On my honor, Reverend Jones, I have never taken a single woman to the belltower."

My first impulse was to ask if he took married women there. My second impulse was to ask if he didn't take 'em to the belltower, where *did* he take 'em? Then I took a serious look at all the muscles on his arms and neck, and my third and most reasonable impulse was to change the subject, which I proceeded to do.

"Brother Quesadilla," I said, "I been looking for a place to establish my tabernacle. As long as Fate has brung me to your doorstep, how much do you think your employers would rent this joint out for?"

He chuckled at that. "This is the Notre Dame Cathedral. It's not for rent, Reverend Jones."

"Well, here it is, four in the morning, and not a soul is milling around except you and me," I pointed out. "It seems a sorry waste of such a nice tasteful building."

"You preach to your congregation at four in the morning?" he asked.

"Well, truth to tell, I had in mind something more in the way of maybe a nightly bingo tournament to help pay the overhead."

"Bingo?" he said, puzzled.

"Well, if the French don't play bingo, I suppose we could set up a craps table and maybe a roulette wheel."

"It's a fascinating concept," he admitted with a grin, "but this is a place of worship."

"Brother Quesadilla, you'd be surprised how often people call upon the Good Lord when they got a pair of dice in their hands," I said.

He considered it for a minute and then shook his head sadly. "They'd never permit it."

"Wouldn't nobody have to know about it except you and me and such various sinners as we manage to attract," I said. "We could set up shop every night from, say, midnight till five in the morning."

"We?" he repeated.

"As in you and me," I said.

"Do you mean you'd really trust the notorious Clubfoot of Notre Dame?"

"Sure," I said. "I just won't go to the belltower with you."

"This is a most intriguing concept," he said. "Would we split the profits down the middle?"

"One-third for you, one-third for me, and one-third for the Lord," I said.

"As the Lord's landlord, I'll hold His share of the money," said Quesadilla.

"I was kind of figuring on holding it myself," I replied, "me being His spokesman and all."

"Fifty-fifty?" he said.

I sighed. "Fifty-fifty," I agreed.

"How do you plan to get word to all the sinners?" he asked.

"I met a batch of 'em tonight," I said. "I'll just go on back to the same place tomorrow and announce that we're open for preaching, salvation, and craps."

"We'll need some craps tables and a roulette wheel," noted Quesadilla.

"Well, I figure if I'm supplying the sinners, the very least the landlord can do is supply the equipment."

He mulled on it for a minute or two and then agreed.

We shook hands, and I left him playing on the pipe organ.

Then I hunted up a nearby hotel, which had seen better days and probably better centuries. I figured I was moving up to more elegant quarters the next night, but I didn't see no need to insult the management, so I registered for a week and the next morning I tiptoed out while the desk clerk was otherwise occupied.

There wasn't much for me to do until after dinnertime, so I decided to mosey on over to the Louvre and soak up a little culture. I saw everyone clustered around this one painting, and I figured it must be something pretty special, so I stood in line until I could get a good close look at it, but it turned out to be a picture of this kind of plain woman who couldn't quite make up her mind whether to smile at the painter or not, and in truth it didn't hold a candle to the picture of Nellie Willoughby in the alltogether that they had hanging over the Long Bar of the New Stanley Hotel back in Nairobi.

I wandered around a bit more, and then I came to this statue of a lady who wasn't wearing an awful lot more than the ladies I'd seen the previous night, and it set my good artistic blood to boiling, because someone had busted off the arms out of sheer malicious mischief, and since it hadn't been covered up or repaired or nothing I figured the guards didn't know about it yet, so I hunted up a gendarme and grabbed him by the arm and led him over to the statue and pointed out what had happened and told him he'd better report it to his superior and maybe double their security until the culprit was caught. He just looked at me like I posed a serious danger, and right on the instant I realized that it was an inside job, and he didn't want to let his superiors know that he'd had any part of it, so I apologized for taking his time, and made a mental note to come back on his day off, and lay out the whole plot to whoever was in charge of the place after first finding out if there was a reward for exposing the culprits.

After I left the Louvre, I found I still had some time on my hands, so I wandered over to the Arc de Triomphe, which I'd always thought was a horse race but turned out to be a kind of big stone arch as well, though for the life of me I couldn't see how you could bet on it. I saw a bunch of Frenchmen standing around not doing much of anything, so I walked over and told 'em that they looked like a sporting lot, and that they could now do their sinning and their repenting all in the same spot if they'd come to Notre Dame a bit after midnight. Most of 'em thought I was kidding, but three or four guys writ down the information, and I told 'em to make sure they passed the word to all their friends and relations.

I stopped at a sidewalk cafe for dinner, and got a little live entertainment with my meal when a couple of bearded Americans wearing turtlenecks and berets got into a knock-down drag-out over which of 'em looked more like Hemingway. In point of fact, the only Hemingway I knew was bald and eighty and ran a hardware store back in Ephrata, Pennsylvania, but I didn't see no sense hurting their feelings by enlightening 'em, and before long the gendarmes came along and dragged 'em both off to the hoosegow just as I was finishing my dessert.

By then it was time to go back to the Folies Bergere. I figured I'd just hunt up M. Bergere and ask him to make the announcement for me, but nobody in the whole place had seen hide nor hair of him, so I waited until the place filled up and then hopped onto the stage. Evidently I interrupted the very same blonde lady I had interrupted the night before, because she bellowed *"You again!"* and took off a shoe and started hammering me with it.

The audience thought it was all part of the show, and I recognized some of the same faces from the last time, so after I calmed the young lady down I told 'em a couple of more stories, including the one about the airplane pilot and the Tasmanian belly dancer, and then, when they'd all stopped laughing, I explained to them that Notre Dame had a new policy of one-stop sinning and salvation, and even though most of 'em laughed at first I kept explaining it over and over until everybody got right serious and the stage manager kept making a gesture with his hand across his throat, which I figured meant he was choking on a peach pit or something, and finally I thanked 'em for their time and hospitality and promised to greet any and all of 'em that came to Notre Dame later in the evening, and before I left the building I'd hired half a dozen refined young naked ladies to provide a little entertainment for our parishioners between midnight and sunrise.

I was thinking of stopping by the Lido and the Moulin Rouge and making the same announcement, but I noticed it was getting on toward ten o'clock and I decided I'd better get back to Notre Dame and see how Quesadilla was coming along with his part of the bargain.

Well, somehow or other, he'd managed to find a couple of roulette tables and three craps tables, and had even hunted up some poker and baccarat tables as well. I asked him if he knew anyone in the beer and wine business, so we could get a little liquid refreshment into them sinners what was running low on energy, and he said that he'd already thought of that, and couldn't see no reason to pay a middleman to set up a bar when we could do it ourselves, and just as he was explaining it to me in came a couple of deliverymen with our supplies.

We broke out a bottle of our best drinking stuff to celebrate our little enterprise, and then we settled back to wait for the sinners to start gathering, and sure enough, just after midnight, in they came, and by three in the morning we must have had a good four hundred evil men and painted women gambling their money away. Then at five o'clock we closed all the tables, and I stood up on a chair and forgave 'em in the name of my merciful and compassionate Silent Partner, and then they all went home, and me and Quesadilla paid off the young ladies and moved all the tables and supplies into a storeroom and counted up our take.

"Sixteen thousand francs!" he said excitedly.

"There's a lot to be said for working on the side of the Lord," I agreed.

"I never realized how well salvation could pay," he said.

"Well, it's all a matter of getting the right class of people in your congregation," I said. "Them what's beyond redemption usually ain't got all that much pocket money, and them what's totally without sin are probably more likely to throw the first stone than place the first bet."

Well, I found to my surprise that he liked talking religion as much as I did, so we kept it up till after sunrise, and then a batch of priests showed up and Quesadilla decided to head off to bed, and I watched the poorbox for a while and decided that the priests were missing a bet and that maybe once I got to know 'em better I'd explain to 'em how to run their church more like a business, but for the time being I decided they probably didn't want no outsiders interfering with the way they practiced their trade, so I headed toward the exit, and just as I did I bumped into a big roly-poly guy in priest's robes.

"Excuse me, Brother," I said. "I hope I didn't do you no lasting harm."

"I'm fine, my son," he replied. "Didn't I see you here very early yesterday morning as well?"

"It's a possibility," I said. "I hang around churches a lot, me being a man of the cloth and all."

"Episcopalian?" he asked.

"That's right generous of you," I answered. "but it's a little early in the day for me."

He just stared at me for a minute. "Well, if you should ever need help, I'm Father Gaston."

"I'll keep it in mind," I promised him. "And if you ever feel the need of spiritual uplifting, I'm the Right Reverend Honorable Doctor Lucifer Jones."

Well, he kept on staring at me for so long that I figured he was a little bit near-sighted and had maybe forgot his glasses, so finally I just smiled at him and continued on out the door, after which I decided that I needed someplace a little more upscale to hang my hat, so I hopped a taxicab and pulled up at the Ritz a few minutes later. I found out at the desk that they didn't give no discounts to clergymen, but I figured that as long as I was already there I might as well rent myself a room, and I spent the rest of the morning and afternoon doing a little serious sleeping.

Business was booming that night, as word of our little enterprise seemed to have spread far and wide, and it kept getting better all through the week. Every morning I would leave just after sunrise, and bump into Father Gaston, and exchange a few pleasantries with him, and every evening I would round up the ladies from the Follies Bergere and cart 'em over to Notre Dame and make sure that Quesadilla didn't invite none of 'em up to the belltower for a little hanky-panky, and I was just about sure I'd finally found my calling, and was even thinking about scaring up some other churches and maybe franchising the salvation business, when one night, just when the young ladies were doing their artistic interpretation of an Indian love dance to Quesadilla's accompaniment on the pipe organ, and the mayor himself had two thousand francs riding on the next roll of the dice, Father Gaston burst into the church.

"What is going on here?" he demanded, and suddenly all our parishioners dropped what they were doing and hightailed it for the exits, except for the young ladies, who weren't exactly dressed for going outside in the cool evening breeze.

"Well, howdy, Father Gaston," I said. "What brings you here at this ungodly hour?"

"Ungodly is the word for it!" he bellowed. "I had a feeling all week that something strange was going on here. What are you doing in my church?"

"Acquiring a first-rate congregation of sinful men and loose women," I explained. "After all, if they didn't have nothing to confess, you wouldn't need them little booths, would you?"

"This is outrageous!" he said. "Look at those women!"

"I can hardly take my eyes off 'em," I agreed admiringly. "Especially the third from the left."

"They're all naked!"

"Nothing much gets past your watchful eye, does it?" I said, figuring a little compliment, one clergyman to another, might help to calm him down.

"Why are they here?"

"Where else are a passel of naked ladies gonna go to find forgiveness?" I said. "I'd say Notre Dame has outdone itself tonight."

"And what were all those other people doing here?" he continued.

"Getting all the sin and corruption out of their systems so they'd be fit for saving," I said.

He stared at the tables. "Do you mean to tell me there's been gambling going on here?"

"No, I sure didn't mean to tell you that," I answered.

"I didn't mean to tell him anything," said Quesadilla unhappily.

"I'm calling the gendarmes this instant!" said Father Gaston.

"It won't do no good," I pointed out. "All our dealers and croupiers are gone. Tell 'em to come by tomorrow about midnight, and to bring plenty of money with 'em."

"You are impossible!" he shouted at me, and then turned to Quesadilla. "I hold you responsible for this, you ugly little clubfoot!"

"I don't care," said Quesadilla. "Reverend Jones is my friend. In fact, he's my *only* friend, and I won't let you do anything bad to him."

"He's a criminal and a fraud!" growled Father Gaston.

"Why don't you come up to the belltower with me and we'll discuss it?" suggested Quesadilla with a funny kind of smile on his face.

"We have nothing to discuss," said Father Gaston. "I'm having you both arrested."

"I don't think that would be a very good idea," said Quesadilla.

"Nobody asked you your opinion," said Father Gaston.

"If I go to court, they might ask me more than my *opinion*," said Quesadilla. "They might even ask me what I saw you doing with Madame Duchard."

"That was seventeen years ago!" said Father Gaston uneasily.

"Oh, I'll just tell them what I saw," said Quesadilla. "You can fill in the dates and other particulars."

"All right," said Father Gaston with a defeated sigh. "No gendarmes. Just get out of here and don't come back."

"That suits me fine," said Quesadilla. "Thirty years of this place is enough for me."

"Hah!" said Father Gaston. "Where is an ugly little clubfoot like you going to find work? You'll starve within a month."

"Father Gaston," I said, "as one man of the cloth to another, I'm ashamed to hear you carrying on like this to a decent Christian like Quesadilla who never meant no one any harm, and we ain't going to listen to no more of it."

I took Quesadilla by the arm and led him out the door, while Father Gaston just stood and glared at us.

"He's right, you know," said Quesadilla as we walked down the empty Paris streets. "I've been cooped up there for thirty years. How am I ever going to make a living? I don't have any job skills."

"Sure you do," I said. "And with a little help from me, you ain't gonna have no trouble atall."

"What did you have in mind?" he asked curiously.

"Did you ever hear the one about the bullfighter and the fan dancer?" I asked.

"No, but—"

"Then shut up and listen."

Well, I told it to him, and as depressed as he was, he practically fell down laughing, so I told him to get himself a pen and paper, and once he did I sat down and told him the one about the poet and the feather merchant's twin daughters, and then the one about the Sumo wrestler and the circus thin lady, and the one about the six-fingered gangster and the one-eyed manicurist, and by the time the sun had come up I'd guv him about a hundred such knee-slappers.

Then, after we had breakfast, I took him over to the Folies Bergere and introduced him to the stage manager, and after he told a couple of jokes they hit it right off, and the last I saw of the Clubfoot of Notre Dame, he was providing the musical accompaniment for the dancing girls at the organ and telling the audience droll stories between acts.

As for me, I took my half of the money and headed off to London, where I hoped to find a church that was more attuned to my particular brand of salvation.

18
The Crown Jewels

The very first thing you notice about London is that it ain't exactly warm. The second thing is that it ain't exactly cold. The third is that it ain't exactly dry. The fourth is that it ain't exactly sunny. The fifth is that it ain't exactly cheap.

Still, London's got a lot of things going for it. For one thing, most of the folks speak a kind of American, which was a pleasant change from Paris, where they don't speak no known language at all. For another, everyone kept saying that it was a pretty class-ridden town, so I figured if I could just find out where the sinful classes hung out I'd know right where to establish my tabernacle.

I took a room at an old, run-down hotel on Basil Street, then went out looking for a sinner or two of the female persuasion, just to test the waters, so to speak. I'd got maybe three blocks away from the hotel when I came across a large crowd lined up to get into some theater, and they seemed so eager and excited that I decided I might as well join 'em and see what all the fuss was about, since in my broad experience on four continents very few entertainments draw that kind of enthusiasm unless they feature a few fallen women in serious need of both clothing and redemption.

Well, we all filed in and sat down, and while I was looking for painted women, of which there was nary a sign, an announcer came out on the bare stage and said, ''Thank you for coming, ladies and gentlemen. Our speaker tonight needs no introduction.

He has consented to give one of his rare public lectures, and so may I present, without any further *adieu*, the greatest consulting detective in the world, London's own Sherringford House.''

Everybody stood up and started clapping, and then this skinny guy, dressed in tweeds and smoking a pipe, came out onto the stage.

"Mr. House," said the announcer, "before you begin, can we impose upon you to display your remarkable powers of deduction for the audience?"

"Certainly," said Sherringford House. "May I have a volunteer, please?"

Well, I could see right off that there weren't going to be no sinners on display, so I got up to leave.

"Thank you, sir," said House, and suddenly everyone started staring at me.

"You talking to me?" I said.

"You have recently been in Paris, I perceive," he said, "and I believe it is not incorrect to state that you toil in the service of your Lord."

"Now how on earth did you know that?" I asked.

He merely smiled, and suddenly everyone started applauding.

"The science of deduction," he said after they'd all calmed down, "can be divided into three separate parts: observation, analysis, and conclusion. Anyone who has been properly trained can do what I just did. You ask how I have solved one hundred and three cases without a failure, and I say to you that had the police learned those three basic principles—observation, analysis, and conclusion—they would not have needed my services in any of them."

"Rubbish!" said a voice from the audience.

"I beg your pardon?" said House.

"I say that's balderdash, and that you're a fake," said the voice, which was suddenly sounding pretty familiar. "What's more, I'm willing to bet five thousand pounds that I can prove it."

"Please stand up, sir, so that I may see you," said House.

The man stood up, and now that I could get a good look at him, I realized that it was Erich Von Horst.

"I will put a challenge to you, Mr. House," said Von Horst. "In three nights' time, I will steal the Crown Jewels, and I'll wager five thousand pounds that you and the entire London Metropolitan Police Force cannot prevent me from so doing."

"Arrest that criminal!" shouted a woman.

"No!" said House sharply. "This man has challenged my integrity. Were I to back down, I would be less than British, which is unthinkable." He turned back to Von Horst. "Sir," he said, "have you any conditions attached to your challenge?"

"I will need one assistant," said Von Horst.

"Professor Melanoma, perhaps?" said House, arching an eyebrow sardonically.

"I need no one else to help me plan the theft," said Von Horst. "To prove it, I will accept someone from the audience, if you will promise that he or she will not be prosecuted."

"That is acceptable," said House. "I will speak to Inspector McIlvoy, and I'm sure he will agree." He paused. "Who do you choose?"

Von Horst looked straight at me and smiled. "It makes no difference," he said. "It might as well be the gentleman from Paris."

"Done, sir," said House. He now turned to the announcer. "Will you be good enough to hold the stakes?"

"Gladly, Mr. House," replied the announcer. House pulled out a checkbook and began scribbling while Von Horst approached the stage and handed over a huge wad of bills.

"It does not bother you that I have seen your face?" asked House.

"Not in the least," said Von Horst confidently, "for you shall never see it again."

"Ladies and gentlemen," said House, "I hope you will forgive me, but I must postpone this lecture while I prepare to apprehend this villain. If the management will agree, your tickets will be honored for a week from tonight, at which time I shall tell you exactly how I captured him and saved the Crown Jewels."

This brought a standing ovation, and then House walked off the stage and everyone except Von Horst started filing out.

"Good evening, Doctor Jones," said Von Horst when we

were alone in the theater. "Fancy meeting you here, of all places. What a small world it is."

"Crowded is more the word for it," I said bitterly.

"Ah," he said. "You're still mad about our little venture in Greece."

"You might say that."

"Then this is my chance to put things right between us," he said. "I'll let you in for one-third."

"Things ain't been right between us since the day I first met you back in Dar-es-Salaam, and they didn't get no better in Morocco or Algeria or Mozambique or Greece. Just get out of my life."

"What kind of attitude is that for a man of the cloth?" he said. "How can I atone for my past sins if you turn your back on me?"

"Von Horst," I said, "there's probably a couple of hundred things I might do to you, but turning my back on you ain't one of 'em."

"How can I prove my sincerity?" he said. "I have a foolproof plan to steal the Crown Jewels. I'm so sure it will work that I put up five thousand pounds against the greatest detective in the world. You will be working for me. You'll know all the details of my plan, the location of my headquarters, everything you need to turn me in if you should decide that I'm trying to deceive you in any way. Furthermore, Sherringford House has given his personal guarantee that you will not be held culpable if I succeed. What more could you possibly want?"

"Everything always *sounds* good when you lay it out," I said, "but somehow or other you always get the money and I always wind up in the hoosegow."

"But you *can't* wind up in jail this time!" he said. "If I'm caught, you go scot-free, and if I succeed, you get a third of the Crown Jewels."

I mulled on it for a couple of minutes.

"What makes you so sure you can outwit Sherringford House?" I said. "Even *I've* heard of him, and I ain't never been in England before today."

"Doctor Jones," he said, "this plan simply cannot fail. I

don't care how brilliant House is, I don't care if the Tower of London is entirely surrounded by police, I will come away with the Crown Jewels.'' He paused. ''And the beauty of the scheme is that it requires no special skills whatsoever. I don't have to be able to climb up the sides of buildings or pick complex combination locks or fight my way past an army of policemen. It took a genius to conceive it, but any fool could carry it out.''

It was at that very instant that my own plan occurred to me. If any fool could carry out the theft of the Crown Jewels, well, I could be every bit as much of a fool as the next man. I figured that I'd go along with him until I learned all the details of his scheme. Then I'd tell House just enough so he'd be waiting for Von Horst, and while he was carting Von Horst off to the calaboose, I'd use the plan to help myself to a couple of generous handfuls of the Crown Jewels and finally get around to building me a tabernacle worthy of my preaching talents.

''Well,'' said Von Horst, ''what do you say? Are you in or out?''

''In.''

''Good,'' he said. ''I *knew* I could count on you. And you won't regret it.''

''Actually, I got a good feeling about this here enterprise,'' I allowed. ''Like you said, there's no way I can lose.''

''Shall we shake on it?'' he asked.

''Just a minute,'' I said, slipping off my watch and putting it on my left wrist. ''Okay.''

''Somehow I have the feeling you still don't entirely trust me, Doctor Jones,'' he said, shaking my hand.

''Maybe I will after you explain your plan to me,'' I said.

''Fair enough,'' he agreed. ''But not here. There's too much chance that we'll be overheard.'' He looked around. ''Do you know the Garroted Goose?''

''It's a kid's nursery rhyme, right?''

''It's a pub on Bond Street. Be there at noon tomorrow.''

He turned and walked out of the theater, and a minute later I hunted up a phone book and found Sherringford House's address, and half an hour after that I was introducing myself to his landlady, who showed me up the steps to his apartment. I heard fiddle music coming through the door, and commented that it sounded right pretty.

"Oh, Mr. House is a great one for the violin," said the landlady. "The house is filled with music whenever he's thinking."

"He thinks a lot, does he?" I asked.

"Practically all the time," she said. Then she whispered, "Just between us, I do wish he'd vary the melody every now and then." We reached the landing. "Well, here we are. It's the first door to your left."

"Do come in," said House's voice, just before I could knock on the door.

"Howdy, Mr. House," I said, entering his apartment, which was filled with books and chemicals in equal proportion.

"Ah, the gentleman from the theater," he said, turning off his Victrola and putting the record back in its package. "Please sit down."

"Thank you," I said, pulling up a chair.

"You have come to me because of the proposed burglary of the Crown Jewels, have you not?" he said.

"Yeah," I said. "How did you know that?"

An amused smile crossed his face. "What other business could we possibly have to discuss?"

"Well, it seems simple when you explain it," I said, "but for the life of me, I still don't know how you figured out I had just got here from Paris and was in the service of the Lord."

"Elementary," he said. "On the sole of your left shoe there remains a trace of horse manure. Beneath your fingernails is the sort of grime that is most easily accrued by working with animals. Your accent is American. Your bearing and demeanor is something less than aristocratic, and I therefore deduce that far from being a sportsman you are a common laborer. Now, where would an American be most likely to find work on a horse farm? In Paris, Kentucky, the breeding capital of the thoroughbred industry. And why would you suddenly come to England? Because Lord Pemberton has only this week moved his racing operation from the Blue Grass country to Britain, and since he is well-known for rewarding loyalty in his employees, it stands to reason that he has relocated all of his American help here in London. Therefore, it was a simple matter to conclude that you have recently arrived from Paris, and that you remain in the service of your Lord.'' He leaned back and puffed smugly on his pipe.

"Well, if that don't beat all!" I said.

"It's nothing," he said, getting to his feet. "Let me observe you further for a moment."

I sat still like I was posing for a picture, until he walked once around me, nodded his head, and plumped himself back down on the sofa.

"You are left-handed, your mother died during childbirth, you are a crack shot with a .38-caliber revolver, and your fondest desire is to translate Shakespeare into Serbo-Croation."

"Truth to tell," I said, "I'm right-handed, last time I heard from my mother she was serving hard time in Colorado for running a bawdy house, I ain't never shot a pistol in my life, and my fondest desire is to raise enough money to build the Tabernacle of Saint Luke."

"Well," he said with a shrug, "it had to be one or the other." He took another puff of his pipe. "And now, what can I do for you, Mr. . . . ?"

"Reverend," I said. "The Right Reverend Doctor Lucifer Jones."

"Doctor?" he said, suddenly alert. "I don't suppose you'd have access to . . . well, no, never mind. Please continue."

"Well, Mr. House," I said, "I been a law-abiding citizen and a God-fearing Christian all my life, and I just don't feel right helping Erich Von Horst steal the Crown Jewels out from under your nose, so to speak, and while I appreciate the fact that no one's going to arrest me no matter what happens, I'd feel a lot better about things if I knew I was helping to uphold the law rather than bust it."

"A most commendable attitude," he said.

"So I got to thinking on it," I continued, "and I figured that the very best thing to do would be to find out exactly what Von Horst's plan is, and to pass it on to you so you'd be ready and waiting for him."

"Well, I thank you very much for your concern, Reverend·

Jones," said House, "but it would hardly be sporting, now that we've made our bet."

"What's sporting got to do with anything?" I said. "This man has stolen and finagled his way all up and down Africa without getting caught, and now he's going after the Crown Jewels."

"Africa?" he said with a laugh. "Not a chance, Reverend Jones. I studied him carefully when he came up to the stage, and I can tell you with total confidence that he has spent the last seventeen years as a bookkeeper in Brisbane, Australia. He is henpecked by his wife, devoted to his seven children—two boys and five girls—and spends his Sundays watching cricket matches from a seat that faces north-north-east."

"I tell you he swindled his way across the length and breadth of Africa," I said.

"Poor fellow," he said sympathetically. "I fear that when that horse kicked you in the head last November—or was it October? No, November—it must have jarred loose some of your memory."

"Can we just agree that wherever he's been, he's here now, and the main thing is to stop him from stealing the Crown Jewels?"

"Certainly," said House. "And prevent him I shall."

"Wouldn't it be a lot easier if you knew his plan?" I asked him.

House shot me a confident smile. "But I already do," he said.

"You do?"

"Certainly," he said. "The man is obviously a master of disguise. At precisely eleven o'clock three nights hence, when they change the guards in front of the jewel room, he will present himself for duty, dressed as a sergeant in the Tower Guard. He will take his post outside the door, snap to attention, and patiently wait for us to lose interest in him and direct our attention elsewhere on the assumption that he has not yet gained access to the Tower. Then, when the corridor is deserted, he will dispatch his fellow guard with a single blow to the back of the neck—the man is obviously an expert at karate; brown belt, I should think—and will enter the jewel room, prepared to make off with millions of pounds of Britain's greatest treasures. But *I*, Sherringford House, will be hidden inside that room, waiting for him.''

"Well, that sure sounds like you got it figured out," I said. "But if you're right, what does he need *me* for?"

"In case the police remain in the vicinity of the jewel room after he has taken up his position, he will need you to create a commotion on one of the lower levels, drawing the police away so that he can have a few necessary moments alone to perpetrate his foul crime." He paused and relit his pipe, which kept going out. "It is a brilliant scheme, as he said it was, and it is indeed almost foolproof. He forgot to take only one single factor into consideration."

"Yeah?" I said. "And what was that?"

"He forgot that he would be trying to fool the greatest consulting detective in the world," said House, who sure wasn't weighted down by no false modesty. "So you see, Reverend Jones, the situation is already well in hand. I thank you for your concern, but Von Horst will be in jail before the Tower clock strikes midnight three days hence."

"You're absolutely sure you ain't made a mistake?" I said.

"A mistake?" he said. *"Me?"*

Well, I could see we didn't have nothing more to talk about, so I took my leave of him and wandered on back to Basil Street. I woke up about ten in the morning, found out that nobody in London knew how to make a good cup of coffee, and when it was getting on toward noon I moseyed over to the Garroted Goose, where Von Horst was waiting for me at a table in the back.

"Good morning, Doctor Jones," he said. "I trust you slept well?"

"Passably," I said. "I had a pretty comfortable room, except maybe for the bed and the mattress and the springs and the pillow."

"Well, three days from now, you can stay in the Royal Suite at the Dorchester," he said. Suddenly he grinned. "And Sherringford House will never even know he's been bested!"

"You keep saying that," I pointed out, "but you don't say *how*."

"I'm about to," said Von Horst. "Have you been to the Tower of London yet, Doctor Jones?"

"Nope," I said. "I thought I'd take a gander at it this afternoon."

"Well, when you do, you will see that the jewels are kept in a heavily guarded room at the very top of the Tower," said Von Horst. "There are guards on duty around the clock, the door has a lock that is said to be unbreakable, and the only way down is by a single staircase. Every great thief in the history of crime has attempted to steal the Crown Jewels," he added, "but none has ever succeeded—until now."

"If I was a betting man, I'd go with the run," I said.

"Ah—but I know something that even Sherringford House doesn't know," said Von Horst with a grin.

"Yeah?"

He nodded. "Most of the jewels on display in the Tower are fake. The *real* jewels are locked away in a vault below ground level—and *that* vault can be cracked. The government has no desire to call attention to it, so it is not guarded, not marked in any way, and indeed looks like any storage room. While House and the police are waiting in the Tower, I shall be directly below them, where I will have all night to steal the unprotected Crown Jewels at my leisure."

"You *sure* of this?" I asked.

"Would I have bet five thousand pounds if I had any doubts?" replied Von Horst. "I got it from an embittered woman who once thought she had a chance to marry Edward and become the Queen of all England. He toyed with her affections and then left her, and for years she has been nursing her bitterness and waiting for her revenge. It was after we were introduced by a mutual friend and I admitted some of my youthful indiscretions to her that she decided to impart this knowledge to me, in the hope that after I had accomplished my mission I would make it public and thus make fools of the entire royal family." He smiled. "And what better way to publicize it than to defeat and humiliate England's favorite son, Sherringford House?"

"Just where do *I* enter into these here plans?" I said.

"You must convince House that for some unfathomable reason you have taken a strong dislike to me and wish to thwart me. You will give him some cock-and-bull story that we will concoct about how I plan to sneak into the jewel room, so that all his efforts are concentrated there, and he never realizes that while he is waiting for me, I have arrived and stolen the *real* jewels directly below where he is standing.''

"And that's it?" I asked.

"That's it," he said. "What do you think?"

What I thought was that he'd be out of the country with the jewels while I was stuck in the Tower and he had never had any intention of paying me my one-third, but I just grinned at him and said, "You were right; it sounds foolproof to me."

"I'm staying at the Savoy," he said. "Come by tomorrow night and we'll work out the bogus plan that you can relate to House and which will keep all his efforts and attentions confined to the Tower."

"What time?" I asked.

"Shall we say eight o'clock?" suggested Von Horst. "We could do it sooner, of course, but I want House to think it took me a full two days to confide in you. It seems more realistic this way."

I got up and told him that I'd see him the next night. Then I went right to a bookstore and bought a map of the Tower of London. The real jewel room wasn't on it, but I found the stairs leading down to its level, and it looked like Von Horst had figured things out pretty well. There were plenty of escape routes, and if things got really tense, he could open a window and just jump into the Thames. In fact, it was a such a good plan that I decided I'd keep it for myself.

I spent the rest of the day getting my first good look at London, which was real long and strong on museums and stuff, but right short on gambling houses. I figured I might take in a little culture, so I went to a theater in the evening, but instead of moving pictures they had a bunch of real live people on stage. Still, it was a pretty entertaining comedy, and when this here prince started talking to a skull, of all things, I broke right out laughing, which led me to the realization that Londoners ain't got no sense of humor because everyone else just turned and stared at me and began trying to shush me up, so I got up, real dignified-like, and walked out, feeling right sorry for all them poor actors who were probably wondering why no one else appreciated all their jokes.

The next day I slept till noon, and figured I'd spend the day at the races, so I asked the desk clerk where I could find Ascot and Epsom, and he gave me two addresses, but evidently he didn't understand plain-spoken American real good, because the first address turned out to be a men's clothing shop and the second was a druggist, and all I had to show for my hopeful afternoon at the track was an Ascot tie and a box of Epsom salts.

I stopped at a local restaurant and had what they assured me was a typical British dinner, which led me to understand why I kept running into expatriate Brits all over the world. The lemonade could have used a little sugar to make up for not having no lemons, and with no ketchup to bring out the subtle nuances of flavor in the Dover sole, I decided they sold the leftovers to cobblers who had appropriated the word for shoe bottoms.

When it was getting on toward eight o'clock I went over to the Savoy, and found out from the desk clerk that Von Horst was in room 533 and was expecting me, so I took the elevator up to the fifth floor and began walking down the hall. Just as I passed room 531 I thought I could hear Von Horst's voice, and as I walked up to his door I could hear him, plain as day, speaking on the telephone.

"Yes, it's all working out beautifully," he said. "The man is a complete and total fool. By now he has doubtless decided to alert Sherringford House to what he believes is my true plan, and to appropriate it for himself at some time in the future." He chuckled at something, and then continued. "No, there's no way it can fail. Half the London police will be in the Tower, and the rest will be watching the storage room, and while they are all occupied, *I* shall sneak into Buckingham Palace and steal all the jewels they have taken out for the King of Norway's state dinner. I never did say *which* Crown Jewels I planned to steal, and while they're watching one set, I'll make off with the other and deliver them to you before sunrise . . . You'll have to sit on them for a couple of years, but since I'm only asking thirty percent of market value, I think it's fair to say that we'll both make out like, shall we say, thieves?''

He laughed again, and I knocked on his door.

"I'll be right with you!" he yelled, and then I heard him say into the telephone, "I have to hang up now. You won't hear from me again until after the job is done."

Then I heard him walk across the room, and the door opened, and he greeted me with a great big smile.

"Good evening, Doctor Jones," he said. "I'm sorry if I kept you waiting, but I was in the lavatory."

"Quite all right," I said, walking in and sitting myself down in a leather chair. "Quite a spread you've got here."

"It's cozy," he agreed. "Can I get you anything to drink?"

I allowed as to how a glass of whiskey might wash away the taste of a typical British dinner, and he poured some for each of us, and then he sat down opposite me and while I finished my drink he instructed me to tell Sherringford House that he planned to impersonate a Tower Guard and have me create a commotion on the lower levels, and that when House and the police went down below to investigate he would disable the other guard with a karate chop, pick the lock, and steal the jewels before anyone returned.

"It's the stupidest scheme in the world," he said with a chuckle. "But I've been reading House's adventures in the magazines, and he's just dumb enough to buy it."

"Yeah," I said. "I'll bet I could get him to go for it."

"Your job," he added, "is to lead them a merry chase without ever going below ground level, where I'll be stealing the real jewels from the storeroom. Do you think you can manage it?"

"I can't see why not," I said.

"Fine. We'll meet at Westminster Abbey at four in the morning, where I'll give you your share of the jewels."

"Fair enough," I said agreeably.

"All right," he said, getting to his feet. "Is there anything else we have to discuss?"

"Not that I can think of."

"Good. Then I'll see you approximately thirty-two hours from now, at which point we should both join the ranks of Britain's richest men.''

I walked on back to my hotel and sat down and started mulling on everything I had heard. Obviously Von Horst was using his bet just to divert the attention of Sherringford House and the London police so that he could have a clear, unhindered shot at all the jewels in Buckingham Palace, and I had known all along he planned to double-cross me, though I didn't know until I overheard his phone call exactly how he planned to do it.

So I got to sorting things out, and it seemed to me that since House already believed in Von Horst's phony scheme even though I hadn't yet told it to him, there wasn't no sense at all disappointing him, so I would lay it out just the way Von Horst wanted me to, and that would take care of the world's greatest consulting detective and the whole of the London Metropolitan Police Force.

Then, since I knew that the gems at Buckingham Palace would be unprotected, and that Von Horst had arranged everything so that he could sneak in and steal them at eleven o'clock, all I had to do was get there ahead of him, at maybe ten-thirty, and once I'd gotten safely back to my hotel I could call the Tower and tell 'em Von Horst was lurking in the Palace grounds, and that would take care of him once and for all, since he'd publicly promised to steal the jewels and they would sure as shootin' get themselves stolen.

The more I thought about it, the more I couldn't see no way it could go wrong, so finally I moseyed over to House's apartment and told him that he was dead right about what Von Horst planned to do.

''Was there ever any doubt?'' he said with a contented smile.

''Then, if it's all the same to you, I'd rather not be anywhere on the premises, since Von Horst has a pretty vile temper and I don't want him taking no pot shots at me when he finds out I spilled the beans.''

''Certainly,'' said House. ''Your job is done, Reverend Jones. I commend you for your citizenship and your service to the Crown, though of course I knew all along what Von Horst was planning, as you'll recall from our conversation two nights ago.''

He walked me to the door and bid me good night, and then I went back to Basil Street, and spent the rest of the night and most of the next day resting up. I knew better than to try another British home-cooked dinner again, so I went out in search of a healthy meal and got myself two egg rolls, a chocolate donut, and a stein of ale, and at ten o'clock I started walking over to Buckingham Palace.

When I got there I saw that the whole building was dark, and I figured that all the kings and queens and aristocrats were indulging in their party games a little early, and that I might have to go from one bedroom to another collecting their treasures, but I'd brung a flashlight along with me, so that didn't bother me none. I walked up to one of the back windows, and since I didn't want to make no noise, I took off my shoes and then climbed in.

I found myself in some kind of drawing room, and since it was empty I opened the door and walked out into a huge corridor, and started opening doors and inspecting rooms one by one, but I couldn't find no jewelry or people or nothing in 'em, and after a few minutes I was beginning to wonder if maybe there was more than one Buckingham Palace, and if Edward and all the royal folks was in the other one and this one was owned by a kindly old couple named Buckingham who were asleep on the second floor.

Finally I made it to the living room, which was maybe a hundred feet long and half as wide, and I figured that if there wasn't no gems to be had, maybe I could at least pick up a knick-knack or two so it wouldn't be a totally wasted evening, and just as I was reaching for a little statue of a lady who was dressed as if she'd just stepped out of a shower and didn't have no towels nearby, all the lights came on and a voice shouted "You're under arrest!" and suddenly I was facing four hundred members of the London police.

"What are you guys doing here?" I asked. "You're supposed to be over at the Tower of London."

"We had a tip that someone would try to rob Buckingham while the Royal Family was vacationing at Windsor Castle," said the officer in charge.

"Well, somebody *is* gonna try to rob the Palace," I said,

"and if you'll just stick around a few minutes you can catch him red-handed."

"We just did," said the officer with a laugh.

"You got it all wrong," I said. "I'm the Right Reverend Doctor Lucifer Jones. Don't that mean nothing to you?"

"It means you'll probably be thrown out of your church when they find out what you were doing," he said.

"But you can't arrest me!" I said. "I got an agreement with Sherringford House!"

"Sure you do," said the officer. "Now put your hands behind your back."

"But I do!" I said as they slipped on a set of handcuffs. "Just ask him."

"Sherringford House is much too busy protecting the Crown Jewels to be bothered right now," said the officer.

And that was that. They led me off to the British version of a paddy wagon and took me to the local station and photographed and fingerprinted me and booked me and locked me in a cell just like a common criminal. They even took away my cigars and my hip flask and my personal pair of custom-made dice, and left me with nothing but my well-worn copy of the Good Book, which wasn't as comforting as it might have been, since it was too dark to read or swat flies with it.

Well, I finally drifted off to sleep, and in the morning who should show up but Sherringford House. He nodded to the guard, who unlocked my cell.

"I'm terribly sorry for this misunderstanding," said the consulting detective. "You are, of course, free to go. The London police have agreed to honor my promise to you."

"Thanks," I said.

"It was the least I could do for you," he said, "considering that I won the five thousand pounds."

"You caught Von Horst?" I said, surprised.

He shook his head. "He never showed up. At the very last minute he must have realized that he could never hope to elude Sherringford House." He turned to me and shook my hand. "It has been most interesting working with you, Reverend Jones. I hope you enjoy the remainder of your stay in London."

He walked off, and I went over to the desk to pick up my belongings.

"You're Lucifer Jones?" asked the desk sergeant.

"The Right Reverend Lucifer Jones," I corrected him.

"Here's your gear," he said, handing me a small cardboard box. "And this letter was hand-delivered for you about an hour ago."

I opened it up and read it.

My dear Doctor Jones:

Once again I have found collaborating with you to be a stimulating and enriching experience. I had been planning to steal the Crown jewels for almost a month, but I had to wait until the perfect partner showed up, so you can imagine my elation when I saw you walking into Sherringford House's lecture three nights ago.

After I had arranged the wager and convinced you to join forces with me, I knew it would only be a matter of time before you betrayed me and tried to steal the jewels yourself. I also knew that House would have most of the London Metropolitan Police Force gathered at the Tower. The trick, of course, was to let you overhear me talking to myself as you approached my room at the Savoy, because I knew that the police would hold a few men in reserve to protect the rest of the city, and I had to find some way to get them all in one place, far from where the actual crime was being committed.

That is where you came in, Doctor Jones. Once you heard me say that I would be stealing the jewels from the Palace at eleven, I knew that I could count on two things: first, that you would keep this information to yourself and not divulge it to Sherringford House, and second, that you would show up sometime before eleven to rob the jewels yourself.

It only took a phone call to the police to alert them to the fact that someone would be breaking into the Palace between ten and eleven—and while they were apprehending you and Sherringford House was wasting his time in the Tower of London, I was free to commit the robbery that I had planned from the beginning.

If you will walk over to Bond Street after reading this letter, you will find a jewelry store owned by a Mr. Alastair Crown. Prior to last night, he had the Moons of Africa, three perfectly matched diamonds, on display in his window. They are now in my possession, and by the time you read this I will be out of the country.

As for the five thousand pounds, if you can convince House that he lost his wager, I happily forfeit all claim to it and gladly give it to you. It was a small enough investment, considering that it resulted in my acquiring some three million dollars' worth of diamonds.

I realize that you may feel ill-used, but the fact of the matter is that I told both you and House the truth: I did in fact steal the Crown jewels exactly when I said I would do so. If you don't believe me, just ask Mr. Crown, who must be somewhat distraught at this moment and could doubtless use such spiritual comfort as a man of the cloth such as yourself might wish to bring him.

> Yr. Obdt. Svt.,
> Erich Von Horst

I crumpled up the letter and threw it on the floor, and then went out into the wilderness—which in this case happened to be a bench in Hyde Park—and had a long heart-to-heart with my Silent Partner, and we decided to pull up stakes and try our luck in some other municipality since we hadn't done all that well since arriving in London.

Then He went off to tend to other godly business and left me to wonder why, where Erich Von Horst was concerned, I could be so stupid when I am so smart.

19
The Loch Ness Monster

I hopped a northbound train out of London, got involved in a friendly little game of chance with three of the conductors, and when I looked up we were not only out of England but had left Glasgow far behind us. I figured the next stop was probably the North Pole, but one of the conductors assured me that the train didn't go no farther than Inverness, which was plenty far enough as far as I was concerned, since I hadn't never heard of it.

Well, let me tell you, Inverness ain't one of the glittering capitals of Europe—or even of Scotland, if push comes to shove. One of the locals suggested I stay at Culloden House, which he told me was right where Bonnie Prince Charlie had been defeated, so I moseyed over and rented a room, but I couldn't find hide nor hair of no prince, so I reckoned he'd given up whatever fight he'd been in and gone on home to lick his wounds.

The chambermaid was a girl named Anna, whose father worked as the gamekeeper for the local laird who owned most of the nearby property, and we hit it off right quick for two people who didn't have much in common—I liked women and she hankered after men. It was after our idyllic little tryst that I asked her what the locals did to amuse themselves, which seemed like a perfectly innocent and harmless thing to ask, but her only response was to climb out of bed and throw a lamp at me. I took this as a gentle reproof to the way I had worded my question, but after she threw a chair and both my shoes at me I could see that she was mildly displeased, so I simply thanked her for showing a stranger some of the brighter glories of Scotland and allowed that I would mosey on down to the local tavern and see if anyone there was more of a mind to direct me to such action as might be taking place in Inverness of a Tuesday evening.

Due to my little interlude with Anna, it was getting on toward midnight when I reached the tavern, and there weren't more than half a dozen old men sitting around, all staring at this great big clock over the bar. There were a bunch of nasty-looking fish mounted on the walls, with little metal plaques saying who caught them and when, and here and there were photos of some Brit wearing a crown, which I thought was probably King Edward but I didn't want to ask, just in case it turned out to be this Prince Charlie and he still had friends in the vicinity.

"Good evening, stranger," said the bartender. "I haven't seen you here before."

"I just got into town today," I said, and since everyone was looking at me, I turned to face 'em. "The Right Reverend Honorable Doctor Lucifer Jones at your service, weddings and baptisms done cheap, with a group rate for funerals."

"Pleased to meet you, Reverend Jones," said the bartender. "And since you're a man of the cloth, the first one will be on the house."

"Well, that's right generous of you, brother," I said. "All them millions of people who swear the Scots are a mean, stingy, miserly race of tightwads obviously ain't been to Inverness lately."

"Thank you," said the bartender. "I think."

"You plan on being here long, Reverend Jones?" asked one of the old guys who was sitting alone at a table.

"I doubt it," I said. "Three or four hours of hard drinking and I ought to be ready for bed."

"I meant, do you plan to stay in Inverness for any length of time?"

"I ain't made up my mind yet," I said. "I've spent the last few years wandering the world, looking for the right spot for me and God to build our tabernacle."

"Just getting the lay of the land, eh?"

Well, I thought I'd already *got* the lay of the land with Anna back at Culloden House, but it seemed ungentlemanly to mention it to strangers, at least until they started bragging about what *they'd* caught lately, so I just kind of nodded in agreement.

"If there's anything we can do to help, places to point out, things like that, just let us know," he said.

"Well, as long as you're being so open and honest to a newcomer, what do you fellers do for excitement of a weekday evening?" I asked.

He looked around. "Should we tell him?"

The others all stared at me, and one by one they nodded.

"First," he said, turning back to me, "you have to promise not to tell anyone."

"You got my word as a man of the cloth," I said.

"All right," he said. "After midnight, when the constable's gone to sleep, and the laird and his gamekeeper are all locked up in their castle for the night, we sneak over to the Loch and poach salmon."

Well, if poaching salmon was their idea of a good time, I could see that Inverness wasn't the most wide-open town I'd ever been to. Personally, I couldn't see that it was any more exciting than poaching eggs, which is also not the most thrilling sport in the world, and I couldn't figure out why they had to wait until the constable and all them other people were asleep, unless there was some law on the books that the only way you could cook salmon was to fry or broil it, but it occurred to me that I hadn't eaten since I got off the train and that a little poached salmon on toast might just hit the spot, so I asked if I could tag along.

"Are you sure you want to get involved in this, Reverend?" asked one of the men.

"Why not?" I said.

"Isn't it against your religion?"

"Show me in the Good Book where it says you can't poach salmon in Inverness," I replied.

"Reverend Jones," said one of the men, getting up and putting an arm around my shoulders, "I *like* your brand of Christianity. You build your tabernacle, and you've got your first customer in Angus McNair."

We had a couple of more drinks, and then Angus McNair decided it was time to go poach the salmon, and we wandered out of the tavern and walked through town, and then we started going across some bog outside of town, and just as I was wondering why we couldn't have used a kitchen that was a little closer, we came to this great big lake.

"Here we are, Reverend," said McNair.

"You're gonna poach the salmon right here?" I asked.

"Couldn't very well poach it back in town, could we?" he said, and everyone laughed, so just to be polite I laughed, too, though for the life of me I couldn't figure out why not, unless they figured it tasted better over an open fire.

"Let's get the boats out," said McNair, and suddenly they pushed back a bunch of dead branches and brought out three boats. "You can come with me, Reverend Jones."

"We're going out on the lake?" I said.

"Unless you feel like rowing on dry land," he replied.

Well, I didn't have no answer to that, so I just climbed in alongside of him, and we rowed out to where the current was mighty swift, and then he tossed a net over the side, and rowed back to shore hell-for-leather, and once we got there he climbed out and started gathering in the net, and there were four or five big salmon in it, and I noticed both of the other boats had done the same and were gathering in their own salmon.

By this time I was hungry enough to eat one raw, but I decided that I might as well be polite and wait till they got around to poaching 'em.

"Ain't you gonna build no fire?" I asked.

"And alert the constable and the gamekeeper?" said McNair. "The whole reason we come here after midnight is to *avoid* them."

"What *are* you going to do, then?" I asked.

"We'll chop off their heads and gut them, and then bring them back to the village."

"I don't want to appear unduly forward," I said, "but does anyone ever get around to actually eating 'em?"

"Certainly," said McNair. "We'll feast tomorrow, eh, men?"

The others all chuckled and nodded, which left me to wondering what we were doing there tonight, but I didn't want to say nothing that would make me appear ignorant, so I just kept my mouth shut and watched while they went to work on the salmon. They tossed all the heads and guts into a big metal pail, and then McNair handed it to me.

"Here," he said. "Toss this into the loch, and be careful."

I walked to the edge of the water, and suddenly I heard a bunch of birds screeching and squawking and looked to see what the commotion was all about, but there wasn't nothing happening, so I turned back to the water, all prepared to dump the pail, when I found myself face-to-face with something that was awfully green and mighty wet and plenty big and mostly scary.

"Give it to her quick, Reverend," said McNair, "before she decides to take it right out of your hand."

This here creature was maybe a couple of hundred feet long, and covered with scales, and it kind of reached out this enormous neck until its head was hovering right over me, and if its face was nothing to write home about, let me tell you that its breath was even worse.

I tossed what I was holding, pail and all, at the creature's face, and it just opened up its mouth and swallowed, and after I finished counting its teeth I looked down its throat and decided there was plenty of room for a man of the cloth to slide right down without causing no serious problems at all, so I did what any reasonable man would do and raced back to the boats like unto an Olympic sprinter.

"What the hell was *that*?" I asked.

"Ah, that was only Nessie," said McNair with a shrug.

"There wasn't nothing *only* about it!" I said. "If I didn't know better, I'd swear I just saw a sea serpent!"

"You did," answered McNair. "You've heard of the Loch Ness Monster?"

"As has been writ up in song and story?" I asked.

He nodded. "This is Loch Ness, and that was the monster." He paused and looked at the ripples in the water, which were the only sign that a monster has recently come around begging for table scraps. "We get dozens of scientists out here every year, looking for her, but old Nessie, she's got an aversion to people. Only time she ever breaks the surface is when she knows we're going to throw her the leftovers from our salmon poaching.''

Which was precisely the moment that my hunger for a little poached salmon got itself overtook by my hunger for a little easy money.

''You mean all you got to do is come to the lake here, and go out on your boats, and she knows you're going to toss her some fish guts?'' I asked.

''That's pretty much the way it works,'' agreed McNair.

''And as long as you feed her, she don't never molest you, or breathe smoke and fire, or gobble up your boats, or nothing antisocial like that?'' I continued.

''She's a nice old girl, Nessie is,'' said McNair. ''We don't bother her, she don't bother us. The way we see it, the salmon innerds and heads are her commission for letting us fish in her loch.''

''Well, that's right interesting, Brother McNair,'' I said. ''And you say she don't never show herself to the august members of the scientific community?''

''Nope,'' he said. ''She's got no more use for 'em than we have.''

''There wouldn't be any such members around here, would there?'' I asked.

''I hear tell there's an American staying over at Glen Mohr,'' he said with a chuckle. ''Been on the loch for two weeks now. I believe he's due to stay here for another week before he goes home and tells all his peers that the monster is just a myth.''

Just about that time one of McNair's colleagues pulled out a hip flask, and we all had a little nip to keep the cold night air at bay, and then we went back across the bog to Inverness, and while they all went to sleep, I lay on my bed in Culloden House and tried to see where the most likely profit was to be had from the monster's existence.

I figured that no scientists, no matter how gullible, would pay me good coin of the realm to lead them to Nessie until they knew beyond a doubt that she existed, but if they saw her, then they didn't need *me* to prove it to them. I mulled on it till daybreak, and as I was having breakfast the solution finally dawned on me: I would buy a camera and take some pictures of Nessie, and once I showed them to this here scientist, he'd be more than willing to pay me a finder's fee for leading him to her.

I hadn't never taken a picture in my life, but as soon as the stores opened I picked me up a camera and half a dozen rolls of film. Anna was feeling a little less angry in the light of day, so I had her show me how to work the shutter and apertures and such, and just to make sure I had the hang of it, I took a practice roll of her standing on the front porch of the hotel.

Then I stopped by a fish market, of which there were an awful lot in Inverness, bought a bunch of heads and guts that the owner was going to throw out, stuck 'em in a pail, tried not to notice the smell as I carted it off to Loch Ness, and went out in Angus McNair's boat. I spent a few minutes on the lake, then rowed to shore and waited—and sure enough, Nessie showed up a minute later, all two hundred hungry feet of her, and I took a whole roll of film of her gobbling up the fish heads and innerds I had laid out all nice and neat on a log between me and her. Then she belched once, and disappeared beneath the surface of the water.

I stopped by the camera store, gave the clerk all my exposed film to develop, and went back to Culloden House, where I tried to catch up on my sleep and Anna tried to catch up on her romancing, and though it was a near thing, I got 'em both done in the proper order.

I just kind of loafed around the next day, and in midafternoon I stopped by and picked up my pictures. Everything had come out clear as you like, and I decided that if I ever gave up preaching, I could probably make a living taking artistic photographs of ladies in their unmentionables for use in calendars and other such vital publications.

First thing the next morning, I left a package of Anna's photos with her and told her to send 'em to her father with my compliments, just so he'd know a new and thoughtful preacher had set up shop in town. I passed Angus McNair and his cronies coming back from a hard night's fishing as I moseyed over to Glen Mohr, which was an old Tudor house that had been turned into a hotel, and I sat myself down in the lobby and waited until the guests started moving around. Finally a young feller with thick glasses and bushy hair walked down the stairs, said good morning to the desk clerk in perfect American, and headed off for the dining room, and I got up and followed him.

"Excuse me," I said, walking up to him once he'd been seated. "But I'm the Right Reverend Doctor Lucifer Jones, out of Moline, Illinois. I been preaching my way across the world for close to a dozen years now, and hearing your accent made me realize just how much I miss the green hills of home."

"There aren't any hills in Illinois," he said.

"But if there were, they'd sure be green, wouldn't they?" I said. "Anyway, I'd be happy to buy you breakfast in exchange for the pleasure of talking to a fellow Yank after all this time."

"Well, that's a different matter," said the man. "Pull up a chair and join me, Reverend Jones."

"Glad to," I said, sitting down opposite him. "You up here to do a little fishing?"

"No," said the man. "My name is Norbert Nelson. I'm a scientist, here to collect data on the Loch Ness Monster."

"No kidding?" I said. "What have you collected so far?"

"About three hundred mosquito bites and a bad cold," said Nelson. "But at least I'm on the verge of proving conclusively that the monster doesn't exist."

"Yeah?"

He nodded. "I'm due to stay another five days, but as far as I'm concerned, I might as well pack up and go home now. I can't imagine where this monster myth got started, but there isn't any basis for it."

"What a shame," I said, shaking my head. "I suppose finding the monster could have made you rich and famous?"

"Well, let's put it this way, Reverend Jones," said Nelson with a smile. "I'll never get rich and famous proving that there *isn't* a monster."

"Right," I said. "You could have proved that about Lake Michigan and saved a bundle in travel expenses."

"Well," he said with a shrug, "at least science will soon be able to state conclusively that it's just another legend with no basis in fact."

"Seems a pity, though," I said, "after all that effort."

"I agree," he said. "Finding the monster would have been the biggest news since Stanley found Livingstone."

"Bigger," I said. "Doctor Livingstone was merely misplaced, but everybody knew he existed."

"All right, bigger," agreed Nelson. "But it doesn't exist, and that's that."

"Brother Nelson," I said, "my heart goes out to you, as one Christian to another. I appreciate all the hard work you've gone to trying to scare up the monster, all the expense and privation you put up with, and I have it within my power to do you a favor for which I think you'll be everlastingly grateful."

"Oh?" he said.

"Yeah," I said, pulling the packet of photos out of my pocket and shoving them across the table to him. "I got something here that just might interest you."

"You do?" he said, picking up the packet and opening it.

"Well?" I said, as he thumbed through the photos. "What do you think?"

He stared at me for a long minute and then said, "All right. I'm interested."

"I kind of thought you might be," I said, shooting him a great big Sunday go-to-meeting grin. "What would it be worth if I was to put you right next to her?"

"I've never indulged in this kind of transaction before," he said. "What do you think it's worth?"

"I know scientists ain't exactly loaded down with cash," I said sympathetically. "I think five hundred dollars would do for now. We can renegotiate after you're rich and famous."

He looked at a couple of the photos again. "Five hundred seems a little steep," he said.

"All right," I said. "Because I got nothing but trust in my fellow man, three hundred."

He considered it for a moment, then dug into his wallet and pulled out six fifty-dollar bills.

"Brother Nelson," I said, "you ain't gonna regret this."

"I'd better not," he said. "Shall we go right now?"

"She's just finished eating," I said. "Let's give her a few

hours to digest her meal, and then we'll go get her. Why don't I meet you at your boat at, say, two this afternoon?"

"I don't feel like waiting," he said.

"I'm telling you, she's been eating all night," I said. "She's gonna be all sluggish right now."

"I don't care," said Nelson stubbornly. "A deal is a deal."

"I'll tell you what," I said. "I can understand you being so anxious to get a look at her, after being up here alone on the lake all this time. Since you're so all-fired eager, why don't you go looking for her now, and if you ain't found her by two o'clock, come on back to your boat."

"She'd better be there," he said, getting to his feet.

"You got my word on it, Brother Nelson," I told him as he walked out of the dining room.

I spent most of the morning walking around town, looking for the best place to build my tabernacle, and finally hit on a spot right between two taverns, which seemed a likely place to attract sinners as they staggered from one bar to the other, and then I had lunch and went on down to Loch Ness. I found Nelson's boat, and waited next to it until sunset. I couldn't figure out what was keeping him, since I knew he didn't know how to attract Nessie but finally I went back to Glen Mohr and asked if he'd returned there.

"Actually, he checked out at noon, sir," said the clerk.

"Yeah?"

He nodded. "And the young lady was with him."

"What young lady?"

"Anna, the gamekeeper's daughter. I believe they were going off to Glasgow to get married."

"Well, if that don't beat all," I said. "I wonder how in tunket he managed to run into her?"

"I believe *you* can claim the credit for that, sir," said the clerk with a smile.

"Me?"

He pulled out a few of the photos I had taken of Anna. "Mr. Nelson showed these to me on his way out, and asked me to identify the building in the background. Well, as anyone could have told him, it's Culloden House. He left in rather a hurry, and returned a few hours later with Anna on his arm."

Just then a kind of pudgy gentleman in a constable's uniform burst into Glen Mohr and walked up to me.

"Are you Lucifer Jones?" he demanded.

"The Right Reverend Doctor Lucifer Jones, at your service," I said.

"Doctor Jones, you're under arrest!"

"What the hell for?" I demanded.

He handed me a batch of photos of Nessie eating the fish guts. "Did you take these?"

"Ain't nothing illegal about taking pictures, is there?" I said.

"But it *is* illegal to fish in the laird's loch," said the constable. He sighed and shook his head. "What I can't understand is why, if you had to break the law, you added insult to injury by sending the photographic proof of it to his gamekeeper."

Well, we argued back and forth for about five more minutes, but in the end I was carted off to the local hoosegow, where I languished alone until dinnertime, when Angus McNair and his buddies heard about what had happened and snuck me in some poached salmon, which truth to tell wasn't worth all the buildup they had given it.

Then, just before midnight, the constable unlocked my cell and escorted me out to the front door of the jailhouse.

"Doctor Jones, you're free to go," he said.

"You finally figured out that you got no legal right to hold me, huh?" I said, brushing myself off.

"I have every legal right to hold you," he said, "but the laird's gamekeeper, in celebration of his daughter's pending marriage, has declared an amnesty for all the local poachers." He lowered his voice. "I've done a little bit of digging around, and if I were you, I'd get out of town before her father, who's about the best shot in the county, finds out exactly how and why his daughter met her future husband, and what her relationship was to the matchmaker."

It struck me as right good advice, and truth to tell, I'd had my fill of rainy weather and fish guts, and me and the Lord decided it was time to set off once again to find the perfect location for our tabernacle.

20
A Tabernacle Is
Not a Home

After my little misadventures with the Clubfoot of Notre Dame and the Crown Jewels of England and the Loch Ness Monster, I was fast running out of European countries in which to establish my tabernacle—and even before that, I was in serious danger of running out of continents on which my presence was allowed. I'd heard tell that Germany had a steady supply of good beer, and since preaching can be mighty thirsty work, I made up my mind that no matter what happened, I was setting up shop there.

The newspapers were full of the antics of some little house-painter who had already corralled most of the sinners in Berlin, so I decided to head over to Hamburg, where I was assured I'd find a passel of souls in serious need of salvation.

As soon as I got there, I started wandering the streets of the city, looking for the proper location for my tabernacle. It didn't take too long to figure out that most of the folks were heading for the Reeperbahn, which was an area loaded down with bars and nightclubs, and I figured that it didn't make much sense bringing Mohammed to the mountain since Mohammed was having a high old time right where he was, so I decided to look around for some For Sale signs, and after a few minutes I turned onto a little street called Herbertstrasse, the likes of which I ain't never encountered before or since.

What it was, was a bunch of buildings, each with three or four great big windows down on the ground level, and in each window was a pretty young German lady in her unmentionables, and for some reason not a single one of 'em had remembered to pull the shades down, and whenever I'd look in and offer 'em a smile of detached artistic appreciation, they'd smile right back at me.

Well, I hadn't gotten halfway down the block when I decided that Herbertstrasse seemed just the place to establish my tabernacle, since it was close to the Reeperbahn, which would supply me with a steady stream of sinners, and it was filled with a bunch of friendly neighbors of the female persuasion who kept smiling at anyone who happened to walk by.

As long as my mind was made up, I figured there wasn't no sense in wasting time, so I walked up to a blonde lady who was sitting by an open window, enjoying the cool evening breeze, to ask her if any of the buildings on the street happened to be for sale.

"Good evening, ma'am," I said.

"Hi, handsome," she replied in a thick German accent. "I am Helga."

"Pleased to make your acquaintance, Helga," I said. "I'm the Right Reverend Doctor Lucifer Jones. Do you know if any of these here hostelries is for sale?"

She just stared at me and frowned, like she couldn't understand simple American.

"The buildings, Helga," I said.

"Buildings?" she repeated.

"Yeah," I said. "Are any of 'em for sale, and if so, for how much?"

"Ah!" she said, her face brightening. "How much?"

"Yeah."

"Thirty marks," said Helga.

"Thirty marks?" I said. "You're kidding!"

She shrugged. "Okay, twenty-five marks."

"Twenty-five marks for *everything*?" I asked.

"For *everything*, thirty marks."

Well, I didn't want no one to move out the furniture or the refrigerator, so I figured I might as well buy the whole place, lock, stock, and barrel, since it was such a cheap price for such a nice building.

"Who do I pay?" I asked.

"You pay *me*," said Helga. "Wait and I open door."

A minute later the front door opened and she grabbed me by the arm and yanked me in off the street.

"You pay me now," she said.

"I kind of thought I'd take a look around first," I said. "You know, kind of inspect the plumbing and the heating and the necessaries and all."

"You pay me now," she repeated.

"Well, what the hell," I said, counting out the money and handing it over, "for thirty marks, how badly can I get took?"

Well, take my word for it, I never in all my experience found a person to be so grateful to make a cut-rate real estate sale. She practically dragged me up the stairs and into her bedroom, and before too long we got to know each other about as well as two people *can* get to know each other on such short notice. Helga kept shrieking and screaming like all get-out, and I kept trying to shush her up so we didn't bother the other tenants, but when I finally got her to keep quiet I heard all kinds of yells and giggles coming from down the hall, and I figured either all the young ladies were entertaining their gentleman friends at the same time or else they had contracted some rare but contagious disease in which screaming and laughing were the two main symptoms.

When we were all done, Helga climbed back into what she was wearing when I'd made her acquaintance and walked back downstairs, but I figured now that I owned the building I'd take a little tour of it, so I walked down the corridor, hoping I wouldn't catch no giggling disease, and pretty soon I came to a kitchen where about half a dozen blonde German ladies were gathered, most of 'em drinking beer or coffee.

"Good day to you, ladies," I said.

"Who are you?" asked one of 'em in somewhat better English than Helga's.

"I'm the Right Reverend Doctor Lucifer Jones," I said. "Are you just visiting, or do you all live here?"

Well, she laughed aloud at that, which made me figure maybe I was right about the disease, and when she was all through giggling she said, "We work here."

"In the kitchen?" I said. "Just how many cooks does this place hire?"

Well, she cracked up again, and this time she translated it into German, and everyone else started laughing, and I figured that the first thing I'd better do the next morning was stop by a doctor's office and get some kind of vaccination if it wasn't already too late.

"Now let me ask you, Reverend Jones," said the lady who spoke English, "what are *you* doing here?"

"I just bought the place," I said.

"You?" she said, looking kind of surprised.

"Right," I said. "I was kind of hoping for something with maybe a steeple, but there just wasn't no way I could turn it down for the price."

"Do you know what this place is?" she asked.

"As near as I can tell, it's an apartment building what's badly in need of window shades and sound-proofing," I said. "But once I clean it up and give it a paint job, it's gonna be the Tabernacle of Saint Luke."

"A tabernacle?" she repeated. "In *Herbertstrasse*?" Suddenly she started laughing again.

"What's so rib-tickling about that?" I asked.

"Reverend Jones, there is nothing in Herbertstrasse but whorehouses!"

"Yeah?"

"Yes."

"You know," I said, "I *thought* all them young ladies in the windows was dressed a little light for this time of year."

"Now that you've bought the place, what is to become of us?" she asked.

"Well, I wouldn't never want it said that a place of worship threw the flowers of German womanhood out into the street," I answered.

"You mean we can keep on working here?"

"Why not?"

"It seems somehow inconsistent with running a tabernacle," she said.

"Nonsense," I said. "A tabernacle can't function without sinners. If there's a better way to attract 'em, I ain't never come across it."

"Reverend Jones," she said with a great big grin, "I think we're all going to get along just fine."

"Never occurred to me that we wouldn't," I replied, grinning right back at her.

"We've been turning over fifty percent of our earnings to the former owner," she said. "How much will *you* charge?"

"As a gesture of goodwill, the Tabernacle of Saint Luke only wants forty percent," I said.

"It's a deal."

"You know," I said, "now that I come to think of it, I ain't got no place to stay. I'll be happy to lower it to thirty percent for any one of you frail flowers who'll give me a night's shelter."

Well, once she translated it I was overwhelmed with offers of shelter along with friendly, nurturing care, and my faith in the generosity and compassion of my fellow man—or in this case, my fellow woman—was reaffirmed.

I got up bright and early the next morning and went to a local sign painter and had him fix me up a sign that told one and all that they were about to enter the Tabernacle of Saint Luke, and I had him do it in German, French, Italian, and English, just so we didn't lose no sinners that couldn't read a foreign tongue. Then I had him add that the casual sinner who entered the tabernacle could find salvation, free beer, and a batch of friendly, caring young ladies who would be happy to listen to his confessions and even help him come up with some new ones.

Once the sign was up and we were open for business, I took over the ground-floor living room, set up a pulpit, and let it be known that I planned to spread the word of the Lord from 8:00 to 8:05 every evening, and maybe even oftener if the situation called for it. Hamburg was another town that hadn't never heard of bingo, but I found an old roulette wheel in a second-hand shop and announced that every Tuesday and Thursday we'd be indulging in friendly little games of chance to raise funds for our overseas missions.

Things went along pretty well for the first week, and even better the second, and I got to thinking that if business kept up like this, I was going to have to start four or five more tabernacles on Herbertstrasse.

I took to spending my mornings in the city's parks, recruiting handmaidens for the congregation, and I did my serious sleeping in the afternoons, when the salvation business was at its slowest. Then word got out that the Tabernacle of Saint Luke was charging ten percent less overhead for such business arrangements as the local females were inclined to make, and suddenly we had a steady stream of blonde ladies applying for positions with the tabernacle. Interviewing 'em was exhausting work, if you catch my meaning, but I figured it was my own special burden, so I done it with nary a complaint, and pretty soon we had three full eight-hour shifts of handmaidens toiling away in the service of the Lord, and an awful lot of the windows in the other buildings were temporarily boarded up.

Then one night I came down the stairs after a vigorous afternoon's nap, and who should I find waiting for me there but Rupert Cornwall.

"Well, howdy, Brother Rupert," I said. "I ain't seen you since we was both courting Lady Edith Quilton back in India."

"Doctor Jones!" he said. "What in the world are *you* doing here?"

"Just spreading the word of the Lord," I answered. "How about yourself?"

"Well, it's a strange situation," he said. "I *own* this building. I've been away for a month, tending to other matters, and I just arrived back not ten minutes ago to find some interloper claims to have bought it."

"I hate to correct you, Brother Rupert," I said, "but I ain't no interloper, and it just so happens that I'm the landlord of these here premises."

"*You?*"

"That's right," I said.

"Who do you think you bought it from?" he demanded.

"Helga."

"Helga's a goddamned prostitute!" yelled Rupert.

"I'll thank you not to use the Lord's name in vain when you're in the Tabernacle of Saint Luke," I said.

"What the hell makes you think Helga had any right to sell this building?" he continued.

"I negotiated it fair and square," I said.

"How much did you pay for it?" he asked.

"Thirty marks."

"*Thirty marks?*" he screamed. "It's worth seventy-five thousand!"

"I thought it was a mite inexpensive myself," I said, "but that don't change the fact that it's mine."

"Where is your bill of sale?" said Rupert.

"It was an informal transaction," I said.

"It was an illegal transaction!" he yelled. "This place belongs to me!"

"Why don't we let the tenants take a vote on who they want to be their landlord?" I suggested.

"They have nothing to do with this! This is my building, and I want you out of here in the next thirty minutes."

"Look, Brother Rupert, I don't see no reason why a couple of old friends like you and me can't work this out."

"We can work it out just fine," he said. "Get off my premises."

"Well, I suppose I could clear out," I said.

"Good."

"Of course," I added, "I ain't got no place to go, and I imagine the local constabularies would pick me up for vagrancy before long, and being the good-natured and friendly man of the cloth that I am, I'd probably try to entertain 'em with some amusing stories while they were fingerprinting me down at the station, and one of the ones that comes to mind is how you stole the Empire Emerald back in Hong Kong, and after we'd shared a laugh or two over that, I might tell 'em how you tried to get your hands on the Flame of Bharatpur when we was in Rajasthan, and sooner or later we'd share a drink or two and I'd tell 'em why you can't never go back to Australia, and that there's still half a dozen warrants out for your arrest."

"That's outrageous!" he said. "Does our friendship mean nothing to you?"

"I cherish our friendship, Brother Rupert," I told him. "But on the other hand, *I* ain't the one who's trying to throw *you* out into the street."

"Doctor Jones," he said. "*Lucifer*, my old friend. Suddenly I feel certain that we can work something out."

"Well, that's right friendly of you, Brother Rupert," I said. "And I want you to know that despite our little contretemps, I never doubted that you was a decent Christian who would do the right thing sooner or later."

"All right," he said with a sigh. "Promise not to go to the police, and you can have a quarter of the take."

"I'm ashamed of you, Brother Rupert," I said. "When you flim-flam *me*, you're flim-flamming the Lord. And betwixt us, me and the Lord have tripled the business in less than a month."

"All right," he said. "A third."

"Sixty percent," I said.

"I can't let you buy more than half my business for thirty marks!"

"You're looking at it all wrong," I said. "I'm *giving* you almost half *my* business for nothing."

Well, we argued and haggled for another hour, and in the end it was decided that I owned fifty percent of the voting stock in the Tabernacle of Saint Luke, Rupert owned the other fifty percent, and the Lord held an option on three hundred shares of preferred nonvoting stock.

Things went along pretty well for the next week. Rupert had taken a room for himself at the Vier Jahreszeiten Hotel, which was a fancy place in the center of town, but I couldn't see no reason to move out of the tabernacle, where I could keep in close contact with all them flowers of German womanhood who were toiling day and night in the service of the Lord, and whenever it looked like one of 'em might fall from grace I saw to it that I was always first in line with an uplifting word and a little missionary work.

We were making so much money that I decided some new preaching clothes were in order, so I stopped by a local tailor and had him make me up a white silk suit, which I figured would reflect the purity of my thoughts, and I also got a couple of nifty green and red and gold Hawaiian shirts to go with it, just to make some of the sailors from the South Seas who stopped by feel more at home.

Then I figured that since I was now sharing the take with Rupert Cornwall, it wouldn't hurt none to do a little advertising to bring in even more sinners, so I made up a bunch of signs directing people to the Tabernacle of Saint Luke and posted 'em all over the Reeperbahn, so folks would know where to go to get their sins redeemed.

All this time I was sweating and toiling in the service of the Lord, I hadn't seen hide nor hair of Rupert Cornwall, except for his nightly visit to collect his share of the money, and truth to tell I was feeling a little resentful that me and God were doing all this work for only half the profits, but being the big-hearted Christian gentleman that I am I kept my feelings to myself, except when the handmaidens would ask why he was still hanging around after I had bought the place, and I had to explain to 'em that the Lord teaches us to be charitable to sinners, though it wasn't a piece of advice I necessarily wanted them to live by, so I further explained that that particular passage was only in the Australian translation of the Good Book and since Rupert was the only Australian they knew, it didn't really apply to none of the other sinners who visited the tabernacle with money to spend.

Then one night, while Rupert was upstairs counting out his share of the money, a group of ten real well-dressed guys walked in all at once, and each and every one of 'em looked kind of unhappy, like life hadn't been treating 'em none too well of late.

"Welcome to the Tabernacle of Saint Luke, gents," I said, walking over to 'em. "Most of our handmaidens are otherwise occupied at the moment, but if you'd like, I can whip through a quick service and get you a head start on your salvation so's you'll have a few sins paid for in advance."

"Never mind that," said the littlest one of the group. "Do you know who we are?"

"It don't make no difference to the Tabernacle of Saint

Luke," I said. "We treat all sinners the same, regardless of race, creed, or political affiliation."

"We are the other landlords of Herbertstrasse," continued the little guy, "and it is not inaccurate to say that we are seriously displeased with this establishment."

"You stole our girls!" shouted another.

"And our customers!" yelled a third.

"In other words," said the little guy, "we don't mind a little friendly competition, but you, sir, are a monopolist."

"That's a lie!" I said. "I ain't never shot a king or a prince in my life!"

He just stared at me for a minute and shook his head.

"We have come to buy you out," he said at last.

"The Tabernacle of Saint Luke ain't for sale," I said.

"You're quite certain of that?" he asked me.

"Lemme put it this way," I said. "If I was you, I wouldn't go laying no serious bets against it."

"You have complicated our task," he said sadly. "We came here to make you a legitimate business offer, and you refuse even to listen to it. That leaves us no other choice but to take over your business by other means."

And suddenly I was staring into the business ends of ten pistols.

"It just so happens that the judge of the local probate court is my brother-in-law," said the little guy. "If something were to happen to you, something shall we say permanent, I think it not unlikely that he would decide to award your possessions to myself and my associates."

Just then Rupert appeared at the head of the stairs, having counted out and pocketed his share of the previous day's income, and suddenly I saw a way out of my predicament.

"I'm sorry, gentlemen," said Rupert, climbing down to the main floor, "but we don't allow firearms in here."

"Who's he?" asked the little guy.

"Gents," I said, "this is Mr. Rupert Cornwall, formerly of Australia, Hong Kong, and India. Brother Rupert, these here fellers are associated with the local court system, and are looking into the ownership of the Tabernacle of Saint Luke."

"Oh?" he said, with a kind of greedy smile on his face.

"Yeah," I said. "Just tell 'em I bought it fair and square and you can be on your way."

"I hate to correct you, Doctor Jones," said Rupert, "but I am, and always have been, the sole owner of this building."

"You don't have to pretend for my sake, Brother Rupert," I said. "Just tell 'em the truth."

"The truth is that you are a mountebank who has no legal claim to these premises," said Rupert.

I turned to the little guy. "Well, I done my best," I said.

"You are free to leave," he said, and then turned to Rupert. "Mr. Cornwall, I wonder if my associates and I might have a word in private with you. We have a business proposition to make."

"Oh?" said Rupert.

"Well, two propositions, actually," he said with a smile.

Rupert led 'em into the next room, and I figured that whichever proposition he took, my stake in the Tabernacle of Saint Luke was up in flames, so I went up to my room, collected my money, kissed Helga and the other handmaidens good-bye, and headed off for fresh territory, confident that having got my feet wet in the tabernacle business, so to speak, I'd do even better with the next one.

21
Death in the Afternoon

There are a lot of ways to see Spain. In my expert opinion, the very worst of them is to be standing in the middle of the arena at the Plaza de Toros while a bull named El Diablo is pawing the dirt about twenty feet away and planning to use you for target practice.

But I'm getting a little bit ahead of myself.

If you ever go to Madrid, you're going to make two discoveries right quick: all the women wear black, and all the men think they're bullfighters. Beyond that it's pretty much like any other city, except that the people there don't speak much American, and they all go crazy for this kind of Spanish tap dance which is always being done by guys in tight pants called Juan or José or Diego.

I'd left Hamburg with a healthy supply of money in my wallet, so I decided to check in at the finest hotel in town, which back in them days was the Palace. There were posters all over the lobby about something called the Fiesta de Toros, which as near as I could translate meant that the restaurant had bought too much steak and was trying to find ways to get rid of it, but I wasn't hungry anyway, so instead I moseyed out onto the street and wandered around until sunset, and then, because wandering can be pretty thirsty work, I stopped by a little tavern about a mile from the hotel.

The place was just about empty, except for this tall, athletic-looking feller with slicked-down hair and a big black mustache who was sitting at the bar, and when he saw me he sort of waved me over to join him.

"May I buy you a drink?" he asked.

"Why, that's right neighborly of you, brother," I said, sitting down next to him.

"You are English?" he asked.

"American," I said. "The Right Reverend Honorable Doctor Lucifer Jones, at your service."

"You have come a day too soon," he said morosely. "The service will be held tomorrow night."

"Yeah?" I said, wondering what service he was talking about.

He nodded. "The women will be wailing in the streets, and they will throw themselves upon the coffin. Ten thousand candles will be lit at the cathedral, strong men will weep, and little children will lose their faith in God. The line to the cemetery will be two miles long, and the Cardinal himself will speak at the graveside."

"Sounds impressive," I allowed.

"It will be a funeral they will talk about for years," he agreed.

"Uh . . . pardon my ignorance, but I'm a stranger in town," I said. "Who's about to die—some president or general or such?"

"Me," he said glumly.

"You?"

"I am Pablo Francisco de Varga," he said. "Perhaps you have heard of me?"

"Didn't you used to play third base for the Brooklyn Dodgers?" I said.

"I am the greatest bullfighter of all time," he said.

"Excuse a personal question, Brother Pablo," I said, "but why are you figuring on dying tomorrow?"

"El Diablo," he said.

"What is that—some kind of disease?" I asked, backing away a bit just in case it was catching.

"El Diablo is the bull I must face tomorrow in the Fiesta de Toros," he said. "He has already killed three matadors."

"Well, I'm right sorry to hear that," I said. "But if you're the greatest bullfighter around, what makes you think you're gonna lose?"

"I have broken a bone in my foot," he said. "I am completely unable to move to the side. El Diablo will kill me on my very first *veronica.*"

"Why don't you call it off, then?" I said.

"Tens of thousands of people have come to see Varga face El Diablo in the arena," he said with dignity. "I will not disappoint them."

"Seems to me you're just about guaranteed to disappoint them what ain't rooting for the bull," I said. "If I was you, I'd get a doctor's excuse or whatever it takes to postpone this thing."

"That is because you are not a Spaniard," said Varga. "You do not understand the concept of honor. This is a matter between El Diablo and myself. I will not be the first to back down."

Well, we got to talking and drinking, and he kept explaining the Spanish concept of honor, whch seemed an awful lot like the American concept of stupidity, but after a couple of hours I gave up trying to talk him out of it, and after he'd finished a whole bottle of whiskey and paid for mine as well, I figured the least I could do to thank him was help him hobble back to his hotel. He was right insistent that no one see him limping, so we snuck around to the back door and went in through the kitchen and found a freight elevator, and a few minutes later I left him and returned to the Palace.

It seemed to me that as long as I couldn't talk him out of canceling the fight, there wasn't no reason why I shouldn't make a little profit out of it, since me and God still planned to build our tabernacle and I didn't know what construction costs were like in Madrid, so I walked up to the desk clerk and asked him where the local bookmaker had set up shop. He must have misunderstood, because what he sent me to was a publishing company, but as I was walking back to the hotel I passed by a casino, and I figured if anyone knew where I could lay some bets on the bullfight, this was the place.

I walked in, and sure enough, along with poker and craps and roulette tables, they had a guy in the corner taking bets on the big bullfight, but the only odds he was giving was on whether Varga would be awarded one ear, both ears, or both ears and the tail.

"Good evening," I said, walking up to him.

"*Buenos noches,*" he replied.

"Well, that's right kind of you, but I've already et," I said. "I'm just here to make a sporting wager on the big bullfight tomorrow."

"Yes, *señor*?" he said. "And what do you choose?"

"I don't see no odds on El Diablo winning," I said.

He laughed so hard I thunk he was gonna fall right off his chair, and when he finally got ahold of himself, he wiped the tears from his face and smiled at me.

"You have a wonderful sense of humor, *señor*," he said.

"Yeah, I been told that many a time," I said modestly. "But I still want to lay a bet on El Diablo."

"Do you know that El Diablo is facing the great Pablo Francisco de Varga?"

"Who's he?" I said.

Suddenly he got a greedy gleam in his eye. "All right, *señor*," he said. "I will give you odds of ten to one."

I pulled out my wad and counted out all but about two hundred dollars of it.

"Okay," I said. "I'll put twelve thousand on El Diablo to win."

Suddenly there was a hushed silence in the room. The guy I'd been talking to looked at me like I was crazy, but finally he shrugged, took my money, and wrote me out a receipt.

"You are a fool," he said. "Varga is the greatest matador of all time, greater even than Juan Belmonte."

"Well, for all you know, El Diablo is greater than Babe the Blue Ox," I said.

"Than *who*?"

Well, I could tell I was talking to a cultural illiterate, so I just bade him good-bye and went back to the Palace, where I had a couple of drinks to wash down the whiskey I'd had with Varga, and then went up to my room and took a shower. I had just climbed out of the tub and dried off when I heard the door open, so I looked out from the bathroom and found three well-dressed Spaniards sitting around the room, one of 'em normal-sized and two of 'em looking like gorillas with suits on.

"Howdy, brothers," I said. "What can I do for you?"

"You are the Reverend Lucifer Jones?" asked the normal one.

"The Right Reverend Doctor Lucifer Jones," I corrected him.

"Then we have come to the right place," he said. "We have some business to discuss."

"Well, given the time of day, I'm afraid I'm gonna have to charge you time-and-a-half for salvation," I said. "Though if any of you are lately bereaved, I got a group rate for funerals."

"Allow me to introduce myself," he said. "I am Manuel Garcia, and these are my two associates. You may call them Mr. Crush and Mr. Smash." Mr. Crush smiled at me, and from where I sat it looked like he had steel teeth; Mr. Smash just glared sullenly. "Did you just bet twelve thousand dollars that Pablo Francisco de Varga would be killed in the arena tomorrow?" continued Garcia.

"You make it sound kind of morbid," I said. "I didn't so much bet *against* him as I bet *for* El Diablo."

"My colleagues and I would like to know *why* you bet against the great Varga."

"Because I think the bull will win," I said.

"Do not play games with us, Reverend Jones," said Garcia. "We represent some of the most powerful men in Madrid."

"You're the lawyers for a bunch of weightlifters?" I asked.

"Enough of this foolishness!" snapped Garcia. "You have bet a substantial sum on El Diablo. We, too, are gamblers, and we want to know if you are privy to some inside information that would lead you to make a wager that, on the face of it, seems laughably foolish."

"Well, I don't see no point in lying to you," I said. "But to be totally honest and even-handed about it, I don't see no point in confiding to you, neither. I mean, it ain't as if you was regular parishioners who had promised to donate, say, five thousand dollars apiece to the Tabernacle of Saint Luke once this here contest betwixt man and beast reaches its possibly tragic conclusion."

"All right, Reverend Jones," said Garcia. "We agree to your terms. Give us your information, and if we elect to make our wagers based upon it and Varga should lose, we will deliver fifteen thousand dollars to you at the conclusion of the event.''

"Well, that's mighty agreeable of you,'' I said, "but how do I know I can trust you to keep your word?"

The three of 'em looked like I'd just stabbed their mothers.

"We are Spaniards," said Garcia. "We live and die by our code of honor."

"All right," I said. "But I want to sit with you guys at the bullfight, just so it don't slip your minds."

"Men have died for lesser insults, Reverend Jones," growled Mr. Crush in broken English.

"Painfully," added Mr. Smash.

"And men have gone hungry for lesser precautions," I said. "Have we got a deal?"

They whispered amongst themselves in Spanish, and finally all three looked at me and nodded.

"Okay," I said. "I happened to run into Pablo Francisco de Varga in a bar earlier tonight, and he's already making plans for his funeral."

"But why?" demanded Garcia. "Surely the great Varga has not lost his courage!"

"Unthinkable!" added the other two.

"What he's done is gone and busted a bone in his foot, and for some crazy reason he don't want to tell no one or call the match off," I said.

"Well, of course not," agreed Garcia. "He has lived by the code; he will die by it."

"You don't find that a mite peculiar?" I asked.

"Absolutely not. We shall pass along your information to our principals, and I'm sure they will act accordingly." He stood up. "Thank you for your time, Reverend Jones."

"Where will I meet you guys tomorrow?" I said.

"We will be waiting outside the box office at the Plaza de Toros," said Garcia, and then the three of 'em walked out, and I finished drying myself off and spent a little time figuring out just how much money I'd be worth after poor Varga went off to the great bullfight plaza in the sky, and finally I climbed under the covers and went to sleep and dreamed about building my tabernacle right next to Varga's grave as a way of thanking him for putting me onto this opportunity.

I woke up bright and early at about noontime, got dressed, and caught a cab out to the Plaza de Toros, where true to his word, Manuel Garcia was waiting for me with Mr. Crush and Mr. Smash. The four of us went to his private box, where we had a few beers and watched a couple of warm-up fights, and by the time the Big Event rolled around the score was Matadors 2, Bulls 0.

We sat there and chatted about this and that, and after awhile we became aware of a kind of uneasy murmuring in the crowd, and when half an hour had passed Garcia said something to Mr. Crush, who left the box and returned about five minutes later to whisper something in Garcia's ear.

"Come with me," said Garcia, getting to his feet.

"I think I'd rather stay here, sipping my beer and getting a little sun," I said.

"Come with me!" he repeated, and suddenly Mr. Crush grabbed me by one arm and Mr. Smash grabbed me by the other, and I didn't have no choice but to accompany them, since they were holding me a few inches off the ground and rushing to keep up with Garcia.

We came to a door beneath the grandstand, and Garcia nodded to the guard, who let the four of us in. Then we went down a long corridor past a number of dressing rooms, and stopped at one with Varga's name on the door. Garcia pushed it open, and there on the floor lay Pablo Francisco de Varga, still in his street clothes.

"Is he dead?" I asked.

"Drunk," said Mr. Crush.

Garcia knelt down next to him and slapped his face a few times. He didn't move a muscle.

"We have a serious problem," said Garcia, standing up and facing me.

"Seems to me that Varga's the one with the problem," I said.

"We have bet more than half a million dollars on El Diablo," he said. "If Varga does not appear in the arena, they will cancel the fight."

"Well, it ain't a consummation devoutly to be wished," I allowed. "But on the other hand, it beats losing our money."

"You do not understand," said Garcia. "I have promised some very powerful men that they would increase their money tenfold by wagering on El Diablo. These are not men who like to be disappointed."

"Well, El Diablo is gonna win by a forfeit," I said.

"The bookmakers do not pay off on forfeits," answered Garcia. "No, *someone* must go into the ring and lose to El Diablo. The question is: *who?*"

Suddenly I became aware of the fact that he and Mr. Crush and Mr. Smash were all staring intently at me.

"Oh, no," I said. "You ain't gonna get *me* in a ring with El Diablo! I ain't never fought a bull before!"

"Then you are precisely the person we need," said Garcia. "I have guaranteed my principals that El Diablo cannot lose."

"Then you tell your principals that they're gonna have to learn to live with disappointment," I said. "Nothing's gonna get me to step into that ring!"

"My dear Reverend Jones," he said, and suddenly Mr. Crush and Mr. Smash were pointing their revolvers right betwixt my eyeballs, "you have two admittedly unhappy choices: you can die in the arena amid the cheers of thousands, or you can die in the next ten seconds, alone and unmourned. I am afraid that there is simply no third alternative."

Which is how I came to be standing in the middle of the Plaza de Toros in Madrid in a fancy bullfighting outfit while El Diablo stared at me through his beady little eyes and pawed the dirt.

Since I was supposed to lose, Garcia hadn't seen fit to give me a sword, so all I had with me was a red cape called a *muleta*. I was more than a little bit nervous at the prospect of hobnobbing in person with the Lord in the next few minutes, and my hands were shaking, and this made the *muleta* shake, and for some reason this annoyed the bejabbers out of El Diablo, who snorted and drooled a bit and then let out a bellow and ran straight toward me.

Well, I figured if he wanted the *muleta* all that badly, *I* sure wasn't going to argue none about it, so I just dropped it on the ground and ran to the far side of the arena while he shredded the thing with his horns and everyone started whistling, though truth to tell I couldn't spot no melody.

After he'd worked off a little excess energy on the *muleta*, El Diablo lifted his head and looked around, and when his eyes fell on me he pawed the dirt a couple of more times and then lowered his head and charged, and I made a dash for the grandstand and reached it about two steps ahead of him and flung myself into the first row while El Diablo plowed into the concrete wall that protected the customers and busted off one of his horns.

He looked a little bleary-eyed as he backed off, and I figured I might as well stay where I was for the rest of the afternoon, but then Mr. Crush and Mr. Smash made their way through the crowd and reached my side and tossed me back into the ring, and El Diablo shot them an appreciative look and started sizing me up again.

I climbed back onto my feet just as he charged, and as he lowered his head I grabbed ahold of his remaining horn on the assumption that he couldn't stab me with it as long as I kept it at arm's length, but then he tossed his head and lifted me way off the ground, and suddenly I found myself sitting on his back. He came to a stop and stared all around the arena, looking for me, while I stayed where I was and tried to figure out what to do next.

Well, neither of us moved for the next couple of minutes, and all of a sudden the crowd started throwing popcorn boxes and beer bottles into the ring and whistling some more, and finally El Diablo charged at a piece of paper that was fluttering on the ground and I fell off with a thud, and he wheeled around and started snorting and drooling and bellowing at me again. Since I didn't have no *muleta* left, I quick slipped off the little jacket they had made me wear and held it out to see if maybe he wanted to eat *it* instead of *me*, and he bellowed again and charged straight at it. I let go of it just before he reached it and started running again, only this time I didn't hear no galloping footsteps behind me, so I turned to see what was going on, and what had happened was that he'd stuck his horn into the sleeve of the jacket and pierced right through it, and the rest of it was covering his face so that he couldn't see nothing.

I figured this was as good a time to take my leave as any, and probably better than most, so I walked back to the door through which Mr. Crush and Mr. Smash had dragged me in, but when I got there I found a bunch of guys in bullfighting outfits all laughing their heads off.

"I never knew you could be so funny, Pablo Francisco!" guffawed one of 'em.

"It has been wildly amusing," agreed another, "but now I see that you have come back for your sword. Here it is." He handed me this long sword and kind of pointed me back into the arena and gave me a friendly shove.

El Diablo still hadn't gotten the jacket off his face, and I figured if I was ever gonna kill him and get out of this in one piece, now was probably the ideal time, so I walked cautiously up to him and got all ready to run him through when it occurred to me that I didn't know where his heart was. I had a feeling it was probably somewhere inside his chest, but there was an awful lot of chest in front of me, and I was pretty sure I was only gonna get one chance to do it right before El Diablo finally got rid of the jacket.

I finally made up my mind where to stab him, but then Mr. Crush jumped into the arena and pointed his pistol at me, still determined to win Garcia's bets for him, and just as he fired I ducked and then El Diablo jumped like he'd been shot, which he had, and fell over dead.

Well, the police surrounded Mr. Crush right quick, and he started jabbering something in Spanish and pointing at me, and by the time I'd finished taking a couple of bows and walked back to the dressing room there were a passel of police waiting there for me, and they took me down to the local calaboose and I spent the night there, still in my bullfighting outfit.

They left me in the cell for three days and three nights with no comfort except my well-worn copy of the Good Book, and let me tell you that it was a pretty morose time, since I soon realized that thanks to surviving my ordeal with El Diablo I was destitute again, which was getting to be a common condition but still not one that brought me any great comfort.

Then, on the morning of the fourth day, I was pulled off my cot and out of my cell, and then handcuffed and brung into court and made to stand before the bench, which was being presided over by a judge named Alberto Coronado, who had kind of a lean and hungry look to him, like maybe his shorts were too tight or someone had just got him out of bed.

"So *you* are Lucifer Jones," he said.

"The Right Reverend Honorable Doctor Lucifer Jones," I corrected him. "Pleased to make your acquaintance."

"Are you really?" said Judge Coronado. "I'm fascinated to make yours."

"Well, I'm right flattered to hear it," I said. "Maybe if you could see fit to remove these here handcuffs, we could slip off to a local bar and lift a few and swap stories."

"I think not," he said. "It seems we have a little business to get through first."

"We do?"

He nodded. "You have been charged with conspiring to fix the outcome of a bullfight, and to make an enormous profit thereby. How do you plead?"

"I didn't make no profit at all," I pointed out. "El Diablo lost, may the Lord have mercy on his poor bovine soul."

"That in no way alters the fact that you did everything within your power to predetermine the result. I am afraid I am going to have to find you guilty. Your three friends admitted everything, and are currently serving their own sentences."

"Well, it seems mighty single-minded and unfair to me, Your Honor," I said, "considering that I wound up dead broke and almost got killed in the process."

"I have taken that into account," said Judge Coronado. "I have even made inquiries to see if one of our European neighbors would let us send you there on the condition that you promise never to return to Spain."

"Sounds good to me," I said.

"It sounded good to me, too," admitted Judge Coronado. "Then we started receiving replies from the various governments we contacted." He looked at me and smiled. "You lead quite an interesting life for a man of the cloth."

"Well, you know how it is," I said modestly.

"I truly had no idea how it was," he replied. "Though I do now." He began riffling through some papers. "It seems that you are wanted in Romania for grave-robbing, and for running a bawdy house in Germany."

"Yeah, well, I can explain that," I said.

"The Italians want you for pretending to be an exorcist, and the Hungarian S.P.C.A. wants to question you about your treatment of a certain show dog."

"A series of misunderstandings," I said.

"The French are after you for running an illegal gambling operation in the Cathedral of Notre Dame." He paused and looked at me. *"Notre Dame?"*

"I thought it was a football stadium."

"The government of Crete wishes to speak to you about your complicity in the death of a Professor Zachariah MacDonald, the Scotch claim you are an undesirable who left the country over a game-poaching scandal, the British have decided you had something to do with the break-in at a jewelry store on Bond Street, and the new democratically-elected government of Sylvania is after you for impersonating a member of the former Royal Family."

"They *asked* me to!" I said heatedly.

Judge Coronado held up a hand for silence. "Finally, the government of Greece has issued a warrant for your arrest for illegally removing salvaged treasure from their country."

"I didn't remove nothing!" I said. "Wait till you hear *my* side of it!"

"Doctor Jones, I'm sure hearing your side of the story would prove most entertaining," said Judge Coronado, "but it doesn't negate the fact that you are a walking disaster. As a responsible member of the European community, I could not in good conscience turn you loose upon our neighbors."

"Then send me somewhere else," I said.

"That is my intention," he said. "Unfortunately, it appears that you have been barred from the continents of North America,

Africa, and Asia.'' He paused and stared at me. ''You have lived less than half your allotted span of years, Doctor Jones, and you are already in danger of running out of land masses that will accept your presence. Fortunately, no one in South America seems to have heard of you, and since that is sufficiently far from Spain, I have elected to send you there. I must confess that I feel enormous sympathy for the remnants of the once-proud Aztec and Mayan civilizations, but this is a matter of survival, and I would be betraying my high office were I to turn you loose in any western country. Case closed.''

''When do I leave?'' I asked.

''You will be transferred to Barcelona tomorrow morning,'' he said. ''Your ship leaves two days later.'' Suddenly he smiled. ''And now that the case is officially closed, let me say that I would be delighted to stop by your cell this afternoon and listen to you explain how thirty-four governments on four continents have so erroneously interpreted your good intentions.''

Well, true to his word Judge Coronado stopped by, and we lifted a few while I told him of all my adventures and exploits and encounters, and the next day they shipped me to Barcelona, which I hear tell is a lovely town but ain't much to write home about when viewed from the inside of a prison cell, and then they put me on a boat bound for Brazil.

I had done my best to bring the Word of the Lord to the depraved citizens of Europe, and this was the thanks I got for it. Still, I ain't one to discourage easily, so I started making plans to build my tabernacle in South America, which I finally did do four years later. But before me and God set up shop, I stumbled upon more than my share of lost civilizations and high priestesses and strange voodoo rites and revolutions and the like, and I plan to tell you about 'em someday, but writing your memoirs can be pretty tiring work, so I'm heading off now to find some friendly and sympathetic soul of the female persuasion and renew my artistic energies.

Mike Resnick was born and raised in the Chicago area. He attended the University of Chicago, where he met his wife Carol ("and majored in absenteeism"). They were married in 1961, and their daughter, Laura, an award-winning writer herself, was born a year later.

Mike and Carol bred and exhibited collies with enormous success during the 1960s and 1970s, which led them to purchase the country's second-largest boarding and grooming kennel, which they still own and operate in Cincinnati.

Mike wrote in a number of other fields prior to 1981, at which time he began concentrating almost exclusively on his first love, science fiction. Since that time he has produced such well-received novels as the best-selling *Santiago*, the Nebula-nominated *Ivory*, *Soothsayer*, *Paradise*, *Stalking the Unicorn*, and of course *Adventures*, the book that brought Lucifer Jones to the world.

He was never very interested in short fiction until the mid-1980s, when he began turning it out in quantity. The downstate returns aren't all in yet, but when last we looked he had won Hugo awards for "Kirinyaga" and "The Manamouki" and had also been nominated for a number of other brilliant stories.

Mike and Carol spend a month in Africa every year, and they are also much in demand on the science fiction convention circuit.